Praise for *A Deadly Inside Scoop*

"Abby Collette has crafted a delicious addition to the cozy mystery world with her superbly written *A Deadly Inside Scoop.* Delightful characters and a puzzler of a plot kept me turning pages until the very end. I can't wait for my next visit to the Crewse Creamery for another decadent taste."

—*New York Times* bestselling author Jenn McKinlay

"Abby Collette pens a delightfully delicious cozy, introducing readers to smart, funny Bronwyn Crewse, savvy businesswoman and ice cream maker extraordinaire. With an endearing cast of characters ranging from her close-knit, multigenerational family to her feisty best friends, this intricate mystery plays out with plenty of suspects, tons of motives and an ending I didn't see coming. I can't wait to see what Win gets up to next in Chagrin Falls."

—Bailey Cates, *New York Times* bestselling author of the Magical Bakery Mysteries

"With a host of quirky friends and family members, Abby Collette's new series is a welcome addition to the cozy mystery scene, and life at Crewse Creamery promises plenty of delectable adventures to come. Only one warning: *A Deadly Inside Scoop* causes a deep yearning for scoops of homemade ice cream, no matter the weather."

—Juliet Blackwell, *New York Times* bestselling author of the Haunted Home Renovation series and the Witchcraft Mystery series

"*A Deadly Inside Scoop* is a deliciously satisfying new cozy mystery series. It's got humor, a quirky cast of characters and ice cream. What more could you want?"

—V.M. Burns, Agatha Award–nominated author of the Mystery Bookshop Mystery series

"What do you get when you put together a tight-knit, slightly quirky family, a delectable collection of ice cream flavors and an original mystery? A tasty start to a new cozy series. *A Deadly Inside Scoop* is a cleverly crafted mystery with a relatable main character in Bronwyn Crewse."

—*New York Times* bestselling author Sofie Kelly

# A Deadly Inside Scoop

Abby Collette

Berkley Prime Crime
New York

BERKLEY PRIME CRIME
Published by Berkley
An imprint of Penguin Random House LLC
penguinrandomhouse.com

Library of Congress Cataloging-in-Publication Data

Names: Collette, Abby, author.
Title: A deadly inside scoop / Abby Collette.
Description: First edition. | New York: Berkley Prime Crime, 2020. |
Series: An ice cream parlor mystery
Identifiers: LCCN 2019055578 (print) | LCCN 2019055579 (ebook) |
ISBN 9780593099667 (trade paperback) | ISBN 9780593099674 (ebook)
Subjects: GSAFD: Mystery fiction.
Classification: LCC PS3603.O4397 D43 2020 (print) |
LCC PS3603.O4397 (ebook) | DDC 813/.6—dc23
LC record available at https://lccn.loc.gov/2019055578
LC ebook record available at https://lccn.loc.gov/2019055579

First Edition: May 2020

Printed in the United States of America
1 3 5 7 9 10 8 6 4 2

Cover illustration and design by Vi-An Nguyen
Book design by Alison Cnockaert

To my mother, Leslie Vandiver.

Always here with me in my heart, my thoughts and my words.

# chapter ONE

Today I was going to touch the stars.

Lying on my back, I stared up at my bedroom ceiling. When I'd moved to my own place, the only things I'd taken from my childhood home were the star-shaped glittered cardboard cutouts my grandmother and I had made when I was seven. I hung them as a reminder of what she'd told me—always shoot for the stars.

She'd also told me on days I had to make ice cream for the store, don't sleep past five a.m.

I sat up in bed and looked over at the red glow of my digital alarm clock.

Four thirty-nine.

Up ahead of time. Already, the day seemed promising.

A smile escaping my lips, I pulled back the covers and stood on the bed. On my toes, I reached up and felt the coarse bumps from the glue on the gold-glittered star that hung the lowest. Closing my eyes, I walked the length of the bed, socked feet sinking into the mattress, and ran my fingertips along the points. Inhaling happily, I jumped off the bed and padded down the hall into the bathroom, humming a tune.

Yes, today was the day that I was going to realize my dream.

As I brushed my teeth, I stared back at my reflection in the mirror and could almost see all the excitement oozing out of me. Running my family's ice cream shop hadn't *always* been my dream, surely not the one I'd left for college and earned a degree in marketing and an MBA for. But when my dad's sister, Aunt Jack, had moved to North Carolina and left our little business without a manager, my grandfather had chosen me, his only granddaughter, to run it. He'd put the key to the shop in a box with a keyring that said "Manager" and a card that said "Carte Blanche" and placed it under the Christmas tree. Tearing into the red-and-gold Ho-Ho-Ho wrapping paper that holiday morning, I'd felt just like a kid—wide smile, nervous giggle and my insides squealing with delight.

That had been nearly a year ago.

I let out a long sigh as I put away my toothbrush and closed the medicine cabinet. I pulled a plastic cap over my short-cropped black hair and stepped into the shower.

Yep, today I was confident about opening the shop, but that confidence had been born out of trouble. After the baton had been passed to me and I came up with the plan to turn our little shop around, I found out the hard way just how quickly plans could go wrong.

I closed my eyes and let the hot water from my brand-new luxury spa showerhead—the only modern amenity in the old Victorian rental—fall down on me.

I had opted to revamp the store, modernizing it with what I deemed strategic, moneymaking renovations. It had a full glass wall at the back of the dining area, a 1950ish soda shop motif (complete with a black-and-white checkered floor), an open-view kitchen where customers could see their ice cream being made and a menu based on the recipes my grandparents, Aloysius Zephyr Crewse and Kaylene Brewster Crewse, had used when they opened shop in 1965.

I didn't have my grandmother's original recipe box—no one seemed to know what had happened to it. But I did have photocopies of some of the recipe cards she'd used, and, having worked alongside her for my entire childhood tugging at her apron strings, I was pretty sure, for the recipes I didn't have, I could remember most of the ingredients and churn out her bestsellers, or at least be pretty close.

Known for being the methodical and analytical one, I had carefully mapped out a blueprint to restore the business to what I called its glory days—when all we sold was ice cream—but all my planning and practical graduate coursework had gone straight out of the window by week two. I learned firsthand about real-world time delays.

I'd never worried so much in my life. My plan had been to relaunch the shop at the Chagrin Falls Annual Memorial Day Blossom Festival. But between the wrong glass shipping for my partition wall, a prolonged crop of rainstorms and an overbooked contractor, it would be closer to our little village's October Pumpkin Roll before I could flip the sign on the shop door to *Open.*

I say "closer" because my vision still hadn't been actualized. The plexiglass wall needed to partition off the kitchen still hadn't arrived. And the supplier of our fair-trade cane sugar had gotten into a ten-car pileup—no casualties, but tons of the white grains had been overturned across the highway, making me have to wait to get the first batches started until another truck could be loaded. It turned out to be only a two-day delay. Thank goodness it had arrived in time.

I reached over and flipped the showerhead to pulsating, letting the water beat down and wash away those thoughts of all the hiccups that had tried to give my ice cream dream a meltdown.

I basked in the spray for a few more minutes before I turned off the water, stepped out of the shower and wrapped a towel around me. I slid my hand across the condensation on the mirror and grabbed a bottle of face moisturizer.

Smearing the liquid under my eyes and across my forehead, I couldn't help but grin thinking about how our little business, with me at the helm, was going to come full circle today. We were back to selling ice cream and *only* ice cream.

I pulled off my shower cap, ran a comb through my hair and felt the first of the butterflies flapping around in my stomach. I whispered a little prayer and headed back to my bedroom to get dressed.

My grandfather had often reminisced about how hard it had been for him and my Grandma Kay to start that little shop. Just relocating to the village of Chagrin Falls, a suburb of Cleveland, from the south, had been an ordeal. My grandma hadn't gotten used to the snow and cold when they took on the business of digging in a frosty freezer every time she served a customer. But then she'd made it her own. Over the years, she came up with flavors that captured everyone's fancy—smooth and lemony luscious ice box pie, sprinkle-splattered cake batter and my grandfather's favorite, pralines and cream—folds of gooey sweet caramel and salty praline pecans swirled into her homemade vanilla bean ice cream.

But selling ice cream in a place where four seasons sometimes slid into two—either hot or cold—meant our family business had hit more bumps than the almond-filled rocky road ice cream my Grandma Kay used to whip up for her famous cakes. So, to keep up, other family members had stuffed the shop shelves with non–ice cream items in an attempt to keep it viable all year round.

Crewse Creamery had become more of a novelty shop—T-shirts, Chagrin Falls memorabilia, hot dogs, lemonade and candy. "No one wants ice cream in the wintertime, Bronwyn," my aunt Jack had said, calling me by my full name, something no one did, while setting up an Ohio lottery machine she'd purchased. "We have to follow the money. Diversify."

With Aunt Jack's changes, our family business had been teetering on the point of no return, especially after she stopped making ice cream by hand. She ordered mix for soft serve and frozen tubs all the way from Arizona. Homemade ice cream had been what set us apart from all the other ice cream shops. But she said it made no economical sense to continue to make it half the year when she could get a year-long contract to supply ice cream to cover the late-spring and summer months. Luckily, she'd found love on the internet and moved to follow her man to the Tar Heel State before the first shipment arrived.

My radio alarm clock had popped on at five and was issuing a weather alert when I got back to my room. *Cold. Wet. Dreary.*

Pulling back the sheer curtains at the window, I took a peek outside. I couldn't read the still-dark sky, and the dry ground illuminated by the yellow glow of the streetlight didn't give a hint of what the forecaster warned.

I pulled out a sweater as the old radiator clanked and hissed, held it up and thought better of it.

"Cold weather may be blowing in," I said, folding the sweater up, "but churning ice cream and waiting on customers is gonna make me work up a sweat." I smiled. "Yeah, lots of customers. Lots of sweat."

I stuffed the sweater back into the drawer and, opening another one, pulled out one of the shop's custom T-shirts. I layered it with a button-down flannel shirt—always best to be prepared—and snaked my way into a pair of jeans. On my knees, I rustled through the floor of my closet. I pushed work shoes down into my knapsack and dug my UGG boots out of the back.

I was ready to start my day—*the* day—the first day of our family's new and improved ice cream shop.

First stop, though, my parents' house.

I grabbed my puffy coat and a hat from the coat rack, picked up last year's Christmas gift from PopPop and stuffed it in my jeans pocket and plodded across the old wooden floor and down the back stairs that led out from my second-story apartment.

The sky spit down droplets of rain on me as I walked outside. Right now it was hit or miss, but something was brewing, I could tell. The wind let out a low howl, blew the autumn leaves across my path and gave me a shiver up my spine. I pulled the hood up on my coat, shoved my hands into my pockets looking for gloves. Nothing. I balled my fists up and tried to keep my fingertips from freezing. The weather forecast was rarely right, at least for Cleveland and its surrounding areas, and—fingers crossed—I hoped the wintery forecast for the day would be a miss.

Around my hometown, snowfall could come with the daffodils in April and not so much for sleigh rides and decorated trees in December. It wasn't odd anymore for Christmas to arrive with sixty-five-degree weather, which was what I was wishing for today.

# chapter TWO

Hey!" I called out. "Mom! Dad!" I walked through my parents' front door, which was always unlocked. "Where are you guys?" I knew no one was asleep in this house.

My parents still lived in the big colonial home where my grandparents had raised my dad, my uncle Denny and aunt Jack, and where they had raised my three brothers and me. They were pretty much empty nesters now, but family was always going in and out. We were a close-knit bunch, and my large family made up the majority of the 0.4 percent African American population of Chagrin Falls listed on Wikipedia.

"We're back here, Win," I heard my mother call out.

I tugged out of my coat, draped it over the newel post at the foot of the stairs, adjusted my knapsack across my shoulder and walked down the center hallway back to the kitchen. Much more updated than the Victorian I lived in. Since the kids moved out, my parents had renovated just about every room in the house.

My mother, sitting at the island, reached out for me as I

emerged through the kitchen entryway. "Happy Opening Day!" She took my hands and, pulling me over to her, planted a kiss. "Oh!" she said. "Your hands are freezing. Where are your gloves?"

"I'm okay, Mom," I said. "It's a short walk down to the shop. I'll be fine until I get there."

"You're not okay. And it's not fine. You're cold." She snapped her fingers, a thought seemingly sparking in her head, and hopped off the stool. "I've got a pair for you right here in your old cubby in the mudroom."

"Hi, Daddy," I said, knowing there was no use arguing with my mother. Plus, she was right, my hands were cold. "What are you two up to?"

"Daddy's making me breakfast," my mother said, bubbly and smiling as usual as she came back from the mudroom shaking a pair of red knitted gloves at me. "We're having a Riya omelet." She placed the gloves into my hands.

I raised an eyebrow. "As in my Riya?" I pushed the gloves down into my knapsack.

"Yep," my dad said, and gave a firm nod. He stood at the stove, bent over close, intense, working on the contents of his small skillet like he was performing surgery. He was the best cook out of our clan. Nobody missed dinner on Family Chef Night when it was his turn. He had on brown dress pants, ready for work, the sleeves of his light blue dress shirt rolled up, his collar button undone. His tie and suit jacket were carefully placed over the back of a chair. "It has a little turmeric, a little garam masala, basil, sweet Italian sausage and—"

"Some red chili pepper!" said my mother, finishing his sentence.

I laughed. "That would be Riya," I said.

One of my two best friends, Riya Amacarelli was half Sicilian, half Indian and fully American. She had always been a firecracker, hot-tempered and determined. She'd followed in the footsteps of more than half my family and gone into the medical field. Something I'd never considered. I peeked over into my dad's sauté pan—somehow he'd captured Riya in an egg dish.

"You want me to make you one, Pumpkin?" my dad asked.

"No," I said, shaking my head. "It just seems wrong eating a dish named after someone I know."

"Suit yourself. You'll miss a treat." He flipped over the omelet. "I'm making one for your Grumpy Pa, though," my father said. "You'll drop it off to him before you head down the hill?"

"Sure," I said.

My grandfather lived in the same house, but he had his own suite where he'd drawn a line—no entering without an invitation—except for me. I was his girl.

"Graham, don't call your father that," my mother said, creases forming on her brow. "He might be in a good mood this morning." My mother, the perpetual optimist. "He wanted Win to take over the store and run it, and today's the day. That has to have him in a good mood."

"Grumpiness is built into his DNA," my dad said. "I've been scouring medical journals ever since my residency days to see if a grumpy gene has been identified. Soon as they find one, I'm extracting it out of him."

My mother giggled. She thought all of my father's dry jokes were funny. The gleam in her eye and her constant smile when they were together would make anybody think that they were newlyweds instead of having been married for thirty-six years.

Other than both being patient and inherently kind, they were complete opposites. My mother, Ailbhe, always joining a Zumba group, a yoga class or a jitterbug dance team, was chubby. Short, with a head of dyed-over gray hair, she was full of energy, joy and laughter. She raised us kids, supported us in our dreams and had helped her in-laws at the ice cream shop from the time she started dating my father.

Besides riding his bike recreationally with my mom and down to the clinic he volunteered at once a week, my dad, Dr. James Graham Crewse, didn't do any exercise at all. He was tall and muscular, sturdy and just seemed naturally fit. He was an orthopedic surgeon at the renowned Lakeside Memorial Clinic. A thoughtful, systematic and careful man in everything he did, from performing surgeries even down to picking out a paint color for the den. I, according to my mother, was just like him. It drove her and her impulsive nature crazy.

I thought I was more like my Grandma Kay.

"I'm sure PopPop will enjoy his breakfast, Daddy," I said, not as fully convinced as my mother seemed to be. "He'll think it's nice that you shared your creation."

"That'll be the day," my dad said. He pulled a plate out of the cabinet and slid an omelet onto it.

Right in sync, my mother took it from my father's hands, grabbed the plastic wrap and covered the plate. "Tell your grandfather I'll stop by before I go down to the shop this morning and see what he needs," she said, handing me the plate.

"I'm sure this will be fine," I said. "His morning coffee, his newspaper and"—I held up the plate—"a couple of eggs—"

"Are all he needs to start his day," the three of us said in unison, and then laughed. That was my grandfather's mantra.

But even though my grandfather had been saying it for years, my father was right. Not even his morning staples could make him satisfied with how any day went. There were only two things I knew that put a smile on my grandfather's face, and my father's cooking wasn't one of them.

"I'M NOT EATING this." PopPop pushed the plate across the table after I had placed it in front of him. Not even bothering to take the plastic wrap off.

My grandfather had met me at the door as I came around the outside of the house to the separate entrance of his living quarters. Already up and dressed like he had a job to go to, he greeted me with a kiss and a smile. It was probably the first one he'd emitted since the last time he saw me.

I was one of the things that put a smile on his face.

I trailed behind him back to the kitchen, where evidently he'd been sitting at the table, probably waiting on me. He knew I wouldn't start today without a talk with him.

My grandfather was just an older version of my dad (or would that be my dad was a younger version of him?). He was tall, and his daily walks up and down the hilly streets of Chagrin Falls kept him fit. He had a penchant for plaid shirts and wing-tipped shoes and all these years after Grandma Kay's death, he still wore his wedding ring.

The small kitchen was neat and tidy. His old radio, loudly playing a sports station, went hand-in-hand with his outdated appliances and old tile floor. He hadn't let my parents remodel his part of the house, saying that those walls knew all about him and they kept him company.

"Why won't you eat it? It's what you eat for breakfast every day," I said, turning down the volume on the radio. He denied it, but I'd swear he was getting hard of hearing. "I brought your newspaper in and"—I eyed the countertop—"I knew you'd already have coffee brewing. That's everything you need, right?"

"What *is* that?" He pointed at the plate.

"Eggs. Just like you like."

"Don't put words in my mouth," he said, shaking his head slowly. "I never said I liked eggs like *that*." He turned up his nose. "That doesn't even look like an egg."

"It's an omelet," I said. I grabbed a fork out of the drawer, bumping it shut with my hip. I walked back to the table, slid the plate back in front of him and handed him the utensil. "Something different from the usual scrambled you eat, but you've had an omelet before." I smiled. "And your son made it. You know what a good cook he is."

He placed the fork on the plate and slid it back across the table. Again. "He should stick to medicine."

"I bet it's good." I sang the words and planted a smile on my face.

"Don't patronize me, little girl," he said, and narrowed his eyes at me. He still called me that even though I wasn't too far from knocking on thirty's door.

"I'm not," I said. I knew better. No matter how old I got, PopPop was still my elder—you just didn't talk back. I was taught to show respect. I bent over and kissed him on his cheek. "I never would."

"I can make my own eggs, you know," he said. "I can still take care of myself."

"I know," I said. "We *all* know." He had told us enough.

PopPop was all about his independence. Although he hadn't run the ice cream shop since my grandma took sick with early-onset Alzheimer's and couldn't be left alone, he always reminded us that even at his age he still could. He said his date of birth wasn't a hindrance to anything other than the draft, and, he noted, they didn't even have that anymore.

"So if you know, stop trying to get me to eat that."

"Okay," I said. I picked the plate up and put it on top of the stove.

"You opening the store today?" he asked. He already knew the answer, but we both liked talking about it. We had been counting down the days.

"Yes, PopPop. Today's the day." I pulled out the chair next to him and sat down. "I'm just sorry it took so long to do."

"Don't worry none about that," he said, and put his hand over mine. "You got it done."

I nodded. "I got it done."

"Yes, you have, and you've done a better job at it than anyone else could have," he said, a proud smile on his face. "I walked by it the other day, decided to go inside, and it's looking just like one of those shops I see in the trade magazines."

"You saw it?" I said, a grin emerging on my face. "I wanted to wait until everything was ready to give you the grand tour."

"Looks ready to me."

"A couple things are still missing."

"Like making your kitchen see-through?"

"Yeah," I said, and chuckled. "I want customers to experience just what we're boasting about. Give them a full view of the love and pride that goes into every handcrafted batch of our frozen creamy goodness."

PopPop laughed. "But that pales in comparison to that glass wall you put up at the rear of the store overlooking the falls," he said. "Anybody sitting at one of those tables you put back there is going to get a treat."

I grinned. "The village was established around that waterfall, named after it, and our store sits right on top of it. Why not showcase it?" I got up, reached for two cups out of the cabinet and poured us both coffee.

"It was a really good idea," he said. "Wish I'd thought of it."

"Well," I said, setting the cups on the table and going to the fridge for milk, "I like your idea of having a vintage soda fountain."

"That was a good idea, wasn't it?" Another smile escaping his lips, he poured the milk into his coffee—he'd never liked cream—and stirred it. "We make a good team."

"Yeah we do," I said, and took a sip of mine.

We sat silent for a few moments, no words passing between us as we sipped our brew. I felt so comfortable with my granddad. Like my dad, he had a calm about him that made everything seem okay.

"I got something for you," my grandfather said after a short while. "Something I've been saving for the right person to have."

"Something for me?" I asked, a smile beaming across my face.

"Don't get too excited," he said. "It's just some little old thing I wanted you to have." He got up and went to the cabinet next to the sink. I stood and followed behind him, excited about what it might be. Taking out a stack of bowls, he reached back into the corner of the cupboard and pulled out a box.

"Oh!" I said, my hand going up to cover my mouth, my eyes wide. "It's Grandma Kay's recipe box!"

"It sure is, and I think—no—I know, she'd want you to have it."

I looked up into the cupboard and back down at the pale green tin box with citrus fruit and leaves painted across the top and spilling over the rim of the container.

"Has that been there all the time?" I pointed up. Everyone over the years had been trying to find it. "All this time? You said you didn't know where it was. Aunt Jack had to use the copies we had."

"No." He shook his head. "I said I hadn't *seen it* in years. There's a difference."

"You hadn't seen it?"

"Right." He nodded. "I had put it away. Your grandmother toiled over those recipes to make them just right, and she'd only want someone who would do right by them to have them."

"And that's me?" I said.

"I think so," he said, and pushed the box toward me. A loud giggle busted out as I reached for it, but he pulled it away. "I know that you've come up with your own flavors and you've got the photocopies already of some of your grandmother's recipes." He tapped the top of the box. "And these aren't one of a kind anymore. I've seen lots of people using her flavor combinations over the years, and the shop will do just fine without them."

"But hers are special," I said, letting him know I understood. "And even if I don't *need* them, I want them."

"Yes," he said, his eyes sparkling. "Her recipes were special. Just like she was."

"Thank you, PopPop!" I wrapped one hand around the box and the other around his neck and gave him a big kiss. "I'm going to start a Kaylene line of ice cream. All Grandma Kay's recipes."

"I knew you'd do the right thing with them," he said. "Now, don't you lose that." He nodded at it. "That little box has been around longer than your father."

"I won't let it out of my sight. Ever. Promise." I opened up my knapsack and pushed it down into a corner—couldn't chance it falling out.

"Now," PopPop said, sitting back down in his chair. "How about grabbing a couple of those eggs out of the icebox?" He nodded toward the refrigerator. "You got time to scramble up a couple for me? I'm starving." He grabbed his cup of coffee and took a sip.

"I always make sure I have time for you, PopPop."

"Thank you," he said, smiling. He pointed to the plate I'd brought over. "And you can eat that thing your father cooked."

# chapter
# THREE

For each step I took toward North Main Street, where Crewse Creamery sat, another goose bump rose up on my arm. I could hardly swallow and there was a smile plastered on my face that may have been stuck because of the cold, but I couldn't be sure.

I had made scrambled eggs for my PopPop before I left, but no matter how much he had insisted, I couldn't eat anything. Everything inside of me was in a knot. I was drenched, through and through, with anticipation.

The store wasn't opening for another four hours and I had a lot to do to get ready. But I couldn't be sure that even my prep work could drain all the nervous energy I had bouncing around inside of me.

I'd made a list mapping out the chores for the day—flavors I wanted to offer, the order I'd make them in and the ingredients needed for each—making sure I didn't miss anything. It was time to rebuild the Crewse brand. Time to spread the word that we were back in the business of making ice cream the old-fashioned, wholesome, natural way. It was time to cultivate a love, like the one my family shared for what we did, that was evident to everyone who walked through our doors. But most importantly, it was time to show the place I'd created, where, I hoped, people would line up out the door, no matter the season, to see and taste what we had to offer.

I patted the side of my knapsack and smiled. Probably all my planning was going out the window. That just seemed the way things had gone lately. But this time it would be a good thing—I'd be including my Grandma Kay's recipes in today's batches. A deviation made with love.

Hopefully I had the right ingredients in-house for at least one of my grandma's recipes. I couldn't wait to take a look at them. My mother was going to be so surprised to see them after they'd been AWOL all these years, and just as excited as I was. She had spent so much time side-by-side with my grandparents in our little shop, even helping my grandmother conjure up those recipes—at least some of them. Grandma Kay could be very secretive when it came to her Crewse Creamery flavors.

I spied the store as I turned the corner off Carriage Hill Lane. The golden glow from the bronze wall-mounted lanterns I'd had installed on either side of the front door made the new yellow-and-baby-blue-striped *Crewse Creamery* awning shimmer. Everything all shiny and new. Everything except for the old wrought-iron bench my grandfather had placed out front for Grandma Kay.

After Grandma Kay had gotten sick, she'd sit there for hours, everyone taking turns spending time with her while she reminisced. She couldn't remember what she'd had for breakfast, or sometimes how to get back home after she'd wandered off, but she could relay, down to the last detail, something that had happened in 1958.

I kept that bench because getting rid of it would have been like losing a part of her.

As I arrived at the shop, I saw someone standing in front of it, a dog in their arms.

*People lining up already?*

That sent a warm feeling all through me.

"Morning." It was a man. He smiled and spoke when I reached the front of the store. "You're not by any chance looking for a lost puppy, are you?" He held it up to give me a look at it.

It was an Ori-Pei. I knew because my down-the-street neighbor had one. The little guy was all wrinkles, with a big head like a Shar-Pei but the floppy ears and thick curly tail of a pug. He was black and white with lots of spots and had big brown eyes that looked right through me.

"No," I said, and reached out and scratched the top of the puppy's head. "Where'd you find him?"

"Right in the stoop of the flower shop next door." He tilted his head that way. "Probably trying to keep warm."

"No ID tag?" I asked.

"Nope." He ran his hand down the pup's head and around his neck, checking in his folds. "Unless his collar fell off. But he looks too healthy to be a stray."

"Awww. Sorry, I can't help you." I leaned in and looked into the little puppy's eyes. "Can't help the both of you." The dog gave out a bark in response.

"It's okay," the man said, and pulled off a red scarf that had been around his neck and wrapped it around the dog. "I'll walk him over to the police station and see if someone isn't looking for him." He looked up the street one way and back down the other. "You're the only person I saw out this early. Figured he might be yours."

I chuckled. "I'm on my way to work." I pointed to my ice cream shop. "Have to get everything made and let it freeze before we open."

"Crewse Creamery?" he said, and looked up at the sign as if he was just noticing where he stood. "I can't believe this place is still here." He leaned forward and peered through the window. "I used to come here, oh man, must have been twenty-five, thirty years ago. Loved their ice cream. That was when it was owned by the Crewse family."

"It still is," I said. "I'm Bronwyn Crewse."

"Get out of here," he said, smiling. "Aloysius and Kaylene's granddaughter?"

A smile beamed across my face. "Yes." I tilted my head and looked at him. "You know them?"

"Yes." Dimples appeared when he smiled, and his blue eyes seemed to sparkle at the memory. "Of course I know them. How are they?"

"Oh, my grandmother passed away a few years back. But my grandfather is doing great. I just left him."

"He still lives on Carriage Hill Lane? I've been living out of town for a while. Just passing through and couldn't miss saying hello to my friends in Chagrin Falls."

"Yep, that's the family house."

"It's funny how things can be so different when you've been away, but some things, the important things"—he looked into my eyes—"seem to stay the same." He stroked the puppy. "I visited at the house a few times with your grandparents. That was when everyone was around—Graham, Denny, Jack. You kids. I remember you guys were big on family. Especially your grandmother."

"Wow, you *do* know everyone," I said. "And, yes, she was. Family meant a lot to her. It means a lot to all of us."

"Well, I owned the store next door here," he said. "So we were like family—in a neighborly sort of way."

I frowned and looked at the wooden sign hanging over the door that read *The Flower Pot*, the village's only florist. It had been open only a year or so, and I realized he was talking about the shop that had been there a quarter century ago. "Clawson's Bike Shop?" I asked.

"You remember?"

"I do," I said. "But you're not Mr. Clawson." I remembered him, too.

"No," he said. "Good memory." Chuckling, he shook his head. "I'm not Dan. He ran the shop. I, along with his wife, was in charge of the back office. We were more like his silent partners. I'm Steve." He switched the dog to the other arm and stuck out his hand for me to shake.

"Nice to meet you, Steve," I said, and took his hand.

"We aren't just meeting for the first time," he said. "You don't remember me?"

"Sorry," I said, my forehead creasing.

"You were young," he said. "But I probably spent more time in your grandparents' store than I did in my own." He winked. "Helped them through a few rough bumps. That was a long time ago, though."

I didn't know what bumps he meant, but trying to run a business, I'd discovered, didn't come without them.

"You probably don't remember, but those were good times. Good memories."

*I have lots of good childhood memories,* I thought.

Steve wore a camel-colored overcoat that looked expensive. He didn't have it buttoned up, and with the wind that was blowing through, I figured he must be cold. His cheeks were flushed, his shoulders hunched. Still, he was better prepared than I'd been. He wore brown gloves that weren't leather and, to me, they—along with the red scarf that he now shared with the dog—didn't match the rest of him. His rubber overshoes were mottled with dried slush and salt, and he wore a gray chunky-knit mock turtleneck sweater that was almost the same color as his hair.

"I should get going. We're re-opening today," I said proudly.

"Then I'll be sure to drop in and get a scoop," he said with a firm nod. "I remember how I loved your grandmother's mud pie ice cream." He licked his tongue across his upper lip. "That rich fudge swirl, then crunchy little cookie pieces. Yum." His dimples seemed to deepen.

I laughed. "Well, I'll see if I can't whip some up for you when you stop back by."

He smiled at me, then looked up the street. "I might even drop in and say hello to your grandfather while I'm here. He'd probably fall over if he saw me."

"I'm sure he'd love to see you. Especially since you remember my grandmother. She is his favorite topic of conversation."

"Yep. I just might do that." He looked down at the dog. "Right now, though, I gotta drop this little guy off at the police station." He turned the dog to face him. Leaning in close, he said, "We gotta find who you belong to, don't we?"

"Good luck," I said.

"I think we'll be okay," he said. "Must've been meant for me to find him. He wouldn't have lasted long out here." He looked at me for a long moment, his eyes seemingly searching mine for something. "I guess it was meant for me to find you, too."

"To find me?" I said.

"Yes." He relaxed his stare. "To remind me where I can buy the best ice cream in Cleveland. You still have the best, right?"

I nodded. "We do."

"Then I'll definitely be back." And with that, he took off in the opposite direction of the police station. I turned to tell him he was going the wrong way, but ended up just watching him walk aimlessly down the street. He tucked the puppy under his coat and started to whistle as he walked. Maybe he had something else he needed to do first.

*Yay!* I thought. *I'll at least have one customer today.*

"What am I saying?!" I flapped my arms. "We're probably going to sell out!"

I hurried around to the side of the building, pulled off one of the gloves my mother had given me and dug down into my jeans pocket. I wrapped my fingers around the key ring, pulled it out and squeezed it tight.

*Blessings abound for the home of a family . . .*

My Grandma Kay's words.

Kaylene Brewster Crewse was all about family and all about home. She even imbued others with that sentiment. Just like she had with the man I'd just met. And that was what she made the ice cream shop about, too. Those words were in my heart and mind from the moment PopPop gave me the keys and every minute after.

I walked around to the side of building, drew in a breath and, standing at the door, stuck the key in, turned the lock and pushed it open.

# chapter FOUR

Are we late?" Maisie rushed through the door, red-faced, words stumbling out, her arms laden with cloth bags and a book bag, and her red, usually curly hair still wet and droopy from what must've been a hasty morning shower. She looked wildly around the kitchen. "I couldn't find my lucky socks, the ones with the ice cream cones on them."

"No," I said, and smiled. I brushed my hands down my apron and looked up at the wall-mounted clock. "You're right on time."

My help had arrived. Well, most of it. My never-on-time mother would be straggling in soon, I was sure. I had given them a start time an hour after mine. I wanted to meet my deliveries, spend time alone to take it all in and be able to create without any interruptions.

The three of them wouldn't be my usual morning crew. Riya and Maisie had jobs: Riya was a resident at the hospital where my dad worked and Maisie was a waitress at Molta's. I just wanted my besties to be there for my first day. My mother's retirement was filled with dance, arts and crafts, and exercise classes. When I realized how late in the year we were opening, I'd hired two people to help, but they were scheduled to come in for the afternoon and evening shifts. When the true ice cream season came along, I knew I'd have to hire additional employees. It had been shop tradition that the family filled in vacancies, especially the younger members. But now it seemed that nearly everyone had grown up and moved on.

"She couldn't find her head if it wasn't attached," Riya said, walking in the door behind Maisie. "I waited for her in the car for twenty minutes before having to go inside and drag her out. I'm missing my morning run for this."

I raised an eyebrow. "You could have run the twenty minutes you were waiting for Maisie," I said.

"Tell me about it," Riya said, and held up a hand for an air high five. "I could've done my whole seven miles."

Riya's olive-colored skin was flushed with frustration. She had a hair-trigger temper. She'd started running and taking tae kwon do to channel her energy and keep a level head. But sometimes Maisie could test her nerves.

"Well, you should have. It would have given me more time." Maisie dropped her bags on the table. "I mean she literally *dragged* me, Win. I'm probably bruised." She rubbed her arm. "I could hardly finish getting my one foot into my galoshes. Wait . . . what's the word for just one—goulash?"

"I think that's a stew, Maisie."

Riya, ignoring Maisie's digression, shook her head and turned back to me. "Which begs the question," she said, smacking her lips as she shrugged out of her coat, "why take time to put on special socks that no one will see?" Riya pointed down at the knee-high yellow plastic boots that Maisie donned.

"Well, I couldn't let my feet get wet," Maisie said. She hung her coat up on the rack by the door. "It's getting bad out there. It's like freezing rain. I could catch my death of cold."

"She's her grandmother's child," Riya said. She pushed up her sleeves and put her hands on her hips. "I've got rounds at the hospital in two hours. And like I said, I'm missing my usual morning run, so I've got a lot of pent-up tension to work off before I go. We need to get down to business." She pulled her spare rubber tie off her wrist and, pulling her hair back into a ponytail, wrapped it around her thick, chin-length black hair. "No time for Maisie and her shenanigans."

"I can stay all day," Maisie said. Always chipper—a big grin on her face, her brown eyes sparkling—she never acknowledged Riya's backhanded jibes and would do all she could to help the both of us. "And I came bearing gifts!" She reached into one of her cloth shopping bags and took out gallon-sized plastic bags filled with goodies for me. She shook one bag—"Vanilla"—then the other. "Cinnamon. All homegrown. All for you. And there's more." She nodded toward her bags. "If you need it."

"Thank you, Maisie." I walked over and took the bags and sniffed each. "Mmmm. Smells good," I said. "Adding a greenhouse to your garden was a good idea."

"Didn't you say this place is all about farm fresh?"

"Yeah," I chuckled. "But I didn't quite envision the farm being a block away, with fresh-grown produce all year round and run by you."

Maisie Solomon was my other best friend.

The three of us had been best friends ever since recess on the first day of kindergarten. After rushing over to pull Riya off Derrick Liefkuheler because he took the swing she wanted, we bonded. I had channeled my mother, rubbing my hands down Riya's arms and making shushing sounds to try and calm her, while Maisie had taken her act from her grandmother's playbook, trying to stuff her with food from her book bag. We'd gotten her to calm down and come play on the monkey bars with us.

"Wow! Do you even need me?" My mother came bursting through the door. "You've got a full house." She yanked off her hat and shook the water from her umbrella on the mat by the door.

"Morning, Mrs. Crewse," the girls chimed.

"Morning." She blew out a breath. "Whew!" she said. "It's getting bad out there."

"C'mon, Mom," I said, going over to help her with her coat. "I'll always need you. I couldn't do it without you."

"Right," she said, then sized up the room. "This place looks fantastic. Doesn't it?" she asked the girls. "I love that you exposed the brick walls."

"Yes, it does look nice in here," Maisie said. "I love all the stainless-steel appliances, too. Makes it look official."

"Official?" Riya asked.

"Yes, I think it looks official," Maisie said. "Although with all the pictures Win took with her phone and texted to me, I already knew it was going to be beautiful."

"I got more notifications from her phone than I got hospital pages," Riya said.

"I still have to get that plexiglass wall up." I pointed to the particleboard that was holding its place. "Once that's in, then I can see up front from back here, and up front can see me."

"Well, I'm itching to see up front," my mother said. "I'm sure I won't even recognize the place. And I am so excited to see that glass wall overlooking the falls."

"Beautiful," Maisie said.

"You've seen it?" my mother asked.

"Only in pictures."

"I stopped by the day they were putting it in," Riya said. "Haven't seen it fully installed, though."

"Well, I'll give everyone the full tour after we get my batches going," I said, looking at my mother. "Plenty of time for all of your *ooh*s and *aah*s. But that won't help me serve my customers."

"I'm ready," my mother said. "I came to work."

"That's what I'm talking about," Riya said. "Let's get to making ice cream."

"Yes," I said. "Let's make ice cream!" I clapped my hands together. "Maisie, you're on flavor duty. I'm making the usual—French vanilla, chocolate—only mine is going to be chocolaty decadence."

"Decadent chocolate? I don't know how you'd do that," Riya said. "But that sounds like it's going to be my favorite."

"I'm betting it'll be everyone's favorite," I said.

"What about strawberry?" Maisie said. "That's a usual one."

"I'm doing it, only I'm mixing it up and making it a shortcake." I turned and pointed to my mother. "Mom, I need you to bake the cake and"—I nodded toward the pantry—"I had ears of corn delivered this morning. They're in a box. I pulled them in there, too. If you can cut the kernels off the cob for me."

"Popcorn?" she asked, her eyebrows arching. "You're making popcorn ice cream?" She didn't seem to like the idea.

"We're not doing popcorn, per se," I said with a sly grin. "At least not what you're thinking of. I'm making a caramel corn ice cream."

"Oh! That sounds yummy," she said, and smacked her lips.

"Glad you like it," I said, and smiled. "So you take care of the corn and I'll make the caramel."

"So what do you want me to do?" Maisie asked.

"Split the vanilla bean and extract the seeds," I said. "And I'll need enough to make vanilla extract, too. I'll give you the measurements. Then cut up the strawberries. I'll make the puree." I grabbed my knapsack and pulled out my notebook. "Oh," I said after perusing it, "I'm also making cherry amaretto chocolate chunk."

"Amaretto?" Maisie said. "As in the liqueur?"

"Yes," I said. I looked at her sideways and batted my eyes. "As in the liqueur. So, I'll need you to pit and halve the cherries and break the chocolate into chunks." I tore the page out of my notebook. "I wrote down how much I'll need." I pointed to the pantry where I'd told my mother she'd find the corn. "Everything's in there."

"And me?" Riya asked.

I walked over to the commercial refrigerator and pulled out a crate of eggs. "Here," I said, and nodded toward the aluminum mixing bowls. "Grab a couple of those. I need you to separate these eggs for me."

"Oh." She looked down at them, then back up at me. "I—I don't know if I can do that," she said, taking the tray from me, her eyebrows knitted together. "I don't think I remember a thing from my surgery rotation."

"It's not like surgery," my mother said, laughing. "It's easy. You'll be fine." My mother headed to the pantry to get started on her assignment. "Crack open the shell and extract the yolk."

"Sounds like surgery to me," Riya muttered. Maisie and I chuckled.

"I've got something to show you," I said, following my mother. I leaned in toward her and lowered my voice.

I looped my arm through hers and walked her back over to the table where I'd put my knapsack.

"Well, you said it. It's getting late, so you better hurry and tell so we can get down to business." She looked at Maisie and Riya. "Although I think you won't have a problem with all your help."

"It's about PopPop," I said. I turned her toward me and let my eyes settle into hers.

"What?" Her eyes got big and she turned to look at the girls. She must have figured it was about them since I'd taken to whispering. "Is it the omelet? Was your dad right? PopPop wouldn't eat the Riya omelet?"

"No." I blinked, then shook my head. "Yes. Daddy was right. But that's not what I wanted to tell you." Without taking my eyes off hers, I reached my hand down into my bag and pulled out the tin.

"Oh my," my mother said, looking down into my hands, practically mimicking my reaction when I first saw it. "It couldn't be." I saw tears well up in her eyes, and that made mine get misty as well.

She reached out her hand tentatively, then pulled back, seemingly afraid that if she touched it, it might disappear again.

"Can you believe it?" I said. "PopPop had it all the time."

She shook her head and chuckled. "Graham is right. PopPop is a grump. Why would he keep this from us?" She smiled down at it. "That little box was like gold to your grandmother. She guarded it with her life." She gave a firm nod. "She would have wanted you to have it."

"That's what he said."

My mother gave me a warm smile. "He's right."

"And," I said, "I'm going to check to see if I can't make one of her recipes today. Mud pie."

My mom frowned. "Mother Kay never made mud pie ice cream."

"She must have," I said. "I met a man today who told me it was his favorite."

"He got that wrong," she said. "Mother Kay used to say that that was what she made as a child, and she wasn't putting it in her store."

"I don't know, Mommy. I don't remember it either, but he did, and he remembered a lot of other things, too."

"People always remember our ice cream."

"He remembered the whole family. Oh!" I said. "You'll know who he is. He said he was part owner of Clawson's Bike Shop."

"Dan Clawson didn't have a partner."

"He was a silent partner. Along with Mr. Clawson's wife."

My mother narrowed her eyes and put her hands on her hips. "What was this guy's name?"

"Steve."

"Steve what?"

I shrugged. "He didn't say. But he's coming back to get ice cream. Mud pie ice cream, so I have to find the recipe." I started to open the box, but she put her hand over it.

"What did this guy look like?" she asked suspiciously.

"I don't know." I hunched my shoulders. "He had graying hair. Deep blue eyes—"

"And dimples!" Her words came out with fire.

"Uhm . . . yeah. Dimples. Because why?"

"Stephen Bayard! That's who that was. That no-good scoundrel."

"What?" I asked, confused.

"His name is Stephen Bayard. He didn't eat mud pie ice cream here. What he did was drag us through the mud!"

"Who?"

"The whole family."

She was breathing heavily through her nose. I could have sworn I saw fire. "And he wasn't Dan Clawson's partner either. What he did was partner up with his wife."

"I'm not following," I said. "He seemed like a nice guy."

She didn't even let me tell her the part about the puppy before she spat back, "He is *not* a nice guy!"

"Okay," I said. "Calm down."

"He is the one who preyed on your grandmother's illness and had her sign over the store to him. We had to scramble to get into court to have her deemed incompetent, something that broke your grandfather's heart, so the contract wouldn't be legally binding. And before we could do anything about him, he disappeared! With Dan Clawson's wife!"

"Oh," I said. I couldn't think of anything else to say. Maybe he wasn't a nice guy . . .

I was twelve when Grandma Kay took sick. When we were kids, we weren't allowed in "grown folks'" business. They spoke in hushed tones around us or we were told to leave the room. That was probably why he didn't seem familiar to me.

"What did he want?" she asked.

"Nothing, I guess." I shrugged. "I don't know. He had a dog with him and was looking for its owner," I said. "He was just talking."

"What did he say?" Her words were quick and stern.

"Nothing, Mom. Just that he remembered the store and all of us. That he was going to stop by and see PopPop."

"Oh, no, he's not!" She turned from me and marched over to the wall rack where she'd hung her coat and purse. "I'm calling home right now to warn them about that scumbag," she called over her shoulder. "Because if he shows up"—she yanked her purse down from the rack and started rummaging through it—"your father might just kill him."

# chapter FIVE

"You girls are going to catch your death of cold down here." Our family discussion was interrupted by Rivkah Solomon. She was a natural-born intruder.

Rivkah was our store's second-floor tenant, Maisie's grandmother, the Jewish owner of the village's only Chinese restaurant, and the only other person I knew of who could make my grandfather smile.

She was thin and had long, slender hands—my grandmother used to say she had piano fingers. Now, like on her face, the skin that covered them was thin and wrinkled. She wore her all-gray hair pulled back, braided and wrapped around in a bun, but she always had strands that strayed.

"Savta!" Maisie said, a big grin on her face. She wiped her hands on a towel, trotted over and planted a kiss on her grandmother's cheek. "I was going to come up and see you."

Rivkah pulled her own sweater close around her, then held up her hands. Her fists were filled with outerwear. "I knew you girls wouldn't be prepared for this morning's weather." She had a sweater for each of us.

How she knew how many to bring, I didn't know.

"Morning, Savta," I said, and followed Maisie's lead. I planted my kiss on the other cheek.

"Hi, Mrs. Solomon." Riya muttered her greeting. She'd refused to call Rivkah the Hebrew word for grandmother. She'd said long ago that the family she had from both sides of her parents were more than enough relatives to keep up with without picking up any strays.

"I'm going to turn the heat up," Rivkah said, and headed over to the thermostat. "It's not good for you not to be warm while you work."

"We're making ice cream, Savta," Maisie said. "It's supposed to be a little cold."

"It's not good to be overheated either," Riya said. "I can tell you that to a medical certainty."

"Nonsense," Rivkah said, and waved a hand. "Is that what they taught you at that medical school?" She spoke to Riya over her shoulder as she fiddled with the thermostat. Satisfied, she turned and looked at us, a gleam in her eye. "I have made you a little something to eat. Maisie, you help me bring it down." She aimed a finger at her with her instructions. "You girls are too skinny, and you need all your energy to get this place going.

"And let me tell you." She waved her hand. "I'm so happy not to have to hear all that construction noise going on down here anymore. I can't wait for the smell of ice cream." She bunched up her shoulders and let her fingers waggle in front of her nose as she gave a sniff.

"I don't think ice cream has a smell," Riya said in a low voice, looking at me.

"Well, good morning, Felice," my mother said, and we all looked toward the back steps from where Rivkah had emerged. And there she was, Rivkah's cat. She should have been called Your Highness. Her white coat flowed as she pranced down the steps and across the kitchen floor with her short, chubby legs, her plume tail swaying. She disappeared into the front of the store without even throwing a "meow" our way.

"What is she doing?" Riya asked.

"I think she's going to see how the window seat turned out," I said.

Riya raised an eyebrow.

"She was here when the interior decorator came with samples for the covering, and she picked out the fabric."

Riya rolled her eyes at me.

I held up my hands. "What? What can I say? The cat knows what she likes."

"Well, I'm going, too," my mother said. "You can take the girls on your prescheduled tour later, if you want. I didn't see it while it was under construction." She jerked her head toward the cat. "I'm like Felice, I want to see it when I want to see it. I've waited long enough." She looped her arm around Rivkah's. "I'll call your father"—she bowed her head at me—"and let him know about your visitor this morning." She tugged on Rivkah. "C'mon, let's see what your cat has contributed to the new store."

"Mom," I said, and flapped my arms. "We've got a lot of work to do. We get distracted and we won't finish on schedule."

She paid no attention to me, and sashayed off on her short little cobby legs just as Felice had, dragging Rivkah beside her.

I shook my head and gave Riya a look that asked, "Can you believe this?"

"It's a good thing you hired help," Riya said. "This is a lot of work."

"Yeah, I know," I said, glancing toward the front where my mother had disappeared. "I've got Candy Cook and Wilhelmina Stone coming in later today."

"Wait," Maisie said, a spark in her eye. "You mean Miss Wilhelmina? The woman who was the greeter at the Mayland Heights Walmart?"

"Yep, that's her." I nodded. "She's working afternoons."

"Isn't she like a hundred and five?"

"A hundred and four," I jokingly corrected, "but she's got years of customer service experience."

"I bet," she said, and we all laughed.

"You know how to pick 'em," Riya said.

"Candy, my other new staff member, seems real cool. She's nineteen and says she's a night owl, so she'll work until close," I said.

"How do you know her?" Riya asked.

"I don't." I shrugged. "She just came in and applied. She seemed friendly enough. Doesn't know a thing about making ice cream, though. Actually, neither one of them did."

"Not a commonly found skill set, huh?" Riya said.

"Go figure!" I said, and chuckled. "So I'm thinking with those two and my family's help that should cover all the hours and foot traffic."

"I'll quit Molta's," Maisie volunteered, "and work for you."

"You're going to quit your job, Maisie?" Riya said. "Not again!"

"That Ari is a micromanager," Maisie said in her own defense. "He gives off bad energy. Crashes my mood and sends my always-twenty-percent-tip servicing skills into a nosedive." She scrunched up her nose. "I don't like him and I can't work with that man. Plus, that restaurant is too fancy for our little village."

Did Maisie think that without her the restaurant would just go away?

"The whole village is going upscale, you know, including this place," Riya said.

"No, we're not," I said, and scrunched up my nose. "We're just the corner ice cream shop my grandparents started."

"Corner shops don't sell ice cream with liqueur in it," Riya said.

"This place isn't on a corner." Maisie said it like it was the first time I was finding that out.

"I mean we're just *like* one. And between family and my two new employees, I think we'll be good, at least until the weather breaks."

"See! You need me," Maisie said. "You're gonna need all the help you can find when all your customers start blowing through."

I couldn't help but break out in a big grin. "You think so?" I asked. "They're going to be blowing through?"

"I know so," Maisie said, her smile matching mine. "Like a high-speed train. Nothing can stop them."

But like in most cases, Maisie didn't have a clue. We blew through the prep, and I knew the day's ice cream flavors would've blown anyone away, if anyone had showed up.

They didn't.

The only thing that blew up to our door was snow. More than a foot and a half of it. And it stopped anyone from coming through.

# chapter

# SIX

I sat on the bench in front of the store. Grandma Kay's bench. I needed to feel her arms around me.

I drew in a breath, then watched it vaporize and swirl around when I blew it back out.

My mother had a habit of sitting in parking lots. Whenever she was feeling low or depressed, if she was out, she'd pull the car over and sit there. She said that sometimes to get clarity you just had to be still.

I didn't need clarity. I knew exactly what had gone wrong. It was the blizzard that blustered in the day I opened a store that usually served the edible kind—on warm, sunny days . . .

And even though I knew what went wrong, I didn't want to move. My mind needed to be still and I was pretty sure my body was frozen in place.

It was dark already and it was only a little past six. I had sent my mom and Maisie home way before the scheduled eleven p.m.

closing and told my new employees not to come in. There wasn't any reason to stay.

I had walked there, and even though Maisie offered me a ride home, I didn't want to take it. I felt like walking, only I didn't get any farther than that bench.

The deep snow crunched underfoot, the cold wind that bristled against my face felt prickly and my fingertips were numb. I pulled the hood of my puffy coat over my head, the fur falling down covering my eyes, stuffed my hands in my jacket pocket, slumped down in my seat and started clicking my nails.

I had planned a grand opening, but after the place didn't get finished until close to Halloween, I thought that I'd wait until then. People came from all around for our Pumpkin Roll. I'd flooded my social media accounts, though, passed out flyers and given my friend who owned a food truck samples to give away on Walnut Wednesdays—Walnut, a street in downtown Cleveland where food trucks gathered at lunchtime on that day each week. I thought all of that would bring people in.

I had been just as wrong as Maisie.

I wondered what my PopPop was going to say about all of this. I had to go and see him and tell him what happened. Let him know what a bust the day had been.

And I wondered if he was going to feel let down about passing the reins over to me.

Me and my big ideas. Maybe they'd been too much. My brothers had said it to me enough times.

"Jasper! Come back!" A voice far off wafted my way. The noise jolted me out of my disappointment. I sat up straight and looked toward the voice. It came from down by the movie theater, marquee lights showing only a shadowy, ambiguous figure.

Footsteps came crunching in the snow toward me, but in the haze of the night, blurry streetlights and the tears threatening to fall, I could only get a glance. And then the figure was out of my sight. The same high-pitched voice near the marquee called out again. "She's not coming back!" it said.

I chuckled. That would never have been one of us kids, running away after being called. I could just imagine what kind of trouble he'd be in when whoever was calling him caught up with him. My senses no longer dulled, I realized it probably wasn't too smart to sit in the cold any longer.

I stood up to go, pain coursing through my nearly frostbitten fingers as I pulled the knapsack over my shoulder.

"I need gloves," I mumbled. I remembered the ones my mother had given me. I reached inside my knapsack to get them and my nails hit the tin.

Grandma Kay.

I pulled it out and sat back down.

I hadn't ever taken the time to look through her recipe box. The morning had been so hectic and the rest of the day so harrowing. I had forgotten all about it.

I opened it up and pulled out a card. The emotion that struck me when I saw which one it was almost choked me. The amber light from the lanterns revealed her little scribblings on the card, her side notes and the date she'd written it.

The recipe? It was for ice cream made from snow.

Snow, the one thing that right now was ruining the business she had started. Still, I had to smile. Snow was also one of the things that my grandma loved. Whenever it would snow, she'd round us kids up, we'd go out, get snow and she'd make ice cream just for us.

My grandmother hadn't ever seen snow before leaving the south and was fond of telling us grandkids the story of how her uncle had at one time traveled north. Once arriving back home, she said he couldn't stop talking about how wonderful everything up here was—people living high, colored folks going wherever they wanted. They even, he had told her, had cotton falling from the sky. For a family of sharecroppers, that was just like equating snow to manna from heaven. And it was what made my grandmother always dream of moving north.

"There has to be at least a foot of it," she used to say about making snow ice cream. "And it has to be fresh-fallen snow. Otherwise it won't taste as sweet."

I chuckled. There was nothing sweet about this newly fallen snow. I dug the toe of my UGG boot into it and gave it a kick. The white particles floated through the air.

No. This snow had been a curse.

But then I thought how my Grandma Kay always made the best out of everything, and she didn't let much stop her. Not even the disease that finally took her from us.

I decided I wasn't going to let this beat me either.

I was going to make the best of it. I was going to make some ice cream. From snow.

"You won't defeat me. And you won't stop me," I said with a nod. I'd even take some to PopPop. It would probably be easier to face him if I came bearing gifts anyway. Especially when it was the kind of gift I knew he'd enjoy.

I put the recipe box back in my knapsack. I stood up, walked around to the side door, pulled the key to the store out of my pocket and went back inside.

I grabbed the top bowl from a stack of aluminum ones, then put it back. It was too small. I was going to make a big batch. I grabbed the bottom one, a scooper and the now-empty cardboard box the corn had been delivered in that morning. I laid my knapsack on one of the stainless-steel prep tables, fished the gloves out, put them on and headed back out the door.

The Chagrin River's two waterfalls bisected our little town. The twenty-foot-high waterfall that ran just out back of our family business was the larger. It had once powered nine different mills, and the industrialization of the early twentieth century that swept our little neck of the woods could be ascribed to it.

On our side of the road, getting up close and personal to the falls wasn't easy. Right next to the shop was a wooden-planked overlook that housed a seating area and a plaque with the village's history, which gave way to a series of stairs and a boardwalk. The boardwalk was as close as you got to the falls. But any kid who grew up in Chagrin Falls could tell you that if you wanted to get to the falls, you didn't use the stairs.

And from being a kid, I knew that's where you'd find the best unadulterated snow. At the bottom of the falls.

I went around to the front of the shop, headed down North Main Street just past the overlook, and turned onto Bell Street. There was a lookout there just beyond a hill, covered sparsely with trees, the earth beneath uneven due to erosion. All of it now covered with snow.

I tore the box I'd brought at one of the seams, tossed it on the ground and flattened out the top and the bottom of it with my feet. I was going to use it to get to the bottom, my own homemade sled. I could walk back up, but going down was tricky.

I sat down on the box, the bowl and scooper in my lap, and gave myself a push.

I smiled all the way down. It was just as much fun as when I was ten.

Hopping up once I hit the bottom, or close enough to it to make my way down to the water's edge, I took off toward the start of the falls. It hadn't been cold long enough for the water to freeze, but I knew it would be better the closer I got to the origin.

I finally found the right spot, and as I bent over to shovel up my first scoopful, I heard a rustling to the side of me. It started off with a thud and lasted a couple seconds longer than I thought it should.

"Who's there?" I called out. Not that I was afraid or anything. Nothing happened in Chagrin Falls. Statistically, I'd read, our little village was safer than 82 percent of all other cities in the U.S. But it would be nice to know who I was sharing the hillside with.

"Hellooo," I called out again.

Nothing.

I looked down at the scoop in one hand, the bowl in the other and then at the snow. Even in the dim lighting cast from the street above, the snow glistened. Fresh. Soft. Inviting. More than the depth required by the recipe. It was a perfect spot to do what I'd come down to do.

But for some reason I decided to see who it was who wouldn't answer me instead.

I walked down the path that followed the river. It was difficult going. Hard to see for want of light and tough to walk because the snow was deep and the path irregular. A couple minutes in, I was starting to get out of breath and was ready to give up, when I heard the noise again.

It was higher up the hill than where I stood, so I followed the sound of the footsteps. The person had to hear mine, too.

"Hey!" I said. "What are you doing down here?"

I'm sure they were wondering the same thing about me.

Then out of the corner of my eye, I saw something. A multi-colored scarf. Long. Loud. A distinct contrast against the dark silhouette trying to make its way up the hill back to the street. Close enough to the light to let me know the intruder had been a child.

"What were you doing down here?" I muttered as I stood and stared as the figure made its way back to the sidewalk and darted out of view.

This wasn't the smartest place to be. Especially alone.

Ah . . . Had the kid been alone? Us kids used to hang out around the falls in groups.

I looked around and listened. But there was nothing other than the sound of the water running over the falls. I shook my head. Here I was worrying about it being unsafe for someone to be down here and I was out here as well.

But I had a good reason.

I chuckled. One I was going to get back to right now.

I veered off to the right, stepping carefully down the small incline I had taken chasing the noise I'd heard.

But before I could get back to the path, my foot bumped into something hard and solid. Something that wouldn't budge, and I took a tumble. I nearly did a head flip, and must have rolled a couple of times before I came to rest facedown in the snow.

"Owww!" I said as I rolled over and sat up. "What the heck!" I rubbed my head and shook it to make sure I was okay. Nothing appeared loose. Finding that I was still in one piece, I stood up. Brushing the snow off me, I walked back up the few feet I'd tumbled to see what had made me fall.

"Oh my God!" I said, trying hard to stifle a scream.

It was a body lying in the snow.

# chapter SEVEN

Flashing red and blue lights lit up the dark, dreary corner where North Main and Bell streets met. Yellow crime-scene tape draped around trees cordoned off the perimeter of the wooden overlook. Floodlights invaded the stillness that surrounded the falls, and voices bombarded my eardrums. I was numb, but not from the cold.

I had panicked once I realized I'd tripped over a body. Not a panic born from fear, but from the fact that I didn't know how I could help. What to do. Blowing out a breath, I'd had to calm myself so I could figure it out.

It was dark and I hadn't been able to see clearly enough to make a decision. Had the person still been alive? Should I try to start some life-saving measures?

Not that I knew any . . .

Should I go get help?

The body hadn't moved, even after my falling over it.

Not a grunt. Not a moan. Not a whimper.

Feeling with my hands in the dark, I found a face. I leaned in, my face close, to see if I could feel a breath.

Nothing.

I laid my head on its chest to listen for a heartbeat.

Still nothing.

I should call for help.

*Crap.* I'd left my cell phone in my knapsack, sitting on the prep table in the ice cream shop. All I had was my aluminum bowl and scoop, so I started banging them together.

"Help!" I yelled out, and hit the scoop on the side of the bowl. "Hey! I need help! Anybody! Somebody help me!"

But all my noisemaking hadn't gotten one response. I looked down at the silhouette of Dead Guy and back up to the street. No lights from passing cars. No footsteps crunching in the snow.

I needed to get up the hill to get help.

But the snow was thick and cumbersome. I trudged up at a slow crawl, my feet sinking into the snow with each step forward, my gloves wet and covered with the powder. It seemed to be deeper and heavier the harder I tried to get up to the sidewalk. Bent over, hands clawing in the snow up the incline, I was out of breath with heavy legs by the time I made it to the top. Once my feet were planted on the sidewalk, I had to place my hands on my knees to catch my breath and slow my heart before I could go any farther.

Knowing what lay at the bottom of the falls made the night more ominous. The streets more deserted. The lights more dim.

I looked one way down Bell Street, then the other, not quite sure where I should go to get help. I just knew that I wanted to tell what I knew. Get someone else there with me. Then my eye caught sight of the woven scarf I'd seen on the kid who'd been down the hill with me. With Dead Guy.

I started to grab the scarf but thought better of it. People always come back to where they've lost their things to find them. The little boy might return. Maybe I'd report the lost item to the police.

*The police . . .*

I had to call the police. Or an ambulance.

I scurried around the block, past the front of the ice cream shop to the side door, and unlocked it. I hastily dumped the contents of my knapsack and had to catch Grandma Kay's tin recipe box as it tumbled out before it dropped onto the floor. Hands slightly shaky, still breathing hard, I found my phone and pushed in the three numbers.

*"911. What's your emergency?"*

AFTER I ENDED the call, I had to make a restroom pit stop to try to collect myself. I wondered if I had done all I could to help. I shook my head. There hadn't been anything I could have done. He hadn't moved. He hadn't made a sound. He wasn't breathing and I didn't know how long it would be before someone came along to help.

I ran warm water over my hands at the sink, dried them off and started to head back into the kitchen to get my knapsack, and ran right into Felice.

"Hello there, muffintop," I said, and stooped down, running my fingers through her white coat. "How did you get down here?"

She looked up at me, fluffed out the end of her tail, then, eyes half-closed, blinked slowly. I picked her up. "You want some kisses, sweetie?" I said, knowing it was me who needed comforting. She rubbed her cheek up against mine. "Thank you."

Holding her, I walked around to the back area where the stairs led to Rivkah's apartment and called up. No answer. "She must still be at the restaurant." I looked at Felice. "Did you just come down for me? To make me feel better?"

"Mrrao," she said.

I met her forehead with mine, but only for a moment. She didn't have time to be gracious. She jumped out of my arms and ran up the steps. I watched as she strutted up the stairs. I didn't know how she'd gotten out. Rivkah never left the door unlocked.

Tonight I was glad she had.

I went over to the prep table and stuffed everything back into my bag, grabbed the bowl and scooper and headed back outside. By the time I got out there, a police cruiser was pulling up in front of the store. The officer got out of the car and walked over to me.

"Are you the person who called 911?" he asked.

"I am," I said.

"What's going on?"

I pointed toward the falls. "There's a guy down there. I think he's dead."

"You wanna show me?" he said.

We walked around the corner, past the overlook to where I'd climbed back up.

"How did you get down there?" He looked at me. His face was red from the cold, vapors shooting out as he spoke.

“I made a sled out of a cardboard box.” I pointed. I was sure it was still down at the bottom where I’d left it.

“That’s pretty dangerous to do.”

I nodded, not mentioning I’d done it hundreds of times before.

“Stay here,” he instructed, and went down the steps at the boardwalk. The easy way down. He was gone for about five minutes. When he came back up, he clicked the radio perched on his shoulder and spoke into it. “I need backup and an ambulance at the overlook.

“C’mon,” the police officer said. He took my arm, gently guiding me back around the corner. He pointed to Grandma Kay’s bench and I sat down.

The police officer took out a small notepad and, for what seemed like an eternity, asked me the same round of questions, rehashing what I told him over and over again. It was exhausting, and I was tired and still freaked out about the dead man and upset that we hadn’t had any customers in the store that day. I wanted to go home and regroup.

But even after telling him everything I knew, repeatedly, he said I needed to wait for the detective to come so I could speak to him.

I guessed I’d be telling my story again.

My mind was swirling around in a whirlwind. I couldn’t even feel the bite of the cold any longer. Still, out of habit, I tugged at the zipper on my jacket, zipping it up to my neck, and pulled my hood over my head. I clapped most of the snow off my damp, glove-clad hands and stuffed them inside my pockets.

Backup arrived. That first officer who arrived on the scene seemed to get assigned to me. He got a bright orange blanket out of the back of the EMS truck, wrapped it around my shoulders and stood, it seemed, guard over me so I wouldn't bolt. But that wasn't my plan, not even when I saw the metal-framed gurney emerge from the side of the hill on the pulley system they'd set up with that black body bag bouncing on top. It made my stomach lurch into my chest, but didn't make me want to bolt and run. I still stood waiting for that detective.

Soon people began crawling out of their homes, the movie theater and stopped cars—everyone, I think, within earshot of the sirens. The throng of onlookers snaked around the parked emergency vehicles pointed, stared and muttered among themselves. I was doubtful if any of us villagers had ever seen anything like it. I knew I hadn't.

The next call I made, after giving all the pertinent information to the police dispatcher, was to my parents. I had to let them know what was going on. My mother answered, and in her frantic my-child-is-in-trouble voice, told me to hold on, she was on her way.

"Bring Daddy, too," I said. But I think she'd hung up by then. I could just picture her scrambling to get her clothes on, coming down the steps one at a time, my father holding his arm out to brace her.

"Here. I thought you might need this." I turned to see Ms. Devereaux, owner of a clothing boutique across the street catty-corner from our shop, pushing a cup toward me. She was dressed in a full-length furry coat, her hands covered in knitted gloves. The steam rose from the mug into the cold night air. As I wrapped my hands around the sides of it, I could feel the heat through my gloves, and took a sip.

"Thank you," I said.

"You told them what you knew?" she asked, her high voice strained.

I nodded, swallowing the warm, aromatic flavor of the lavender tea she'd filled my cup with.

"Surely he got what he deserved," she said, then took a sip out of her own cup.

I looked at her, not sure what to make of her statement.

"Who?" I asked.

She peered at me over the rim of her cup. Taking her lips away, she said, "Drink up. It'll do you good." Then she turned and walked away, heading back to her store, Exquisite Designs, not bothering to clarify what her words meant.

It wasn't like her. Deborah "Debbie" Devereaux was an undercover purveyor. It never seemed she sought out information—I'd never heard her going around asking questions—she just always knew what was happening around town.

Nearly seventy, she was slim, shapely and savvy. Well-dressed, she was always sparkling—dangling rhinestone earrings, bedazzled baseball caps, crystal stones on the sides of her overly large Wayfarer-rimmed glasses, twinkling brown eyes—although she claimed there was nothing fake about her or anything she wore. I found it hard to believe that all her "dazzlingness" was real. Not everything she owned could truly be diamond-encrusted.

I also didn't believe her real last name was Devereaux.

She and her sister, who ran the village's sole B and B, were the only other blacks in our community. Debbie lived over her store. And tonight, despite the bad weather, she appeared to still be hanging out and had more information about who I'd found at the bottom of the hill than I did.

Before I could call out to stop her so she could tell me what she meant, I got a tap on the shoulder. I spun around and came face-to-face with a man. Black leather jacket. Houndstooth apple cap. Black slacks. Rubber-soled shoes. Lines etching out the corners of his eyes. Brown facial hair. Musk cologne. He was so close that everything about him was amplified. I had to take a step back to keep our noses from touching and bring him into focus.

"Hi," he said. "I'm Detective Liam Beverly."

"Oh," I said, a smile tugging at the side of my lip. I was happy he'd finally arrived. "I think I'm waiting for you."

# chapter EIGHT

His eyes were the color of pistachio ice cream, even down to the flecks of gold. Not as cold, but they seemed all about business. They bore into mine and held my gaze. Long enough to make me feel uncomfortable. My smile faded and I opened my mouth to speak, but he didn't give me time. Without missing a beat, he started ticking off questions.

"You found the body?"

"I did."

"What's your name?" he asked. He took no notes. I guessed he had a better memory than the police officer.

"Win," I said, then thought this conversation probably wasn't going to be informal, and I shouldn't be either. "Bron*wyn.* Bronwyn Crewse."

He pointed up to the awning over the store. "As in . . ."

"Yep." I nodded my head. "Yes," I corrected, remembering this was official.

"And what were you doing down at the falls?" He cocked his head, his jaw tight, face expressionless. "It's pretty bad out tonight."

"I wanted to get snow," I said. I held up my bowl and scoop, realizing how silly it was for me to be clinging on to them.

"Snow?" he asked, and tilted his head to the other side.

"To make ice cream."

"Lots of snow up here." He stomped his feet one at a time. "You couldn't use any of it?"

"Wasn't the right kind," I said. "Plus"—I pointed to his feet—"it's been walked on."

He pursed his lips and nodded his head slowly as if he was processing what I'd said. Fortunately for me—I was cold and tired of answering the same questions—he hadn't come up with a response or another question before one of the police officers walked up beside us and got his attention. The detective, turning to speak with the officer, brushed his shoulder against mine and left it there. I sidestepped the other way.

"EMS is ready to go," the officer said.

"Has the body been identified?" Detective Beverly asked, looking past the officer, over at the ambulance, and giving a head nod.

"Nope." The police officer dug his hands in his pockets and shook his head. "We didn't find any ID on him."

"Do you know who he was?"

"Me?" I raised my eyebrows and turned my gaze from the police officer back to the detective. He was back to questioning me.

"Yes. You," he said, a small grin curling up his lip.

"Oh, no. I don't think so." I shook my head. "I didn't see—couldn't see—his face down by the falls. It was too dark."

"Win, are you okay?" It was my mother. Finally. I was happy to see her. I turned from the tête-a-tête with the detective.

"Mom," I said, grabbing on to her. I was taller than she was, and pulled her head close into my chest for a hug. She smelled like flowers and sandalwood. "I'm so glad you're here."

"What happened?" she said.

"Where's Dad?" I asked.

"Uhm." She pulled away from me and looked around like she'd find him close by. "He's coming. I tried to wait for him, but I wanted to get to you. He'll be here soon."

"He was at work?" I asked. He didn't usually get home so late.

"It's okay," my mother said, not answering my question. "I'm here. Now tell me what happened."

"I don't know, Mom. I went down by the falls to get some snow, and I tripped over this guy."

"What guy?"

"I don't know," I said, hunching my shoulders. I leaned in and whispered to her. "He's dead. They had him in a body bag."

"Oh my," she said, and held her palm up to her cheek.

"Hel-lo." Detective Beverly turned to face us, drawing out the word.

"Hi," my mother said, and stuck out her hand. "I'm Bronwyn's mother. Ailbhe Crewse."

"You make ice cream, too?" he asked, shaking the hand she had offered.

"I do," she said.

"Out of snow?"

My mother gave me a crooked smile, then looked back at the detective, narrowing her eyes. "No," she said.

"Bronwyn—can I call you that?" he asked. "Or do you prefer Win?"

"Bronwyn is fine," I said. I didn't feel like being friendly, and I'd already decided this was all official.

"Was there anyone else out tonight?" he asked. "Anyone that may have seen you or the gentleman you found?"

My mind and my eyes wandered back to Ms. Devereaux and her store. *He got what he deserved* . . . She had to know who he was, otherwise how would she know that he'd merited his fate?

The store was set directly in front of Bell Street.

Maybe she had seen something. But when I brought my eyes back to meet with the detective's, I saw that scarf.

The multicolored one.

It was wrapped around the neck of a young boy. Probably the young boy I'd spotted under the streetlight as he'd scrambled back up the hill coming up from the falls. A woman stood behind him, her hands on his shoulders.

"*He* may know something," I said, and led the detective in the direction of the boy with my eyes.

Detective Beverly looked over his shoulder, following my gaze, then turned back to me. "Who?" he asked.

"That little boy," I said. "I saw him down by the falls."

"You saw him?"

"I think I did," I said, and focused my gaze on him. "I saw his scarf."

"Hold on." He turned to the officer and asked him to go and get the boy.

I heard the detective say something to me, but my attention was on the boy and the woman. Through the sea of faces and movement, it seemed that briefly her eyes had locked with mine. It was as if she knew, somehow, that I had spoken about her—or the child—and she started to edge away.

The officer must have radioed his intent, because before he got to her, another officer came up behind her. He leaned in and spoke to her. I saw her acknowledge the officer as he headed over.

"Bronwyn." *Snap! Snap!* Fingers were in front of my face making the noise. "Bronwyn!"

"Yes," I said, diverting my thoughts and refocusing my eyes on the detective.

"You got lost there for a minute," he said. "You alright?"

"Yeah. I am," I said. "Just cold and tired."

"Do you need another blanket?" He tugged on the one I still had wrapped around me.

"Mm-mm." I shook my head. "This one is fine."

"Detective Beverly." It was the officer speaking. He had escorted the woman and boy over. She didn't seem too happy about it. "Here's the woman you wanted to speak with."

Her red lipstick was faded and dull. The mascara laid thick on her eyelashes had begun to run due to the dampness in the air. The curls in her blond hair—dyed, as evidenced by her dark brown roots—had flopped. She held her head up, her grip on the boy tight.

"What do you want?" she said. Her voice was gravelly, like she'd been smoking ten packs of cigarettes a day for the past forty years. She didn't look that old, though. "I have to get my son home. Out of the cold."

"Ms. Crewse here"—the detective pointed to me—"said she saw you down by the falls."

"Not her," I corrected. "Her son." I flapped an arm in his direction.

"He wasn't there," she said, not even taking the time to consider my claim.

The detective looked at me.

"I saw that scarf around someone's neck. A child's neck," I said. "That's how I found the body. Chasing after it. Him. Then I saw the scarf again lying on the ground when I came back up to get help."

"She must've seen another scarf," the woman said dryly.

"Exactly like that one?" I asked, sarcasm threaded through my words.

She shrugged. "It wasn't my son's. He wasn't anywhere near the falls tonight. Or anytime today."

"Then why are you over here?" I asked, and before she gave an answer, I suggested one for her. "You come looking for that scarf?"

She blew out a snort. "No. I came to see what was going on, just like everyone else." She looked at the detective.

"Where were you coming from?" I asked. "Did you go to the movies tonight?" I remembered the voices I'd heard earlier. I had heard a woman calling out something . . .

The woman raised an eyebrow. "Is she working for you?" She directed her question to the detective.

"No." He chortled at the woman's words, his green eyes lighting up. "But do you have any more questions, Bronwyn?"

I wasn't amused. "It was his scarf," I said. "And it was him."

"Is this why you asked me to come over here?" she said, slowly taking her eyes from mine and looking at the detective. "So she could accuse me—or my son—of something? I don't know what this is about, but I can't help you. And neither can he."

"What's your name?" the detective asked the boy, but the woman spoke up.

"Why?" she asked indignantly.

"Because I'm an officer of the law, and you have to tell me if I ask," Detective Beverly said, his voice calm but steady.

"I don't think that's true," she said.

"We can take you in. Talk about whether it's true or not down at the station," he said. "That way your boy can stay warm."

She didn't like that remark. "His name is—"

"Jasper," I said, suddenly remembering the earlier incident while I'd sat sulking on the bench. I remembered how she had called out the name as he ran from her.

"Jasper," she said at the same time I did.

"Do you know him?" Detective Beverly asked me.

"No," I said. "I don't know him. I heard her call him that."

"When?" the detective asked.

"Not long before I found the body.

"And, Mom, what's your name?"

"Glynis Vale," she said. "And my son, Jasper. Vale. Who is only ten years old." She put her hand on top of his head. "He wouldn't be out wandering off by himself."

"He was tonight," I said.

"He didn't see anything," she countered, seemingly daring me to contradict her again.

"Is that true?" the detective asked the boy. "You didn't see anything?"

Jasper strained his neck to look up at his mother standing over him.

"Of course it's true," Glynis said.

"I'm asking him," the detective said.

Glynis Vale smacked her lips. "Answer him," she told the boy.

"I didn't see anybody."

"Any *body*?" the detective asked, separating the word. "You didn't see anyone or you didn't see a body?"

Jasper looked up at his mother again. She nodded. "Both," he said. "I didn't see no one, and I didn't see no body."

"See," she said, looking at me as she spoke. "There wouldn't be anything to talk about if you took me in."

"How about this?" the detective said. "You give your information to this officer. Address. Phone number. How to contact you—if we need to—and you can be on your way."

"Can my daughter be on her way, too?" my mother asked.

Detective Beverly looked at her and then at me. "You have anything else to tell me?"

"Nope," I said. "Not here. Not even at your station."

I saw a grin curl up one side of his lips. "Okay. Then, yes. You can be on your way, too." He pointed to our store. "I can find you there?"

"Every day. Eleven to eleven."

He turned from me without saying anything else and walked away.

I looked at my mother. I was sure she could see on my face that I was more than ready to go. Then, over her shoulder, I saw my father walking up. He had a look of concern, or determination, I couldn't tell which—maybe both—on his face. Each long stride he took seemed measured with purpose as he walked over to us. He was dressed in gray sweats, Timberland boots and a jacket. His leather gloves were wet, and his usually mocha-colored cheeks were red from the cold.

"What's going on?"

"A man died. Win found him," my mother said.

"You okay, Pumpkin?" he asked. I nodded. "Who was this guy?" My father looked around the scene.

"We don't know." Mom reached over and rubbed my arm. "But he must've been someone from around here."

"We should go home," my father said, putting his arm around me and giving me a squeeze. "You look cold."

"Where were you, Daddy?" I asked.

"At work," he said, and gave me a smile. He took his arm from around me and grabbed my mother's hand. "C'mon. We should leave." He looked down at my mother. "Did you drive? Where's your car?"

She pointed, and I watched as they walked toward it.

My father hadn't been dressed like that when he left for work this morning. I'd seen what he had on when he was making omelets. And I'd never known him to wear anything but a suit to work. Never a pair of sweatpants.

I didn't know why he said he'd been at the hospital, but I did know that Glynis Vale wasn't the only person tonight not telling the truth.

# chapter NINE

I rode in the back seat of my mother's Volkswagen Passat on the drive home like I was an errant child. I didn't know where my father's car was, or how he'd gotten down to the shop.

Over the course of the short ride, my parents spoke in hushed voices. Whether to keep what they were talking about secret from me or because it was late and everyone was tired, I didn't know. Maybe no one had the energy to speak any louder.

But my mind was far away from anything they said. All I could do was think about getting home and climbing into bed to sleep off the disappointment of the day. How was I going to get people into the store? The view from that full glass wall I was so proud of showed nothing but snow and the crime scene where a dead body had been found. By me.

After my parents dropped me off, I dragged myself up the stairs to my apartment, still holding on to that aluminum bowl and scooper. I shrugged off my coat and shoes and got under the bedclothes, covering my head with the bedspread.

Running my family's business wasn't what I had come back home to do. But I thought it must've been what I was meant to do.

After college, I'd been recruited by an ad agency in New York City. I had been their rising star. Good at what I did. And my team were true go-getters. Together we tried to build brands that would catapult unknown businesses from side streets to Main Street. But then I got sick and panicked.

Tossing and turning, I thought about what had brought me back home.

My memory had been shot. I was forgetful. Sometimes even confused. And it seemed like I was always tired. By two o'clock in the afternoon, I was dragging. And then I almost blew a pitch my team had worked tirelessly on for weeks—thank goodness the operative word was "almost." I had time to fix it, but not my frayed nerves.

Little-girl memories of Grandma Kay's illness came flooding into my mind as fast as the water rushed over the falls outside our family shop.

At twelve I didn't know what was really happening to her. At twenty-six, when I started feeling bad, I knew, without doing any research, that I probably didn't have what she'd had. But I also knew—without doing any research—that what she had was hereditary and that maybe one day I could get it. That scared me. And that made me think of all the love and support my grandmother received from family being close.

Then I realized I didn't want to be in New York anymore. Whatever was wrong with me, I wanted to be at home. To deal with it with my family.

Plus, my father was a doctor at a renowned hospital. He would make sure his little girl got the best care possible.

So, I quit my job, although not without my employers trying everything they could to get me to stay and promising to always have a spot open for me. I gave up my apartment on the Lower East Side and came home. From the time I drove into the driveway on Carriage Hill Lane, I knew I'd made the right decision.

My mother mollycoddled me and my father used his clout to push me to the front of the line in every testing queue at the hospital.

It turned out to be nothing serious. My calcium was high—extremely high—and it mimicked symptoms of a heart problem. Easily taken care of by a good doctor friend of Dad's—this one an endocrinologist—who removed my parathyroid gland. That took all of thirty minutes and an overnight stay with my mother asleep in the chair next to my bed in the observation ward to bring everything back to normal.

But it didn't make me want to go back to New York. Why should it? According to an article in *Forbes*, Cleveland was "hot," ranked number two in emerging U.S. cities. I could easily find a job at home. My brothers had. I'd been the only one to venture out of the backyard of our little village.

I didn't know if I'd ever felt "homesick" while I was away, but it took my being sick to realize I needed to be home. Then Pop-Pop gave me that Christmas gift and I took my résumé down from Monster.com, thinking all of it had happened because it was meant to be.

But now what?

Months of planning. Sleeping with my vision board. My notebook full of multicolored sticky notes covered with every idea that popped into my head. Now, after one day of snow and a dead body, I was in the bed with my head burrowed under the covers?

My grandparents had built a little shop that had weathered all kinds of storms. The race riots of the turbulent sixties. The long stretch of recession in the eighties. And then there was 1994—Cleveland's coldest winter ever—but PopPop said that was one of the shop's best years ever, Crewse Creamery steadfastly holding on. Staying the course.

So what was wrong with me?

I peeked my head from under the covers and with one eye open looked at the clock on my bedside table and huffed. This wasn't how I'd pictured me managing the shop. It certainly wasn't how I ran my team back in New York.

I couldn't let snow slow me down. I jerked the covers from over my head with a thump and got out of bed. I looked down at myself—clothes still on. "What the heck?" I said. I put my shoes and coat back on and grabbed my car keys. I ran down the hallway toward the steps, but before my foot could hit the first step, I turned around, ran back and picked up my bowl and scooper, then headed back down the hallway, down the stairs and out the door.

I threw everything in the car and started it, letting it run while I cleaned off the snow.

The foot of snow.

Ah, that pesky snow.

I hummed all the way down the hill as I devised a plan to get people out in the cold to buy ice cream. I was a millennial. An entrepreneurial spirit. Social media savvy and technical prowess were encoded into my DNA!

I turned the corner on North Main Street, drove past the store and did a U-turn to park in front of it. I got into the side door with all my stuff and turned on all the lights.

I set up my laptop at the little corner nook where I'd created an office area, made myself an ice cream cone—three scoops—and sat down and got to work.

I got on the internet, and for the next four hours, I hovered over my keyboard and emailed, texted and posted about our ice cream. I sent an email to the plexiglass manufacturing people to give them a little push, and I made "Free Scoop" coupons to hand out to customers, printing fifteen, to use on subsequent visits.

With melted ice cream all over my fingers—seemed like I got more on me than in my mouth—I washed my hands and let my eyes wander around the room. "Now what?" I said, clicking my nails.

I could make ice cream. That's what Grandma Kay did when she had worries.

*Hmmm . . .*

I trudged over to the walk-in freezer and swung it open. I had ice cream in the freezer, plenty of it, but I thought I could make something else . . .

Something that would get people excited enough to put on their boots and a coat and come out of the house into the snow to get ice cream.

*But what?*

I closed the freezer door and went to the front of the store and over to the jukebox on the far wall. I'd installed it because music in the store always reminded me of Grandma Kay. No iPod speakers or Wi-Fi radio back then, she used to bring a portable turntable and play her albums all day long. She loved jazz and rhythm and blues by singers like Dinah Washington, Brook Benton and Ray Charles, and because of her, I did, too.

The jukebox was red, silver and shiny. There were fake 45s that sat inside the glass front, and between songs, there was a clicking sound like the records were changing. They weren't. Preprogrammed, it took just a push of the start button to listen to the smooth sway of music. There was no order to the songs it played.

Brook Benton's "This Time of Year" came on . . .

Ha! I knew what to do. Themed ice cream!

People around our parts loved Halloween and our Pumpkin Roll. Why not get the season started early?

I snapped my fingers and smiled. I could make a pumpkin spice roll ice cream. And maybe something Halloweeny. "Maybe," I said, nodding, "something with candy in it." An early taste of trick or treat. Mmm . . . lots of candy. Candycopia!

And then, I thought, why not something ghoulish? "Something blue," I announced to an empty room. "I've got it!" I snapped my fingers. "Blueberry ice cream."

I ran back to the kitchen. I didn't have what I needed. I knew I'd have to go to the grocery store. I sat at my desk and wrote out a shopping list, then looked up twenty-four-hour grocery stores before heading out.

The heck with snow and dead bodies. Customers were going to come in droves just like they did in my grandparents' day. Fingers and ice cream scoops crossed.

------

I LIFTED MY head from the table and swiped my fingers across each eye. The sweater wrapped around my shoulders fell off onto the floor. The sun, streaming through the windows, lit up the room. I had to think for a minute to remember where I was.

I looked at the time on the phone I had gripped in my hands and shot straight up in the chair.

"OMG!"

It was ten fifteen. In the morning! I looked down and realized it was a new day, but the old me. I had fallen asleep. I needed to shower and change my clothes.

Felice was staring at me from the window seat. I picked up the sweater and shook it at her. "Has your momma been down here?"

"Brrrreow." She tilted her head to one side and winked at me.

"Why didn't you wake me up?" I said. I needed to get home to bathe and change. I had forty-five minutes. Good thing I had driven down the hill.

She blinked her eyes at me slowly, as if to say she had, then stretched and lay down for a nap.

"Well, unlike you, I can't sleep any longer," I said, hopping up. "I have an ice cream shop to run." I turned the jukebox off, grabbed my coat and rushed out the door into the cold morning air, not putting on the brakes all the way up the hill to the old Victorian. I hustled into the house and showered, dressed and was out and headed back down the hill by ten til eleven.

I parked around the corner—didn't want to take parking spaces from my soon-to-be-many customers. Happy that yesterday was over, even though I'd had almost no sleep, I felt energized and ready for the day.

Satisfied with my middle-of-the-night and early-morning social media blitz, I set out the ice cream, replacing three of the flavors from the day before with the Pumpkin Spice Roll, Candycopia and Ghoulish Blueberry I'd made. I ran around the dining area and made sure all the chairs and tables were straight. Pushing Felice over, I vacuumed up her cat hair from the bench—she hadn't moved while I was gone—turned the jukebox back on, hit the power button on the cash register and put money I'd gotten out of our safe in the kitchen into the drawer for change.

I blew out a breath and looked around. Everything looked good, I nodded to myself. I grabbed a couple of cat treats from under the counter and walked over to Felice.

"You keeping watch?" I asked. She still hadn't moved. I sat next to her on the bench, stroking her down her back and over her wide, fluffy tail.

"I only need people to taste it." She climbed halfway onto my lap. "They'll love it."

"Erreow," she trilled, seemingly agreeing with me.

"Yesterday was one heck of a day for me," I told her. "But today will be different."

"Brrreow."

I turned to look out of the window. The soft glow from the front-mounted lanterns still on from the night before made me feel warm and comfortable. A shining beacon letting me know I was doing the right thing.

Those thoughts faded away as I saw a police car sitting in

front of the flower store next door. A grim reminder of what had happened the day before.

*They must still be working on finding out who that was down by the falls,* I thought.

I broke from my reverie and looked at my watch.

"Time to get this day started," I said to Felice. I picked her up and nuzzled her before setting her back on the window seat. I got up, turned the outside lights off and flipped the switch for the cool orange neon *Open* sign that hung in the window. Glancing up, I noted the cloudless blue skies. Maybe no snow today, but I already knew that Chagrin Falls had officially started its winter and selling ice cream was going to be an uphill battle.

Speaking of the cold, I felt quite warm. I went over and checked the thermostat. It was on eighty.

*Rivkah!*

# chapter TEN

I went in the back to wash my hands. I was warm, so I took off my long-sleeved shirt, leaving on just the T-shirt with the shop's logo.

A song in my head, I was humming when I heard the side door opening. It startled me. I wasn't expecting anyone this early. I looked toward the door and saw PopPop step inside. He'd come in with his own key. Closing the door behind him, he stomped his feet and smiled at me.

"Morning, little girl," he said.

"Morning, PopPop," I said, surprise in my voice. I hadn't expected to see him at the shop. "I didn't come to see you this morning." It was a statement, but I meant it as an apology.

"I don't need you to tell me that," he said, an amused look on his face. He pulled off his hat, holding it in one hand, and adjusted his backgammon board and newspaper stuck under his other arm. "I'm fully aware of what happened this morning."

"I was here all night."

"Were you, now?" He looked around, taking in the kitchen area. "Did you get any sleep?"

"A little," I said, looking toward the front of the store where I had nodded off, arms folded, head lying on top. It seemed sufficient, though. With the anticipation I had buzzing all through me, I probably couldn't have slept much longer even in my own bed. "I feel good."

"Ready to sell ice cream?"

I held my breath. Did he know I hadn't sold any the day before? I bit onto my bottom lip, not able to think of a word to say to him. I had done enough tweeting and posting to let people know and get people in, but facing PopPop gave me pause. I started clicking my nails.

He smiled. Walking past me, he grasped my hand and gave it a squeeze. "It's okay," he said, and headed out to the front of the store. Standing at the entryway between the kitchen and dining area, he let out a whistle. "Now this is what I call an ice cream parlor."

A smile beamed across my face. "You like it?" I asked.

"I love it," he said. He turned and looked at me, and I swore I saw a twinkle in his eye. "And so would your Grandma Kay."

I didn't think my smile could get any wider, but it did.

"Thought I'd come and sit with you awhile," he said.

"You came to help serve ice cream?"

"I said 'sit,'" he said, his brow wrinkling. He patted the bundle under his arm. "Brought something to pass the time. Don't plan on doing any work. At least not today."

He shrugged out of his coat, folded it over, laid it down on the booth seat, put his hat on top of it and slid it to the end of the bench. He sat down, wiggling and patting the seat. He seemed to be testing it. It must have passed his inspection, because he nodded and unfolded his newspaper.

"I don't have any coffee," I said, glancing over at the counter as if I didn't know whether a coffeemaker would be there or not.

He snapped his fingers. "I brought some from home. Must've left it in the car." He used his hands to press down into the bench and scooted his way out of it. "I'll just run and get it." He picked up his coat and hat and slipped out the front door. I watched him walk past the big window, tugging down on his hat and pulling his coat closed, and it wasn't long before he returned carrying a yellow-and-purple-plaid thermos.

"Where's the runner for the front door?" he said, stepping back inside and stomping his feet. "You don't want the floor getting wet and somebody falling when they come in."

*If someone comes in . . .*

"I've got it in the back," I said, and pointed over my shoulder. "I'll go get it."

I rushed to the back and found it in the corner of the utility closet. I put the black rubber rug in front of the door. PopPop was standing in front of the dipping cabinet, peering down into it.

"This ice cream looks good, Win. Makes my mouth water just looking at it."

I came and stood next to him. "I made some seasonal flavors." I tapped my fingers on the glass, pointing to the three new flavors. "I wanted to get the village ready for Halloween and the Pumpkin Roll."

He shook his head. "I hate that thing. Whoever thought rolling pumpkins down a hill could be fun? Pumpkins all in the streets, kids out at midnight making all kinds of noise."

"I know you hate it, PopPop, but those kids might just come in here and buy ice cream, plus all the spectators that come out with them."

"I guess so," he said. He bent forward, looking through the glass again. "Well, you've come up with some winners there." He nodded toward the case. "You've got your grandmother's touch. Not everyone can make up flavors like that or make ice cream look smooth and glisten like you do."

"It's the lights, PopPop." I pointed up. "I had them strategically placed."

"No, I think that's all you." He pointed through the glass. "The soda fountain. That jukebox. Gives the place a whole new vibe."

"A good vibe?"

"A real good vibe." He chuckled. "Have I told you lately how proud I am of you?"

"You tell me all the time, PopPop."

"I probably don't tell you enough." He headed back over to the bench where he'd left his newspaper and backgammon board and went through the same routine of taking off his coat and hat, but this time he didn't sit. He turned and looked at me. "I heard you had a visitor at the store yesterday."

"He didn't come *into* the store." I hedged around the answer. Didn't know how I should talk about it, even *if* I should talk about it. My mother had told me what that man had done to our family and business. That was enough hurt caused by him that my mother would think that my father would stoop to murder if the guy just showed his face. "I saw him out front. He had a little lost puppy."

"Whose puppy was it?" he asked.

"I don't know, PopPop, and he didn't either," I said, and shook my head. "That's why it was lost."

"Wouldn't be surprised if he stole it." His eyes narrowing, he spoke through tight lips.

After learning what a con man he was, I wouldn't be surprised either.

I noticed talking about the guy was building up a little steam, and anger started bubbling through. I thought that maybe I should change the subject.

"Who you playing backgammon with?" I said, and pointed to the board sitting on the table at the bench he'd occupied. Although I'd seen PopPop play by himself plenty of times, I just didn't know what else to say.

His eyes followed my finger toward the table, then they turned back and looked at me. "I don't want you worrying about that fellow," he said. "He won't be bothering you anymore."

I looked at my grandfather. He wasn't frail by any meaning of the word, but he was old. Nearly eighty, he was slim and stood tall, but nothing about him was menacing. I glanced over at the table and understood. He had come today to protect me. To make sure I'd be okay.

"He wasn't trying to hurt me," I said. "I didn't feel scared or anything." Other than finding the dead guy down at the falls, in all my years I'd never known anything going on in our little village that would cause me to be afraid to go out or talk with people.

"He was a con man, Win. Took advantage of your Grandma Kay. Of all of us."

I could tell that those words bit into my grandfather's very being. He wasn't one to tolerate anything that had caused his wife pain.

"He did say things that weren't true," I said, remembering his comment about my grandmother making mud pie ice cream. "And I guess"—I hunched my shoulders—"in his eyes, he was playing a game with me, but he didn't hurt me."

"Like I said, he won't be hurting anyone else in this family, that's for sure."

I raised my eyebrows and tried to imagine my grandfather as Liam Neeson in *Taken*, going out to avenge me for some wrongdoing. I would have chuckled at the thought, but PopPop's face was serious and he was looking right at me.

"Okay," I said sheepishly. "I know you'll take care of me."

# chapter ELEVEN

I heard the chime over the door go off, and my stomach leapt into my chest. A customer. My very first customer!

I glanced over at PopPop. He didn't even look my way. He had sat down and picked his newspaper back up. Evidently, he hadn't come down to watch me making sales.

"Hi," I said to our customer. "Welcome to Crewse Creamery."

"Are you the person that found the dead body?"

"Excuse me?" I said. I turned and looked at PopPop. He looked up momentarily, then back down at his paper. The woman hadn't wasted any time getting to her point. And what she needed apparently wasn't ice cream.

"I don't think we've ever had a murder in Chagrin Falls," the woman said.

"I don't think there's been one now either," I said.

"Of course there has." Her words came out with incredulity. "You should know, you discovered it. You must not have seen the morning paper." She was wearing a black wool overcoat, mid-calf-high boots. Her hair was brown, parted on the side and cut even with her mouth, her face pale from the cold. She looked as if she could have been the Prada version of the Grim Reaper, but I wasn't sold on her facts of the case.

"Nope," I said, my lips tight. I slowly shook my head. "I've been here making ice cream."

"*You* make the ice cream?"

"Yes, we do."

"Here?"

"Right in the back." I pointed to the particleboard placeholder. "We'll have a see-through wall soon so you'll be able to see us do it."

"That's cool," she said, then let her eyes fall down on the dipping case. "What kind of ice cream do you have?"

"They're all listed there." I pointed to the chalkboard sitting on top of the back counter. "But today's special is Pumpkin Spice Roll."

She laughed. "It is that time of year, isn't it?"

"Yep."

"My son can't wait. Too old to go trick-or-treating around these parts just means you're old enough to go out in the middle of the night and roll pumpkins down North Main."

"I'm sure he'd love some, too," I said, pointing at the deep orange ice cream.

"Who eats ice cream in the middle of winter?"

"Everyone," I said, and grabbed one of the dipping spoons. "And technically, it's still fall."

"You'd never know with this weather."

I took the spoon and dipped up some of the pumpkin ice cream. "We're going to get a little sunshine today," I said, and handed the sample to her.

She hesitantly wrapped her mouth around the tiny spoon, her

lips sliding the ice cream into her mouth. "Oh! My!" She covered her mouth as she spoke. "This is so good!" Her eyes beamed with appreciation. "Do I taste cinnamon?"

"Maybe," I said.

"I do!" she said. "And how did you get this to taste like real pumpkin?"

"I used real pumpkin."

Her eyebrows shot up. "Get out of here." I nodded. "Did you really?"

"I did," I said, a proud smile beaming across my face. I held up one of the pint cups. "You'd like some to go?"

"I would," she said.

While I filled her container, I could see her as she took in her surroundings.

"I used to come here. Haven't been in a while," she said. "What happened to the lottery machine?"

"We just sell ice cream now," I said.

"Oh, will you look a-there!" She pointed to the back wall. "You can see the falls."

There'd always been a window there, though not as impressive as my wall. But until I took over the shop, all the clutter of the non–ice cream and novelty items had distracted from the view.

"Aren't you the savvy saleswoman," she said, coming back to the counter.

"How's that?" I asked, walking over to the cash register.

"I only came in to find out about the body you found." She shook her head. "Horrible business." Then she smiled at me. "And then you got me to buy ice cream at eleven o'clock in the morning with a foot of snow on the ground." She handed me a five-dollar bill.

"I heard it might melt," I said, knowing I hadn't heard any such thing. I handed her her change and a coupon for her next visit.

"Well this won't, I'm sure." She held up her container and turned to head out the door. "It'll be gone before that could ever happen. I probably should have bought two."

"We'll be here tomorrow. Come back. Use your coupon."

"I might just do that," she said, waving it in the air. "Oh!" she squealed before she made it out the door. I looked up at her just as she turned to me, eyes wide. "I thought that was a stuffed animal." She pointed at Felice. "It just blinked."

I laughed. "Meet Her Royal Highness Felice. All fluff, regal and real."

"Oh my," she laughed. "She scared me. But she's a cutie! Thanks for the ice cream." She held up her container again.

"You're welcome," I said. "Come back soon."

"I will," she said, and was out the door.

Yes! I pumped my fist and stole a glance at PopPop.

*My* first customer. Family business, surely, but I knew this rebranding was all on me.

I pressed the "No Sale" button on the cash register and pulled out the five-dollar bill she'd given me. It wasn't the first money our little shop had ever made, but it was the first for me. It may have been a corny thing to do, but I was going to frame it. Even if the person who gave it to me hadn't planned on buying ice cream when she came in.

"Is that Rivkah's cat?" PopPop spoke for the first time since the woman had come in. A big smile showing all his teeth emerged across his face. "Is she here, too?"

# chapter TWELVE

The hands on that old clock on the wall dragged around at a snail's pace. If I wasn't watching it, I was watching the door or PopPop. Looking for customers. Looking to see if he was watching me or the door like I was.

About an hour after he got in, PopPop had a friend drop by who bought two scoops of ice cream and then sat down to play backgammon with him.

I wiped down the counters. Twice. Checked the temperature of the freezer. Three times. And paced the length of the space behind the dipping cabinet and register, phone in hand, a dozen times. I was nervous. Anxious. Waiting . . . Hoping for customers.

"I know I'm late." My mother came rushing out from the back, still tying her apron around her. "But my morning was just hectic."

I didn't know what kept my mother from being on time. She piddled around that big old house most mornings and some afternoons, all by herself, and took a lot of classes.

"It's okay, Mom," I said. "We only had two customers."

"We had customers?" She looked toward the door, as if they were still lingering around it.

"Isn't that what we want?" I asked.

"No." She shook her head, her little tight ringlets bouncing around. "Yes. It's what we want. That's not what I was saying. I meant I knew they would come. Lots of them." She cupped my face with the palm of her hand. "So don't be worried," she said, like she could read what I was feeling. "Oh." She stopped. Peeking around me, she lowered her voice. "What is PopPop doing here?"

"Right now he's playing backgammon. But I think mostly he's here to protect me."

"Protect you from what?"

"From who," I said.

"Okay, who?"

"The guy with the puppy." She frowned up at me. "You know, yesterday morning."

"I know who you're talking about," she said. "But you don't have to worry about him anymore."

I narrowed my eyes. "That's exactly what PopPop said." What had my family been up to? "Why does everyone keep telling me that?"

"What? Telling you not to worry?"

"Yeah," I said.

"Oh." She waved a hand. "We just don't want you to be afraid."

"Afraid? Why would I be afraid of him? He didn't act threatening. Or menacing."

"So 'afraid' wasn't the right word. Alarmed," she said, and

looked at me as if gauging how I weighed in with that word. I groaned. "Worried." She changed the word again and I blew out a breath. She seemed satisfied with that reaction.

"Worried," she repeated, as if saying she'd go with that. "We didn't want you to worry about him."

"I wasn't worried about him," I said. "I'm fine."

"Of course you are," she said, and gave me a pat on the arm. She turned her attention to PopPop. "I'm going to say hi."

Two more customers, one after the other, came in while my mother was saying hi. Either that was the longest hello ever or they had their heads together about something. Probably protecting me from Puppy Guy. But I was happy to serve our customers by myself. One bought two scoops of the Ghoulish Blueberry and the other had a scoop of the strawberry shortcake I'd made the day before. They both got the "free scoop" coupon and promised to come back.

"Hey, Mom," I said after the last customer left. "I'm going to run and get something to eat."

She looked over at me. "You hungry?"

"Yes." I rubbed my belly, realizing I hadn't eaten anything, other than tasting the ice cream I'd made in the wee hours of the morning, since yesterday.

"You want me to go and get you something?"

"No, I'll go," I said, undoing my apron strings. "Can you mind the shop for me?"

"Of course, sweetie," she said, and smiled. "But I have to leave soon. I have a Zumba class at two." I looked at the clock. It was twelve forty-five. I held back my chuckle. She sure didn't keep long work hours. I was always happy for her help and company, and I knew she was enjoying her retirement. "It's okay, Wilhelmina and Maisie are going to come in. I actually thought Maisie would be here by now."

My stomach was growling as I walked to the back of the store and grabbed my coat off the rack. "People are trickling in," I said. She followed me to the back. "I hope it won't be too much to do alone. But you should be okay until those two get here."

"I'll be okay," she said. "I'm sure backup will arrive soon. Plus"—she tilted her head toward the front—"PopPop is here."

"He's the bouncer today," I said. "I don't know if he's doing double duty as the soda jerk, too."

She giggled like she did with my father's jokes. The chime went off and my mother's eyes got big. "We have a customer!"

She was excited about helping me with the store. When Aunt Jack ran it, my mother never came down to help. Even though Grandma Kay was Aunt Jack's mom, my mother was more protective of my grandmother and the way she had run the store. My mother didn't approve at all of what Aunt Jack had done.

Before she went to take care of the customer, she turned back to me. "This isn't a parking lot kind of moment," she said. "Don't dwell on yesterday." She rubbed her hands up and down my arms. "More customers"—she pointed over her shoulder—"just like this one will come. It's early yet."

"No worries, Mommy." Her optimism always made me feel better. "I'm just walking to get some soup," I said. "I'm not even taking the car."

"That never stopped me."

"I assure you," I said, chuckling, "there will be no loitering involved."

I walked down North Main and around the bend in the sidewalk as it started the first leg of the town square, then turned onto North Franklin Street and smiled. I was happy with the customers who had come in. Four was good to start—actually, five with PopPop's friend getting a couple of scoops. My parking lot moment, if I were going to have one, would have been last night when I'd parked myself on Grandma Kay's bench to pout.

The Zoup! line was long. Nearly out the door. Envy tingled through me and I made my way to the back of the line. I was cold, not because of the weather, although I probably should have put my long-sleeved shirt back on before going outside. But my chill was because I was full of anticipation. I rubbed my hand down my arm. I was good at marketing, and hoped with all my might that I was good enough to sell the proverbial ice to an Eskimo, because that had basically been my plan.

*It's early yet.* The words of my mother echoed in my ear.

"A penny for your thoughts."

I looked up to see a man smiling, and it looked as if it were directed at me. But who knew. Maybe he had a Bluetooth in his ear.

"Hi," he said, and leaned into me. Another guy who didn't understand about invading other people's space.

"Hi," I said, and did a half step back. I gave him a smile. Mine was on the weak side. "Haven't heard that in a long time," I said. "A penny for your thoughts."

"You looked like you were deep in thought."

I drew in a breath and gave a half nod. "Guess I was," I said.

He pointed up ahead to the counter. "Soup not only warms you up, it can heal your soul."

I chuckled. I would end up standing next to the corny guy. "Sounds like that should be written on a fortune cookie."

He laughed. A throw-your-head-back kind of laugh. His eyes sparkled and he did a half step forward. Closer to me. I hadn't thought it was that funny.

"I hope they have loaded baked potato soup today. I need something hot and good." He had turned to face me.

"To heal your soul?" I asked.

"To keep me warm," he said, a smile beaming on his face. "Just what a body needs after yesterday with the snow. Today, it's just cold. Brrr!" He did a fake shiver.

I shut my eyes and let out a moan. I didn't want to hear about the cold and people wanting to keep warm. I was too ambitious to understand such a simple concept—I'd been trying to sell ice cream all morning to boot-wearing, hat-and-scarf-clad folks.

"You okay?" he asked.

"Yep." I pursed my lips and nodded. "All I need is something warm to heal my soul."

He chuckled. "Are you making fun of me?"

I pointed, indicating that the line was moving forward. He hadn't seemed to notice. "No," I said, after we moved a couple of feet. "It's just the irony of it all."

"Of what?" he said, still smiling.

*He must be having a good day.*

"I opened an ice cream shop yesterday."

"Oh no!" he said, that grin still on his face turning into a pitiful puppy-dog frown. "In the snow?"

"Yep."

"Did anyone come?"

"Nope," I said, and swung my head back and forth. "Not one person."

"What are you going to do?" he asked.

"That's why I'm here," I said. "I'm going to buy a gallon of something." I waggled a finger toward the soup selections. "As part of my marketing strategy, I thought I'd pass out a free cup of piping-hot soup to everyone who bought a scoop of ice cream. I'm thinking that might pull customers in."

He laughed again. Louder. More eye sparkle. I just seemed to tickle his funny bone.

"Oh," he said after taking a moment to process. "Is your shop Crewse Creamery?" He pointed toward a wall, but in the direction of where the shop was located.

"That would be me." I raised up a hand like when you're in class. "Win Crewse. Winter purveyor of frozen concoctions."

He chuckled and stepped closer. "I loved that place when I was a kid. I bet you'll have a store full of customers in no time."

I didn't know why he'd have confidence in me, a complete stranger, but his words made me feel good. But looking at the long line and the weather conditions outside, I knew Zoup!'s customer base was the opposite of mine, and it made me curious.

When it was my turn in line, instead of putting in my order, I first posed a question. The answer from the smiling server gave me hope.

"Do you guys sell soup in the summer?" I asked.

"We sure do," she said. "And the line is still out the door."

# chapter THIRTEEN

I took my soup back to the ice cream shop. Not because I was really planning to pass it out like I'd told that guy, but because I didn't want to stay away too long. Mom had to leave and I wasn't exactly sure what time Maisie would come.

Plus, I was afraid Penny for Your Thoughts Guy might try to sit next to me. Once again invading my space and trying to lurk inside my brain with nothing more than a mere pittance as an admittance fee.

"There she is," my mother said when I came in through the front door. "I was just schooling Maisie on the new flavors and the free scoop coupons."

I waved to Maisie. "Did we have any more customers?" I asked. "Did Wilhelmina get here yet?" I turned and glanced at the clock on the wall.

"I just got here," Maisie said.

"Yes, we had customers!" my mother said, a look of delight on her face.

"But no Wilhelmina yet," Maisie added.

"She's not due quite yet," I said. "I didn't realize how early it still was. So how many customers?"

"Three," PopPop said without looking up from his game. His friend must've left, because he was playing solo. His eyes deep in thought, he was still concentrating like he had an actual opponent.

"Three," I repeated. A sizzle of electricity snaked through me. Slowly but steadily, people were finding us again. Even in the snow.

"Yep," my mother answered. "And they couldn't stop talking about how good the ice cream is. Some remembered your Grandma Kay's and said it was just as good."

That made me happy.

"And someone called to see what time we close," my mother added.

"What time do we close?" Maisie asked.

"We close at eleven," I said.

"Ten," PopPop said. He looked at me. "We always close earlier in the winter."

I glanced out of the window. It was definitely winter.

"I'm going in the back to eat," I said. "You guys okay?"

"Of course we are," my mother said.

"I like your new flavors," Maisie said, following me into the back. "I tasted them and they are really good."

I smiled at her as I pulled off my gloves and stuck them in my coat pocket. I sat the bag from Zoup! on the desk counter and took off my coat. "I was in a panic last night," I told her. "So upset after yesterday with no sales."

"You'll be okay," she said, and smiled reassuringly. She pointed to the bag holding the soup. "Soup is good for you, it boosts your confidence."

I chuckled. "Someone just told me it's good for the soul."

"That too," Maisie said, nodding in confirmation. "And I'm here for you, Win. I'll help all I can. You know that, right?"

"Thanks." I smiled at her. "I know I can count on you."

"Always. Sooo," she started. "When did you make the ice cream?"

With the look she gave me, I knew she knew I'd made it to relax myself. It was easy to see that after all we'd made the day before, we didn't need anything more.

I sat at the desk and pulled the container of soup out of the bag. "Sometime in the middle of the night," I said.

She frowned at me. "You should have called me. I thought you'd left right after we did."

Opening the soup container up, I grabbed the French bread that came with it, broke off a piece and dipped it in my cup of chicken potpie soup.

"What happened?"

"When?"

"In the middle of the night to make you make ice cream?"

"Other than opening day without customers?"

"Yes, other than that."

"I found a dead guy down at the falls."

"No!"

Apparently Maisie hadn't seen the day's paper either.

"Yes. Police came. Asked a bunch of questions." I looked at her. "I couldn't sleep," I said, chewing up the bread.

"Oh wow. I wouldn't be able to sleep either." Her eyes drifted off before returning to focus a look of concern on me. "What were you doing down by the falls?"

"I went down to get snow to make ice cream."

"Like your grandmother used to make?"

She was being patient, waiting for the part about the guy.

"Right," I said. "I thought it would make me feel better."

"So who was the guy?" she asked. I could tell her mind was turning. Something was swirling around in there. Something more than concern for me. "What was his name?"

"I don't know." I crunched down on the bread and tore off a big chunk with my teeth.

"What did the guy look like?" she asked.

"I don't know." I sipped a spoonful of soup. "It was dark when I found him. I tripped over him."

"That's creepy," she said.

"I know." I stuck another spoonful chock-full of chicken, peas and potatoes in my mouth. "I'm okay though."

"No. That's not . . ." She stopped talking.

"Well what, then?" I said. "You're acting strange."

"Soooo," she said, pulling up a stool next to my chair and plopping down on it. "How did he die?"

"I don't know that either. And now you're being creepy," I said, and wiped my mouth with a napkin. "Probably a heart attack or something. He must have fallen down the hill. I'm not even sure it wasn't the fall that killed him. Maybe he slipped on the ice and went tumbling."

"You saw the dead body, then made the ice cream?"

"Nothing as morbid as that," I said, frowning. "Things happened in between." I looked at her. "Why?"

"Things like what?" she asked.

I huffed and hunched my shoulders. "I don't know, Maisie. You're beginning to sound like that detective." I took another mouthful of soup. "Like I made coupons. I posted on social media. *Lots* of social media. I went to the store to get a pumpkin and some blueberries. Just things."

"Ghoulish Blueberry is my new favorite," she said absently. "You can't see one piece of the fruit, but you can taste it."

"Is this why you're acting strange?" I said. "You think the dead body inspired my ice cream flavor choices? Because it didn't."

"No."

"Then what?"

Maisie scooted her stool closer, sidling right up next to me. I could feel the hairs on her sweater tickle my arm. "I've got something to tell you," she said.

"So tell me," I said. "And stop acting so weird, you're making me worry."

"I think I know who the guy was."

"What guy?" I dipped another piece of my bread in the soup.

"The dead guy."

"*My* dead guy? The one I found at the falls?"

"Yes." Her tone was conspiratorial.

"Who was he?" I asked. "What's his name?"

"I don't know," she said.

I frowned.

"Okay. I don't know him, know him," she said. "I just know who he is—was. At least I *think* I know." She bit her lip. "And I *do* know his name, if I'm right. I just for the life of me can't think what it is right now."

"Why do you think you knew him?"

"He worked at the restaurant."

"At Molta's?" I asked. Now I could see why she was acting strange. It must have been weird working with someone one day, then finding out the next day that they'd died. "He worked yesterday?"

"Not exactly."

"What does 'not exactly' mean, Maisie?" I asked.

"And," she said hesitantly, "I think I know who did it."

That wasn't an answer to my question. She had just added another layer of confusion to the pile. "Who did what?" I asked.

"Killed him."

"Ki—" I sputtered and almost choked on the soup. I swallowed hard before saying anything else. "Killed him?" My brows were knitted in confusion. "No one said anyone's been *killed*, Maisie." Other than my first customer. "Why do you say that?"

"Customer!" my mother yelled out from the front even before the chime went off on the door. "We're going to need more coupons."

"Oh brother," I said, jumping up. "I made fifteen. We need more already?" I went over to the sink to rinse my hands. I threw a glance at Maisie. "I'll be back."

"I didn't finish telling you," Maisie said.

I swiped my wet fingers on my apron and started out front. "Tell me after I see about our customer," I said. I put on a smile and walked out to the counter.

It was the guy from Zoup! I lost the smile. As he walked over to the dipping case, Felice jumped from her window seat, the first movement I'd seen her take all morning. She followed him as he walked, circling his legs as he walked the length of the dipping case, peering down into it.

"Hey, little cat," he said, stooping down. She wasn't to be ignored. "Where'd you come from?" He stood up straight. "Is this your cat?"

"Officially, she belongs to our upstairs tenant. But Felice does what she wants."

"You're Felice, huh?" he said, stooping to pick her up and giving her a scratch behind the ears. She bumped her nose with his.

"Errreow. Erreow." That was a love trill Felice made if ever I heard one.

"I'm going to print off more coupons," my mom said.

"Do you know how?" I turned my attention from the love affair Felice was having with Zoup! Guy.

"Of course," she said.

"Sooo, can I help you?" I asked.

"Yes," he said, and put Felice down. "I'm here for dessert. And to see what kind of soup you're serving."

"We're only serving ice cream," PopPop said. My grandfather didn't know about the silly little conversation I'd had with him at Zoup!

"Mr. Crewse?" Zoup! Guy walked over to my grandfather with his hand extended. "I remember you from when I was little."

"You used to come in for ice cream?" my grandfather asked. He half stood, hovering over his seat to shake his hand.

"What kid wouldn't want to?" our customer said. "The ice cream here was the best." He licked his lips. "I remember your wife, too. She told my mom the first time we came in that she made all the ice cream herself."

"She did." My grandfather had a proud smile on his face. "Now Win makes it."

"Win," he repeated, and turned to look at me, that same stupid grin on his face that he'd had at the restaurant.

He wasn't bad-looking. He was dark, with skin as smooth as the chocolate I melted in my double boiler. Maybe five-ten or -eleven, his hair was black, in a low-cut curly afro. He had deep-set eyes and teeth that were white and straight. But I didn't have time for him or his charming smile. I had a business to run, and the snow and dead guy were enough of a distraction.

"Bronwyn. Win is my nickname." I said. "But hardly anyone calls me Bronwyn."

"Pretty name," he said. "My name is Morrison Kaye, by the way." He stuck out an awkward hand. "But everyone calls me O."

I shook his hand. Nice, firm grip . . .

"Kay?" my grandfather interrupted. That got his attention. "That's your name?"

"My last name, yes, sir. It's spelled with an 'e' on the end."

"Why do they call you O?" I asked.

He turned and looked back at me. "When I was little, I'd always say 'okay' to everything. It stuck and was shortened to just 'O.'"

"I like this fellow," my grandfather said. I shook my head. He would like the guy who was stalking me. It didn't seem to me that PopPop was going to be too good at protecting me.

"I don't remember ever seeing you around here," I said, wondering how much of his story was true. I guessed he was about in his late twenties or early thirties, and I knew nearly all the people in Chagrin Falls around my age.

"I didn't live around here then," he said. "I grew up in South

Euclid. But we used to come out here in the summers. You know, Fourth of July. The Memorial Day Blossom Festival. I even came once for the Pumpkin Roll." He pointed out the window in the direction of the big hill.

My grandfather grumbled.

"He doesn't like the Pumpkin Roll," I said.

"Yeah, I only came the one time," O said, as if he needed to explain and not get on my grandfather's bad side. "But the store was different that time." He swung around looking at it, then pointed to the window. "Like that. That wasn't there."

"It's new," I said.

"That's a really nice view."

"Win put that in," PopPop said. "Good touch, wouldn't you say?"

"Yes, I would," O said, and looked at me. "But last time I was here, I was under the impression it was owned by someone else. The store was different. Candy. A hotdog stand. Not so much ice cream."

"That was my daughter, Jaqueline," PopPop said, his mouth turned upward like he had a bad taste in it. "She did all kinds of things." He shook his head. "But Win here rebuilt it with the original plans in mind."

"I like it," O said, looking around.

"I think he likes you," Maisie said in a low voice right in my ear. She startled me and I jumped. I hadn't realized she'd come out from the back. Standing close to me, she hit me on my thigh.

"Who?" I asked.

"That guy." She brought her hand up slightly and pointed. "Who else?"

"He does not," I whispered. "He came in for ice cream."

"I don't see him with any," she whispered back.

"You playing backgammon by yourself?" O asked PopPop.

"You know this game?" PopPop asked. "Not many young folks do."

"Sure, I know it," O said, and slid into the bench opposite PopPop.

"I had a partner earlier," PopPop said, "but he had to go. You wanna play?"

"Doesn't he have somewhere to go?" I asked Maisie, speaking in hushed tones again.

She smiled. "Seems like he wants to be here."

"Who is that?" My mother came out from the back. Apron off, she had her coat and hat on.

"Someone who is evidently unemployed and has no life," I said.

"He likes Win," Maisie said.

"Who is he?" my mother asked again.

"I met him at Zoup! when I went for lunch."

"And he followed you here?" she asked.

"I don't know if he *followed* me. We were talking while we were standing in line and I told him I worked here."

"He likes her," Maisie said, nodding her head knowingly.

"Sounds like it to me," my mother said. "And your grandfather seems to like him. Grumpy Pa doesn't talk that much to anybody."

"His last name is *Kaye*," I said.

"Ohhh," my mother said, nodding. "He's got your grandma's name. He'll probably make that guy his best friend." She pushed her purse up on her shoulder. "Well, I'm off to my class. You want me to come back later?"

"No." I shook my head. "We're good. I've got Maisie and Wilhelmina." I shrugged. "And PopPop."

"Thought you said PopPop wasn't working today?"

"I'm sure he'd help out if we got busy."

"Okay, then. Sounds like you've got it covered," she said. "So, I'm off."

"Wait," I said, stopping her. "Where are the coupons?"

"I couldn't figure out how to work that printer," she said.

My eyes rolled upward and I chuckled. "No worries. I'll do it."

"Okay," she said. "Stop by the house on your way home and let me know how the rest of the day went."

As she headed out the front door, it opened and a customer came in. My mother turned after she passed him and gave me a thumbs-up.

"Welcome to Crewse Creamery," I said, and put a great big grin on my face.

# chapter FOURTEEN

Maisie and I served a few customers after my mother left, then I went into the back to print off more coupons. Maisie followed right behind me.

"So about the dead guy," she said.

"The one you knew?" I opened up the laptop and started it.

"The one that was killed," she said.

"Maisie?" I slid the mouse across the pad and clicked on the file folder at the bottom of my screen. "Like I told that lady earlier today, we don't get murders around here."

"We do now, thanks to Ari."

"What did Ari do?" I asked.

"I think he's the one who killed him."

I stopped what I was doing and turned to look at her. She couldn't be serious. "You mean your boss? Ari Terrain? That's who you think killed someone?"

"Yes," she said. "Ari Terrain. My boss. I think he killed a guy that worked at the restaurant."

"Whoa," I said. "That's a huge accusation." Which I couldn't understand how she could have thought of. I didn't know Ari as well as she did, but he seemed like a nice guy. The kind of nice guy who doesn't commit murder. "And what does that have to do with the guy I found by the falls?"

"Ari killed him."

"I'm confused," I said. "Are you saying 'too'? He killed him, too? Like Ari killed *two* people?"

"No. I'm saying that the guy I'm talking about and the guy you found are the same guy."

"Oh." I let that sink in for a moment. "And that this guy was murdered by Ari?"

"Yes."

"How did you come up with that?"

"Ari called off from work last night."

"Okay. And?"

"And he was supposed to be at work."

I thought about my father saying he was working when he hadn't been. But that would never make me think he'd been out committing murder.

"Okay," I said. "But I don't see how you think just because Ari wasn't where he was supposed to be that he might have been involved in a murder."

"Because the police called," she said matter-of-factly, like that would clear everything up.

"Called who? You?"

"The restaurant."

"I'm not understanding," I said.

"Remember yesterday I told you I could stay all day and help you?"

"Yeah," I nodded. "I remember."

"That's because I wasn't supposed to work."

"Okay."

"Then I got a call after I left the ice cream shop that I needed to come in. The new guy who was supposed to work hadn't shown up, one lady who just started called to say she wouldn't be in, and then Ari was MIA."

"Okay." I still didn't understand how she was making the connection. But I figured she'd get to the point sooner or later.

"So why wouldn't Ari come into work?" Maisie asked, holding out her hands.

"I don't know, Maisie." I was trying hard to follow her. "Why?"

"Because he was out killing the new guy!"

I wanted to laugh, but Maisie was serious and I would never make her feel bad.

"And what did the police say when they called?" I asked.

"They asked where they were calling."

I frowned. "They didn't know?"

"No. They didn't know."

"Oh," I said. "I would have thought that fishy, too. Then why would they call?"

"I have no idea," she said.

I hung my head and tried to keep from laughing.

"I think they were using the new guy's phone."

I tilted my head, considering what she said. "Sooo . . . the police used the phone that belonged to this guy who was supposed to come to work to call the restaurant?"

"Yes," she said, giving a resolute nod like now I was getting it. Only I wasn't.

"Why would they do that?" I scrunched up my face.

"Oh my goodness!" Maisie said, and slumped her shoulders. "Don't you watch TV?"

"Evidently not the same shows you watch," I said, and laughed.

"They always call the last number dialed on the vic's phone."

"The vic?" Then I held up my hand. "I got you. The *victim.* Okay. So the last number dialed on the phone they had was to Molta's?"

"Right," she said, seemingly happy I was finally following her.

"So what does that mean?"

"Really, Win?" She flapped her hands on her thighs. "Just really?"

"I mean I get how you could think that something might be amiss with the police having a phone and calling the last number dialed. But it might just have been a lost phone."

"Or the phone of a dead guy."

"I don't know about that," I said, shaking my head.

"And what about Ari just not showing up? He owns the place. He shouldn't ever do that. And then this new guy not coming in?"

"Coincidence?" I offered.

"Murder gets my vote," she said.

"We're voting on whether there's been a murder committed? Maisie! We shouldn't jump to conclusions like that."

I heard the chime on the door.

"We've got a customer," I said. "Oh shoot!" I glanced at the printer. "I didn't print any more coupons. Can you do that for me real quick and bring them out?"

"We have to do something about the murder," she said, her arms folded in protest.

"There hasn't been one," I said. She opened her mouth to

speak, but I put up a hand. "But if we do do something," I said to placate her, "we'll have to do it after I wait on this customer. Can you print up some coupons for me, please?" I wiggled my fingers over the keyboard.

I walked to the front of the store. When I got to the cash register, ready to greet my customer, Maisie bumped into the back of me. She had followed right behind me. Guess this customer wasn't going to get a coupon.

She went around the corner and over to Felice, picking her up and giving her a kiss. "Hey, sweetie," Maisie cooed. Felice purred right back.

I put on a smile and started my usual salutation. "Welcome to—" I stopped mid-sentence. It wasn't a customer. It was the back of Detective Liam Beverly. I knew that leather bomber jacket anywhere.

I blew out a breath. *What does he want?*

Maisie talking about murder and then he shows up. *Geesh.*

I glanced over to see what PopPop was doing, but he wasn't in his booth. I looked around the small eatery and saw he'd left altogether. *Missed opportunity for him,* I thought. Here was something I would have loved him to protect me from—the detective's questions. I was sure he'd come back to ask me more.

At least Felice was taking a stance. Literally. She'd gotten out of Maisie's arms and was on all fours, seemingly ready to pounce if given a reason.

*That's right.* I tried to telepathically get my thoughts over to Felice. *He's a menace. Get ready to attack!*

"Hello, Detective Beverly," I said, directing my attention back to him, a sly grin on my face. If he only knew my thoughts. "Are you here for a scoop of some of our delicious confectionary delights?"

He turned from looking out of the door and walked over to me. He was dressed much like he had been the night before—leather jacket, apple cap—but today his pants were brown and those pistachio-colored eyes looked tired. I did notice something new: he was bowlegged.

"Are you really selling ice cream?" He swung around from his waist and glanced out of the window, then swung back to me. "In the cold?"

"It's just that good," I said, and smiled.

"You had any customers today?" he asked.

"Of course we have," I said, thankful it wasn't the day before that I was being questioned about.

"Not many?" It sounded as if that was his question and his answer.

"We had a few," I said. He turned the ends of his mouth down and slowly nodded his head, indicating he was impressed. "You ask a lot of questions, don't you? I mean, just about anything."

He chuckled. "Yeah, I guess I do. I'm just an inquisitive kind of guy," he said.

"Lucky me."

"And as luck would have it, I have a few more questions for you about last night."

"That doesn't sound lucky to me," I said. "Why so many questions anyway? Is this routine when someone dies?"

"It is when they die outside on the street."

"I found him at the falls," I said, even though I knew what he meant.

"Same thing," he said. "We investigate any unexpected deaths. It's just routine."

"Did you find out who he was?" I asked.

"I'm not at liberty to say right now," he said. "I was hoping you might have something else to add."

"Well, I've told you everything I know—last night," I said. "And I told that police officer everything I know more than a few times."

"Which police officer?" he asked.

I let out a sigh. "The one that kept me company until his 'backup'"—I did the air quotes—"came. Which, I'm assuming, included you."

He nodded. "Like I say, this is routine. I'm waiting for the autopsy report to come back. Thought I'd follow up with a few of the witnesses."

"Were there other witnesses besides me?" I asked, surprise in my voice.

His eyes lit up and I saw a small smile curl up his face. I didn't think he expected me to be as inquisitive as he was.

He forged past my question. "People forget things sometimes when they're faced with a traumatic event, then remember later." He tapped his finger on his temple. "Something jars their memory."

"Nope," I said, shaking my head. "I'm sure I told you everything last night. No jarring here." I tapped on my temple.

"You forgot about the boy and the scarf," he said, a smirk on his lips. "You didn't mention him until you saw him."

*Hmmm . . . He was right. I had done that.*

"So can you think of anything else?" he asked.

I decided not to just brush him off. I earnestly thought about everything that happened the night before. I squinted my eyes and tilted my head. Could I have forgotten something?

"You thinking?" he asked.

"I'm trying," I said, squinting my eyes even tighter.

"Well, while you're thinking, let me ask about something else."

"Okay," I said.

"Did you find a lost puppy yesterday?"

"No." I shook my head. "But I saw someone who did." I glanced over at PopPop's now vacant bench and was glad he wasn't there to hear this line of questioning.

"And what happened?"

"Nothing," I said, hoping my expression would belie the fact that I knew something about *the guy* who had the lost puppy. I didn't want to start that conversation if I didn't have to. It seemed to upset everyone I knew when I said anything about him. "A guy asked me if it was my puppy, I said no, and he said he was going to take it to the police station."

"It never made it to us," he said.

"Oh," I said, recalling how I'd seen him walking the opposite way of the police station. I hoped the puppy was okay.

"Did you know the guy?" he asked.

"Nope," I said, which wasn't a complete untruth. "I didn't know the guy. And I can't think of anything else I might have missed telling you yesterday."

I had officially joined my dad and Glynis Vale in the Village League of Liars.

*chapter*

# FIFTEEN

As soon as the detective left, Maisie's imagination went into overdrive. She put Felice back down on the window seat and hurried over to me.

"You think he suspects Ari?" she asked.

"He didn't ask me one question about Ari, Maisie."

"Won't be long." She ran over to the window and peeked out of it. "I bet he's on his way over there now."

"Where? Molta's?"

"Yep."

"Good," I said. "Let him ask other people questions."

"That phone call Dead Guy made before he died is probably all the proof they need."

"That would be some pretty flimsy proof, Maisie. I don't think anyone could be convicted on that."

"Why did he ask you about the puppy?" Maisie asked, my comment going right past her. "That was weird."

"I know," I said. "How did he even know about the puppy?"

"I don't know, but he knows something about it," Maisie said. "Maybe he was testing you."

"Testing me how?"

"He knows information about the puppy and he's checking to see if you know the same information."

"Why would he do that?"

She shrugged. "They like to get people tangled up in a web of lies."

"Well, I'm not lying about anything," I said. It was a little difficult getting those words out. "I didn't see anything, and I told them everything I knew."

"He's got his work cut out for him," Maisie said.

"Finding the puppy?"

"Catching the murderer."

I rolled my eyes.

"And I remembered his name."

"Whose name?" I asked.

"Dead Guy's."

"Oh," I said. "What is it? Or what *was* it?"

"Peter Sellers."

I scrunched up my face. "Like the actor?"

"Actor?" Her eyes got wide with the realization. "Never thought about that until now. That was the name of an actor, wasn't it?"

"Yes," I said. "You remember that guy?"

Maisie, like me, had hung around her grandparents as much as her parents and had knowledge about a lot of topics that most people our age didn't. Movies from the sixties was one of those topics.

"*The Pink Panther*?" she asked. I nodded. "Then maybe that wasn't my guy's name," she said. She squinted her eyes. "But I'm almost sure it was."

"I'm sure the police took fingerprints or something to identify him."

"Or we can go to the restaurant."

"And do what?"

"Find out his name. He had to have a time card or something. We could look around."

"Whoa!" I said. "Don't get me involved."

"Don't you want to see if we can't figure out if there is a connection between Ari and this guy, whatever his name is?"

"No."

"Yes," she said. "Yes, you do."

"Why would I care about who Dead Guy is?"

"That'll work." She smiled. "We'll call him Dead Guy." She weighed the decision with a side-to-side tilting of her head. "At least until we find out what his name is for sure."

"And who you don't know for sure is the guy I found at the falls."

"I do know for sure," she said.

"That and that Ari killed him, right?" I said.

"Right," she said.

That was Maisie. She wasn't always up on everything, and sometimes didn't have a clue on anything. But when she set her mind to something, it was next to impossible to get her to change it.

"Why would Ari kill a guy who worked for him?" I asked.

"Did he really work for him?"

"I don't know, Maisie, that's what you said."

"He wasn't there but for one day."

"Did you see him and Ari fighting or something?"

"No."

"Well, I say let the cops find out who your Peter Sellers is—if that was his name—and if Ari had anything to do with his death. And if your guy and my guy are the same guy."

"While we're at the restaurant we should search his office, too."

"What?" I turned to look at her. "Whose office?"

"Ari's." She just seemed so calm about her new illegal proclivities.

"Oh no, *we* shouldn't and neither should you." I wiggled a finger at her. "We can't go to the restaurant to look for anything."

"Why? We need to find out. They do it on all my British amateur sleuth shows. They snoop and find out what they need to do. We need to find out about him."

"In *real* life, that's against the law," I said.

"You don't really have to do illegal things to find out about people." O had walked up to the ice cream display case. Evidently he'd been listening to my and Maisie's conversation.

"Where did you come from?" I asked.

"The restroom." He pointed in that direction.

"Were you eavesdropping?" I asked.

"Who, me?" he asked, a grin on his face.

"Yes, you."

"Nooo," he said, and smiled. "I just like to be helpful."

"And how can you help?" I asked.

"Your person dilemma. You can find out a lot about people just by doing a little research online. Use a search engine," he said, his voice authoritative like he was giving a dissertation on the subject. "Type in what you want to know. It'll fill in the blanks."

"What can we find online?" Maisie asked. She nudged me over so that she was standing in front of him.

"Addresses. Age. Phone numbers. Criminal records."

"Criminal records." That was all Maisie needed to hear. She was on board. "How would I do that?"

"Well, Cuyahoga County's court documents are online and they are really easy to access. You can plug in a person's name and see whatever cases they've had in court—civil or criminal."

"I can find out what they've done?" She was excited.

"Yes. You can find out the date they were arrested. The charges filed against them and the disposition of the case."

"What does disposition mean?" Maisie asked.

"What happened during the case," he said. "And in Ohio, if they went to prison, you can look up their inmate record. Shows their picture, what crime they were convicted of and when they were incarcerated."

Maisie looked at me as if she'd just learned she'd hit the lottery. Her eyes were full of excitement. I knew this was a bad thing for her to know. She had already had it fixed in her mind that a crime had been committed. She knew who the victim was and who had caused his demise all from an innocent phone call from the police department. Weaponizing her with all the information Google could bestow couldn't be a good thing.

"You can look up property ownership on the auditor's website." He was building his list of where to find anything needed to snoop.

"This is so awesome!" Maisie said. "All this information at your fingertips."

"You can look up gravesites on Find A Grave—find out if a person is dead or not," he continued, seemingly happy to engage Maisie. "Lots of times you'll find relatives and associates of people by checking out Facebook. A wealth of information right at your fingertips, indeed." He moved his fingers like he was typing on a keyboard.

This man was dangerous.

"Who *are* you?" I asked, narrowing my eyes at him.

# chapter SIXTEEN

We finally got Mr. 1-800-Learn-How-to-Snoop-Online, otherwise known as Morrison Kaye, out of the ice cream shop. We needed to get busy printing coupons and prepping for new ice cream flavors. And Wilhelmina came in and I needed to show her the ropes.

But work wasn't going to stop Maisie.

"On *Agatha Raisin*," she was saying over the hum of the printer. I had assigned Wilhelmina the task of tasting each one of the ice creams so she could make informed recommendations, and Maisie had followed me into the back. "Agatha, the main character, moves to a seemingly quiet village, just like Chagrin Falls." She raised her eyebrows and gave me a knowing tip of her head. "And there's a murder."

I expected her to say, "Just like in Chagrin Falls," but she didn't.

"So Agatha becomes a murder suspect," she continued. "Then she has to solve the murder. You should watch the show because you'll see what we need to do."

"I thought Ari was the murder suspect," I said.

"He is."

I couldn't see how she thought that related to her theory of murder and wanting to find out "who done it," but I wasn't going to ask.

As soon as I printed up more coupons (twenty-five this time!), the chime over the door alerted me to another customer and gave me an excuse not to hear any more about Maisie's shows. Perfect timing.

I left Maisie chopping nuts for the banana nut ice cream I wanted to make and rattling on about some show called *Vera*.

"I'll get it," I said to Wilhelmina as she came out front. She looked at me wide-eyed with a mini spoon hanging out of her mouth.

My customer turned out to be Debbie Devereaux. Owner of Exquisite Designs clothing boutique and as of late, mysterious tea whisperer.

*Maybe Detective Beverly should talk to her,* I thought. She seemed to know more about the guy I'd found by the falls than I did. Or than Maisie did, for that matter.

"Oh, it looks gorgeous in here." She walked around the room, from one wall to the other, then back to the window overlooking the falls. Pointing her finger back over her shoulder and walking toward me, she said, "That is a nice touch."

"Welcome to Crewse Creamery," I said, happy that she liked what I had done with the store. Ms. Devereaux had good taste. Everyone knew it and it made her store a hot spot in our village when it came to buying fashionable clothes.

"I feel welcomed," she said, and smiled.

Today she had on a furry headband that matched the fur of

the coat she'd had on the night before. Her leather gloves and mid-calf boots that laced up the front had fur around the tops and were the same deep chocolate brown.

"Did you come in for some ice cream?" I asked.

"Oh, no," she said, shaking her head. "It's too cold."

I didn't know what to say to that.

I found I didn't need to say anything because she kept on talking. "I came in to check on you." She laid her hand on top of the dipping case, and her small cocoa eyes seemed to study me. "Are you okay?" she asked.

"I'm fine," I said.

"It's not every day that you stumble over a dead body."

"No. It's not," I said. "But really, I'm okay." I chewed on my bottom lip, debating whether I should ask her if she knew the person I'd found at the bottom of the falls. With the comment she'd made, it was easy to think she'd seen him before he went down.

I decided to ask my question in another way.

"Have you spoken to the police about last night?" I asked.

"Oh. No. I haven't," she said. "Not about last night."

*Then what did she talk to the police about?* I shook my head to clear it. "Do you know the guy who died?"

"Do you?" She answered my question with one of her own.

I didn't know how to respond. "The detective—Detective Beverly—I don't know if you saw him or not, but he asked me about other witnesses," I said. Maybe she had seen something.

"Witnesses to what?" she asked, her eyes big as if she had completely forgotten about what she'd said to me.

"What happened last night? How that guy may have fallen to his death."

"Fallen?" she chuckled. "I don't think that could have happened. Who tries to go down to the falls with all that snow on the ground?"

I wanted to raise my hand and say, "Uh, that would be me." But she already knew that and was seemingly playing dumb. I wasn't trekking into that territory again, relaying something I knew was true only to find the person would lie to deny it. I'd done it with that woman Glynis Vale and her son, Jasper.

So I hunched my shoulder and played dumb right along with her. "I don't know," I said. "Who indeed?"

She laughed again and touched the side of her nose. She knew I was on to her, but still insisted on this cat-and-mouse game.

That was fine with me. I'd grown up around her and had a lot of respect for her. My grandmother had loved her, saying she had a good head on her shoulders that many people didn't have. I remembered they used to talk often.

"Well, I'm going to go," Ms. Devereaux said. "Your Grandma Kay wouldn't have ever forgiven me if I hadn't stopped by to make sure you were alright."

"Come back and buy some ice cream," I said.

"I will," she said, waving bye to me. "As soon as it gets warm out."

After Ms. Devereaux left, I figured it was as good of a time as any to train my new employee.

"Did you taste all the flavors?" I asked Wilhelmina. I wanted her to be able to share her experience with the customers.

"Some twice," she said. I smiled. "My favorite is the caramel. Tastes just like caramel popcorn."

"I used fresh corn in that."

"Easy to tell," she said.

Wilhelmina Stone didn't look anywhere near a hundred, like Maisie and I had joked. But she was old*er*. She had a pep in her step and was always stretching out her arms and legs. "Old lady yoga," she told me when I gave her the first questioning look. She wore a reddish wig, and no glasses. "They're still twenty-twenty," she'd told me when I asked her if she knew where we were located, and then added, "I'll find you." But what she found when she walked in the store her first day of work was PopPop. She gushed and blushed and wanted to know who he was. I think I even saw her wink at him. She patted on her wig and brushed her hand down her dress. "Size six," she said proudly. The reason for that, she leaned over and whispered, was that she had smoked for fifty years, quit for more than ten years, but by then the nicotine had killed all the fat cells. Permanently.

While I talked with Wilhelmina, Maisie kept herself busy cutting and chopping. I made the banana nut ice cream but just didn't have the energy to make anything more. I'd have to put the mise en place that Maisie had readied for me for the other flavors away.

I was tired. The lack of sleep from the night before and all the things that had happened during the day, including—big grin on my face—all the customers we had, were weighing on me. Nowhere near as many visitors as all the likes I'd gotten on my posts, but it was a start. And my marketing magic hadn't dried up yet. I had more tricks up my sleeve.

I pulled up one of the stools from the back to the entryway so I could see customers when they came in, and eased down onto it. I really needed that plexiglass to come, then I could see through to the front without sitting in the middle of the floor. The email response the vendor had sent me said early next week. That was disappointing. I just wanted it to get here. You'd think by now I'd be used to delays.

Maisie, with earbuds, sang softly as she worked. And Wilhelmina, I'm sure thanks to skills learned from her time as a Walmart greeter, was great with the customers. She insisted that she was fine, so I pulled my feet up to rest on the rung of the stool and let out a sigh. I tried to prop my weary eyes open just enough to see out of them. On top of my no-sleep-steady-stream-of-customers day, just being around Maisie and my mother could zap anyone's energy. They were always buzzing around and into something. Watching them could make anyone tired. But it seemed like Maisie had wound down some. Even her talk of British shows and murderous restaurant owners had dissipated.

I was just starting to put up the ice cream when the chime went off over the door. Wilhelmina was taking care of two customers. Thought I'd better give her a hand.

I tried to blink away the sleepiness in my eyes and put on a cheerful smile. "Welcome to Crewse Creamery," I said, stifling a yawn.

"Hi," the woman said. She walked over to the dipping case and peered inside, a smile appearing on her wide, round face. "I've heard rave reviews about your ice cream," the woman said, looking up at me. "It looks delicious."

"Would you like to try a sample or two?" I said.

"May I?" she asked.

"You sure can. We have a trio of seasonal favorites, but I think you may enjoy this one." I thought I might have had her pegged. Grandma Kay always knew what to offer a newcomer. I scooped her up a taste of Decadent Chocolate in one of the pink sample spoons.

"Try this," I said.

"Oooh, chocolate," she cooed. "I love chocolate." She wrapped her lips around the spoon and her small, wide-set eyes lit up. "Oh boy," she said, putting her fingers up to her lips, mulling the ice cream around in her mouth. "I have never tasted chocolate ice cream this good. It's smooth, and creamy and . . . Oh. So. Rich! It has to be bad for me." She dragged her teeth across her bottom lip. "But I don't care. I just want more."

"It's Decadent Chocolate," I said.

"It sure is," she said.

"No." I laughed. "That's the name of it. Decadent Chocolate."

"Ohhh," she said, giving her cherry-colored lips one last once-over with her tongue. "That's a perfect name for it."

She stuck her hand over the top of the dipping cabinet. "Hi, I'm Clara Blackwell."

"Nice to meet you, Ms. Blackwell." I shook her hand. "I'm Bronwyn Crewse," I said. "But you can call me Win."

"Win it is," she said, and gave a firm nod. "You're just the person I was looking for. And you can call me Clara."

"So, Clara, would you like two scoops? A pint?"

"Actually, I'd need more like a few gallons." She waved her hand in the air as if it was going to be an endless stream of ice cream.

"Gallons?"

"This is going to be really short notice, I know," she said. "The other place we booked had a problem getting their ice cream."

"We won't have a problem," I said, not even knowing what she needed yet.

"I had to come out this way to take care of some business and I heard you make your ice cream here." She turned her head and looked out the corner of her eye. "I had to see for myself. Is that true?" she asked.

"Yes," I said, and pointed toward the back. Oh, how I wished for my plexiglass window right about now. "I make it most every day."

"Wow," she said, delight dancing in her eyes. "You don't order it and have a big refrigerated truck drive it to you, do you? Because that's the problem we had with the company we booked."

"Why? Did something happen with their refrigerated truck?" I asked.

"It broke and it wasn't going to be fixed in time." She hunched her shoulders and held her hand out. "How do you only have one truck if you want to stay in business?"

I puckered up my lips and shook my head. "I don't know," I said.

"Well it won't be open for long, not with how they take care of business, I can guarantee that," she said. "But you don't use those, right?"

"No. No refrigerated trucks used here," I said. I held up my hands and wiggled my fingers. "We make it all by hand."

"And you don't pour a premade mixture of flavored milk into a big churning-slash-freezing machine? Because I'm not looking for slushy ice cream either."

"We start with fresh, whole products. Most locally grown." I pointed to the tray of vanilla bean ice cream. "The vanilla used in that was grown in the Village Community Garden."

"The one around the corner?"

"Yes," I said. "The person that runs the garden, Maisie, put in a greenhouse. We're able to get some of our products from them even at this time of year."

"Professor Kaye told me that, and I didn't know if it could be true. That you made everything right here. And that you go to local farms all around Ohio for your ingredients. He highly recommended you."

"Professor K?" I questioned. I was trying to keep up with the conversation. "Are you talking about someone from Wycliffe University?"

"Yes, I work there."

Wycliffe was a local university, the next suburb over. I started thinking that it would be a great place to market our wares.

"I don't think I know a Professor K," I said, "but we've had lots of customers from there over the years."

How could I have forgotten about the college right down the road? I made a mental note to do some marketing at the school. Maybe whatever Clara Blackwell wanted me to do would get that ball started and get our name out around the campus.

"He's at the law school," she said. "I'm sure you know him, he certainly knows you. Morrison." She wrinkled up her face. "Oh! You probably just call him O." She nodded. "I forgot, that's what his friends call him."

"Oh. O," I said.

"You do know him, right?" Concern flashed across her face.

"Um, yes," I said. "I do. I know him. He was just in the store today playing backgammon with my grandfather."

*Striking up a conversation with a guy in a soup line might not have been such a bad thing to do. But him stalking me is a different matter . . .*

"And you can help me?" she asked.

"I'm sure we can," I said. I was holding my breath that that statement was true. Could I really be able to provide what she wanted? "When do you need your *gallons* of ice cream?" I joked, half of me wanting it to be true, the other half not so sure.

"I'm the dean of student affairs, the chaplain for Gamma Phi Pi sorority and the chairperson for this year's President's Dinner."

*Good lord, I hope she doesn't need ice cream for all of those things. At least not all at once.*

"And as our mascot is a polar bear, I was thinking that the theme should be frosty and festive."

"For which event?" I asked. Doing a quick analysis in my head, I knew there'd be more students during a student affairs event, and a lot of high-wheeling benefactors at a President's Dinner.

"I thought about setting up a malt-slash-milkshake station." She was still talking. "A sundae station and maybe even a banana split station might be fun." She had taken a breath reciting her laundry list and hadn't answered my question, so I tried again.

"For which event?"

"I see you already have a soda fountain. Is it portable?" She stood on her toes to peek over the dipping case. "It's adorable. Does it work?"

"Yes, it does." I stopped asking her questions. I figured she'd get to the point sooner or later.

"Or we could go classy and do cakes. Do you do ice cream cakes?"

"Yes. We do a variety of ice cream cakes." I had said the words out loud, but they didn't really mean anything. What I had was Grandma Kay's recipes for ice cream cake, not the actual cakes. I didn't even have a display freezer for any.

"Maybe even ice cream pies." Her mind was moving faster than the blades on my mixer.

"All of that sounds yummy," I said. "We can do just about whatever you need."

"Good," she said. She pulled her hand away and placed it over her chest, then blew out a breath. "You are a lifesaver." She gave me a megawatt, all-white smile.

I thought I'd try again. "When is the event?" Maybe a different question would elicit an answer from her.

"That's the thing," Clara said. "With such short notice, the other vendor pulled out."

"The delivery disaster." I had already heard about that.

"Yes. The delivery disaster. I could have just marched over to their store and choked someone." She made the choking motion with her hands, gritting her teeth. "Seems like they'd have some backup plan, doesn't it?"

"You would think," I said. I figured I'd agree with her until she told me what I needed to know.

"But I guess it might have been for the best." She shook her head. "I'm sure I would have let them go anyway if I had found out first."

"Found out what?" I asked.

"There'd been some shake-up in management. Shady dealings

and all that may have reflected badly on the school. And in hindsight, I think that may've been the real reason they pulled out."

I nodded while she talked.

"Still, they got their comeuppance for backing out so close to our event."

"Without the choking on your part?"

She chuckled. "Oh, heavens yes. I wouldn't do anything like that. Couldn't. It just isn't in my nature. But my assistant . . ."

"That's a different story?" I finished for her.

"Yes!" she said. A glint in her eye. "She pulled out her phone and left a few choice words to let people know and a one-star rating that will hurt them way more than me going over to inflict any bodily harm."

"Oh," I said. "Online?"

"Yes! Online!"

"She left them a bad review, huh?"

"Scathing," she said. "I'm sure it'll make anyone else think twice before they book that company for anything."

# chapter SEVENTEEN

Winter hours for the shop were not in effect with Clara Blackwell in the store. It took nearly twenty minutes for her to tell me what she needed and that was after a fifteen-minute discussion about Felice being a real cat. It seemed Clara had a stuffed one when she was a child. Felice couldn't take it anymore and sashayed out mid-event-info discourse, as did Maisie. She promised to come back the next day if I needed help, though. Felice left no indication when she'd return to her window seat perch.

I had popped in the back to get a pad and pen and found Maisie packing up to leave. She told me she was thinking about quitting Molta's. She couldn't fathom working for a murderer.

I didn't have time, but I knew I'd have to have a talk with her to convince her that Ari wasn't a murderer and that there hadn't even been a crime committed. And, I thought, I should probably see if I couldn't encourage her to stop watching those British sleuth television shows.

Maisie wanting to be an amateur sleuth to solve an undetermined death surprised me. She never wanted to fix anything. If something was broken, she'd say not to use it. Whether it was a sink, the banister at her house or a clock, repair wasn't an option. Now she wanted to fix something that wasn't broken.

I closed up shop after getting Clara out. Nicely. Didn't want any one-star scathing reviews from her or her assistant. I put the ice cream in the freezer, even though I'd decided I would replace most of it the next day. I dusted, mopped the front and back of the store, and wiped down the dipping cabinet and countertops before bundling up and heading up the hill to walk home, humming the entire time. All my thoughts were on the big event I was going to do at Wycliffe, and that made me feel good. Professor Kaye, although I hoped he wouldn't show up again so soon, had gotten me more exposure than my tweets.

It was only when I got as far as my parents' house that I realized I had driven to work that morning. I stopped, turned around and looked back down the hill. Did I want to go back and get my car?

No, I decided. But I was going to stop and let the family know about the catering job we'd gotten. I turned and cut through the neighboring lot to go around to PopPop's. I wanted to tell him first.

The walkway and stoop in front of PopPop's place was shoveled and salted. I was sure he'd done it himself. He always wanted to make sure that we knew he could take care of himself.

I knocked at the front door. There was no answer.

I glanced over at the three-car garage. PopPop rarely drove anywhere. Like me, he enjoyed walking. I probably picked that up from him. The car being there wouldn't have meant he was at home, so I skipped looking inside the garage for it.

I stepped off onto the grass and crunched through the snow to peer into his front room window. The curtains were drawn and there was no light from inside peeking through.

He had left the shop abruptly and I didn't know why. He'd been hanging around all day and then, *poof!* He was gone. Every time the bell jangled on the door to the store, I looked up, expecting him to walk back in.

Now he still wasn't around. And I had good news.

I doubted if he was in my parents' part of the house—he'd rather people come to him—but I decided to check anyway. I hadn't seen my mother since before lunch and I was excited to tell her, too, that we'd not only gotten a few more customers in, but that I was going to be a party planner. She'd love that.

I came around to the back door. I remembered that I wanted to put the gloves my mother had given me back into the cubby in case I ever needed them again. I'd know right where to find them. Today, I had remembered my own.

I came out of the mudroom into the kitchen, but it was eerily quiet. I looked around. Pots sat on the stove. The cutting board had yellow and red peppers partially diced. It looked as if someone had been in the middle of cooking and had been interrupted. My parents took late-night snacks to a whole new level.

I heard voices toward the front of the house. One was familiar, but not one that belonged to our house.

As I came down the center hall toward the front, I realized who it was.

Detective Liam Beverly.

*What is he doing here so late?*

"Where were you last evening?" the detective was asking.

Detective Beverly's presence made me nervous and I didn't want to interrupt. I pressed my back up against the wall, and tried to still my hastily spent breaths so I wouldn't be heard.

"That depends on what time you're asking about." My father didn't seem as rattled by the detective as I was.

"Before seven p.m."

"I was at work," my father said.

"And you weren't anywhere near your family's ice cream shop?"

"I was there," my father said. "I arrived after you did."

"You saw me?" the detective asked.

"I did."

"Why were you there?"

"My daughter, Wi—" my father paused, seemingly hesitant about saying my nickname. "My daughter, Bronwyn, called and asked that we come down. She told us what happened."

"She did." That was my mother's voice. It sounded just as calm as my father's.

My chest was rising and falling like a yo-yo. My father hadn't come with my mother. He didn't arrive until later and hadn't been dressed the same as he had when he'd left for work that morning. I wondered if he was going to mention that to the police . . .

"How long had you known him?" the detective asked.

"I didn't know him," my father said.

*Known who? Who are they talking about?*

"You didn't know Stephen Bayard?" the detective responded, his voice threaded with disbelief.

*Stephen Bayard . . .*

Why did that sound familiar?

"Not personally, no," my father said. I could just picture him there with his arms crossed across his chest. He could stay calm under most circumstances. I, on the other hand, was starting to sweat bullets.

I didn't know what Detective Beverly was after, but the whole conversation was making me queasy.

"He was a menace," my mother said. No spit or fire in her voice, she spoke matter-of-factly. That was unusual for her. "No one around here cares what happened to him."

"Let me answer the questions, Ailbhe," my father said.

"I may have some questions for you as well, Mrs. Crewse. I hope that'll be alright with you, Dr. Crewse."

I didn't hear a response from either one of them.

The detective sounded more official than he had the night before or when he'd come into the shop earlier in the day. "It's interesting," he said, his words coming out slowly, "that your wife knows him, Dr. Crewse, and you don't."

Neither one of my parents said a word.

"What was your relationship with Mr. Bayard, Dr. Crewse?" I guess Detective Beverly thought asking the same question differently might trick my father into answering.

"I told you, I didn't know the man. I didn't have any kind of relationship with him."

"What was it that you did know of him?"

"He was a con man."

"That he was," the detective said.

"He turned our family upside down," my mother, who wasn't supposed to be answering questions, offered. "He tried to steal our family store from us."

*Oh . . . that Stephen Bayard.*

Now I knew who he was. Puppy Guy.

Wait! I drew in a hasty breath. That's who I tripped over? Puppy Guy?

Dead Guy was Puppy Guy?

*Crap!*

"In the course of your work, Dr. Crewse, do you use succinylcholine?" the detective asked.

*What is that?* I thought.

"No, I don't," my father said.

"Are you sure?" Detective Beverly asked, his voice sounding stronger.

"Of course I'm sure," my father said. His voice didn't sound like he was backing down. The detective's bravado wasn't bothering him.

"I'll ask again—" the detective started, but my father cut him off.

"You don't have to ask again. It seems you don't understand how the drug is used. *I* don't use it. Not as the surgeon," my father said. "An anesthesiologist would, however. I can give you the name of a good one if you need it."

"Maybe I will get that name from you, but right now I want to understand what you're saying."

"What don't you understand?" My father's voice flowed with irritation.

"So," the detective said, "it's in the operating room with you, right? You have the drug succinylcholine in there during that time?"

"I suppose," my father said. "I don't concern myself with another doctor's work unless it affects my patient. I need the anesthesiologist to put my patient to sleep. I don't concern myself with him doing it."

"But you would have access to the drug, is that not correct?" he asked.

"Access?" my father said.

"Why?" my mother wanted to know.

"Because, Mrs. Crewse, succinylcholine was the murder weapon used to kill Mr. Bayard."

*Murder weapon?*

Then I realized what was going on. That detective was questioning my dad as a suspect in the murder of Stephen Bayard. He had to be. My mother had just told me that my father would kill him if he saw him.

Did the detective think that, too?

I rested my hand on my heart, closed my eyes and hoped she hadn't been right.

# chapter EIGHTEEN

I stumbled out of the house, trying to be as quiet as I could, but it seemed I couldn't find my balance. I fell into the wall, stumbled into the kitchen island and tripped over the doorjamb going through the door outside of the mudroom. Usually those kind of noises would have brought my mother running. Raising us four, especially three boys, any off sound set her on high alert.

I was sad to admit that Maisie was right. There had been a murder. And the police thought my father had something to do with it.

I stood still, the cold whipping up my nose and sending another shiver down my body, but it wasn't as formidable as the one caused by what I'd just heard.

My parents were pillars of our community. My mother an elementary school teacher in the district for more than thirty years. My father a respected doctor. I turned and looked back at the house and then across the street at the black Dodge Charger I hadn't even noticed earlier.

Was the detective going to walk my father out in handcuffs? Was his late-night ambush meant to catch him off guard? Was he going to throw him in jail? Was my father now going to be one of those people whose—per O, or Professor Kaye—criminal records could be found online?

*Oh my God . . .*

I felt faint and sick to my stomach.

I didn't know what to do. I didn't think I could make it the rest of the way up the hill to my house. I didn't have the sturdiness or strength to do it. And I couldn't just stand there, I couldn't take it if I saw that detective march my father out, or hear my mother fussing about listening at things I shouldn't.

And where was PopPop? I could go to him for help if he'd been around. Maybe he could straighten out this mess. Explain that there was no way his son could have done anything like what that detective was accusing him of.

I watched my breath evaporate and swirl up around as it came out of my mouth. I closed my eyes to ward off the dizziness that was trying to grip me and saw my father. There he was, I remembered, dressed in sweats and Timberland boots. I cringed as I replayed watching him walk up to that crime scene and lie to me about where he'd been.

I WASN'T GOING to be able to sleep. I knew that. It was going to make the second night in a row. This time it was because I was completely drenched with dread.

I ended up walking back down the hill to the shop. Figured I'd get the car and drive home. Even though it was the same distance to my house as it was to the shop, getting to the shop was downhill and the only direction I didn't need my own momentum to go. I initially thought I'd make ice cream—that had always been therapeutic—but there was no way I could do that. I was sure I wouldn't be able to concentrate.

Instead of going to my car, I walked around to Bell Street and stared down the side of the hill where just the night before I'd stumbled on that man.

*Stephen Bayard.*

The Crewse family nemesis.

Like last night, it was quiet out. The hum of a few passing cars, the glow from car lights and dim streetlights making the streets look dreary. Getting colder, it seemed, by the minute. The snow had been pushed back—sidewalks and streets free of snow now had ice starting to form over them.

I tried to understand Stephen Bayard.

Why had he come back to Chagrin Falls? Why had he been roaming the streets at five thirty in the morning? Why had he told me all those lies? Had he really known who I was and done it to taunt me? Or my family? And what had he been doing coming down by the falls, in a snowstorm, getting himself killed?

Stuffing my hands down into my jacket pockets and my face into the collar, I found that staring down in the darkness gave me no answers. And answers were what I needed.

Maisie and Professor Kaye seemed to have the answer to finding out information—oh heck, I'll just call it what it was: snooping. But that didn't seem right to me.

I decided that I should go to the source. The only person I knew who had any answers. Detective Liam Beverly.

I blew out a breath, squared my shoulders and tugged on my bottom lip with my teeth. Yes. I was going to talk to him. To that inquisitive, misinformed detective.

I looked down at my watch. Eleven thirty p.m. Maybe he'd be back at the police station by now. That is, if he was finished harassing my parents.

I hopped in my car and buckled up. Putting the car in gear, I drove to the police station—a whole block and a half down the street and around a corner.

The Chagrin Falls Village Hall was located at 21 West Washington Street. The administrative office was in a redbrick, two-story building with white columns, white-framed windows and a white door. It looked more like a house than a government facility. On the side were a yard and a sidewalk that led to the attached one-story police station. A white post-and-rail fence separated the parking lot.

It, of course, was open, but I wasn't sure if the wily detective was inside. So after sitting for thirty or so minutes getting the lay of the land (or more likely the nerve to go inside), I perused the parking lot. Driving down the rows of cars, I noticed they all looked alike. If they weren't black-and-white patrol cars, they were black Chargers. Just like the one that had been parked at my parents' home. I parked and went inside. A pudgy, too-tight-uniform-wearing desk clerk police officer informed me that Detective Beverly wasn't due in until eight a.m. the following morning.

What was I going to do until then?

That was when I found out I couldn't sleep. I went home, changed into my pajamas, got into the bed and tossed and turned for what seemed like hours. I thought about what I was going to say to Detective Beverly. How I was going to tell him that he had the wrong man if he thought my father did it.

I even thought of a myriad of stories to tell about my father. How he took care of underprivileged and underinsured children and seniors at the clinic he'd helped my brother Bobby start. How he'd been rated one of the hundred best in orthopedic surgery and given a Choice Award every year for the last fifteen years, and how he worked at the Lakeside Memorial Clinic. Everyone the world round knew how good the doctors were there. I was going to tell him how when we were kids, my father had bandaged up half the neighborhood and every one of them still called him first when they weren't feeling good.

"Tell me, Mr. Detective," I imagined myself saying. "How could a man like that commit such a crime?"

I knew it wasn't possible that my father had done such a thing. And I was going to convince that detective of it, too.

Ugh! I sat up, pulled the covers off, and got out of bed. Hair sticking straight up, shoulders slumped, I padded down the hallway to the bathroom. Coming back into the room, I glanced at my alarm clock. That was when I discovered I'd been in bed for only two hours. It was 1:52 a.m.

What was I going to do for almost six more hours?

I wasn't going to be able to make it through the night. Not at this rate. I smoothed my hair down with a hand, stood in the middle of the floor and tried to figure out how I was going to pass the time.

Then I realized there was only one thing I could do.

I got dressed, grabbed a book and got back into my little Toyota. I drove down to the police station, again, and parked in front of it. I was just going to wait there for Detective Beverly. Keep an eagle eye out for his arrival and flood his sensibilities, if he indeed had any, with the knowledge of the unequivocal innocence of my father.

I cracked open my book, flipped through the pages and thought I might just finish it before daybreak. But that was the last thing I remembered. I didn't know when he got there, and he certainly saw me before I saw him. I only *thought* I couldn't fall asleep. Being so close to the place where I knew I'd be able to clear my father's name must have lulled me into some sense of comfort, because it was Detective Beverly tapping on my car window that made me realize I'd dozed off. I rolled down the window.

"Some people inside that building"—he pointed to the police station—"might consider you loitering."

"Good thing none of those people came out to arrest me," I said.

His shoulders were hunched to ward off the early-morning chill in the air, and there were red blotches on his face and the tips of his ears. I had the heater and radio on and had been, evidently, feeling quite comfy.

"Did you come to see me?" he asked. "Thought of something else from the other night?"

"I did come to see you," I said. "But not because I thought of anything other than what I've already told you."

"Well, it's cold out here. Can we take this discussion inside?"

I rolled up the window, turned off the car and got out. He waited for me at the door, holding it open. Once inside, I waited for him to lead me to his desk.

Once past the lobby of the police station, the bulletproof counter and the chairs scattered about, we went through one door and then another. The room had two desks, a chair behind each and one on the side.

He gestured to one of the chairs alongside a desk, telling me to sit.

Now that I was inside, I didn't know if I could be still. I was nervous and anxious and I could feel a tinge of anger bubbling down somewhere inside of me that I hoped wouldn't come rising up and out.

"What can I help you with?" he said, and pushed aside a couple of folders, then collected a stack of papers and piled them on top.

"I'm here to help you," I said.

His eyebrows went up and his forehead creased. "How is that?"

"To tell you that if you think my father killed anyone, you're wrong. I have complete faith in my father and his actions."

"Is that a fact?" he said. It wasn't sarcasm I heard slipping into his voice, but, I thought, an air of advantage. Like I didn't know what he did, and couldn't possibly make a determination like that.

"A *fact* that you don't seem to be aware of," I said.

"My job is to follow the facts."

"What facts were you following when you questioned my father last night?"

"I don't know if I'm able to share that with you," he said.

"And why is that?" I asked.

"Because I'm investigating a murder."

"A murder, if I have my facts straight, that was committed almost under my nose. Surely not fifty feet from where I sat."

"That's true," he said. "A murder, though, that you have continually told me you don't know anything about."

"I know one thing about it," I said.

"What's that?" he asked.

"That my father didn't do it."

"I can't be too sure of that," Detective Beverly said.

"I can." I leaned in to him. "Don't you think I would have seen my father if he had been there that night? I saw the boy. Jasper Vale. I saw his mother. There was no one else. And if my father had been lurking around the corner ready to pounce on Mr. Bayard and kill him that night, I would have seen that, too."

"I don't know that you would have seen your father. What I would like to know, however, is would you tell me if you had?"

I sat back in my seat. He'd gotten me there, because I most definitely would not have.

"I can tell you this, Bronwyn," he said, with a familiarity that made me uncomfortable. "Stephen Bayard was killed in a very unusual manner."

"I've heard," I said.

"Have you, now?" He stopped and looked at me questioningly. I raised an eyebrow, letting him know it was all I was going to say. "Okay," he started back, "not a lot of people have access to what was used to commit his murder."

"I don't know, Detective Beverly," I said. "The Lakeside Memorial Clinic has more than fifty thousand employees. And more than seven and a half million visitors every year. I would say that's a lot of people."

"Not all of them would have access to what was used."

"How many people do have access to what was used?" I asked. I was sure he didn't know.

"I don't know," he said.

I gave him a smirk. "Yet," I countered, "you zero in on my father as the person who did it."

"We haven't—"

"Who is 'we'?" I asked. "How many people are accusing my father of this?"

He closed his eyes momentarily and swayed forward. "I," he said, opening his eyes, "I haven't zeroed in on him. I just had questions for him."

"You and your questions," I said.

"Just looking for answers."

"Here's a question for you. Maybe you can look for the answer to this. What was that woman doing down by the falls?"

"Woman?" he said, and tilted his head, letting his eyes drift upward. "Oh." He tapped two fingers on his desk. "Glynis Vale?"

"Yes," I said. "And her son, Jasper. Have you questioned them?"

"So let me get this straight, Bronwyn." He sat back in his chair and cocked his head. "Are you proposing that the ten-year-old boy did it?"

I tried not to roll my eyes. I wasn't sure if such a gesture directed at a police detective in a police station was illegal. But it was hard not to do.

"To me, Detective Beverly," I said, "that sounds just as absurd as you thinking my father did it."

"Let me tell you something about murder, Ms. Crewse." He sat up straight and turned on his official demeanor. "The killer is more than likely known by his victim, he has easy access to the murder weapon and likes returning to the scene of the crime. All those things fit in with your father being at least a person of interest if not a full-fledged suspect."

"Returning to the scene of the crime?"

"Yes," he said, and nodded. "In this case, the crime was committed in the exact place your father felt he'd been wronged. The ice cream shop."

"My father didn't know that man. Stephen Bayard." I thought I'd sound less empathetic about the man's death by using his name. "And Mr. Bayard had never wronged my father."

"He wronged his mother," he said. "And the method used—poison—makes it even more egregious. Because that means he thought about it. Planned for it. And waited for the opportunity to do it."

"My father is not that kind of man," I said.

"To find the truth of that proposition, we'd need proof. Because right now, all the proof I have points to showing me he is that kind of man."

# chapter NINETEEN

Maisie's community garden had grown by leaps and bounds since the last time I'd visited.

The cobblestone walkway that wound throughout the garden still had remnants of snow that stuck in the crevices of the pebbles. Some plants were cut back, some covered with tan-colored burlap bags, but the greenery inside the greenhouse was in plain sight.

I'd stomped out of the police station so mad that I could have spread my arms and spun around in circles so fast it would have created a windstorm. Instead, I'd gotten into my car and beat on the steering wheel with my hands and head until I started crying. Partially from the pain, but mostly because I hated that detective.

Okay. So "hate" was a strong word. But I had strong feelings about him, and they were not of the good kind.

He'd said he needed proof that my father wasn't that kind of man, and all my stories I had conjured up about what a good man my father was hadn't even found a voice. They didn't seem adequate to leverage against the detective's speculation and accusation.

But if it was proof he needed, it was going to be proof I gave him.

By the time I'd left the village's administrative offices, it was eight thirty. Two and a half hours before I needed to open the ice cream shop. I had promised myself I was going to go in early to make ice cream, but after last night's revelation, I didn't have the will to do it.

Now I was bursting with determination. But it wasn't of the ice cream–making kind.

Maisie Solomon, green-thumber that she was, had taken a little plot on the side of a vacant building and turned it into an oasis of green, even in the middle of winter. She had donated materials to build a greenhouse and seeds to grow food to help feed the homeless. Like her if-it's-broke-don't-use-it philosophy, Maisie didn't stick with things. She changed jobs and hobbies as often as a traffic light changed colors. But this one she seemed to be sticking with.

"Maisie," I called after opening the greenhouse door. It was warm inside, the smell of dirt and herbs settling around me after I set foot inside.

She didn't look up. She was concentrating on the plant in front of her, struggling to uproot it. She looked determined, her curls falling into her face, but it seemed like the plant was winning.

"Maisie!" I yelled in her ear. I'd walked up to her and leaned in without her noticing. That got her attention. She looked startled. She jumped back and stared at me bug-eyed. I put on a cheesy grin and waved.

"You nearly scared me to death."

"Sorry," I said. "Tried to get your attention before I shouted in your ear."

"Oh geesh, Win. Next time try harder." She brushed her garden-gloved hands down the sides of her smock. "What are you doing here? Isn't it time for you to open the store?"

"Almost," I said. "But I think I need your help."

"Sure," she said, pulling off her gloves. Not even asking what it was I needed. "I'll help. Is it about that lady that came in last night booking a party?"

"No," I said, and shook my head. "It's about . . ." I swallowed, making an exaggerated effort to do it. "I think that maybe you're right."

"Me?" she asked, as if it were a novel idea. "About what?"

"We should find out if Ari killed . . . you know . . . Dead Guy."

"What?" she said, a smile crossing her face. "You really want to be an amateur sleuth?"

"No," I said, but I doubted she'd heard me.

"Like *Agatha Raisin*," she was saying. "Did you watch that show? I told you to watch the show. You said you would."

I was sure I hadn't given her any reason to think that I'd watch it. I wanted to dissuade her from watching it. Now, I thought, her having some knowledge about sleuthing might come in handy.

"Or *Vera*," she was rattling on, "but she doesn't really count because it's her job. Oh, but like *Rosemary & Thyme*." She giggled. "It's spelled like the herbs. That could be us."

I held up my hand. "No. Haven't watched anything. And that's not why I want to do this."

"What's the reason?" she asked.

I hadn't thought I had it in me to do any sleuthing. But that detective coming to my parents' home. Talking to my father like he could have done something so terrible . . .

"I overheard something."

"Overheard what?"

"Detective Beverly questioning my parents." I closed my eyes and drew in a breath. "Mostly my father."

"Come and sit down," she said, and pointed to a bench. "You hungry? I should get you something to eat."

"No," I said. "I'm good."

"Okay, right here." She plopped down on the garden bench and patted the seat next to her. "C'mon, now. Tell me what happened."

"Looks like there *has* been a murder."

"I already told you that," she said.

"I wasn't thoroughly convinced when you said it."

"Now you are?"

"Heard it with my own ears. And they think my father may have done it."

Her eyes went wide. "Who thinks that?" she asked.

"The Chagrin Falls homicide detective."

"We have one of those?" She scrunched up her nose. "We've never even had a homicide before."

"I'm sure we may have had one before, just not one we can remember," I said. "And, honestly, I don't know what he is. A detective is all I know. And one who thinks my father killed that man I found."

"Well, that detective is a bumbling idiot. Because I know that Mr. Crewse didn't kill anyone."

"Thanks for that, Maisie," I said, and tried to muster up a smile. "But we're going to need proof that my father didn't do it. Because, according to Detective Bumbling Idiot, my father looks like the number-one suspect."

"So what do you wanna do?" Maisie asked.

"I don't know. That's why I came to you," I said. "Thought maybe you'd know what to do."

"I think we should search the restaurant. And Ari's office. Bet we'd find proof there."

"Proof of what?"

"Proof that Ari Terrain killed Peter Sellers and your father did not."

"His name was Stephen Bayard."

"Whose name is Stephen Bayard?"

"The guy I found at the falls."

"I thought the guy who worked at the restaurant was the guy you found at the falls."

"Maisie, that was your assessment, not mine. We had no proof that they were one and the same. Except," I said thoughtfully, "there's only been one body that's turned up so far."

"This is so confusing," she said. "But it's a puzzle to figure out. And maybe another body to locate."

"Do you really think that Ari did it?" I asked. I know how bad I felt about someone accusing my father, and while I didn't know Ari Terrain all that well, what I knew about him I liked.

"Of course he did it," Maisie said. "And it's better he go to jail than your dad."

I didn't want anyone to go to jail.

"I can't be sure that it was Ari," I said.

"Why?"

"Because this guy—Stephen Bayard—was killed with a poison that's found only in hospitals."

"So?"

"So how would Ari have gotten it?"

"He stole it from the hospital. He knows someone that works in a hospital." She ticked off other possibilities. "The black market. From a drug dealer. Where do they make it? Maybe he stole it from there. Heck!" She grabbed my arm. "Maybe he bought it off the internet!"

"You think?"

"Where there's a will, there's a way. You don't have to be a doctor to get drugs. If Ari wanted a drug to kill someone with, he could have gotten it. Haven't you heard of the drug epidemic sweeping the nation? You think they get their stuff from hospitals?" She tugged on my arm and gave it a shake. "We can look at people other than those that have hospital affiliations."

I left that greenhouse with my heart just as heavy as it was when I'd gone in.

Maybe Maisie was right.

I drove to the ice cream shop and thought about what she'd said, her list of possible procurement places and how they just rolled off her tongue.

I got to the store and parked the car across the street, then leaned back against the headrest.

Trying to clear my father wasn't going to be easy, especially . . . a tear rolled down my face . . . especially when a thin veil of suspicion clung to me. What had he been doing that he wouldn't tell me the truth about where he'd been? He didn't have on work clothes. He couldn't have been at work, but that was what he told me.

Maybe it was nothing. An innocent act, whatever it was, now misconstrued.

*Simple.*

And it was simple, too, that that smug detective, Liam Beverly, had his reasoning twisted.

I pushed open the car door and hurried into the store. I liked being in the shop first thing all by myself. It gave me time to create and think.

Today, though, it wouldn't be about ice cream.

Maisie and I had decided we'd go to the restaurant around three o'clock. Wilhelmina would be in by then to cover my absence. I wasn't sure what my mother's schedule was. She was voluntary help and pretty much made up her own hours.

Maisie's plan had us getting to the restaurant before it opened at four. She thought that way we could snoop without anyone seeing us. I had cautioned her not to tell anyone what we were doing.

I turned the lock on the side door of the shop, pushed it open and smiled. Everything gleamed and was bright and welcoming. I could just picture my Grandma Kay standing there with her apron on, arms open wide, ready to embrace me and assure me that when family stuck together there wasn't anything we couldn't do.

I could only hope that was true.

# chapter TWENTY

Her Royal Highness Felice was asleep on the window seat when I went out front with the first batch of ice cream to put in the dipping case.

"The day's just getting started," I said to her. "You tired already?"

She lazily opened one eye as if telling me not to disturb her.

"Okay," I said. "Just thought you were ready for a treat."

I heard her snore.

I chuckled and went back to work.

My mother hadn't made it in, and come to think of it, I hadn't even had the chance to speak to her about what time she'd be there. After Detective Beverly's late-night visit, she might just be sitting in a parking lot somewhere.

The shop wasn't open five minutes when I heard the chime over the door go off.

I called out, "Be right with you." I ran water over my hands and tugged my apron off over my head.

I put on a smile and hurried to the front of the store. "Welcome to Crewse Creamery," I said.

"Hi, Pumpkin."

It was my daddy. As soon as I saw him, tears started to well up in my eyes. I left from behind the counter and practically ran over to give him a hug.

"Hey, Daddy," I said. "I'm so happy to see you."

"Well, you wouldn't know it," he said, patting me on my back. "You haven't stopped by the house in two days."

I couldn't let go. I stood on my tippy-toes, arms flung around his neck and my head lying on his shoulder.

"You okay?" he asked, trying to pull back so he could see me.

"I'm fine," I said, holding on tighter.

"You'd think you hadn't seen me in years."

"Nope," I said. "Only two days." I let go and swung around to go back behind the counter without letting him see my face. "A *long* two days." I swiped at the tears and put on a smile before facing him again. "Did you come to get ice cream?" I asked.

"I came in to see how you were doing," he said. He was dressed for work. A gray suit, a white shirt and a black-and-wine-colored paisley tie. His Italian loafers were covered with rubbers. He had on a camel-colored coat, and even though I'd let go of him, I could still smell the subtle notes of the sweet amber and buttery oakmoss of his cologne. "I haven't seen you since the other night after you found that man down at the falls."

I blew out a breath. Was he going to tell me about it? Did he think maybe I couldn't handle it? That's how he'd often treated me. Fragile. Innocent. I was the only girl in the family, and the baby, and he had always thought he needed to protect me.

But after going off to college and living in New York, I'd hoped he'd formed a different opinion of me. Felt different about my strength. My endurance over life's bumps and ditches. Add to that my taking over the management of the shop and overseeing the renovations, and it had to have alerted him to the fortitude in my character.

Maybe I should just bring it up to him . . .

"Daddy, were you down by the falls earlier that night?" I asked.

"No," he said. "Not before I came after your mother called. She was frantic. We didn't know what had happened to you."

"At the time I didn't think it was such a big deal," I said, eyeing him to get a reaction. "But as it turns out—"

He didn't let me finish that sentence.

"I heard you made up some ice cream for Halloween," he said, a proud smile on his face. "Seasonal flavors. Just like your grandmother used to do. She'd be real proud of you, you know."

"That's what I strive for, Daddy, every day. To make Grandma Kay proud."

"My mother used to say, when I'm gone, I want Win to be the one to carry us on."

"Did she really?" I said, another tear popping up in my eye. "You never told me that before."

"Yeah, I think she probably rolled over in her grave when Jack took over. Especially after she turned it into a novelty shop."

I laughed. "Why did PopPop let her take it over?" I asked.

"He was waiting for you."

"Waiting for me?"

"Waiting until you were ready," he said. "Waiting for you to realize that this was what you were supposed to do."

"Do you feel like that, too?" I asked.

"I do," he said. "I always knew you'd run it someday. We all were just waiting for you to realize that your 'someday' had arrived."

"I loved being in New York," I said. "I loved my job and the feeling it gave me when we nailed it—the pitch, the client—then I wanted to come home. Not because of anything bad."

"I know," he said. "I've often wondered if you felt like you were giving up anything to move back. Like you had made a step backward?"

"No," I said. "I never did. I didn't even realize I wanted to take over the shop when I made my decision. I figured after I got well from whatever was making me sick, I'd just get a job downtown somewhere. I just knew, when I started feeling bad, I wanted to be home."

"I know you don't think that I think you're strong. But I know that you are."

"Sometimes I wonder," I said.

"Don't ever think that. Because I do know it." He put his head down. "I would have never taken on the renovation of this store."

"I just felt it was right," I said. "The right thing to do."

"Keep doing the right thing," he said. "Keep being who you are."

"Mom says I'm like you," I said. "I think I got my strength from you and Grandma Kay."

"Sometimes, I don't feel strong at all," my father said. I saw a darkness come over his face and it broke my heart.

"Something you want to tell me, Daddy?" I said.

"Nothing for you to worry about," he said. "You have your hands full with this place. Which, by the way, is a marvel. You have done wonders."

"Thank you, Daddy." I blushed. "And you know that I am here for you."

"I know," he said. "Be here for your mother, too. Promise me."

"Promise?"

"Yes," he said. "Promise."

"Are you going somewhere?" I asked, my mouth getting dry. I wasn't sure what he was trying to tell me.

"Not for a long time," he said. "At least that's my plan. But I still want you to promise that you'll see after your mother."

"That's what we do in this family," I said. "We take care of each other."

My father bought two pint-sized cartons of ice cream—cherry amaretto chocolate chunk and Ghoulish Blueberry. Then we had to find a plastic bowl with a top to give him the gallon-sized tub of French vanilla he wanted to buy, emptying out the tray. He kissed me on my cheek, then on my forehead, and gave me a big hug before he left.

I didn't know what was going through his head, why he'd decided to stop by the store, or why he'd had that conversation with me. All I knew was that I felt that same urge, that same determination I'd felt when I'd taken over the store. Nothing was going to stop me from finding proof that my father hadn't done anything wrong. And certainly nothing as heinous as murder.

"We're here." My mother blew out a breath and she and PopPop burst through the front door. PopPop wiped his feet, took off his hat and headed over to the bench he'd occupied the day before. My mother trotted around the counter, unbuttoning her coat and tugging at the scarf around her neck.

"Hey, you made it," I said to her.

"I had a hair appointment." She shook her head, her ringlets bouncing. "Can't let all that gray show."

I tried to keep a straight face. "No worries, I have Wilhelmina coming in and we still don't have more customers through the door than we can handle."

"You will soon," my grandfather reassured me.

"But I did need you," I said, and ducked my head, trying to keep from smiling.

"Needed *me*?" she said, and touched her hand over her chest. "My independent daughter?"

"Uh-huh." I nodded. "I have to make ice cream and plan for the event I booked over at Wycliffe."

Both of them stopped in their tracks.

"A what?" my mother said, a grin spreading across her face.

"You booked an event?" PopPop said. "When did that happen?"

"While the two of you were missing in action," I said. "The guy who followed me over from Zoup! yesterday recommended us."

"O?" my grandfather asked. "He did tell me he was a law professor over there."

"A law professor?" my mother said. That caught her attention.

"Said before that he used to be a police officer," PopPop added.

"A police officer," I mumbled. No wonder he wanted to get inside my head.

"Is that the one who likes you?" my mother asked.

"He doesn't like me," I told her. "That's just Maisie's craziness." I turned to my grandfather. "I didn't know that about him. Not until Clara came in. How did you know?"

"I asked him," PopPop said. "That's how I know. Had a little conversation with the fellow. You could have, too."

"Who is Clara?" my mother asked.

"Clara Blackwell." Like she knew who that was.

"Is that who booked the event?" Mom asked.

"Yes. Actually, she booked two," I said.

"Two!" My mother screeched and threw up her hands. "Two events! Oh my."

"And I want you to help me with it, please." I looked at PopPop. "Both of you."

"We will," she said, and gave a nod as confirmation. "It's a good thing you hired help. Candy and Wilhelmina can take care of the store while we plan the event."

I heard PopPop grunt.

"What's wrong, Dad?" my mother asked.

"I don't know if I like that Wilhelmina woman."

"Why not?" my mother asked.

He grunted again.

"She has a crush on PopPop. She even winked at him," I whispered. "I think she makes him nervous."

My mother giggled. "Never too old for love. He's pushing eighty and still has women gushing over him."

"It's the Crewse Curse," PopPop said, without looking up from his game. "All the men have it. We're charming without even trying."

We laughed at that, including PopPop.

"So tell us more about this event we're catering," my mother said. "We need to get brainstorming."

"It's Monday."

"Monday?" my mother said. "Today's not Monday. Oh wait." Her mouth dropped open and she put her hands on her hips. "Are you saying that's when . . . Do you mean this event is . . ." She counted on her fingers. "Five days from now, Monday?"

"Yes." I nodded.

"Good heavens!" she said. "How would anyone wait until a week before their event to get the menu together?"

"She didn't wait," I said. "She had another caterer, but there was a problem . . ."

I didn't finish that sentence. I couldn't. Clara Blackwell said that the other caterers had exhibited behavior that wasn't conducive with the school. Wycliffe was a Christian-based college.

I was sure they wouldn't give a second thought about dumping us if she learned that we were an establishment where one of the owners was suspected of being a murderer.

There was no telling what kind of scathing review would accompany that one-star rating they'd be sure to give us.

# chapter TWENTY-ONE

PopPop, Mom and I brainstormed about what to prepare for Clara Blackwell's events. For the ice cream social, we were the main event. As the chaplain for the sorority, she had pretty much mapped out what she wanted. That one would be easy. I'd serve the usual-flavored ice creams—vanilla, strawberry and chocolate. But I'd make something different for the sundae and banana split toppings, and a few specialty flavors to serve as single scoops.

For her President's Dinner we only needed to supply dessert, but what should have been a simple decision turned out to be the hardest for us to decide.

PopPop wanted me to serve Grandma Kay's chocolate cherry and almond ice cream cake. It was luscious, with sliced, frosty dark cherries covering the top and slivers of almonds sprinkled about. Inside were alternate layers of chocolate crumble, thinly sliced vanilla cake and a smooth cherry ice cream made from puree and almond extract. A short-stacked cake, one spoonful filled the palate with tangy and sweet, smooth and crunchy, rich and salty all at the same time. It was elegant and sophisticated and probably the best fit for the occasion.

I thought we should do individual cakes. Raspberry java ice cream cake. A chocolate-espresso mocha-flavored frozen delight, I'd use a moist flourless chocolate cake for the base, but the one-and-a-half-inch-diameter desserts would only have ice cream inside. I'd pile it two inches high, and cover it with a thin satiny chocolate ganache glaze dripped over the top and down the sides, with tons of raspberries scattered atop and a shard of pressed chocolate as a garnish.

My mother pooh-poohed the suggestions PopPop and I came up with, saying that both included chocolate, the usual fare for dessert, and we should do something different. She wanted me to do a seven-layer strawberry tart ice cream cake. Between the four layers of soft, spongy and fluffy cake that had an almondy back note was strawberry ice cream chock-full of the sweet berries. A vanilla rosette-patterned buttercream frosting topped it, and then it was adorned with whole, plump, juicy red strawberries. The dessert was one she'd created when she first started working in the store.

In the end, after much debate—um, discussion—about where we'd find ripe fruit, which one would keep better, how well it paired with the main course being served, and a quick check of Grandma Kay's recipe box, we decided to serve all three. I was in charge of finding strawberries and cherries so late in the year. Something I'd have to get right on if I was going to have them shipped to me and arrive in five days.

We got it all settled and Wilhelmina came in the door at two thirty, batting her eyes at PopPop in time for my three o'clock rendezvous with Maisie.

I left the car parked and strolled toward Molta's. I said a little prayer as I walked. It was twofold—one, that we wouldn't get caught, and two, that I wasn't doing something stupid. I had nothing to go on that Ari was the murderer other than Maisie's harebrained conclusion. But if she was right, he could be dangerous.

I stuck my hands in my gloves and pulled the collar up on my coat. Molta's wasn't far. It was located on West Orange Street—down the street and around the corner—about a half mile away. The restaurant looked like someone had taken two squares and attached them together. One, smaller, was the entryway. It had big dark wood double doors with huge wrought-iron handles. The larger square was attached to the back and right of that one and was where the restaurant was housed. The building was stucco with a whitewash covering. It had black accents—the trim and the wrought-iron fence that delineated the porch eating area.

It was new and modern and chic. Nothing like the restaurant it had replaced. It reminded me of Riya's comment that the village was going upscale. Something most of the community resisted. She'd even said that Crewse Creamery was taking a part in the gentrification. I didn't know if I thought that was a bad thing, but if moving our quaint little village up to the twenty-first century meant that murder was invading our boundaries, my family's ice cream shop and I wanted no part of it.

I saw Maisie walking up from the other side of the parking lot, waving. Her red hair stuck out from under a blue hat that matched the blue in the dress that hung from under a purple jacket speckled with yellow stars. Her feet and legs were covered in red-striped leggings and navy galoshes. She looked like a box of Skittles. I wondered if she had on lucky socks underneath.

"Hi," she said as she arrived by my side, pulling her backpack off. "You ready?"

"As ready as I'll ever be," I said, still not completely happy with my decision of spying on people.

"It'll be easy," she said, recognizing my hesitation. She dangled keys in front of me. "Don't feel guilty, Win." She tugged on my arm and we headed for the door. "I have permission to go in early and to go into the office."

"Not to find out if Ari murdered anyone," I said. I stepped inside and waited for her to turn on the lights.

"If we get caught we could just plead ignorance," she said, heading off toward the back. "Act as if we didn't know we were doing anything wrong."

"Or we could call O to come and bail us out of jail," I said, following her. "Come to find out he teaches law over at Wycliffe."

"He's a lawyer?" she asked. "You go, girl! He's turning out to be one fine catch."

"One fine stalker is what he is," I said. "Although I'm not going to balk about him sending me Clara Blackwell. That was one market I hadn't thought to explore yet."

"This is the office," she said, lowering her voice. We'd gone through the kitchen and down a short hallway and stood at a locked door. She found the key she needed, slid it into the lock and turned it with ease.

Once inside, she shut the door behind us. The windowless room was pitch black. It took her a minute to find the switch and flick on the lights.

"Oh!" I said. "That's bright."

"Shhh!" she said.

"Don't shush me," I said, but still, I lowered my voice. "Why are we whispering, anyway? No one's here."

Maisie shrugged. "It just seems appropriate."

I blew out a breath. "Then we probably shouldn't have the lights on."

"How else are we going to see?"

I pulled out my phone. "Flashlight," I said.

"Oh, okay." She nodded. She pulled her phone out of her back pocket, then went over to the wall and turned off the lights.

"Now what?" I asked, turning on my light and shining it at her.

"Let's look for the folder with applications in it. Or the time sheets," she said. "Maybe we can find him."

"You're not sure of his name."

"Yeah, but I know everyone else who works here. He'd be the only new name."

"Well, I don't know everyone else's name."

"If you find the sheet," she said, "just show it to me."

"Okay," I said, and started looking. "So with the guy only working here a short time, per you, he might be on only one sheet of paper."

"I've been thinking about that," she said. "I had a couple of days off. Maybe he started before and I didn't know about it. But either way, there should be some record of him being hired."

"Unless he was working under the table."

"Yeah," Maisie said. "I hadn't thought about that."

"Okay," I said. "I'll take that stack of folders over there on the credenza."

"Yep. And I'll check out the file cabinet. Maybe he filled out a W-2 or something."

"We'll just look though any papers and file folders to see what we come up with," I said.

"Got it," she said.

We went to our designated areas in the small room. There wasn't much in the room. One file cabinet, a desk, a couple of chairs and the wooden credenza. I flipped through some multicolored folders, and inside they looked like the folders I kept for the store. They were filled with invoices and receipts. One with a legal notepad with what must have been Ari's notes of what seemed like ideas he had for the restaurant.

"Nothing here," I said, and turned around to face Maisie. "What are you doing?" I went over to her. "I thought you were going to go through the file cabinet?"

Maisie had turned on the computer that sat on the desk and had the mouse scurrying across the pad like it was after cheese.

"I'm going through the files, like you told me," she said.

"I never told you to go through *electronic* files," I said. "I meant paper files. In the file cabinet." I pointed to it. "How did you get into his computer anyway? Isn't it password protected?"

"I saw him put in the password once." All I could hear were clicking sounds of the mouse.

I slapped a hand across my forehead. "We're going to jail."

"Look at this," she said. "This email is from the Pink Panther."

"Email?" I said. "Don't go through his email!"

"I'll bet that's Peter Sellers," she said, giving me a knowing head nod.

"We've had this conversation," I said, going behind the desk to stand next to her. "His name is Stephen Bayard. And we should probably go. There's nothing here."

"Don't you want to know what it says?"

"No!" I said.

"Oops," she said as I heard the click of the printer starting.

"Maisie!"

"What?" She clicked a few more times, turning off the computer. Then, standing up straight, she looked at me.

"What are you two doing in here?" The woman's words came out as she swung the door open. A flick of the switch flooded the room with light again.

"Nothing," I answered her question reflexively. I turned off my flashlight and readjusted my eyes to see her.

"Looking," Maisie said at the same time.

"Looking for nothing," I said, and tugged on Maisie's arm, pulling her close to me. My eyes glanced over at the printer, which had just pushed up the printed copy of the email.

The woman raised an eyebrow and tucked a strand of her brown hair behind her ear. "There's nothing in here to take," she said.

Maisie furrowed her brow. "We're not looking for anything to take."

"And we were just leaving," I said, giving Maisie's arm a tug.

"You don't have to run on my account," she said, a small smile forming on her thin, shiny, lip-gloss-covered lips. "And you didn't have to go snooping around in the dark either. That is, if you're not trying to take anything."

"We're not trying to take anything," I said. "And we're not snooping." I let my eyes meet with hers, partly to show her I meant what I said, but mostly so I wouldn't let them stray over to the printer, that one sheet of white paper ready to reveal what we'd done.

"I don't have to run," Maisie said with bravado I didn't know she possessed. "As a manager, I come into his office all the time."

"When there is business to be taken care of," the woman said, raising a brow to suggest we were not doing anything official. "And with the lights on." Then she shrugged and looked at Maisie, a smirk on her face. "No worry. I won't tell Ari."

"Are you working today, Althea?" Maisie asked. There was a snooty quality to her voice like she had some authority.

"Are you?" she asked in return. Then she turned and looked at me. "I'm sure she isn't."

Althea, as Maisie called her, was smart-looking. She was dressed in a pair of nice gray slacks, a cable-knit sweater and flats. She had her coat over her arm like she'd come in to hang it up.

"Why are you here?" Maisie said. "And how did you get in? Doors aren't opened yet."

I was going to have to come visit Maisie at her job more often. She was a completely different person.

"Why are you in here?" Again Althea answered Maisie's question with one of her own.

No time for them to go another round, though. We all diverted our attention to the voice that came from the door.

It was Ari.

*Oh shoot!*

# chapter TWENTY-TWO

Ari Terrain was of Middle Eastern or North African descent. I didn't know for sure which, and had never felt a need to ask or felt comfortable doing so. One thing I did know for sure was that he was handsome. And fit. Brown-skinned, he had big almond-brown eyes, his dark eyebrows were thick and naturally arched, and his lashes were dense and long. He sported a neatly trimmed beard and mustache that shaped his perfectly formed lips—defined cupid bow, even and full. And it was easy to see his muscular definition through the fitted button-down shirts he wore. He had an easy smile and his scent reminded me of a cool breeze.

"I came to check on the schedules," Maisie said, not missing a beat in addressing Ari's surprise visit to the office. I didn't know she could lie so quickly or easily. She grabbed the paper off the printer. "Got everything I need." She waved the paper in the air.

Ari looked around the room at us, and his eyes settled on me. I knew I was the odd man out, and his looking at me—which made everyone else turn their attention my way—made me nervous. I stood behind the desk with Maisie, locked in, no foreseeable easy way out. But before he could say anything, Maisie added, "And Win walked over with me. To keep me company."

"Are you scheduled for tonight?" he asked. "Is that why you're here?"

"No," she answered, not even blinking. She had a new look on her face. Not determination like when she spoke to the woman she called Althea, but defiance. Maybe even disdain.

Ari looked at me again with narrowed eyes. I lowered mine and tried to slow my breathing. I was sure my heart palpitations were evident even through my coat.

"Your last name Crewse?"

I nodded. "Yep," I said, barely getting the word past the knot in my throat.

"You're in charge of the ice cream store now, right?"

I nodded again.

"I saw yesterday that it was open." I nodded again. I felt like a bobblehead doll. "I said I was going to stop by. I used to go there, years ago. When your grandparents—?" He stopped mid-sentence, making his words into a question, to check he had it right.

"Yep. My grandparents owned it."

"Right. When they owned it. Wow. I loved that ice cream. Even back then they had it right. Making it from scratch right in the store. You still doing it that way?"

"Oh . . . um. Yeah. Yes." I couldn't stop stumbling over my words. This illegal stuff was not for me. "We're all about sustainability. Local farmers. Fair-trade ingredients." I cleared my throat. I knew I was talking too much. "Come on by." I had to wrap up my babbling. "We've got something yummy for your tummy."

I knew saying "yummy for your tummy" was corny. And I so disliked corny. But I was nervous.

"Yummy for your tummy?" Maisie turned and mouthed the words to me. Her lips pursed, nose crinkling. "I've been helping her out," Maisie said, turning to Ari, I'm sure to get us past my dumb comment. "I'm in charge of the flavor." She looked at him as if she dared him to dispute it.

If he was the murderer, as Maisie complained, being so brash probably wasn't a good idea. It might make him snap.

I'd known who Ari was for a while, as evident by our present conversation. I didn't know, however, if we'd ever been formally introduced.

He'd come around when I was a teenager. I was finishing high school when he opened up Molta's. I'd gone there a time or two while home on break from school. He'd always seemed nice, although Maisie knew more about him than I did. Still, I didn't want this moment to be the one where I found out that wasn't true.

I was feeling light-headed. Amateur sleuthing was too nerve-racking for me.

"You're in charge of the flavor?" Ari raised one of those perfectly arched eyebrows. "And what does that mean?"

Thank goodness Maisie didn't have a chance to answer. We were staying way too long in that little bitty office. I knew I was going to start sweating at any minute. The knocks that saved me came hard, heavy and in quick succession. It was like whoever was at the door wasn't averse to knocking it down to get in.

"Someone's at the door," Althea said, stating the obvious as she turned toward it.

"Who is it?" Ari called as he headed out of the office, his voice forceful. We followed him.

"Police. We're here to speak to Ari Terrain."

Maisie grabbed my arms. "Oh my!" she said. "Keep back, they might come in shooting."

Ari didn't seem to have anything to hide, nor was he worried about guns blazing. He opened the door wide and held on to it. "I'm Ari Terrain," he announced.

And in walked Detective Beverly.

"Shoot!" I said.

"It's Detective Bumbling Idiot!"

"In the flesh."

"Maybe he's wised up and now came to arrest Ari."

"I'm Detective Liam Beverly with the Chagrin Falls Police Department," he said, and flashed his badge. "You mind if I ask you a few questions?"

"Not at all," Ari said. "Come in." Ari seemed to be filled with mettle.

The first thing Detective Beverly saw when he set foot inside was me.

"Bronwyn," he said, surprise in his voice. "What are you doing here?"

"She's here with me—"

I grabbed Maisie's arm and squeezed it before she could say anything else. She had stepped forward, seemingly ready to attack even the police officer. I pulled her back.

"And you are?" Detective Beverly asked Maisie. He tapped the side of his forehead. "Didn't I see you at the ice cream shop?"

"Maisie Solomon," she said. "Win—Bronwyn's best friend."

"She works for me," Ari said, looking back over at us. "I know why she's here." He turned his gaze to the detective. "But I don't know why you are."

"I just wanted to ask you a few questions, Mr. Terrain."

"About what?" Ari asked.

The detective looked at the other three occupants in the room. Althea pressed her lips together and evened out her lip gloss, then tucked a hair behind her ear. She was as calm as everyone else. Seemed like I was the only one in a panic. I had to ball up my fist to keep from clicking my nails.

"I can go," Althea said, and put on a polite smile.

"You're fine," Ari said, and held out a hand to stop her from leaving. "Just ask what you need to ask." Ari looked at the detective.

"I just had a few questions." He pulled out a little notebook and a pen. First time I'd seen him taking notes. "I wanted to know if you knew Stephen Bayard," he said, making sure he made eye contact with Ari when the dead man's name came out.

Ari paused as if he was thinking about it. He scratched his beard and showed no other reaction. "No," he said finally. "Should I?"

"No," Beverly said. "If you don't know him, you don't know him."

"I don't know him," Ari said.

"Okay. Now, you've said that you don't know him, but did you get a phone call from him night before last?"

"Didn't get a call from anyone by that name. No."

"And where were you from around five to eight p.m. that night?"

Before he could answer, two more people came in the door. Not police officers. They must've been employees coming in for their shifts, but they stopped as soon as they saw the small crowd gathered in the entryway.

"It's okay," Ari told them, then gestured for them to come in with a large circular motion of his hand. "More employees," he told the detective. I had guessed right. "They need to get to work. How about we go in my office if you have more questions?"

"I do have a couple more," Detective Beverly said.

"That's our cue," I leaned over and whispered to Maisie. I tried pulling her behind me but she wouldn't budge.

"Cue for what?" Maisie asked.

"To leave." This time I gave her a yank. "We're leaving now." I pushed her through the front door.

"Didn't you want to hear what else the detective is going to ask Ari?" she said, trying to hold her ground.

"And how were we going to do that?" I asked. I made sure the door shut behind her. I put my hands on my hips and looked at her. "Unless we followed them into his office."

She made a face that told me she didn't see a problem with that.

"I'm going back to the ice cream shop," I said, vowing never to let her draw me into wacky schemes again. "Where are you going?"

"I'll walk back that way with you, I guess," she said, disappointed.

"Okay," I said.

"Hey, is that your grandfather?" she said, looking down the street.

"Where?" I followed her gaze. "I don't see anybody," I said. I didn't see anything, let alone my PopPop. "I'm sure he's still at the ice cream store where I left him."

"Hmm. Looked just like his car," she said.

I glanced over at her. "It felt like I didn't even know you in there," I said.

"In where?"

"The restaurant," I said. "You going into emails, talking tough to that woman. And what kinds of faces were you making to Ari?"

She smiled. "Someone has to stand up to him."

"Doesn't have to be us," I assured her. "You were just ready to take on the world."

"It was two people."

"Still," I said, and shook my head. "And who was that woman?"

"Althea Quigley. She works at Molta's."

"She seems nice enough."

"I don't trust her," Maisie said. "She dresses way too nice to live on a waitress's salary."

"You don't like anyone over there, do you?"

She hesitated. She seemed to be going through the Rolodex of employees in her mind. "Nope," she said finally. "That's why I'm quitting and coming to work for you."

Maisie never liked anything for long.

"Okay." I smiled. "You know I'm happy to have you. But you just can't up and quit on me like you always do."

"Of course not," she said. "I'll love working at the ice cream shop."

"Okay."

"I did good, huh?" she said, getting back to the matter at hand. "Getting us evidence. Standing up to that murderer."

"'Good' is not the adjective I'd use to describe you in there," I said. "It was like you turned into some kind of psychopath or sociopath. I don't know the difference between the two, but you were so far from the Maisie I know."

"I know, right?" Her face lit up and she pumped her arms out in front of her and did a jump, hop, stomp. She was quite pleased with herself.

Narrowing one eye, I shook my head. "I'd expect this weird flip in personality from Riya. You never know which bag she's coming from. But not you, Maisie."

"Well, whatever I turned into, it worked," she said, and wiggled the paper in front of my face. "We got a clue!"

I leaned back—didn't want a paper cut on my nose. "We got a copy of an email." I waved a hand at the paper. "We don't even know if it's a clue. What does it say?"

"Oh yeah," she said. "I guess we should read it."

"What does it say?"

She stopped walking and looked down at the paper. "It says, 'Coming to town. You owe me. I need you for a job.'"

"That's all?"

"That's all." She flapped the paper.

"What does that mean?" I asked.

"It means that Dead Guy was blackmailing Ari."

I rolled my eyes. "It does not mean that."

She was starting to develop a newfound gift for leaping to conclusions.

"Yes, it does. And now we know the reason why Ari killed that guy."

I glanced at her. "The police came looking for Stephen Bayard," I said. "You know that means they've identified the guy who called Molta's as him."

She shook her head. "Maybe. But I'm sure that's not the name of the guy who was missing from work."

"Maybe that guy—Peter Sellers or whoever—quit. Or was too sick to come to work."

"Or dead," she said. "Maybe Stephen Bayard used an alias."

"Maybe," I said. "But we have no way of knowing that."

"Just because his name is something else doesn't mean that Ari didn't kill him."

"I have to give it to you," I said, pursing my lips, "you did guess right about it being a murder."

"And I'm right about this, too."

I wasn't sure of that and didn't say anything.

"Althea must have come in with Ari," Maisie said after we'd walked in silence for a while. "I wonder if she knows he's a killer."

"*We* don't know that," I said, even though the whole mission had been to discover something that would prove he was.

"Well, I hope she doesn't get involved with him," Maisie said.

"You didn't seem to be too friendly with her," I said.

"That doesn't mean I want her dead," Maisie said.

"We didn't get any information that would convince her not to," I said, "or anything to convince the detective that my father didn't do it."

"I think that will happen," Maisie said. "With a little help from us. And"—she tapped my arm—"that detective going to Molta's and wanting to talk to Ari should tell you we're on the right track."

"That detective came to my store, too," I said. "What does that tell you?"

"That they think your father killed Peter Sellers."

"Oh my God!" I said. I stopped and bent over. "Ugh! I can't believe you just said that."

"And." Her voice raised a few decibels with the word. She came and stood in front of me. "There was going to be an 'and' in there, Win," she said, "just let me finish. I was going to say more."

"I don't know if I can take what else you have to say." I rested my hands on my knees and looked up at her.

"Annddd, you were the one that found that guy. That's why he came to talk to you. They wanted to know if you could identify the victim."

"His name is Stephen Bayard," I said. I stood up and started walking. She followed behind me. "And that detective is crazy if he thought I would tell him I saw my father doing anything like that."

Maisie grabbed my arm from behind. She turned me around to face her and looked me in the eye. "Did your father do it?" she asked.

"Oh." I let out another groan and tried to walk away. But she held on to me.

"Tell me."

"No." I put my forehead to hers. It was too heavy for me to hold up. Our noses practically touched. "My father didn't kill anyone."

"Okay, then," she said, and let go of me. She gave me a look that said "Get over it," and started walking. "That's what I thought. That means we have to push through and find out who did it."

Sleuthing Maisie was a side of my best friend I'd never seen before. She was scary.

I trotted to keep up with her. "I think we should go to the library," I said.

"For what?"

"So we can find out more about this Stephen Bayard. It might help us find out why someone wanted to murder him."

"Not someone. Ari."

"You are so stuck on Ari doing it," I said. "It could be somebody else, you know."

"I know you think I just latched on to Ari and won't let go." She looked at me. "And I know I'm just projecting my dislike for the guy into all of this. But, Win, we have to start somewhere."

"And see where it leads us?"

"Exactly. Put the clues together. And Ari is as good a place as any to start."

"Okay." I nodded, giving in. "So what do we have so far?" I asked.

"The dead guy called Ari. We know that. And we know that Ari lied about it."

"Dead Guy's name is Stephen Bayard." I snapped my fingers. "Maybe Ari thought the guy's name was really Peter Sellers," I said.

"Mmmm," Maisie said. You could see the cogs in her brain turning.

"Or," I said, tapping her on her arm, "Ari knew his real name but because of whatever business they had"—I pointed to the paper—"he didn't want to let on to the detective that he did."

"And Ari thought since Dead Guy was using an alias, the police wouldn't be able to find out the connection," Maisie continued with my hypothesis. "That's why he said that he didn't know Stephen Bayard."

"Right," I said. "Because as far as anyone else is concerned, he only *knows* Peter Sellers." I digested what I'd just said. "Oh. But wait. The phone call? The police identified the phone call as coming from Stephen Bayard."

"Well, Ari didn't talk to him when the police called," Maisie said. "I did. So they can't prove he knew him or that they had a conversation."

"That's true," I said. "Still, Stephen Bayard could have called before then. Maybe his phone records show other conversations."

"Yeah," Maisie said, thinking about that. "But that would work in our favor, because then the police would have caught Ari in a lie."

"Yes, him lying to the police would be good." I nodded. "But we do know that they used other means to communicate. Like that email."

"Right." She flapped her arm that was still holding the paper.

"But answer me this, Maisie," I said. "If Ari missed the phone call from Stephen Bayard the night he was killed, and that was the only email you saw from him, how would Ari know how to find him to kill him?"

"Maybe after Dead Guy called the restaurant and couldn't reach Ari, he called Ari's cell phone."

"Oh. That's a thought," I said. "If they had Dead Guy's phone records, then there's a reason the police may have stopped by and another way they knew Ari was lying."

"Right," Maisie said.

"So," I said, wrapping up our little scenario, "Stephen Bayard reached Ari on his cell phone, they met and—"

"Ari killed him," Maisie said, finishing my sentence. "And as soon as the police figure that out, they'll arrest him and have him drawn and quartered right before they put him in front of the firing squad."

"You really don't like Ari, do you?"

# chapter TWENTY-THREE

"What's Riya's car doing here?" Maisie asked. "Is she helping out today?"

"I don't know," I said. "If she is, it's because she just popped in. She didn't tell me she was coming."

We'd made it back to the ice cream shop, faces cold, sniffling and eyes runny.

"Hi," I said as we walked in the front door, the chime echoing our arrival.

"Welcome to Crewse Creamery," Riya said, smiling at us over the counter.

"Hey, Riya," I said.

"Look at Dr. Amacarelli serving up scoops," Maisie teased.

"Yes," Riya said. "Mrs. Crewse has worked me to death. I don't get this tired working twenty-four-hour shifts."

"No one works twenty-four-hour shifts," my mother said, coming out of the back. "Stop crying."

"Hi, Mom," I said. "Where's PopPop?" I glanced over to his usual bench.

"I don't know," she said, and looked at his vacant seat. "I thought he was here."

"He left right after you did, Win," Riya said. "Said he was going home to eat."

"Thought you'd be gone for the rest of the day, Win," my mother said.

"No, I'm back and I can close up if you have to go," I said, walking around the counter. "Did we get a lot of customers today?"

"God yes," Riya said, and leaned up against the counter. "I didn't think they'd ever stop coming."

My mother rolled her eyes and shook her head. "We had four or five."

"Really?" Riya said. "Seemed like twenty to me."

I laughed. "I'm going to hang up my coat. You guys can take a break. I got this."

"I'm here to stay, too," Maisie said, and followed me.

"What have the two of you been up to?" Riya asked as she came in behind Maisie. "And how come you left me here to work and not take me along?"

"We haven't been up to anything," I said.

"Win went with me over to Molta's."

"I thought Mrs. Crewse told me Win had gone out to check with her vendors for an event she was planning," Riya said, giving us a disapproving eye.

"My mother said that?" I asked.

I hadn't told anyone where I was going. I mean, what was I going to say? *I'm trying to clear Daddy's name so he won't go to jail for murder?*

"I ran into Maisie," I said. "While I was out on business."

Technically, what I'd been doing counted as taking care of business. Family business.

I didn't so much care about Riya knowing what we'd been doing. I would have included her, and I would clue her in, too, after my mother left. I'd only gone to Maisie because she seemed to know more about what to do. Even if her knowledge stemmed from the television shows she watched.

"Next time include me," she said.

"I will," I said. "I promise." I pointed at the trash and raised an eyebrow. "What's going on there?"

"I told you your mother worked me until I dropped," Riya said.

"Doing what?" I remembered my mother said we hadn't had a lot of customers.

"Maisie had cut up the ingredients for ice cream that you didn't get around to making, right?" Riya asked.

"Oh, yeah, she did," I said. "And no, I didn't."

"Yeah, so I had to make it," Riya said.

"*We* made it," my mother shouted from the front. "Mostly me."

"Mostly me," Riya mouthed and pointed to herself. "And"—her voice back to a normal volume—"I waited on customers and cleaned the back and the front and carried Felice upstairs."

"That's a whole lot of 'ands,'" I said. I walked over to the freezer and swung the door open. It was full. I smiled. "And a whole lot of work."

"You said that already," Maisie said. She took a big bite out of a banana she had peeled.

"Good job." I nodded at the freezer as I shut the door. "And you know how much I appreciate you," I said, and flung my arms around Riya's neck and kissed her on her cheek. "A girl couldn't ask for a better best friend." I let go of her and grabbed my coat back off the rack where I'd just hung it and stuck my hat on top of my head. "I'll take out the trash. It's the least I can do."

I got it together and went out the side door.

"Hi, Mrs. Cro," I said. She was taking out her trash at the same time.

Isabella Cro was the owner of The Flower Pot. She'd owned the store for the last year or so. It had sat vacant for a while after Mr. Clawson closed down his bike repair shop. I remembered my mother saying she'd gotten a good deal on it. Mrs. Cro had told me that owning a flower shop had been her lifelong dream, although she wasn't able to open one until, according to her, her life was almost over.

"Hi, Win," she said, pushing the top down on her garbage dumpster. "I'm so glad you're finished with all that remodeling over there."

"Sorry if it bothered you," I said. "Rivkah said the same thing. Too much noise."

"If it hadn't stopped soon, I was going to sell my store."

"Was it that bad?" I asked.

"Worse than you could imagine."

*Older people must be more attuned and sensitive to loud noises,* I thought. I couldn't recall it being loud at all.

Mrs. Cro was probably around sixty-five. She was tall and thin and reminded me of a ballerina. Her long black hair, which she usually wore in a bun, had been mostly replaced with gray.

"Well, it's all over," I said. "So you don't have to sell your store."

"Are you selling any ice cream?" she asked.

"Yes, we are." I smiled. "My Grandma Kay's recipes bring people out for ice cream even in the cold."

She closed her eyes and smiled. "Yes, Kaylene made the best ice cream. We spoke often about doing what you love and making your dreams come true."

"My grandma didn't mind passing out encouragement," I said. "In big scoops or small ones."

"No, she didn't." She nodded in agreement.

"Mrs. Cro, you didn't happen to lose a puppy the day before yesterday, did you?" I asked. I knew that Stephen Bayard had gotten that puppy from somewhere. My grandfather believed he'd stolen it. Standing here talking to her, I thought maybe he'd stolen it from her. He had said that he'd found it on her stoop.

"A puppy? No. But there was a commotion at the store that day."

"The day before yesterday?"

"Yes," she said. "It looked like someone broke into the store. Came down through here." She pointed to the ground.

"Through here?" I said, and looked up the alleyway to the street.

"Yes," she said. "To break into the door." She pointed at it.

"Oh my," I said. "I saw a police car outside here. But I thought it had to do with the guy who died. What did they take?"

"That's the thing," she said. "They didn't take anything. At least as far as I could tell. They were in the back storage room. Some kind of in-wall safe was behind a fake wall that I didn't know was there. I hadn't done anything in there after I bought it but store things. I don't know that I would have noticed that wall anyway. It was concealed."

"What was in the safe?"

"Nothing," she said. "At least not after whoever broke in left. I don't know what was in it before." She shook her head. "They made such a mess and left the safe standing wide open. But they did lock the outside door. Unusual because that's a dead bolt."

"So they had a key?" My eyes got big.

"I'm assuming."

"That's terri—" I started to say, but we were interrupted.

"Hi there." A woman's voice I recognized came from around the front. "Just wondering if the flower shop was open."

"Oh yes," Mrs. Cro said, projecting her voice. "Go back to the front and I'll be right there."

But the woman had already come around the side.

"Hi, Althea," I said. It was the woman from Molta's.

"Hi," she said, and smiled warmly. "I just saw you, didn't I?"

"Yes," I said. "I'm Win Crewse." I jerked a thumb over my shoulder. "My family owns the ice cream shop."

"You guys open in the winter?"

"Yes, they are," Mrs. Cro said. "And you'll want what they make all year round." She wrapped her arms around herself. "I'm cold, I'm going back in. Are you coming?" She looked at Althea. "Do you want flowers?"

"I do," Althea said. "And I'll just go back around and go through the front."

"Okay, I'll see you inside," Mrs. Cro said to her. "Bye, Win. I'll come over for some ice cream soon."

Mrs. Cro left, Althea headed to the front and I finished pushing the trash into the dumpster.

"You know," Althea said, coming back my way. "Ari's not so bad. He's really a nice guy."

"Why would you think I'd think anything differently?" I asked.

Althea gave a chuckle. The kind characters give in 1930s movies. The kind where the woman throws her head back and her eyes twinkle. "You just had to take one look at Maisie, it was easy to see. I didn't want you feeling like that, too." She shrugged. "You should give him the benefit of the doubt before you pass judgment. Plus," she said, "I was with him that night." She looked at me out of the corner of her eye. "All night."

This woman acted as if she knew what we'd been up to. What Maisie and I suspected—or rather were trying to suspect Ari of doing. And not only did she know, she was his alibi.

"I do," I said. "Make my own judgment, that is. And I don't think Ari isn't nice."

That wasn't exactly a lie. Maisie didn't like him, but other than micromanage her, I hadn't heard of anything bad he'd done. Although keeping an eye on Maisie wasn't a bad idea.

"Good." She looked at me for a moment, then said, "I guess I better let you get back to your trash." She jabbed a finger at it. "And I better get my flowers."

*Hmmm,* I thought as I watched her leave. I pulled my hat down over my ears. *I wonder why she cares what I think of Ari.*

I went back inside, swiped my feet, shook the cold from my hands and hung my coat and hat back on the rack.

Everyone was up front, but before I had a chance to join them, the phone rang.

"Crewse Creamery," I said, picking up the landline that had been in the store since my grandparents ran it. "May I help you?"

"May I speak to Win Crewse, please?"

"Speaking."

"Hi, Win. It's Clara."

"Hi, Clara." I tried to sound chipper, but my stomach was in a lurch. I was hoping she hadn't called to cancel.

"I just wanted to follow up with you and see when we can get together to sign the contracts for the two events we talked about."

"We just wrapped up discussions on what we wanted to serve this afternoon," I said. "I can draw up the contracts—one for the banquet, one for the ice cream social—tonight and come by tomorrow, if that's okay?"

"Could you do that?" she asked.

"Yes. No problem," I said. "I'd be happy to do it."

"That would be so awesome. Can you come around three?"

"Sure can," I said. "I'll see you at three tomorrow afternoon."

"Oh, Win," she said, catching me right before I hung up.

"Yes?"

"I heard that there was a murder just around the corner from your shop. Did you hear about that?"

My mouth went dry, and I had to swallow and lick my lips before I could speak. "Yes, I did," I said. "Isn't it awful? I don't know that we've ever had anything so awful happen this close to home before."

"No, I can't recall anything so bad either." She paused. "I just wondered if you knew anything."

"No, Clara," I lied. "I don't know anything about it."

I hung up feeling bad that I'd lied to her. But talking about it seemed too much like gossip. And what exactly was I going to say? *Oh sure, I heard about it, and the police think my father did it . . .*

"Win," my mother called, bringing me back from my reverie. "You've got a customer."

"A customer?" I mumbled. The three of them couldn't take care of one customer? Once I washed my hands and went out front, I saw why.

"Hi, O," I said.

"Hi, Win," he said. "I see you have some new ice cream out. I can't wait to try some."

I looked at my mother, Riya and Maisie all staring at me with stupid grins on their faces, as was O. They were playing Cupid.

"O, I don't think you even ate any ice cream when you were here yesterday."

"I guess I got wrapped up playing backgammon with your grandfather." He glanced over to where PopPop had been sitting the day before. "He's not here today."

"He already left," my mother offered. "You'll have to come earlier tomorrow." The size of the grin on her face was ridiculous.

"Do you want any ice cream today?" I asked.

"I was thinking about a sundae. Do you have sundaes?"

I pointed up to the board.

"We have lots of sundaes," Maisie said. "And Win makes the best ones."

"I bet," he said. "Uhm, I think I'll just go with a hot fudge sundae. With vanilla ice cream and nuts. Can I get extra nuts?"

"You can have whatever you want," my mother said. I hoped she wasn't talking about me.

I started dipping ice cream and he walked over to where my mother stood behind the register. He reached inside of his coat and into his back pants pocket, pulling out a wallet.

"This one is on the house," my mother said, pushing his hand away. "We know you sent Clara over to us."

“Yes,” I said. “Recommending us without ever tasting our wares.”

“I remembered how good the ice cream here was.”

“And we appreciate that,” my mother said. “Thank you.”

“You’re welcome, Mrs. Crewse.”

“Call me Ailbhe,” she said. “And go wait at the table for your sundae. I’ll have Win bring it over.” I looked at her and shook my head. “You are eating it here, aren’t you?”

O looked at me before he answered. I stood perfectly still.

“Yes. That would be nice,” he said.

I didn’t know what the crew at Crewse Creamery was up to, but I wasn’t letting them push me into anything. I had a shop to run and it came first.

“I’ll make the sundae,” Riya whispered. “You go and keep him company.”

“I can make the sundae,” I protested.

“We got this,” my mother said, coming over. “Go!” She pushed me to the end of the counter.

I shook my head and ambled over to where he’d sat. “They’re making your sundae,” I said.

“Oh,” he said, glancing at them. “I thought you made the best sundaes.”

“Apparently, my job right now is keeping you company.”

“That’s a good job,” he said.

“Is it?”

“I like it.” He smiled. “Did you and your friend find what you were looking for online?”

“Maisie,” I said. “My friend’s name is Maisie, and no, not yet.”

"Let me know what you find out," he said. "Or if you need more help."

I cocked my head to the side. "My PopPop tells me that you used to be a police officer."

"I did," he said. "Didn't see much justice there. Thought I'd try it from a different perspective."

"Do you practice law?" I asked.

"No. I teach it."

"Yeah, I heard that, too, that you're a law professor."

"I am."

"I have a question for you."

"Sure," he said. "Ask away."

"Say someone lay in wait and poisoned someone with something that isn't readily available, the person died and the killer got caught."

"Which they should."

I looked at him a moment before I finished. "I guess you're right," I said. "What kind of sentence would they get?"

"Is this someone you know?" he asked.

My heart did a flip-flop and I had to take a moment to breathe. "No," I said. "No one I know. It's hypothetical."

He nodded. "Because I heard about that body you found, and then the two of you"—he nodded toward Maisie—"were trying to find out information."

"No one I know has done anything like this. Trust me."

"I can help," he said earnestly.

"Thank you," I said. "Helping me right now would be telling me what would happen. You know, if someone did those things."

"Well," he said, studying my face. "That's premeditated murder, which is a capital offense everywhere in this country. In Ohio, though, we have the death penalty for those kinds of crimes. And that's probably what they'd get."

"The death penalty?" I asked, fear darkening my being.

"Yes," he said. "Death by lethal injection."

# chapter TWENTY-FOUR

I didn't see how the day could get worse.

I was so sad. I felt like getting in my little blue Toyota Corolla and driving to a parking lot. Several parking lots. They must've had some kind of therapeutic effect considering how much time my mother spent sitting in them.

But I had to keep busy. Thank goodness a steady stream of customers came in.

"Hello." It was my new employee, Candy Cook. She'd arrived for her five o'clock shift at four thirty, minutes after my mother and Riya had left. She pulled her earbuds out and took her book bag off her back.

"Hi, Candy," I said, glancing up at the clock. Her first day and she was half an hour early. I liked that. She had been scheduled for opening day, but as it turned out, I hadn't needed her help.

Candy Cook was nineteen, and, per her own words, a serial foster kid. While she'd aged out of the foster care system, her last foster mom loved her like her own and she'd opted to stay even though there were no legal ties. She'd been transferred around so much she hadn't finished high school, and was presently working on getting her diploma.

"I came early," she said. "Didn't know if there'd be a change in anything. Wanted to be prepared, just in case."

"Things are usually pretty routine around here," I said, and smiled. "You can count on that." Candy was short and round, and smart. When she interviewed, and today, she held on to her iPhone like it was an additional appendage. She had shortish ginger-colored hair, pulled back into a messy ponytail. Her black-rimmed glasses had neon-green arms, and she wore jeans that she'd rolled up at the bottoms and gray canvas sneakers with no socks. Her cotton top fit snug around her belly rolls.

"You ready to get started?" I asked Candy.

"Yep. And my mom"—she looked down at her feet—"I mean, you know, my foster mom, told me to be sure to tell you thank you for this opportunity."

"I'm glad to have you," I said. "And super glad you came early, because Maisie"—I pointed to her—"and I have an errand to run."

"You leaving me by myself?"

"I trained you, and I think you mastered everything right off. You feel comfortable being here alone?"

"I've been alone all my life," she said.

I didn't have anything to say about that. It was too sad to think about.

"You ready to go?" Maisie asked. I think she knew to get that conversation steered in another direction.

I let out a sigh and glanced up at the clock.

"I guess," I said. "You know I don't like doing this. Trying to be an amateur detective."

"I do," Maisie said, and smiled.

THE LIBRARY WAS all glass and wood. It had large sliding partitions inside and big windows across the front. There were wooden bookshelves, tables and chairs scattered all about.

Maisie pushed up next to me once we got inside. "We should use the computers in the basement," she whispered in my ear.

"Why?" I asked.

"So no one will know what we're doing."

I hadn't thought about that. "Maybe we should do this at home?" I raised a brow. "We could go to my place. We'd have to pick up the laptop from the store first, though."

"No," she said, grabbing my arms and pulling me along. "The police might do a trace on your computer. You know, if they raid your house for evidence."

"Maisie!" I said. "Don't say things like that. Why would they come to my house?"

"Precautions," she said. "We're just taking precautions." She pointed to the stairwell. "Basement."

We walked down the aisle between the stacks of books, a faint, sweet smell coming from the leaves of the old tomes. I loved the smell of books. I sat at one of the computers and Maisie pulled up a chair next to me.

"Where should we start?" I asked.

"I don't know," Maisie said, and shrugged.

"How about we look up Stephen Bayard's prison record?" I suggested. "See if he actually got caught for anything. O said that the prison site would have a picture of him."

"You know he likes you," Maisie said, leaning in and giving my shoulder a push with hers.

"Who?" I said.

"O," she said.

"Oh, brother," I said, and turned my attention back to the computer. "Shoot," I said. "I need a library card to sign in. I don't have mine with me."

"I've got mine," she said, digging down in her book bag.

We put in her card number and password and I looked up the site. We figured out how to get in and I read the instructions.

"Looks like we might not find him here," I said, and tapped my nail on the screen. "Unless he meets all of the criteria listed here."

"Doesn't hurt to try," she said.

I typed his name in and hit enter. Puppy Guy was the only face that popped up.

"That's him!" Maisie said.

"Who?" I asked. "Peter Sellers?"

"Yes," she said. "Oh wow. That feeling I had was right. I just knew the guy who worked at Molta's was the one you found down by the falls."

"Yep, that's the guy I met that morning," I said, staring at his picture. "He had seemed like a nice guy."

"Until your mother set you straight."

"You heard us talking?"

"Your mother can't whisper," Maisie said. "Especially when she's upset."

"You heard what she said about my dad?"

"That he would kill the guy?" Maisie asked. "Yeah, I heard her say that."

I groaned. "Don't repeat that to anyone," I said.

"Like I would," Maisie said. She poked out her hand for a fist bump. "I got you."

"Thanks, Maisie. Okay"—I blew out a breath—"let's see what we can get from this." I pointed at the screen. "It looks like he went to jail for fraud, passing bad checks and theft."

"Terrible man," Maisie said. "Here it says he was down for eighteen months."

"Down?"

"You know, locked up."

I groaned. Maisie was too into this.

"I wonder what he did," Maisie said.

"I don't know." I shook my head. "But doesn't that just create another mystery for us?" I said. "That realization doesn't clear up anything and it makes it harder to narrow down the killer."

"How?"

"Because." I pointed at the monitor. "He did something bad to someone somewhere else. Maybe it wasn't someone here that killed him. This says that the crime was committed in Hamilton County. Maybe someone followed him here, killed him and left."

"You can't look at it as a bad thing," Maisie said. "You have to think about it as another piece to the puzzle."

"Puzzle?" I sucked my tongue. "What puzzle? I don't see how this helps," I said. "Knowing what he looked like. Which I already knew. And what crimes he committed." I flung a hand toward the computer monitor. "This is going to be hard." I had to chuckle at the absurdity of me thinking I could solve a murder. "How am I going to make them stop thinking of my dad as the prime suspect?"

"Did that detective say that?"

"He may as well have said it."

"What exactly did that Bayard man do to you guys?"

I shrugged. "I'm not sure, exactly," I said. "Something bad enough for my mother to say what she said."

"We know your father didn't do it," she said, "but that's a good point."

"What is?"

"We have to find out what Peter Sellers did that made someone mad enough to kill him."

"How?"

"Yeah. I don't know," Maisie said, and took in a breath. "On all the shows I watch, they go around questioning people."

"Who are we supposed to question?" I asked, my voice squeaky. "Ari? Because searching the restaurant didn't help any."

"It gave us a clue," she said. "A cryptic one, but a clue. And we didn't *talk* to him."

"Okay, say we do," I said. "What are we going to say? 'Did you kill Stephen Bayard?'"

She hunched her shoulders. "Why not?"

"For some reason, Maisie," I said, squinting one eye, "I don't think that'll work. Whatever we do, I think we need to be more analytical about it."

"That's your strong suit," she said. "You're analytical."

"Thank you," I said, and gave a weak smile. "But me being that way isn't working so well for us right now."

I thought about my whiteboard at home. My stacks of sticky notes.

"We'll figure it out." She rubbed my shoulders. "I brought bananas and orange juice from your store," she said, and went into her book bag, pulling out both. Holding one in each hand, she offered them to me. I shook my head no. "Here," she said, unscrewing the top of the juice. "It might help."

I took the bottle from her. I didn't give a second thought about Maisie carrying food around. After all, she'd been raised by Rivkah Solomon. "I mean it's all so weird," I said, taking a sip out of the plastic bottle. "Why was he here? In Chagrin Falls." I swiped a hand across my forehead. "Did he really come just to harm my family?" I turned in my chair and looked at her. "I mean, he'd already done that. Years ago. And how would he know he'd run into me in front of the store?"

"Maybe he'd been watching you," Maisie offered.

"How?" I asked. "It was the first day the store was open. I'd gone to the shop every day, sure, but not at five in the morning. I wasn't making ice cream any of those other days. And he didn't say anything mean or threatening to me even though my family thinks he did." I shook my head.

"Not one mean word?" Maisie asked. I shook my head.

"And why kill him with succinylcholine?" I turned back and stared at the computer. "Had someone set out from the beginning to frame my father?"

"Succi-what?"

"Succinylcholine. It's a muscle relaxant used during surgery."

"Ohhhh . . ." she said, her eyes wide. "Your father is a surgeon. That's why they think he did it."

"With your insight," I said, shaking my head and closing down the prisoner-search site, "we'll have this thing solved in no time." I turned the bottle of orange juice up, took a big gulp and set it on the desk.

Maisie overlooked my sarcasm. "Well, you never told me *why* they suspected him," she said.

And I hadn't told her. I hadn't had to. I'd asked for help, and she'd blindly come to my rescue. No questions asked.

I needed to be nicer.

"Sorry," I said. "This is so frustrating."

"I know," she said. "And no reason to apologize. Here, have a banana."

I took the banana.

"You know what might help?" she said, scooting up in the chair. "Knowing about the instrument of death."

"The instrument of death?" I wanted to laugh, but instead I peeled back the skin of the banana and took a bite. "And how does knowing that help?" I said with my jaw full.

"Because," she said, "maybe we could narrow down the pool of suspects."

I couldn't help but laugh that time. "We don't have a *pool* of suspects, Maisie. We don't even have one."

"We have Ari."

"Okay, but one does not a pool make." I shifted in my seat to face her.

"Let's look at this logically," she said. "Women, when they

commit murder, like to use poisons and heavy objects. Men like guns and knives."

"Is that what you learned from watching all those BBC television shows?" I said, shaking my head.

"No." She blinked her eyes a few times. "Yes." She rocked her head back and forth. "Maybe."

"Well, if your theory is true, Ari Terrain can't be the killer."

"Why?" she asked.

"Because I'm pretty sure that injecting succinylcholine into someone would be considered poisoning. That would mean a woman did it."

"Injecting is sort of like stabbing," she said. "So it *could* be a man."

"We're not going to go about this scientifically, huh?"

"Of course we are. How about this for being scientific? It probably was a man because whoever did the deed would have had to overpower this Stephen/Peter guy, use that stuff on him and push him down the hill. That would take strength."

"That makes sense." I nodded. "And I guess it narrows us down to looking for a man."

"Right."

"Okay. What else can help us narrow it down? Maybe even down to the *exact* man?"

"Other than snooping?" Maisie asked.

"Snooping on who?" I asked.

"Good point." She sat back and thought for a moment. "Okay, let's look at this from a different angle."

"Which angle were we looking at it from before?" I asked.

"Just listen," she said. "How could someone have gotten the . . . sucki . . . cylowin stuff in the first place?"

"Now that's a good question," I said, not bothering to correct her pronunciation. "Because that's the reason, I think, that they are thinking it's my dad. Maybe other people have access to it, and we can see which people around here could have gotten ahold of some."

"Right," Maisie said, and nodded excitedly.

"Okay," I said. "Let's look that up." I took another sip of my juice, then typed, *Where do I get succinylcholine?*

"Okay," Maisie said, leaning over my shoulder. "Let's look at that one." She pointed to a link that read, *Succinylcholine: Is it the Perfect Murder Weapon? Not Exactly.*

"That's a blog," I said, and pointed underneath to the URL address. "It's not what we're looking for."

"It might help."

"Alright, I'll try it." I clicked on it and we both started reading it silently. At least for a few minutes, until Maisie needed to share her reading of it with me. Aloud.

"It's a neuromuscular paralytic drug," she said.

"I know," I said, still reading the article. "I read that. Not that I know what that is."

"Oh my gosh!" she said, pointing to the screen. I swatted her hand out of the way. "It says that it paralyzes all the muscles of the body and the person can't breathe." Her voice slowed as if she was telling a scary story. "They die from asphyxia while they are wide awake. Argh!"

"Yeah, I see that now," I said. "Let me read, please."

"It's used in anesthesia," she said, ignoring me. "To help get the tube down a patient's throat so they can breathe while they're asleep."

I took to reading out loud. Quietly. Moving my lips, I mumbled each word so I could understand what I was reading. It was the only way I could concentrate with her reading in my ear.

"And they use it in lethal injections," she said. "It's part of the three-drug cocktail they give to inmates on death row."

I gave up and sat back in my chair. There was only one more paragraph left in the article. I might as well let her tell me about it because she wasn't letting me find out for myself. Plus, I probably didn't want to read about lethal injections for prisoners anyway. Not after what O had told me.

"It says that succinylcholine must be injected and it works very quickly—within seconds to a minute. It also says that succinylcholine is hard to test for in an autopsy." She sat back in her seat. "So how do they know that was what killed him?"

"I don't know," I said. "But that part about how quickly it kills really gets to me." I turned and looked at her. "I was sitting on Grandma Kay's bench for at least twenty minutes before I decided to go down there and get some snow. It might be possible that I was sitting there when he was killed."

"Oh, that would be awful," Maisie said. "And scary. Did you see anyone?"

"No, not really. Just that little boy with the scarf."

"What boy?"

I told her the story about Glynis Vale and her son. How I'd seen the scarf on him and on the ground, and how she'd lied.

"You couldn't think a little boy killed him?"

"That's the same thing the detective said to me when I told

him my father didn't do it." I looked at Maisie. "And no, I don't think he did it."

"Good. Because that would be awful."

"Right. And we've already decided it was a man, well, more than likely a man, that was the killer, so that would probably leave his mother out as a suspect."

"Yeah, probably," Maisie said. "Well, did you see anyone else?" she asked. "Like did you see Ari?"

"No." I shook my head and tried to think about if I'd noticed anything.

"Ms. Devereaux might have seen something," I said. "She said something weird to me that night after the police arrived."

"What did she say?"

"She said, 'He deserved it,' or something like that."

"Who deserved what?" Maisie asked.

I shrugged. "I don't know. It's just what she said."

"We should ask her about that."

"You know," I said, "come to think about it, I went inside to get a bowl and scoop to get the snow with. I went to the restroom and stopped to talk to Felice." I shook my head. "I probably was inside when it happened."

"Awww, that's sweet."

"What?"

"Felice, my little sweetie pie, saved you."

"How?"

"Because if you had been sitting on that bench when the murderer was around, he would have had to kill you, too, because you were a witness."

"Don't go all Jason Bourne on me, Maisie."

"It's true."

"Well, I wouldn't have ever thought of it that way. And it's probably true that the killer had to have committed the crime there." I started clicking my nails. "Stephen Bayard couldn't have gotten there on his own after he was injected, it works too quickly." I turned back to the screen and tapped it. "In a minute or less."

"Seconds even," Maisie said. "Seeing that you didn't see anyone, that means the killer was there committing the murder in the short time it took you to get that metal scooper."

# chapter

# TWENTY-FIVE

So many thoughts were running around in my head that the things in the room started to blur.

One thing stuck out: Detective Beverly was right. Someone had planned this. They would have had to lure Stephen Bayard to the falls with the intent of killing him there.

*Or maybe,* I thought, *they gave him the drug in a car and pushed him out.* No. I shook my head. He would have landed in the street or on the sidewalk. The edge of the hill didn't come out far enough. If that had been the case, they would've had to drag him out of the car, across the sidewalk, and drop him down the hill.

*Was I gone long enough for anyone to have done that?*

"Shoot," I said.

"What?" Maisie said.

"I was just thinking," I said. "About how this could've happened."

"We probably need to keep this information," she said. "We'll probably want to go over it a few times."

"What information?" I said.

"What we found out. The prison record, the info on that succinyl stuff," she said. "Let's print it out."

I clicked print and checked a few of the other links before circling back to the prison website. I printed the page that told the crime he'd committed, his release date, birthdate and place of incarceration. I didn't know if I'd ever need it for anything.

"This isn't telling us anything, you know." I grabbed the papers from the printer and stacked them up.

"We found out he had been in jail."

"That's not surprising."

"And we found out about his other crimes. Other than what he did to your family."

I shook my head. "We need something else. Something more."

"Well, you're going to talk to Ms. Devereaux, right?"

"Yeah. I guess." I pressed my lips together and let my eyes drift. "I just think I need to find out more on the victim if I'm going to find out who the killer was. Someone who knew him. Or knows where I could find out more about him than this." I waved the small stack of papers we'd printed. "You know, like a guy who knows a guy who knows a guy."

"We have a guy like that."

"Who?"

"O."

I sucked my tongue. "He doesn't know anything."

"He used to be a police officer. Now he's a lawyer—"

"Law professor," I interjected.

"And he told us how to find information on Dead Guy."

I looked at her with a deadpan face. "He is not a go-to guy."

"And he likes you."

"He does not like me, Maisie," I said. "I wish you'd stop saying that."

"It's true."

"It's not true."

"He's come in to the shop every day," she said.

"To buy ice cream," I said.

"Who buys ice cream in the winter?"

"Oh my gosh, Maisie," I screeched. "I'm banking on people buying ice cream in the winter."

"Oh yeah," she said. "But you should call him."

"What? Why would I call him?" She wasn't going to stop with this guy. "He can't help, Maisie. We need someone who might know what this man was up to that got him killed."

"We don't know anyone that knows him." She looked at me sheepishly. "Except . . . maybe your family."

"Oh my goodness!" I turned and faced her. "Maisie, we can never tell my family that we are doing anything that concerns Stephen Bayard."

She nodded, her red ringlets bouncing. "Okay. Okay." She held up her hands, gesturing a surrender. "I know."

"It seems like just the mention of him sends my family over the rails," I muttered. "It's like they've turned into a family hit squad. My mother saying just the sight of Stephen Bayard will send my father into a murderous rampage. My father acting suspicious after the guy turns up dead—showing up in non-work attire, without a car, and late. My mother saying I didn't have anything to worry about. Then PopPop coming down to the ice cream shop, hanging around, camping out at tables like he's in the mafia. I felt like I should be serving spaghetti with marinara sauce."

Maisie started giggling.

"It's not funny, Maisie." I shook my head.

"Yes, it is." She covered her mouth with her hand, but all her giggles squeezed out from behind it. "I'm sorry, I can't stop laughing. I'm just picturing your mother in a hit squad and PopPop in the mafia. 'Mr. Bayard'"—she was trying to imitate PopPop's voice—"'I'm going to make you an offer you can't refuse.'"

"Yeah. Don't picture that." I shook my head more vigorously, giggles starting to bubble inside of me as well. But by shaking my head telling Maisie to stop, I must have shaken something loose, because just then I had an idea.

IT WAS FAMILY Chef Night at my parents' house.

Once a month, one designated family member took the role of head chef, and the rest of us acted as sous chefs. We cooked and dined together—a Crewse gathering of culinary delights. Or disasters. More often than not, the fare for the evening was served after we'd made a big mess, spilled liquids and burned food. But we happily sat, no matter the outcome, around my parents' twelve-foot table, complimenting the chef, eating, laughing and reminiscing.

It was the perfect time to corner a brother and find out what he knew about Stephen Bayard. The only question was which one I would pounce on . . .

My brothers, four, six and eight years older than me, were a font of information on things gone by. One of them, unbeknownst to him, was going to be my "go-to guy." That had been the idea shaken loose after my conversation with Maisie.

I stuffed the papers we'd printed into my knapsack, and Maisie and I left the library. I didn't tell her my newly revised plans. My brothers were very protective over me. It would take all my baby-sister skills to get them to talk. Maisie wouldn't help that cause.

They had been the ones to pull me in my red wagon to the ice cream shop, they'd taught me how to get down the falls on a cardboard box, and it was they who rode in the car with Dad, following me on my first date.

Sometimes they forgot I was all grown up now.

"You're going to your parents' tonight, right?" Maisie asked.

"Yep. Gotta go and get ice cream for dessert first. It's been a long time since we had some made in the store."

"Okay, see you tomorrow," she said, and waved a mittened hand to me.

I headed back to the store, filled up two gallon cartons and headed up the hill. I put my hands to my mouth and blew warm air into them. It was cold out, so cold I felt like I was going to turn into a Popsicle.

My oldest brother, James Graham Crewse, named after my father, was in sports medicine. He was the worst cook of us all. We dreaded Family Chef Night when it was his turn. He, however, never could see (or taste) how awful his creations were. He lived in Orange, the next suburb over, but worked downtown. His patients were players from the area's sports teams—the Browns, Cavaliers and Indians.

Most times I had to remind him he wasn't my father. But when he was around, I didn't have to worry about a thing. He had my back and had always been the one I went to for advice when Dad wasn't available. And being the oldest, he'd probably remember the most about "the incident" with Con-Man-Puppy-Guy. But James was also the most stuck-up. I didn't mean that in a bad way. He was just so serious. About everything. Too serious to entertain a hypothetical about Dad being in danger of being arrested for murder and my needing to play amateur sleuth to help him. Especially if I had enlisted Maisie to help. He thought Maisie was a bundle of fireworks hovering over an open flame. He said no one would ever know when her fuse would catch fire or what direction she'd take off in. She was festive, he said, but potentially dangerous.

The next oldest, Llewellyn Jackson Crewse, "Lew" for short, was a dentist. He had a small practice and kept us all with beautiful, straight white teeth.

*A dentist*... I thought as I trudged up the hill, not worried one bit about the ice cream melting. *I wonder, does he have access to succinylcholine? Hmmm*...

"Oh geesh!" I said, and stomped my foot.

I was supposed to be finding a way to prove my father's innocence, and here I was thinking that maybe my brother had done it.

Then there was the youngest of my older brothers. Robert "Bobby" Bantham Crewse. He was still able to put a "Dr." in front of his name. Bobby had gotten a doctorate of nursing at Case Western Reserve and opened a clinic. The same one where my father volunteered once a week. The only medical member of the family who didn't have a big practice and a big bank account, Bobby was all about helping the homeless, being an activist for those less fortunate and making sure that everyone, no matter their station in life, counted. He'd help anyone with whatever he could, and he was not only funny, but was a lot of fun.

Only, I knew as soon as I told him anything, he'd tell Dad or PopPop. He couldn't help it, he was like a sieve—everything just ran out of him. Just being in close proximity to my father and grandfather made him want to tell everything he knew. My mother had tried unsuccessfully to get him to stop by bribing him with gifts and candy, but he'd go and tell them that, too.

Asking him to tell me what happened when Stephen Bayard came to town and not let my dad know I'd asked was completely out of the question.

I pushed open the front door and could hear and smell the start of what I knew was going to be a fun evening.

I smelled onions and green peppers simmering, and bacon sizzling and popping in my mother's cast-iron skillet. I didn't know what was on the menu tonight, but I was already hungry for it and for the company of family.

"There you are!" my mother said, and came over and hugged me.

"Took you long enough," Lew said. He came over and took the ice cream from me.

"I had to walk up the hill carrying all of that." I pointed to Lew, who was putting the ice cream in the freezer.

"Walk?" my mother said. "Didn't I see your car at the shop today?"

Everyone stopped and looked at me. "Ahh! I forgot!" I said, slapping my hand on my forehead and meeting each of their eyes. "I'm so used to walking."

My father and my brother James looked at each and shook their heads. Seemingly silently agreeing that their girl still needed their help.

"It's alright, Pumpkin," my daddy said. "I can drive you back down the hill to get it after we eat."

I looked over at Lew. He, I decided, was the one I was going to needle for information. "That's okay, Daddy," I said, then smiled at my middle brother. "Lew can take me."

# chapter TWENTY-SIX

On the ride down the hill, sitting next to Lew in his car, I got nervous. I wasn't exactly sure how I was going to broach the subject. *Hey, Lew, I need you to help me prove that our father isn't a homicidal maniac.*

I turned to stare at him, wondering how that would go over.

"Something wrong?" he asked, glancing at me.

"Nope," I said.

"You're acting like it is. Staring at me." He turned the corner onto North Main.

"Sooo . . ." I started.

"Spit it out, Win. I know when something's bothering you." He pulled up in front of the shop. "Is that why you wanted me to bring you to your car?"

"Yeah." I scrunched up my nose. "I wanted to talk to you."

"Okay," he said. He put the car in park, turned off the radio and shifted in his seat to face me.

James and Lew looked a lot like Dad and PopPop. Tall, fit. Light-skinned with upturned eyes and wide noses. That made me more nervous, because it felt like I was talking to Dad.

"Well?" he said. "Something wrong with your teeth? Is that what you want to tell me? You got a cavity or something?"

"No," I said in exasperation. "Why would I not tell you that?"

He punched on the overhead lights. "Let me see."

"No! Not here!" I folded my lips in and made them tight.

"Let me see your teeth."

"Mmm-mm," I said, shaking my head, lips and eyes clamped tight. I stayed like that for a minute to get him to stop, then covered my mouth to speak. "I just need you to tell me about Stephen Bayard."

He popped the light back off. The glow from the streetlight wafted into the car.

"Stephen Bayard." He repeated the name almost in a whisper.

"Yeah. He's the guy who—"

"I know who he is," he said. "I also heard he's the guy you found dead at the bottom of the falls."

"You heard that?" I asked. He nodded. "Who told you?" Then I shook my head. "After you heard that, why didn't you call to see how I was?"

"Dad said you were fine. And we don't talk about that man any more than we have to."

"You talked to Dad about it?"

"Yeah. I talk to Dad. Why wouldn't I have talked to Dad about it?"

*Well for one,* I thought, *Mom said any mention of his name would send him off in a homicidal rage . . .*

But I didn't say that.

"Do you keep succinylcholine at your office?" I said instead.

"Do I keep what?" I could see the confusion on his face even in the dark car.

"For oral surgery, I mean. You know."

"I don't do oral surgeries," he said flatly. "I refer my patients to an oral surgeon."

*Okay, so he doesn't have access to it. Not that I ever considered him a suspect . . .*

"So, what did Dad tell you about the dead guy?"

"What I just told you." He pulled air in through his nose. "That you found him."

"He didn't say anything else?" I asked.

"Like what?"

"I don't know." My voice was slipping into something akin to a whine. "Maybe something more?"

"What do you want, Win?"

I needed to get my nerves together, that was one thing I wanted. The other, as I'd been saying, was information. But getting info from Lew Crewse, DDS, was as hard as pulling teeth.

Maybe I should stop beating around the bush. It wasn't that I was scared to ask my brother anything, but that I might be scared of the answer. But I pushed onward.

"I have something to tell you, but I don't want Daddy to know I told you."

"What did you do, Win? Mess up at the store? Because I'm going to have to tell PopPop or somebody that."

I sucked my tongue. "No. The store is fine. It's about Stephen Bayard."

"We don't talk about him," he said in a soft voice. He wanted me to know he wasn't being mean about it, he just didn't want to talk about it.

"The police questioned Dad about him."

He didn't say anything. He kept his face forward, sticking to the Stephen Bayard Non-Discussion Rule.

I pushed his arm. "They think he did it."

"Who?"

"Daddy."

"I'm sure they don't."

"They do."

He looked at me for a long moment. "They're going to question a lot of people about it," he said. "They have to have started a murder investigation. Dad was just one of those people."

"Yeah, but they think Daddy did it."

He rubbed his hands up and down his thighs. Closing his eyes, he licked his lips. I could tell he didn't like having this conversation.

"It's true," I said, not giving him time to cut me off. "I talked to the police detective about it and he said that Daddy was on his radar."

"Radar? What kind of talk is that, Win?" He shook his head. "Why are you talking to the police detective anyway?"

"I found the body," I said, not admitting to seeking him out on my own. "And remember, you just said they'll be questioning a lot of people. I was one of them."

"Well, don't volunteer any information. It's easy to get railroaded when it comes to murder investigations." He looked at me. "Especially here in the village. Especially when you're black.

Our police don't have a lot of experience investigating murders. They might jump on any little stray clue and try to make a case out of it."

"They already jumped on one," I said. He looked at me and we locked eyes. "Succinylcholine."

My brother swiped his hand over his low-cut hair, then across his clean-shaven face. I could tell that word upset him. I also could tell that my dad had said more to him than what he was telling me.

"I don't think Dad did it," I said, trying to move the conversation down the path I needed it to go.

"I'd hope you wouldn't think that," he said.

"But that man who we don't talk about talked to me that morning. Now PopPop is acting all strange about it. Showing up at the shop every day like he's Kevin Costner in *The Bodyguard*. I just want to understand what happened back then."

"Why don't you ask one of them?"

"Who?"

"Mom. Dad. PopPop."

"Didn't you just tell me 'we don't talk about that'?" I mimicked his voice. "Plus, they really don't seem to handle conversation about that man too well."

"I'd guess not," he said.

"I don't really remember what happened," I said. "Tell me."

"What do you mean, 'they don't handle conversation about that man well'?"

"Because when I told Mommy that Stephen Bayard was around and that he was going to go visit PopPop, she 'bout had an aneurysm. She said that she'd better warn Daddy, because if Daddy saw him, he might just kill him."

"She said that?"

I nodded my head.

Lew leaned back on the headrest. He sat for a long moment, contemplating, his hands folded in his lap. "God, I hope she didn't say that to anyone else."

"So see, that's why I need to know."

"That makes no sense."

"Lew." That was definitely a whine.

"That man . . . Stephen Bayard . . . took advantage of Grandma Kay and then she died," Lew said. "We were taking care of her. PopPop didn't want to put her in a home or have any outsiders come in. He wanted to do everything himself. And he didn't want anyone to know."

"We helped," I said. "And he couldn't have kept it hidden."

"That's not what he thought." Lew shook his head. "And I didn't mean take care of her by himself, literally. Everyone understood it was going to be with the help of the family. That was what he was counting on. And of course everyone was willing to help. Mom and Dad. Aunt Jack. Uncle Denny and all the cousins. Even the community, you know. The shop owners"—he pointed out the window—"all along North Main and around the triangle. Everybody loved Grandma Kay and was willing to help."

I smiled. "I know everybody loved her," I said.

"And Stephen Bayard took that from us."

"How?"

"The shop was only in Grandma Kay's name." He drew in a

breath. “For whatever reason, I don’t know why, you’d have to ask Mom or Dad about that. I’m sure PopPop would never discuss it. And because she was the owner and he is—was—a master con man, Stephen Bayard convinced Grandma Kay, in her fragile state of mind, to sign over the store to him.”

“Sell it to him?”

“I don’t know if there was even any money involved. He proposed that he could help make it better for the family or some nonsense like that, and even sick, Grandma Kay was all—”

“About family,” I said, finishing his sentence.

“Exactly.”

“Then what happened?”

“PopPop had to go to probate court. Prove that Grandma Kay was incompetent,” he said. He stared down at his hand. “That broke his heart. He never wanted that said about his wife, the love of his life—that she was incompetent. Incapable of doing anything—let alone for it to be in court documents for the world to see.”

I remembered O said nowadays you could find just about anything about a person online. I wondered whether those records were out there on the web for all eyes to see.

“Without it being declared that she wasn’t of sound mind,” Lew continued, “the contract for that . . . man . . . to take over the shop could have been found valid.”

“Oh,” I said, nodding, “I see.”

“But that man didn’t just hurt our family. He hurt other people in the village, too.”

“Like who?” I asked.

Lew shrugged. “Like Dan Clawson, for one.”

"Oh right," I said. "Mommy told me about that. He caused his marriage to break up."

"His whole family," Lew said. "When Mr. Clawson's wife left, she took their son, and Mr. Clawson didn't see him for a long time."

"Oh wow," I said. "Is Mr. Clawson still around? He might be a good suspect."

"Mr. Clawson, I think, is around the same age as PopPop. So maybe." Lew stared out the windshield. "His son, Danny, is still around, though. He might be a good suspect."

"The son that went with Mrs. Clawson when she left with Stephen Bayard?"

"If that's where Mrs. Clawson went when she left, yes. I don't know that for sure."

"It's what Mom said," I said.

"All I know is that Mr. Clawson's son came back to be close to his father."

"Back to the village?"

"Yeah. Because I think Mr. Clawson is in a nursing home somewhere or something. Danny lives in their old house. I saw him at the grocery store not too long ago. I believe that's what he told me."

"Who else?"

"Who else?" he asked.

"Who else did Stephen Bayard do something to?"

"Oh. Um. Ms. Devereaux. Wallace Keller—"

"Mr. Keller?" I interrupted.

"Remember he owned Nico's Family Restaurant?"

"Of course I remember," I said.

"Yeah, well, I think something happened with his restaurant because of something Stephen Bayard did. I'm not sure what. I think for a while every business that had trouble blamed it on that man. I heard he had his hand in everything. I remember Mom saying he was a sweet talker. Had an angel's smile and a devil's tail."

"I've seen him in action," I said. "I met him outside the ice cream shop and he made me think he was the best of friends with the whole family and that he was a kindhearted, puppy-loving guy."

"Yeah, Mom told me. That's how I know all of the stuff I know about him. She told me."

I frowned. "She didn't tell me anything."

"She thinks she needs to protect you. Just like Dad and Pop-Pop do."

"Yeah," I said, a confused look on my face. "Why is that?"

He chuckled. "Because you're the baby."

I rolled my eyes. "They couldn't still think like that," I said. I'd heard that enough in my life. "Anyway," I huffed, "back to the restaurant. Stephen Bayard took it from Mr. Keller?"

"No. That's when Ari Terrain got it. After Stephen Bayard got through with Mr. Keller, he left town and Ari got it."

"Ari, huh?" I said thoughtfully.

*Maisie's number-one suspect.*

Maybe the email Maisie got really was about blackmail. Stephen Bayard had said that Ari owed him. Was it for getting the restaurant for him?

"Did Stephen Bayard help Ari out in getting the restaurant?" I asked.

"I don't know," Lew said.

"What did Stephen Bayard do to Mr. Keller? I mean, how could he have taken the restaurant?"

"I don't know that either," he said. "I've heard a few things. One involved something like a Ponzi scheme. Some sort of dubious investment scheme." He hunched his shoulders. "I'm not sure."

"So Mom told you that, too?" I asked.

Seemed Lew had been the right brother to ask. I had no idea Stephen Bayard had caused so much hurt and damage all over our little village. That really opened up the suspect pool.

*I wonder if Detective Beverly knows about all of that.*

"I've heard PopPop, Ms. Devereaux and Mr. Clawson talking a few times about it, too," Lew said. "They used to have their own little chamber of commerce group. As shop owners, they'd meet, sometimes at the house. Talk about their businesses."

"They still do," I said, although I had yet to go to any of their meetings. "So, if Stephen Bayard did all of this stuff to so many people, why didn't he go to jail for it?"

I'd only found one prison record. I remembered the site noted that a convict wouldn't be listed unless he was still in prison, judicially released or still under supervision like probation. It was possible he'd been in jail lots of times. Wronged lots of people.

"I don't know that he didn't," he said. "I just remember hearing that he left here pretty quickly. But maybe they caught him." He stopped talking, his eyes drifted. I could tell he was thinking.

"I wonder why he was back in town," I said. "You'd think he'd be afraid to return here."

He shrugged. "I was just thinking the same thing. It's been a lot of years." He slowly shook his head, seemingly in disgust. "That man had no shame. Probably thought no one would make him answer for all the wrong he'd done or else he wouldn't have kept doing it."

"You think he was here doing wrong?"

"What else could he have been doing?"

I didn't have an answer for that.

"Where was he staying?" Lew asked.

"I don't know. Why?"

"That's what the police should be looking into."

"Why?"

"Because no one here liked him. Whomever he stayed with must have been hiding him. Or covering for him." He shook his head. "I can't believe he was just so bold to come back and spout lies to you about PopPop and Grandma Kay."

"He was bold, but someone else was even bolder," I said. "Someone killed him right on a street corner."

"Hmpf." He ran his hand over his hair. "I guess you're right about that."

"I need to find out who that could be."

"No, you don't." He looked at me. "The police will find that out, Win," he said. "Don't you go and do anything."

I looked at him, weighing whether I should tell him what Maisie and I had already been up to.

"Too late," I said.

"Too late?" He let out a laugh. One that came with a warning. "Don't go snooping around, Win." He pointed a finger at me. "It's always best to let the police do their job—"

"Not when their job includes arresting my daddy," I said defiantly.

"No one is arresting Dad."

"You said they might not know what they're doing. They're not used to investigating murders."

"I didn't say that for you to go poking your nose in."

"I just want to help Dad," I said. "You should want to, too. That man was killed with succinylcholine. It's used in surgeries."

"I know what it's used for," he said.

"Daddy uses it during surgery."

"He doesn't," Lew said, his forehead creasing. "An *anesthesiologist* would use it during surgery."

"Yeah, that's what Daddy told the detective, but that detective didn't care. He knew Daddy had a reason to hate Stephen Bayard and access to the drug that killed him. That was all he cared about. Plus"—I blew out a breath—"Daddy told me he was at work when I found the body and he wasn't."

"How do you know he wasn't? Dad wouldn't lie."

"Yeah, well, he did. He had on sweatpants and Timberland boots when he came down to get me after I found that body. And when I asked where he'd been, he said at work."

"In sweats?" Lew's eyebrow went up.

"Yep."

His hand swiped across his eyebrows. "Oh. That's not good," he said.

"Tell me about it," I said. "Why would our father lie?"

"So what are you trying to do?" he asked.

"Maisie thinks that Ari killed him."

"You got Maisie helping you?" His face showed amusement.

"She watches detective shows on the BBC or Acorn or something."

He chuckled. "You haven't questioned Ari, have you?"

"Uhmmmm . . ." I hummed out the word. "Nooo. Not really," I said, my voice getting tinny. "But we did find an email from someone we think was Stephen Bayard that made us think he was blackmailing Ari."

"That you think was from Stephen Bayard?"

"Yeah."

"How did you get it?"

"Uhm . . ."

"Never mind," he said, holding up his hand to stop me. "It was from Stephen Bayard's email address or something?"

"No. It was from the Pink Panther."

"And why do you think the Pink Panther is Stephen Bayard?"

"Because he was working at Molta's under the name Peter Sellers."

"Who is Peter Sellers?"

"An actor."

"I don't get the connection."

"He played the Pink Panther in movies."

"I thought that was Steve Martin."

"Steve Martin was in the remake."

"Oh. Well don't let Maisie lead you down some stray path," he said. "Follow the clues. Stay under the radar. I'm sure you doing your own investigation could get you in trouble with the police. Obstructing justice or something."

"Yeah, I'm trying to be careful." *If only I could get Maisie to be, too.* "And honestly, I don't know if I'm any good at this. I don't know what to do. That's why I came to you."

"The only way to get answers is to ask questions."

"Like what?" I said. "And to who?"

"Find out where he stayed. Find out who he talked to"—he shot me a glance—"other than you. I'm sure the police probably have already done anything we can think of."

"Ask questions," I said contemplatively.

"Then find out—I don't know how you'd do it—but find out how Ari was able to purchase that restaurant," he continued. "Maybe they were working together and you're on the right track. He tried to blackmail Ari and Ari killed him. You *don't* want to talk to Ari, though, because if he did do it—kill Stephen Bayard to stop him from interfering with his life or business or whatever—he'd probably have no qualms about killing you, too. You don't know, maybe the way Ari acquired that restaurant was shady and he is shady, too."

"Oooh. Shady," I said, and shivered, feigning fear. He seemed to be describing one of those old black-and-white AMC films instead of the goings-on in Chagrin Falls.

"You gotta take it seriously, Win, if you're serious about doing this."

"I am," I said. I was surprised I'd won him over. Who knew he'd think it was okay for me to play amateur sleuth?

"See what you can find out," Lew said. "But be careful."

# chapter TWENTY-SEVEN

Lew said I had to ask questions. Maisie said we had to ask questions.

We hadn't asked anyone any questions. I'd just lifted emails from people's private accounts, or at least hung out with a girl who did, and looked up prison records online.

Oh. Lew. I had asked Lew plenty of questions. But he wasn't a suspect.

Who *were* my suspects?

I got into my car, buckled the seatbelt and turned the ignition. I didn't pull off right away because I was lost in thought.

I could ask Ms. Devereaux questions. She might have answers. Then again—I cocked my head to the side—she could be a suspect. Especially now since Lew had told me Stephen Bayard might have wronged her.

But why would Debbie Devereaux have succinylcholine? And because of the way the drug acted, Maisie and I had concluded it probably was a man who took Stephen Bayard's life. Debbie was a woman. A nearly seventy-year-old woman. She had a lot of stamina, but I didn't think she could handle a body. Still, I could ask her questions . . .

I got a notification beep on my watch. I had a text message from Maisie.

> Where are you?!?!! Drove by house and shop, no you!!
> Don't go snooping without me!

She had fist jabs, crying faces, googly eyes and way too many exclamation marks peppered all through the short text.

"Now *she's* spying on *me*," I muttered. "Oh!" I screeched, and threw the car into gear. "My house!" I'd forgotten.

Mr. Wallace Keller, who owned the restaurant that Ari had gotten, whether legally or not, was now dead. He'd died more than five years ago. Nothing suspicious. Just old age and years of smoking. But his wife was still alive. And she was my landlord!

I heard an angelic chorus hit a high note.

I had someone to ask questions to!

I did a U-turn and headed back toward North Main.

I decided I should go and see her with a gift in hand. I knew she'd love some ice cream. A little frosty, tasty bribe might make her more willing to talk. My Grandma Kay used to say that our ice cream could warm even the coldest soul.

Not that Mrs. Keller was mean. She wasn't, she was sweet. But she'd gone through a lot of loss lately. First her husband, and then her little pet dachshund, Max. She had loved that wiener dog and looked lost without him for company. My mother had said without him, she probably would have withered away after the loss of her husband.

It was late, and I had my fingers crossed she'd still be up. I wanted—no—needed to know how Mr. Keller had lost the restaurant.

I whooshed into the ice cream shop, grabbed an ice cream scooper and two pint-sized containers, and swung open the freezer. I didn't know what she'd like. Three of the trays were filled with ice cream my mother had made. She made good ice cream, but I was trying to woo Mrs. Keller into giving me information about what I was sure had to be a sore subject. I wanted the one I used for bargaining power to be one I'd made.

I decided to go with the fruity ones. I still had some of the Ghoulish Blueberry, just enough to fill the container. And I spooned up some of the banana nut.

God, I hoped she had good teeth. There were a lot of nuts in that one.

I re-covered the trays with the plastic wrap, placed lids on top of the containers and closed the freezer back up. I ran out to my car. I didn't want her going to bed on me, and I didn't want her nodding off while I asked her questions.

Hopefully, the sugar would help with that.

I made it home, pulled the car all the way back in the driveway and noticed her lights were still on. "Thank goodness," I muttered. I grabbed my knapsack and the two pints of ice cream. I wished I'd put them in a bag. My hands were freezing.

I tucked one in the crook of my arm, knocked on her door and waited.

Mrs. Marguerite Keller was in her eighties or close to it. She was short and stout, just like a teapot. And so was everything about her. Her white hair was short, and so were her fingers and her nose. She had thin slits for eyes, a face full of wrinkles and age spots everywhere. She always wore a flowered housedress, with knee socks and house shoes, and she smelled like rosewater.

After what seemed like forever, I saw the light to the interior door come on.

"Who is it?" she asked, trying to make her voice loud.

"It's me, Mrs. Keller," I said. "Win."

"Win? Okay, hold on a minute. I have to get the key."

*Who comes to the door without the key?*

"Okay," I said. At least I didn't have to worry about the ice cream melting.

I tapped out her minute with my foot and started trying to think about what I was going to ask her. My questions needed to be ones that might lead me to a killer.

How was I going to manage that?

I wondered if Maisie would know what to ask. And as if my thoughts had gone out into the air and to Maisie's house, the notification ding went off on my watch again. Without looking, I knew it was Maisie, but there was no time to check her message.

"I got it. I got it," Mrs. Keller said, coming back to the door. I heard her fiddling with the lock and wished I could help her. "Hold on."

"Okay," I said. "Take your time."

"Got it," she said again, this time referring to the lock and not the key. "Come on in, Win. I know it's cold out there."

"Hi, Mrs. Keller," I said, stepping inside. I stomped my feet to get any excess snow off.

"Is everything alright?" she asked, stepping back inside to let me in. "Is it warm enough upstairs?"

"Oh yes. It's fine," I said, walking just inside the door. I set everything on the floor and took off my boots.

"Oh good," she said. "I thought I might have to bleed those radiators. With weather like this you never know."

"Nope," I said, and picked up the ice cream. "It's nice and toasty, just like down here."

"Well, what brings you by?" She looked back out the door as if I had something else.

"I brought you ice cream," I said.

"For me?" she said, and placed her hand on her chest. "I love it, but isn't it too cold for ice cream?"

"It's never too cold for ice cream, Mrs. Keller. I thought you knew that." I gave her a sly smile.

"Well, c'mon back. I'll get us some bowls."

Didn't take much to persuade her.

"I'll help," I said. I took off my coat, draped it around the back of a dining room chair and followed her into the kitchen.

"I haven't heard you overhead the last couple of days," she said. "I didn't know where you'd gotten to."

"I've been at the store. Remember I told you we were opening?"

"I remember," she said. "But it had taken so long, I wasn't sure if you did or not."

"We did," I said. I was familiar with her kitchen, had been in it plenty of times getting things she couldn't reach. So I grabbed the two bowls from the cabinet while she was still deciding what she'd come into the kitchen for, and two tablespoons from her silverware drawer. "C'mon. Let's sit at the table in there."

"Good idea," she said.

I headed back into the dining room. Sitting down, I opened up both containers. "Which one would you like?" I asked her.

She peered inside, a smile spreading on her face. "Oh my, they both look so good," she said, clapping her hands together. "Did you make these?"

"I sure did." I picked up one of the spoons. "How about a little of both?"

"That sounds fine."

I started dipping up the blueberry ice cream. Her eyes were watching me, so I figured I'd start my inquiry. Distracted, she might answer my questions without wanting to know why I was asking.

"Have you been doing okay?" I asked.

"Oh, I'm okay," she said. "I miss my little Max."

"I know," I said.

"And Wally. Max was the only thing that kept me going after Wally died."

"I know," I said.

"I miss him," she said. "He was a good husband. He had his faults, but I loved him."

"You two were together a long time," I said. I knew how long, I'd heard the story before, but I wanted to steer the conversation around to the restaurant.

"Fifty-plus years," she said.

"Fifty years is a long time," I said. "I remember you telling me you did everything together."

"We did."

"My brother just reminded me today that you two ran Nico's on Orange."

"Yes, we did." She nodded. "Nico's Family Restaurant. Wally named it after my father." She took a spoonful of the blue ice cream. "Oh." She smacked her lips. "This is heavenly!"

"Thank you," I said. I let her take another spoonful before I started again.

"What did you do at the restaurant?" I asked.

"Oh, a little of this and a little of that."

"Did you cook?"

"No." She pursed her lips and ran her fingers along the linen tablecloth. "That was Wally's job. At first, you know. After we started getting a lot of customers, he hired someone. I took care of the front, but that got a bit much for me to do as well."

"A lot of good times there," I said.

"Oh yes, there were," she said. She studied the bowl. "I'm going to try this other one."

"Be my guest," I said. "That's why I brought it to you."

"Aren't you going to have any?" She nodded toward my empty bowl.

I was so busy trying to find a way to get her to talk about the restaurant, I had forgotten to get some. "I'll have some of the banana nut with you," I said.

"Is that what it is?" she asked. I nodded as I spooned some in her bowl. "What's the other one called?"

"Ghoulish Blueberry."

"Oh, you made it with blueberries?"

"Yes, ma'am." I nodded. "Fresh blueberries. I came up with it for Halloween."

"I used to make the best blueberry cobbler," she said. "We sold it at the restaurant."

"I bet it was good," I said.

"It was delicious."

"I went to that restaurant where Nico's used to be the other day," I said.

"Bet it's nothing like the days when we owned it. Everything is so upscale now," she said. "We were a family restaurant."

"That was the best part of it, huh?"

"Yes, it sure was," she said.

"How long did you guys run that restaurant?" I asked.

"Oh, twenty-five years or so," she said. "Until we lost it."

"You lost it?"

"Yeah. Wally took out a loan with some shady character. I told him to go to the bank and do it, but he wouldn't listen to me."

Shady. Just what Lew had said.

"What happened?" I asked.

"The taxes on the property got behind," she said. "And the guy who owns it now paid them."

"As a favor?"

"No. We didn't know him," she said. "He wasn't doing us any favors." She took the last mouthful of the banana nut ice cream, scraping the side of the bowl.

"And that was Ari?" I asked.

"Yeah. The man with the last name that means dirt. Because that's what he is. Dirt."

"Ari Terrain," I said. "His last name is Terrain."

She smacked her lips.

"What happened with that?"

"Come to find out anyone can go down to the county tax board and pay the taxes owed on any property."

"I didn't know that. So what happens then?" I asked.

"Then you owe them instead of the county. And," she said, pushing the bowl back, "whoever paid the taxes can foreclose on your property."

"Really?"

That did sound shady.

"Yes, really," she said.

"So that's when Mr. Keller took out a loan?"

"Yes, from a young man who had ingratiated his way into the village's business community. We were a close-knit group. When he got to know one of us, he knew us all. We trusted him. At first." She looked at me. "Your grandfather came around earlier and told me that that man had been murdered. Right down at the falls."

"PopPop told you that?" I asked, surprised.

She nodded. She was sucking on the nuts, maybe making them soft enough to chew.

"Here," I said. I slid the carton of Ghoulish Blueberry in front of her. "I brought it all for you anyway."

She grinned. "Thank you," she said, and stuck her spoon in.

"What else did my PopPop say?" I asked.

"That now Wally could rest in peace."

"So why didn't Mr. Keller pay the taxes off with the money he got? Or pay off Ari?"

"The check that Mr. Bayard gave him wasn't any good."

"Ohhh," I said.

"I think they were in on it together. Him and that dirt guy."

"Ari and Stephen?"

"Yes. And we only owed eighteen thousand dollars."

"On taxes?"

"Yes, now mind you that might seem like a lot, but our business was worth much more than that."

"So I don't understand."

"What don't you understand?" she asked.

"If the business was worth more and you only owed taxes, how could someone else get it?"

"If you owe taxes to someone, they can foreclose on your property after a year."

"Oh," I said, and nodded slowly.

"That Ari offered Wally little to nothing on the building and all the equipment. Said he was saving us from having to go through the court process of a foreclosure. We were old by then. Had had a good run with the business and just figured it was for the best."

"That's terrible," I said.

"They hurt a lot of people around here."

I wondered how Ari still showed his face around the village. Maisie was right, he wasn't that good of a guy.

"I've heard," I said. "I wasn't really old enough to understand what all the legal and business stuff was when it was happening. A lot of people got hurt."

"When I first heard it—and don't you mention a word of this to anyone"—she lowered her voice like she was divulging a secret—"but I thought it might be Danny Clawson that did it. I'd never say anything if he did, though. That man hurt that boy more than anyone else."

"I heard," I said. "You think Danny knew that Stephen Bayard was in town?"

"I don't know." She shrugged. "He's got a steady job and visiting with his father keeps him busy. But he comes and checks on all of us. All the people wronged by that man. Helps us out. Maybe somebody told him that Mr. Bayard was back in town."

"Danny helps out?"

"Yes, he does. Mows our grass. Rakes our leaves. Shovels our snow. He always keeps your grandfather's walkway clear. Whether it's winter's snow or fall's leaves."

"I thought PopPop shoveled his own snow."

"Nope. Danny did it. He puts my storm windows in for me every October and comes back in the spring and puts in the screens. Does odd jobs for me, too. Like going to the store and such."

I scrunched up my face. "I don't remember seeing him around."

"He doesn't like to be seen. Real good at not being seen, too," she said. "That's why I was thinking if he did kill that man, he'd probably be able to get away with it."

# chapter TWENTY-EIGHT

It wasn't my alarm that woke me from the first good sleep I'd had in two days, it was the knock on my door.

*Who in the world . . .*

I slid out of bed and dragged my feet down the hallway. My eyes still not completely opened, I peeked as best I could out the hole in the door.

"Ugh," I groaned. "I should have known," I muttered as I undid the dead bolt.

"How come you've been ignoring my texts?"

"Morning, Maisie," I said.

"And how come you're not up? It's four fifteen."

"My alarm is set for four thirty. But I don't have to make ice cream today. Riya and my mother made some yesterday. So I really don't have to be up early."

"Oh," she said.

"What do you want?" I asked. "Why are you up so early?"

"Because you didn't answer any of my texts last night." She

scratched her head. "Didn't I just say that? Don't try to get me confused."

"I'm sorry," I said. "I meant to answer your text."

I waved her in, and she had hardly gotten into the apartment before she started asking questions.

"What were you doing? Out with O?"

"Oh my goodness, Maisie." I plopped down on the couch.

"What?" she said, sitting in a chair across from me. "He likes you. Stands to reason he'd ask you out."

"I don't like him," I said.

"Why?" she asked, a look of utter confusion on her face.

I stopped to think about that. There really wasn't any reason. He was nice-looking. Smart. And a good customer. He hadn't missed a day coming in since he found out that we were open.

I shook my head. I didn't want to think about him.

"Want to know what I found out about Ari last night?" I knew that would make her get off the subject of Professor Morrison Kaye.

"About Ari?" she asked, her eyes lighting up. "Tell me."

So I did. I filled her in on what Lew had told me and what I'd found out from Mrs. Keller about one Mr. Ari Terrain.

"See why I don't like him?" she said when I finished that part of the story. "He is rotten to the core."

"Knowing that might also explain what that email you had was about."

"Oh yeah," she said, nodding in agreement. "Ari owed him because he helped him get that restaurant by not giving Mr. Keller the money."

"Right," I said, and yawned.

Then I told her what Lew and Mrs. Keller said about how so many of the village's business owners had been wronged by Bad Boy Bayard. And how she was thinking that Danny might be the killer.

"You know, this case might be like that book *Murder on the Orient Express*. Everyone stabbed him."

"Stephen Bayard wasn't stabbed."

"The guy in the book was stabbed," Maisie said. "My analogy goes to the way the murder was committed, not what it was committed with."

"Oh. Sorry." I held back a giggle. I knew this was serious, especially to me since it involved my father. And Maisie wasn't joking about anything. Not even about showing up to my door at four in the morning.

"Lew is right," Maisie said. "We need to start asking questions."

"I agree," I said.

"So you know what we have to do now then, right?" she said.

"What?" I asked.

"Talk to Danny Clawson."

"Lew said to not ask questions to a potential murderer."

"He was talking about Ari."

"He was talking about anyone who had it in him to kill someone."

"Danny Clawson wouldn't hurt us. We're part of the people he's trying to protect."

"He is not the people's vigilante," I said. "If he could murder one person, he could murder two. Or three." I swung a finger back and forth between us.

"Well, we should at least watch him," she said.

"Watch him do what?"

"Because maybe he plans on killing Ari next. If so, he'll probably go shopping at Home Depot or something. Pick up duct tape, rope, shovels. We should keep an eye on him."

"Oh brother," I said. "If he did kill Stephen Bayard, he didn't stop at Home Depot first. Remember? He was killed with succinylcholine."

"Then by following him, maybe we can find out where he got the succinylcholine from," Maisie said. "That would definitely give the police enough to go on so they wouldn't suspect your father anymore."

There was an idea.

"Wait. I thought you thought Ari was the killer."

She blew out a breath. "He still might be. But now we have a new suspect, with just as good of a motive."

"What was Ari's motive?" I asked. "He and Stephen Bayard were con artist buddies."

"Blackmail," we both said at the same time.

"Yep," I said. "I forgot about that, although I did think about it when I spoke to Mrs. Keller." I bit my bottom lip and let my head bobble. "Okay. So now we have two suspects."

"Yep," Maisie said. "Two."

"If we're watching Danny Clawson, shouldn't we watch Ari, too?" I asked.

"I guess," she said.

"Only that's impossible unless we split up," I said.

"I don't want to do that."

I looked at her. "Well, we'll figure that out later. I do want to see what's up with Danny Clawson, so we can watch him first."

"Maybe have a conversation with him."

"Maybe," I said.

Lew had told me to be careful, but I wasn't going to find anything out by just watching people. As soon as I had said it to Maisie, I knew that it wasn't going to work. Not if I wanted to clear my father's name.

I didn't let Maisie know I'd come around, though. I would just let the opportunity present itself and we'd go from there.

Right then, however, it was too early in the morning to do any talking or watching. The only people in the village who were up besides the two of us were probably the garbage collectors.

"Whatever we do," I said, "it'll have to wait at least until daybreak."

"Okay," she said. "How about while we wait, we make a murder board."

"A what?"

"Get all of your different-color sticky notes and one of your vision boards."

"Write down our clues." I looked at her and gave an abbreviated nod. "List the things we know?" I was right with her on that. It was how I liked to operate.

I tore the cellophane off brand-new sticky notes for this project. I had a fresh stash under the bed that I kept in a plastic tub along with colored felt-tip pens and new journals.

Maisie and I jotted down everything we knew, which admittedly at this point wasn't very much. We brainstormed on how we might find out more, googled Danny Clawson's address and tried to figure out how the victim and the murderer got past me, all while eating Cheetos and drinking Cotton Club Cherry Strawberry for our breakfast.

But really what we were doing was biding our time until it got to be a reasonable enough hour to go and spy on Danny Clawson and find something usable.

Something that might clear my daddy from being a murder suspect.

# chapter TWENTY-NINE

"We need to stop by my parents' house," I said.

We were in Maisie's little green VW bug, headed out on our spy mission. She had insisted we go by her house so she could change into "spy" clothing. Whatever that meant. I'd thrown on a pair of jeans, a black turtleneck sweater and black military-like boots.

The sun was shining on us and it did seem it might be a little warmer out than it had been the past few days. It was ice cream weather.

"Where's your sun visor?" I asked, pulling mine down. We were headed east, and the newly risen sun was beaming through the windows into our eyes.

"It kept falling down."

"So?"

"It was nerve-racking," she said. "I just tore it out."

"Is that what those little wires are?" I pointed.

"Yeah." She glanced up at them. "They were for the lighted mirror."

"Did you think maybe, since it kept falling, you could get it fixed?"

"It was broken, Win." She said it like her actions made perfect sense. "I couldn't use it."

"Right," I said.

"So why are we stopping at your parents'?" Maisie asked. "We don't want to miss Danny."

"I don't know that we'll even see Danny"—Maisie started to balk—"even though I know that's our plan," I said. "But I want to check in with them and PopPop."

"Good idea," Maisie said. "Keep them unsuspecting."

"I don't think they would suspect me of going around playing amateur sleuth," I said. "Especially with something this serious."

"That's why we're doing it," she said. "Because it's very serious."

"I know," I said. "But I'd rather they not know."

"Don't they think you could do it?"

"You know my parents, Maisie. In academics, I'm an independent shining star. And even though they supported me one hundred percent in renovating and reopening the shop under my management, they still worry."

"My grandmother, not that I'm telling her," Maisie said, "wouldn't mind me playing sleuth at all."

"That's because your grandmother likes to have her nose in everything," I said.

"I'm telling Savta you said that."

"Don't tell her," I said. "I'm truly sorry I said that out loud."

"Oh, but it's what you were thinking?"

"I plead the fifth."

"Oh!" Maisie's eyes got big. "What about Lew?"

"What about Lew?"

"He might tell." She gave me one of her all-knowing nods.

"He won't tell. I made him promise not to." I glanced over at her. "Plus, I could tell that he thought I should do it. Even told me what to do and what not to do."

"That's true," she said. "And you can use that against him if he decided to spill the beans."

We pulled up in front of my parents' house.

"Okay," Maisie said. "Don't be long. We have to see what we can find out and be done by the time you need to open the shop."

"I got it," I said, and hopped out of the car.

I strolled up the walkway to my parents' house, I'm sure at a much slower pace than Maisie would've liked. But I was nervous. Lately when I'd seen my father, I'd started to cry. There had been too many people at our family dinner to get misty eyes, but I didn't want to cry again. I was sure that was nothing Miss Marple or Maisie's Agatha Raisin would do.

And I didn't want to give away what I was doing either. I didn't want them to worry. Lew had said it right. I was the baby. And a girl. After three rambunctious boys, my parents had been so proud and happy to have me. And cautious. They still were.

"Morning!" I called out as I opened the door.

"We're back here," my mother answered.

I walked down the center hallway, not bothering to take my coat off. I wasn't sure Maisie was giving me that much time.

"What are you guys doing?" I asked when I got to the back.

My parents and PopPop were sitting in the breakfast nook.

"No," my father said.

"Nothing to worry about," my mother said.

"We're talking about getting your father a lawyer," PopPop said.

"Dad," my father said, clearly perturbed with his father.

"She needs to know," PopPop said. "Everyone's going to know sooner or later."

Those non-sleuth-like tears started welling up in my eyes again.

"Did something else happen?" I asked. "Is Detective Beverly wanting to arrest you just because you work with succinylcholine?"

All three of them turned and looked at me.

"Looks like she might already know," PopPop said.

"I overheard him questioning you the other day," I said. "I came over. Through the back." I motioned my head toward the mudroom. "I heard you three talking."

"Well, it's nothing for you to worry about," my mother said.

"I don't see why you think you can't tell me things. I'm almost thirty years old. I lived in New York. Not the safest place in the world. You were fine with that."

"We worried about you every minute," my mother said. "I went through more hair dye than I ever have."

"We can't help but worry about you, Pumpkin," my father said. "But I don't want you to worry about this. Or me. Everything is going to be fine."

"Well, I can't help but to worry, Daddy." I held out my hands. "I love you. And you should tell me what happens with you. You tell the boys."

"That's different," my mother said.

"No, it's not," I said, shaking my head vigorously. "And I can help."

"You can't help," my father said. "Plus, there's nothing to worry about right now."

"What's happening?" I asked.

This time the three of them looked at each other.

"Tell me," I said.

"Detective Beverly just wants to question me again," my father said.

"At the station," my mother added.

"Right," my father said. "And we were just thinking if I should get a lawyer to go down there with me."

"Are you scared, Daddy?" I asked.

He chuckled. "No, Pumpkin. I'm not scared. No reason to be." He looked at me. "I didn't do anything."

"I know you didn't," I said. "And I'm going to make sure that Detective Beverly knows it."

"What is that supposed to mean, Bronwyn?" my mother said. That was her I-mean-business voice.

*Oops,* I thought.

"Nothing," I said. "And I have to go. Maisie is waiting for me out front."

"Don't try doing anything," my father said. "We're going to take care of this."

"I'm not."

"Then why did you say you were going to make sure that detective knew your father hadn't done anything?" my mother said. She stood up from her chair.

"I just meant," I said, "that since I am the only eyewitness, I would let him know, again if necessary, that I didn't see Daddy that night."

"Yeah, well, make sure that's all you say to that man," my mother said. "And why are you out so early? You don't need to make any ice cream this morning. Riya and I made enough yesterday."

I hated lying to my parents.

I drew in a breath. "I have a business to run. A family business." Not a lie.

"Okay," Mother said. "I'll be down later."

I turned to walk away, then turned back. "Daddy, when do you have to talk to Detective Beverly?"

"Either this afternoon or tomorrow. I told him I'd have to let him know my schedule at the hospital. Why?" he asked. "I don't want you coming down there."

"Not even to show my support?" I asked.

"No, Pumpkin. I already know you support me." He got up, came over and gave me a hug. "And that means more to me than you'll ever know."

I gave each of my parents a kiss on the cheek before I left, and told them I loved them.

"OKAY," I SAID, hopping back in the car. "Let's go."

"Everything okay in there?"

"No," I said. "And we need to find out who killed Stephen Bayard before it will be."

"What happened?"

"My father is going to call a lawyer to go and talk with that Liam Beverly."

"For what? I thought he already talked to him," she said.

"This time he wants to talk to my father at the station."

"That can't be good," Maisie said, visibly shaken by the news. Even her little curls on her head were trembling.

"It's not good," I said. I looked at her. "Well, are you going or not?" I gave her knee a push as if that would move the gas pedal. "Let's go. We've got a killer to catch."

Maisie drove the few blocks over to Danny Clawson's house like we were going to a fire. I had to hold on as she hit all the bumps and potholes that were typical in the streets of Cleveland with its shilly-shally weather.

"We should've brought the Cheetos," Maisie said. After driving past it a couple of times, we parked a few houses down and stared at the house. "Because what are we supposed to do while we wait?"

"This does seem rather silly," I said. "We watch the house. We watch him come out of the house." I glanced at her. "That helps how?"

"Murderers always do things to give themselves away," Maisie said. "That's what we're watching for."

"Let's hope that if he is the murderer, he hurries up and gives himself away," I said. "I don't know what that Detective Beverly is thinking and I don't want him doing anything to my father."

"We'll catch him doing something," she said. "I'm sure of it."

"Good, because I'm thinking that's him right there."

A man was coming out of the house we'd determined had belonged to Dan Clawson Sr. before he took up residence at a nursing home. We hadn't been able to find a picture online for Danny. Not on Facebook, LinkedIn or the prison inmate locater we had used to find Stephen Bayard.

This guy was tall, but he walked with his shoulders slumped

and head down. He took measured, pointed steps, barely letting his heels touch the ground as he moved.

He wore a plaid hunting cap, a brown corduroy winter jacket and canvas sneakers. I hoped he didn't wear those when he was out shoveling snow.

"That has to be him," Maisie said.

He walked down to the tree lawn and put the trash he was carrying in a plastic bag into the trash can that was parked there, then disappeared around the side of the house.

Maisie put her hand on the door handle. "We should go talk to him," she said.

"What happened to watching him?" I asked, reaching over to grab her hand if necessary.

"What do you mean? We decided to talk to him."

"We decided that we would try," I said. "But that doesn't mean we ambush him at his house to do it. Only if the opportunity presents itself." I could read the look of frustration in her eyes. "Anyway, we can't now." I pointed. A car was pulling out of the driveway. "I'm thinking that's him."

"Okay, we follow." It was a half question, half statement. But I knew she was ready to go.

"Yes, Maisie," I said. "We follow."

And she took off. Red lights, babies, children and old people beware!

"WHY ARE WE hiding?" Maisie asked. I still had a tight grasp on her arm. She had that same look of determination she'd had the whole drive over.

We were at the Falls Park Senior Complex, standing behind a wall. It was where Danny Clawson—although we had yet to positively identify him—came after he'd made two stops. Neither stop, however, to the chagrin of Maisie, was to a Home Depot.

His first stop had been to the bakery on South Franklin Street and then he'd gone to the CVS on Plaza Drive. Both times he'd come out of the store with a single plastic bag. He climbed back into his old brown Jeep, never lifting his head, and each time I'd had to restrain Maisie from swooping down to browbeat him with the myriad of questions she had come up with while we were tailing him. His last stop was where we were now.

Falls Park was a combination of assisted living, senior rehab and nursing home. I believed it to be the one where Dan Clawson resided, although, as it were, we were now too busy hiding to ascertain the truth of the matter.

"We're standing here because I don't want her to see me," I said. "She'll think I'm spying on her."

"Who is 'she'?" Maisie asked.

"Glynis Vale."

"And who is that?" Maisie said a little louder than I cared for her to, while at the same time popping her head out to get a peek at her.

"A suspect."

"She's not a suspect," Maisie said. "We only have two suspects. Ari Terrain and Danny Clawson."

"I forgot to tell you about this one."

"How could you forget?" she asked.

"Because we decided that the killer had to be a man."

"Is that something else you've changed without telling me?" Maisie asked.

"No," I said. "But look where she just went." Maisie popped her head back out to see, and I had to jerk her back. "I didn't mean that literally."

Glynis Vale, dressed in cobalt-blue scrub pants and a white scrub shirt that had pictures of stethoscopes, thermometers and Band-Aids on it, had appeared not long after Danny came in. She pushed a little medical-like cart down the hallway and stopped right at the doorway that Danny had disappeared into. She'd sauntered in and had been in there ever since.

"Amateur sleuths aren't afraid of being caught snooping," Maisie said. "They just make up a story and wiggle their way out of it."

"Yeah, I noticed that was your attitude when Althea caught us in Ari's office."

She gave me a look that said that was the way it was supposed to be.

"We're not on television," I said. "There's no guarantee that we'd come back for next week's show."

"What does that mean?"

"This is real life, is what I mean. Danny and that woman"—I pointed around the corner to where they were—"might just be murderers who might just kill us, too, if they find out we're onto them." I gave her arm a yank and pulled her behind me, going the opposite way. "We have to be careful."

"Where are we going?" Maisie cried as I dragged her out the door.

"To regroup."

I marched her out to the car and made her get in it.

"We need to think," I said as we sat inside of it.

"We need to ask questions," Maisie said. "And we can't do that from here."

"Things have changed and we need to figure out what we want to ask."

"What has changed?" Her eyebrows went up and her hands went out. "And who exactly is Glynis Vale and how is she a suspect?"

I explained to her who Glynis Vale was. When I let her know how she was a liar and that her son had appeared by the falls at the same time the dead man did, she calmed down by at least fifty degrees.

"Why didn't you tell me about her?" she asked.

"I told Detective Beverly and he dismissed it. And then, like I said, we decided the killer was probably a man."

"Did we change our mind about that?"

"No. Not necessarily. But if Glynis Vale knows Danny Clawson and she works at a nursing facility, maybe she was the supplier of the succinylcholine."

"Oh yeah," Maisie said. "They were in it together."

"Right." I shifted in my seat to face her. "Didn't you say that if we followed Danny he might lead us to his source?"

She nodded slowly.

"And that the murderer always does something to give himself away?"

She nodded slower.

"Well, maybe he just did that."

"And now we need to decide what to do next."

"Exactly," I said.

"Why would Glynis want to kill Stephen Bayard?" Maisie asked.

"I don't know," I said. "We have a motive for the other two suspects." I studied my fingernails as I clicked them together. "Maybe"—I wanted to try this theory on for size—"Glynis didn't have a grudge against Con Man Bayard at all. Maybe she did it for Danny."

"Because she loves him and will do anything to help him, including exacting revenge on the man who ruined his life." This time Maisie was nodding at her own conclusions.

"Oh brother," I said, and rolled my eyes. "You do watch too much TV."

# chapter THIRTY

Maisie and I determined we'd have to find out more about Glynis Vale. We decided we'd watch her—going with Maisie's theory that guilty people always do something to tell on themselves.

Although, somewhere down deep, I hoped that wasn't true, because then my family would know that I'd lied to them.

I had a hard time convincing Maisie that we needed to first just watch what she did. She thought that would take too long to get to the bottom of everything.

"Well, if you're not going to talk to her, how will we find out if she did it?" Maisie had asked.

"What are we supposed to ask her?" I asked. "We found out a lot just watching Danny."

"We need to ask her something," Maisie said. "Maybe we could get her to confess."

"Or maybe we would just make her mad and she wouldn't say anything," I said.

"Okay. So we'll follow her and watch her."

"Yes."

"Then, after that," she said, "we'll figure out what we're going to ask her."

Maisie wasn't giving up.

We headed to the ice cream shop and made plans to get together to work on what questions we'd ask her and set a time to follow her. We weren't sure what shift she worked, but Maisie said she'd try to find out. I didn't know how she was planning to do that.

There wasn't much to do at the ice cream shop to get ready for the day. We'd had no more than ten customers trickle in the day after opening and after my social media blast. And although after I'd counted up sales for the third day of operation and found we'd had about seventeen people come in altogether, I hadn't done anything to get more people coming through the door.

Not long after we pulled up, PopPop pulled up behind us. I smiled and waved, waiting for him to get out of his car.

"Morning again," I said. "You hanging out with us today?"

"If you'll have me," he said.

"PopPop," I said. "It's still your store."

He laughed. "It's *our* store."

I let the three of us into the side door and Felice was there waiting.

"Hey, little sugar," I said. I stooped down and kissed her on her forehead. "You been wondering where I was?"

She blinked her eyes at me and meowed.

"I'm here now," I said, standing up. "You can go sit on your throne now if you want."

With that, she turned around, her tail dragging low to the floor, and sashayed out to the front to take her place on the window seat.

"I wonder what Rivkah is up to," PopPop said, and glanced toward the back stairs.

"I'm sure she's getting ready to go over to the restaurant," I said.

"Maybe I'll just pop up and say hello," he said, his eyes lingering.

Maisie and I smiled at each other.

My mother breezed in just as PopPop headed up the steps. "Hi. Morning. Morning," she said with her usual energy. So different than when I'd seen her two hours ago.

"Hi again, Mommy," I said.

"Today is the day," she said. "It's going to be nice out. Like forty degrees. It's ice cream weather."

I chuckled. That was the same thing I had thought.

"Cleveland's the only place where people think forty degrees is good weather," PopPop said, coming back around the corner.

"I thought you were visiting with Rivkah," I said.

"She's ready to leave. Go over to her restaurant," he said. "I'm going to drive her."

"It's three doors down, PopPop," I said.

"When you get to be our age," he said, putting his hat back on his head, "you like to go for rides."

"I'm surprised you drove," I said. "You always walk down here."

"Lately," he said, "I've needed the car."

I wasn't sure what that meant. He and my mother had been cryptic lately, so I didn't ask.

"Mom," I said, turning back to her. "Tell me again why you're here. I thought you had an appointment."

"Because you said you had to get ready for the events the shop is doing over at the college," she said. "I didn't want you getting bogged down."

*Oh yeah . . .* I *had* told her all the things I had to do. Most of them I hadn't needed to do, I just told her I did to answer her questions about my being out and about so early.

"I'll go out front," my mother said. "PopPop, when you get back from frolicking with Rivkah, you can help out."

"I've got help coming in," I said, wondering if I needed to remind her of my hired help.

PopPop got back about an hour after he'd left and sat on his bench. Maisie left right after twelve o'clock with a conspiratorial wink and an Arnold Schwarzenegger–accented, "I'll be back." We'd had maybe five customers when my father came through the door.

"Surprise!" my mother said. "I told him you needed help."

*Guess I do need to remind her I have hired help.*

"Hi, Daddy," I said, going around the counter to give him a hug.

"Hey, Pumpkin," he said.

He was dressed in black jogging pants, a light gray Crewse Creamery sweatshirt and a matching gray baseball cap, and Nike tennis shoes.

"Don't you look cute?" I said.

"Thank you," he said, and squeezed me tight. "You been busy today?" He stretched his neck, looking around the store.

"Busy as it has been so far."

He squinted. "And that means what?"

I shrugged. "Five or six customers."

"That's better than the first day," he said.

"One customer is better than the first day," I said. "But it's been picking up a little in the evenings."

"That means I got here just in time."

"Yep," I said, not mentioning my help, who would be in shortly. "And I appreciate you coming."

"I love coming to help out in the shop," he said. "Reminds me of when I was little and my mother was here."

"I've never known you to come help out."

"Well, when you were little, I was trying to build my practice, and then when Aunt Jack took it over—"

"I know," I said, putting up a hand to stop him, "there is no getting along with Aunt Jack."

"No, there isn't," he said, and chuckled. "I'm wondering how that man she found on the internet is faring. I bet he's pulling his hair out by now."

I laughed.

"So should I put on an apron or something?" Daddy said, looking around.

"That's up to you." I nodded. "But I think Mommy just wants you here."

"She's worried about me." He glanced toward the front of the store.

"I'm worried about you, too," I said.

"My two girls." He shook his head. "I'm supposed to be taking care of you so you don't have to worry about anything. Especially me."

"Why aren't you at work?" I could just imagine the hospital putting him on leave or something until everything was resolved.

"I took off to talk to that detective." He blew out a breath. "But the lawyer I retained couldn't do it until day after tomorrow. He's in court or something until then." He looked at me. "Guess I'll have to call off again."

I chewed on my bottom lip, clicked my nails and looked at him.

"What is it, Pumpkin?" he said. "I know when you start that annoying clicking of your nails, something is up."

"Is that annoying?" I said, and looked down at my hand.

"You want to ask me something?" he said instead of answering my question.

"I do," I said. "But I'm scared of the answer."

"Scared? Why?"

"I don't know."

"You don't ever have to be afraid to ask me anything. Go ahead. Ask me." He took my hand and held it.

"Why did you tell me that you'd come from work that night when I found the body? You weren't dressed for work."

He looked down at his clothes like they were the ones he'd had on and they could give him answers. There was a confused look on his face.

"I—I was at work," he said.

"Daddy," I said, disappointment written into my face. "I've never seen you go to work looking like that. Sweat pants. Boots."

"Oh," he chuckled. "That's because I don't usually see my patients at a snowy, muddy sports camp." He must've noticed the puzzled look in my eyes. "James wanted me to see one of his patients. I went to meet James and he took one look at me in my tailored suit and said that wouldn't do. Not where we were going.

Those were James's clothes you saw me in. He gave them to me to wear."

I could've fallen on the floor with relief. My brother James and a whole sports team were my daddy's alibi.

"Did you tell the detective that yet?" I asked.

"No, by the time he asked me that question I had decided not to answer anything else. I told him I'd wait to get a lawyer," he said. "You were there that night, you didn't hear me?"

"I didn't hear the whole thing, I guess," I said. "I came in after you had started talking and I left before you finished. I don't remember hearing that part." I thought about it. "Although, with all the blood that had drained from my head listening to that conversation, I might have been there but missed it."

He shook his head. "You shouldn't eavesdrop."

"Yeah. I'm learning that." I looked at him and smiled. "So, Daddy, this is good. Why do you even have to go in to speak to him about this? Tell your lawyer to tell him your alibi."

"Oh, no." My father shook his head. "You don't understand. There is still a time discrepancy. I'm not out of the woods."

"What do you mean?" I asked. "You said you were with James."

"You asked why I had been dressed like that," he said. "And that was why. But it seems like from the timeline that detective gave, it puts me close enough to home to have been around when it happened."

"Were you around?"

"I was, I guess," he said, and huffed. "After I left the sports camp, I stopped by the cemetery to see Ma. Ailbhe had told me that man was in town and it made me think about her. I wanted to go and talk to her."

My grandmother was buried in Evergreen Hill Cemetery. Not five minutes from where Stephen Bayard was found.

That wasn't good.

"How long did you stay there?"

"I don't know." He shrugged. "A good while. I pulled one of my vinyl chairs out of the trunk of my car. And I sat and had a long chat with her."

"Did you tell the detective that? Because I'm sure there are security cameras for him to look at to prove where you were."

"I don't know how much movement they get at a cemetery, Win. Or theft. Probably no need for video cameras at a place like that."

All that despair I'd felt when I heard the police detective questioning my father came crashing down on me again. I started trembling and my mouth went dry. My father must have seen all the grief that had started to envelop me.

"Aww, Pumpkin. It's going to be okay," he said, and wrapped his arms around me. "I didn't do it. And they don't have any evidence that I did."

"People get railroaded," I said, remembering Lew's words.

"They do, but I won't." He pulled me tighter into his bear hug. "I'm sorry you have to go through this. That man caused us so much grief in life, and now he's trying to do the same thing to us in death. But I won't let that happen."

# chapter THIRTY-ONE

Ohio has three big cities situated at the top, bottom and in the middle of it. Nearly everything in between is farmland.

Chagrin Falls, albeit a suburb of the city that is home to the Rock & Roll Hall of Fame, was on the outskirts of Cleveland and just a hop, skip and jump away from its rural areas. Wycliffe was set right beyond the village's boundaries. About a twenty-minute drive. Beyond it was cornfields.

The university was expansive, expensive and all about academia. The alumni were active and the surrounding community supportive. There were always endowments for new, modern buildings that comingled with the finely weathered structures still standing from the school's inception in 1902. The university had various graduate colleges within the school, including one of the state's ten law schools and a school of pharmacy.

Clara Blackwell's office was at the back of campus, a little fact I was unaware of when I had Maisie park at the front. She had insisted on driving me out so we could finish discussing plans on how to get information from Danny and Glynis. Our conversation didn't get that far after I told her that my father was hiring a lawyer. That was all she could talk about the rest of the way out.

It had taken me a good ten minutes to find Clara's office, stopping to ask for directions three or four times. Two of my brothers had attended the institution, but the only thing I could manage after their matriculation was how to find the dorm room buildings.

The snow along the walkways had all been cleared. Pushed back to the edge, it was dirty and crunchy. Piled up like ice on a snow cone. Certainly not anything satisfactory enough to be used for ice cream. I saw a melting snowman next to the sign in front of Stanton Library, snowboards leaning against the front of the University Center and college kids dressed in colorful parkas, hats and scarfs, and some in just sweatpants and hoodies.

"Hi, Win," Clara Blackwell said. Her office was in a small building by itself. A square-shaped one-story, it opened to a lobby with lots of flyers and pamphlets, multicolored upholstered chairs and tables with yearbooks and odd periodicals strewn across them. She stepped out of her office some five minutes after her receptionist announced my arrival.

"Hi, Clara," I said, and held up the paper bag that had the two pints of ice cream she'd asked me to bring and gave it a little shake.

"Oh good!" she said. "C'mon in. I was just finalizing everything with our caterer." She stood back, holding the door open and gesturing for me to come in. I smiled politely and acknowledged her greeting with one of my own as I stepped inside her office. I turned my gaze to take in the rest of the room, and there, sitting in front of her desk, was Ari Terrain.

He was the caterer.

"After you said you'd come by here, Win, and Mr. Terrain wanted to schedule a meeting, I thought it might be good for you two to meet each other." Her head went back and forth between us as she spoke.

"Hi, Ari," I said, trying to sound cheerful, giving a quick wave of my hand. Still a little embarrassed from being caught in his office, I tried not to let that show. After all, even though I'd seen Danny and Glynis together, who in my eyes were a better pair of suspects than Ari, he was someone I still considered a part of this whole murder thing I was trying to figure out.

I eyed him, trying not to give away what I was thinking, and wondered how he could go around acting normal if he really had done something like that.

Ari licked his lips and ran fingers over his chin, smoothing down the hair of his beard. He rose from his chair to greet me. His winter jacket was draped over his arm and he was dressed casually in brown slacks and a tan sweater.

"Hi, Win," he said.

"Oh wait," Clara said, a surprised look on her face. "Do you two already know each other?"

"Sure we do," I said, putting the phoniest smile I could muster on my face. "My friend Maisie works at his restaurant. Plus"—I glanced at her—"the business community in the village is close-knit." I used Mrs. Keller's words. "We are all acquainted."

"Oh," Clara said, and looked between the two of us. "So, will your friend help out serving at the dinner?"

I didn't say anything. I knew how much Maisie disliked Ari

and I was sure she wouldn't want to help him out. I wasn't even sure she was still working at the restaurant. I couldn't even remember the last time she'd gone into work.

"No," Ari said. "I can't take my people away from the restaurant. I have a special crew."

"Oh, of course," Clara Blackwell said. "Okay." She rubbed her hands together and took in a breath. "Ari, you're going to check out the kitchen and the dining area, correct?"

"Yes." He gave her a businesslike, courteous smile. "I would like to do that. If that's okay."

"That'll be fine," she said. "And what about you, Win? Would you like to see the area where you'll be working as well?

"Sure," I said.

My plan was to bring our frozen dessert cart, which I had just ordered, and set it up there. I didn't think I would need any of the university's facilities except for maybe a freezer. But it was my first event and I didn't want to act as if I didn't know what the pre-event drill entailed, even if I didn't. If he needed to see the area, I figured I needed to see it, too.

Clara signed the contracts while Ari waited in the lobby. She assured me that if we needed anything, especially since it was such short notice, the university would be happy to help out.

We met back up with Ari, and Clara, in her heels, walked with us over to the banquet facility. We passed by the smaller room where the ice cream social would take place the following week, and she pointed it out to me.

"And we can use any of the ovens in here?" Ari asked. We stood in the middle of the full-service kitchen. His questions made me think that he'd been hired last minute just like us.

"As I explained to you earlier, and as I told Win before we left the office, everything we have is at your disposal," Clara said. "We're just happy you both could accommodate us on such short notice."

Ari walked the area a few more times and I followed suit. Then Clara had to go, and left the two of us alone.

I didn't have the same feelings of anger for Ari that Maisie held. But after hearing Mrs. Keller's story and my best friend thinking he had to have been the one to kill Stephen Bayard, I felt some enmity for him. Before, I hadn't felt anything for him, and my newfound feelings gave me a little courage. Despite what Lew had warned, I decided to question him. It was the perfect opportunity, and I didn't think Ari would try to harm me. At least not at the university. Too many people around. I didn't feel he'd confess anything to me either. But I was hoping he might give me something more to go on.

Thinking like Maisie, I knew I needed more pieces to the puzzle. Lew had said I had to put all the clues together. This was the perfect opportunity to do that.

"This is good business for your shop," Ari said. I knew he was making polite small talk, but that wasn't the way I wanted to steer the conversation.

"I heard you were hiring criminals to work at your restaurant," I said.

"Excuse me?"

"Stephen Bayard," I said. "He worked for you."

"You heard me tell the police that I didn't know a Stephen Bayard."

"I heard you tell the police a lie," I said.

He looked as if he was about to say something, but instead he just turned and walked away.

I turned on my heels and followed him.

"You know they think my father killed him."

"Killed Stephen?" he asked. He turned and glanced at me, but didn't stop walking.

"Yes. But I've been thinking maybe you did it."

"What part of 'I don't know him' don't you understand?" he said.

"So," I said. "Do you know the Pink Panther?"

"What is it that you want?" This time he stopped moving.

"I want to know if you killed Stephen Bayard."

"No, I didn't," he said. "Now if that's all . . ." He started walking again.

I followed him.

"Is your plan to follow me until I confess?" he asked, a wicked smile on his face.

"Mrs. Keller told me how you got the restaurant."

"How I got the rest— Oh," he said, and nodded. "I didn't do anything illegal. Foreclosing on tax-delinquent properties is set up by the court. It's done all the time."

"That part was probably legal, but what you had Stephen Bayard do, offer Mr. Keller a way out with no intentions of making good on it, was wrong."

"That was all on Stephen Bayard," he said.

"The man you didn't know," I said.

"The man I didn't know," he said.

"Was Stephen Bayard blackmailing you?"

"You sure are full of information," he said. "What makes you think that?"

"You had to have a reason to kill him."

He noisily pulled up air through his nostrils. I could see them flare. He didn't like my questions.

"I didn't kill him, but there were a lot of reasons that I could have."

"You wanted to?" I asked.

"As I'm sure a lot of people did. But I didn't do it," he said. "I just needed him to leave me alone."

"Leave you alone," I said. "How was he bothering you?" I wanted to laugh at the thought.

"Look, Stephen Bayard was a bad guy," he said. "And for a while I was traveling down that same path. Right with him." He raked his fingers on his beard. "We did some things together. In the past. Things I wasn't proud of. But I have a different life now. A life I like, and I wasn't turning back, and that's what he wanted me to do."

"How did he want you to turn back?" I asked.

"You're not going to stop, are you?"

I raised an eyebrow.

"I'll tell you because I didn't do it." He shrugged. "I have nothing to hide."

"Okay," I said. "Tell me."

"He wanted to get his old crew together. Do another job. But I wasn't in on it. He came here to convince me. But it didn't work."

"Is that why you killed him?"

"I didn't kill him," he said.

"Where were you the night he died?"

"Not that it's any of your business," he said, "but I was at home. I wasn't feeling well, so I stayed in. By myself. And before you ask"—he glanced over at me—"I don't have anyone to corroborate my story."

He walked off, and this time I didn't follow. We had made it to a parking lot and I assumed it was where he'd parked. I stood and watched as he got into his car and drove off, not moving a muscle until he was out of sight.

Then I thought about how uncomfortable it was going to be to work with him at the President's Dinner.

"Hey, Win." I turned at the sound of my name to see who had called me.

"O," I said. I *would* run into him.

"What are you doing here?" he asked.

I turned to make sure Ari had driven off. I didn't want him to see me standing around. Then I turned back to speak to O. "Just finalizing everything with Clara Blackwell for the event."

"President's Dinner."

"Yes." I nodded. "Thank you again for that," I said. "It couldn't have come at a better time."

"No problem," he said. "I was happy to recommend you."

"She's also booked us for an ice cream social for a sorority that's coming up. So that's two things to thank you for."

"I'll be there," he said.

"At the ice cream social?" I asked.

"No." He chuckled. "At the President's Dinner." He put his head down. "Although, I could stop through at the other event. But it is a, you know, undergraduate event."

Why was he telling me he could stop by? This was getting weird.

"Well," I said, looking up at the sky. The universal sign of noting the weather. "I guess I'd better be going. It's too cold to be standing around out here."

"Where'd you park?" he asked. "I'll walk you to your car."

All I needed was for Maisie to see me with O. All she'd known to say after we'd met him was that he liked me.

"Oh no, you don't have to," I said. "I'm only parked out by the registrar's office." I stretched out my arm and pointed. "I can make it."

He took my extended arm and moved it forty-five degrees to the right. "The registrar's office is that way." He looked back toward where I'd come from. "You're heading the wrong way. Have you been wandering around?"

"Um . . . no." I didn't want to tell him about my little detour. I looked around to get my bearings and realized I'd strayed more than I thought following behind Ari.

"I can walk you back," he said, and gave me one of his lopsided grins. "I don't mind."

*Oh brother . . .*

"Okay," I said, and gave him a slight smile. "That'll be nice."

No need for me to be rude.

"So how is your little investigation going?" he asked.

I coughed, surprised at his statement. "Excuse me?"

Did he know we were trying to catch a killer?

"You and Maisie, you were trying to find out some information."

"Oh yeah," I said. I turned back to glance at where I'd last seen Ari. "It's going, I guess."

"I can help," he said. "I know a thing or two about the law."

"Yes, I know," I said. "But we're good."

"So what do you think about that murder around your parts? Pretty nefarious, huh?"

I swallowed hard. Why had he brought that up? I certainly

couldn't let him know I was poking my nose into that. He kept showing up at the ice cream shop, and since he and my grandfather were getting chummy, I didn't want him to let what I was doing leak.

I shrugged. "I don't think anything about it," I said.

"Really?" he asked. "Not curious at all."

"Well, I don't know that I'd say that," I said. "I mean, I am the one who found the body."

"I heard," he said.

I turned to look at him. "How did you hear that?"

"The law community around here is pretty small. We all know each other."

"You know Detective Beverly?" I asked.

"I do," he said, and gave a curt nod.

"Oh jeez," I said. "What did he tell you?"

"Not much," he said. "He told me what the guy had been killed with." He glanced over at me. "That's a pretty unusual way to murder someone."

"Tell me about it," I said. "Specific to only one thing."

"You mean the field of medicine."

I didn't answer that question. And that answer was much too broad for what I was thinking.

*Specific to surgery, Mr. Law Professor.*

I didn't know if O knew anything about my father. PopPop could have easily mentioned that he was a surgeon, but I didn't want him connecting the two in case Detective Beverly hadn't told him.

"Why did Detective Beverly say anything to you about it?" I asked.

"You know, I used to be a police officer," he said. "And I teach criminal law over here at the law school." He glanced at me. "And I may have written a book or two on crime here in Ohio."

"A book or two?"

"Or three," he said, and smiled. "You know, you don't get a lot of murders over in Chagrin Falls."

"I know."

"So it's important that the police catch someone."

"You mean anyone."

"In a way, that is what I mean. I teach my class about circumstantial evidence. You know what that is?"

"I've heard about it," I said. "Don't know that I can explain it to you."

"If there is no snow on the ground when you go to sleep, but there's snow there when you wake up, what do you think happened over night?" he asked.

"That it snowed."

"Right. You wouldn't know that for a fact," he said. "But the circumstances—the snow on the ground—would tend to prove your point. It would be evidence."

"And why did you tell me that?" I asked.

"Sometimes the police don't have anything but circumstantial evidence. Can't prove a person committed a crime beyond a reasonable doubt."

"But that's what they have to do, isn't it?" I asked. "Beyond a reasonable doubt. I've heard that before."

"No," he said. "That's not what the police officer is supposed to do."

I looked at him from the corner of my eye. "Are you sure?"

"I'm sure," he said. "The prosecutor has to prove it beyond a reasonable doubt. It's not the police officers' job. They collect the evidence. So sometimes, they get all they can and then give what they have to the prosecutors. Leaving them, and the jurors, to figure out what they can."

"Why did Detective Beverly contact you? Does he have circumstantial evidence or something?"

"He called me for advice."

"What did you tell him?"

"Hey! Hey!" It was Maisie, standing just outside the car, waving at us. We were still a good twenty feet away from it.

"She seems happy to see you," he said.

"I don't think it's me," I said.

"You think she's happy to see me?" he said, his eyes wide like he didn't think that was a good thing.

"Not exactly," I said. "It's complicated."

I'm sure Maisie was happy to see the two of us. Together. But I wasn't sharing that with him.

"Get back in the car, Maisie," I said as soon as we got close to it.

"I just wanted to speak to O," she said. "Hi, O!"

"Hi, Maisie."

She got back in the car but rolled down the window on the passenger side, where we were standing. "What are you two up to?" she asked, leaning across the seat.

"Nothing," I said. "He walked me back to the car."

"Oh," she said, and did some kind of exaggerated wink before sitting back up.

"I have to go," I said to him. "I guess I'll see you at the President's Dinner."

"Oh, I was stopping by for ice cream this afternoon."

"I just bet you were," Maisie said through the window.

"You got any new flavors?" he asked.

"No," I said. "I'll be making more tomorrow if you want to come by then."

"I like the old flavors just fine," he said. "I'll see you later?"

"Sure," I said.

"Bye, Maisie," he said, bending over to look in the car window.

"Bye!" Maisie leaned across the seat and waved.

"See you later, Win," O said.

I climbed into the car and acknowledged him with a smile.

"He likes you," Maisie said.

"You should stop saying that," I said, rolling up the window. "He just likes ice cream."

"Yeah, right," she said.

"I saw Ari," I said, buckling my seatbelt. I knew how to change the subject with her.

"Where?" she said, turning to look at me. "Here?"

"Yep," I said, nodding. "He's the caterer."

"Did he say something to you?" she asked.

"I said something to him."

"You did not!" She had a big grin on her face like she was proud of me. "You didn't just *watch* him?"

I rocked my head back and forth. "I did that, too."

She laughed. "And did you find out anything that way?"

"No," I said. "Looks like you're right about actually having to talk to someone to get any information."

"Asking questions. Not a bad concept, huh?"

"No, Maisie. Not a bad idea at all."

"So tell me, what did Ari say?" She started the car. "Tell me everything." She looked over the back seat to pull out of the parking space, then glanced at me. "Did he confess to killing Stephen Bayard?"

"No. He just said he hated him enough to do it."

"I knew it!" Maisie said. "He's the killer. Now we just have to figure out *how* he did it."

# chapter THIRTY-TWO

I brought you something to nosh on." Rivkah stood at the table, a bowl of boiled eggs in her hand. She set them in the middle of the table. "You look hungry."

"Savta," I said, "we just ordered food." I pointed toward the server, Daiyu, who was heading back into the kitchen.

We were at Rivkah Solomon's Village Dragon Chinese Restaurant. It was all red with golden dragons everywhere and mural landscapes on the wall. Maisie and I sat in our favorite booth. The one we'd claimed as our own since second grade.

We had stopped by the ice cream shop after we'd gotten back from Wycliffe, but not for long. My mother and father were behind the counter with a sprinkle of people lined up and sitting at the tables. PopPop and Bobby were playing backgammon in a booth. If O had stopped by, I didn't know about it. Maisie and I headed right back out and I didn't ask.

Rivkah waved a wrinkled hand at us and said, "When was the last time you ate?" She put her hand on top of mine. "A few eggs won't hurt."

I had to admit, I hadn't been eating lately. The only reason I was getting food now was because Maisie and I had decided to rendezvous at the restaurant before we went on our stakeout mission. Maisie, like her grandmother, was all about a body having enough fuel to make it through.

Maisie, in an earlier undertaking, while I pretended to be busy at the ice cream shop, had found out what time Glynis got off from work. Seemed as if she worked twelve-hour shifts and would be at the senior facility until seven thirty. She must've just gotten to work not too long before we saw her there. If we wanted to follow her to see where she was going, we needed to kill some time or sit in the car for hours.

"You don't have to worry, Savta," Maisie said. "We've been eating."

Rivkah shook her head and held out her hands. "What kind of mother would I be if I didn't worry?"

"Doesn't she know she's your grandmother?" It was Riya, who walked in as Rivkah walked off. She sat down next to Maisie, forcing her to move over. Rivkah headed back into the kitchen, no doubt to see about our food.

"How did you know we were here?" I asked.

"I didn't," she said. "I came in to get tofu."

"Do you always dress like that to go out to get tofu?" I asked.

Riya looked pretty. She had on makeup—mascara, dark red lipstick and some kind of sparkling amber-colored eye shadow and black eyeliner that complemented her olive-toned skin and shiny black hair. She wore blue jeans, a rust-colored turtleneck and fringed suede boots of the same color.

"I got stood up," Riya said. "So I felt like pigging out."

"On tofu?" I asked.

"Someone stood you up?" Maisie asked. "Are they still standing upright?"

Riya's temperament didn't tolerate people doing her wrong, not without repercussions. But she was working on that and it seemed like her stint as an emergency room doctor at Lakeside Memorial had been good for her. The quick thinking needed in that type of work kept her mind busy and calm.

"The whole concept about being stood up, Maisie," Riya said, "is that the person doesn't show up. So that means I didn't see him. Thus"—she slammed her palms on the table—"I couldn't do anything to him. Not that I was going to." She made her voice soft. "Although, I actually had an ulterior motive for seeing him."

"And what was that?" I asked.

"To question him."

"What?" Sleuthing seemed to be contagious.

"I don't know if I should say . . ." Riya looked at the two of us. "Where are you two dressed up to go? All in black."

"We're going on a stakeout," Maisie said.

Riya looked across the table at me. She knew that Maisie had a tendency to not always say what she meant. She could learn a thing or two from the Mad Hatter—say what you mean, mean what you say. But I gave a nod, confirming that was what we were doing, and added, "I just have on a black top. I have on blue jeans." I patted my thighs. "But it wasn't my intention, it just happened to be what I put on."

"Why are you two doing a stakeout?" Riya asked.

"To prove that Win's family isn't in the mob," Maisie said.

"The mob?" Riya said, amusement dancing in her eyes.

"Yeah, that they didn't put out a hit on Dead Guy," Maisie finished her explanation.

"Dead Guy?" Riya asked. "You don't know his name?"

"She's talking about the guy at the falls," I said. "There had been some discrepancy about his name. But we got that all worked out. Didn't we, Maisie?"

"Oh." Riya nodded slowly with the realization. "That dead guy you found. He was murdered?"

"Seems that way," I said.

I realized that Riya hadn't been around much. She hadn't taken any part in our little investigation. Maisie was going to catch her up, it seemed, even if it was with misinformation.

"I hadn't heard," she said.

"I only initially found out because I overheard it," I said.

"That wasn't a good thing, huh?" Riya said, looking at me. "Sorry that happened to you."

"Thanks."

"That's not the worst part of it," Maisie said.

"Anyway," I said, speaking over Maisie. I didn't want to get her talking. "Getting back to the stakeout business, I am not trying to prove that my family is not part of the mob."

"Or that they ordered a hit?" Riya asked, a serious expression on her face.

"Really, Riya?"

"Hey." She held up her hands. "I've seen your dad around the hospital. He has been known to put fear in more than a few people."

"Respect," I said. "They show him *respect*."

"Exactly," Riya said. "Just like a godfather."

"No one ordered a hit," I said, frustration in my voice. "Neither my father, nor anyone in my family, had anything to do with that man's death."

I was sorry that I'd used that term to Maisie.

"Then what are you worried about?" Riya asked.

I didn't want to rehash all the little innuendos my mother and grandfather had been throwing around or their strange behavior. Nor did I want to mention that my father was unaccounted for at the time of the murder. At least in the eyes of the law. I believed him when he said that he went to Grandma Kay's grave, but there was no one to corroborate that.

And I didn't want Riya to know what my mother had said about my dad killing that man the first day in the shop, seeing that Riya evidently hadn't heard her.

My long silence must have made her realize that I didn't want to talk about it, so she decided to.

"Is it because your mother said your father would kill him?" Riya said, and picked up an egg.

She had heard.

"The detective doesn't know that Win's mother said that," Maisie said. "And without that information he *still* thinks Mr. Crewse did it." Riya raised her eyebrows and looked to me for confirmation. I nodded. "He came to see him the other day," Maisie continued. "He was going to arrest him, but Mr. Crewse lawyered up."

"Really?" Riya said, her eyes wide, brows knitted. "I didn't think a lawyer could keep you from getting arrested."

"Detective Beverly wasn't going to arrest my father. And my dad called a lawyer to accompany him to the station for a second interview," I said. "Which is different."

"How is that different?" Riya asked.

"Oh my!" I flapped my arms, my hands landing on the table. "I don't want anyone thinking my father did anything. Or accusing him of anything."

"So how is this stakeout helping?" Riya asked. She must have appreciated my frustration, because she changed the way she asked questions.

"We've been doing some snooping—" Maisie started.

"Snooping?" Riya asked. "Other than what you have planned now?"

"Yes," I said.

"What kind of snooping?" Riya asked.

"Ari might be the murderer," Maisie announced. Talk about not answering the question and getting to the point. Not flinching, she wasn't swaying in her accusation.

"Your boss Ari?" Riya asked.

"He isn't my boss anymore," Maisie said. "I refuse to work for a killer. I've quit." Riya seemed amused. "So we looked through his office," Maisie continued, "to see if we could find some incriminating evidence."

"Why do you think he's the killer?" Riya asked.

Tag team–style, we filled her in on what we knew about Ari from our snooping and my questioning of Mrs. Keller. Riya sat forward the whole time, listening with anticipation.

"Where is the stakeout?"

"At Falls Park."

"The nursing home?" Riya asked.

"The senior citizen facility," Maisie said.

"Why are you going there?"

"We saw Glynis Vale at the nursing home this morning," Maisie said. "And she might be the key."

A blank look came over Riya's face. "What does that even mean?" She squinted her eyes. "What key? And who is Glynis Vale, and what were you doing at a nursing home?"

"Well . . ." I started, stumbling over my words. This was the link to my father. "Dead Guy—"

"Stephen Bayard," Riya said.

"Yes. Stephen Bayard." I nodded. "He was killed with succinylcholine."

"Oh my," Riya said, and fell back in her seat. "What a horrible way to die."

"So we've learned," Maisie said, cracking her second egg and peeling off the shell.

"And Glynis works at the senior care facility," I said. "She was there at the falls the night I found the body and she lied about it. Working at a nursing home, she would have access to drugs."

"Not succinylcholine," Riya said matter-of-factly.

"Why not?" I asked.

"It's only used for surgery."

"We read that," I said. "We know."

"So then you should know that any place that doesn't do surgery—like a nursing home—wouldn't have a need to keep it in stock. She wouldn't have gotten it from there. That sounds like a dead end."

I felt my jaw go slack and my eyes droop. "It's the only thing we have to go on," I said, my voice shaking from the disappointment I felt from her words. "I was thinking that our suspect, the one that injected him, might have met her there and conspired with her to get it for him."

"Not if you think she got the drug from there." She looked at me, and I could tell she knew how I felt. "But a medical facility is not the only place the drug could have come from."

I glanced at Maisie. "So I've heard. What do you know?" I asked. Maisie's answer to that question had been speculation. Maybe Riya had definitive answers.

"It's manufactured at facilities. It's stored at warehouses before it gets to a place that performs surgery. It could have come from one of those places."

That matched with what Maisie had said. "How?" I asked.

"I don't know." Riya held up her hand. "It could have been stolen, maybe. I'm just saying you don't have to think someone was in the medical profession or worked in a medical facility to get it."

"That's what Detective Beverly is doing," I said.

"Well, he's an idiot, then," Riya said.

"Told you," Maisie said, and took a bite of her egg. "Detective Bumbling Idiot. I knew from the beginning it didn't have to be a doctor. You already knew it didn't." Maisie looked at me. "Because you knew your father hadn't done it."

"I guess," I said, knowing that Liam Beverly was anything but an idiot. And even though Riya's comment gave me pause, I wasn't going to let it stop me from going to see if Danny and Glynis hadn't cooked something up together.

"So you think this woman and Ari did this?" Riya asked.

"No," I said. "We have another suspect."

"Who?" She leaned in closer over the table.

"Danny Clawson," I said.

"And who is that?"

"Dan Clawson's son," I said. "Remember, he used to own the bike shop next to our store?"

"No, I don't remember," Riya said. "I mean, I remember the bike shop. But not the owner."

"Anyway, Danny Clawson's mother ran off with Dead— Stephen Bayard, leaving his father and taking him with her."

"Oh, that's not nice," Riya said. "So you think this Danny guy did it because of what Stephen did to his family?"

"That's one theory," I said.

"And you were thinking Danny has a connection with Glynis. The two were in cahoots to commit murder?"

"I don't know," I said, not wanting to let Riya's revelation dash my idea of Glynis's involvement. "I think it's worth watching her."

"So that's your plan?" Riya asked. "You've tried snooping and googling and now you're resorting to stalking?"

"We're not stalking," Maisie said.

"You found out where she works and now you're going to go there to follow her and see what she does?"

"Okay," I said. "We're stalking her. You wanna go?"

"Wouldn't you guys rather go out for a drink?" Riya said, sitting up straight, putting her elbows on the table and leaning in. "We could go to the Flats. We could go to Lago's on the East Bank. We could eat there, too."

"We just ordered food," I said.

"Boiled eggs?" she asked.

"No, Rivkah brought those as . . ." I tried to think of the appropriate word. "An appetizer," I said, thinking that was close enough. Riya should know that Rivkah never thought we had enough food.

"What happened to fortune cookies?" Riya asked.

"You get those at the end of the meal," Maisie said.

"Do you want to go on the stakeout with us or not?" I asked Riya. "You were just saying we've been leaving you out. Now I'm offering an opportunity for you to go with us."

"What the heck," she said. "Count me in. You two seem clueless, you probably need me."

"It's just a stakeout," Maisie said. "We're not in any danger, so technically we don't *need* you."

Riya eyed Maisie. "Is that all I mean to you, Maise? Protection?"

"I wouldn't go down a dark alley with anyone else," Maisie said.

I tried not to laugh.

"What time is this stakeout?" Riya asked. "Do I have time to go home and change into my cat burglar clothes, too?"

"We don't have a set time," Maisie said. "We were just going to go after we finished eating and near the time Glynis would be leaving work."

"Experts at work," Riya said, and shook her head.

Daiyu brought our food over and I asked for an extra plate so I could share my food with Riya.

"It's not tofu," I said. "But if Rivkah sees you not eating, it'll be more boiled eggs for you."

Riya looked up at our server. "Would you bring me a fork, too, please?"

# chapter THIRTY-THREE

So, you guys finished?" Riya asked.

I looked down at my picked-over General Tso's chicken dinner. "I'm ready," I said. I knew I was too nervous to try to eat anything, even the half of it that was left after I shared with Riya. I had to get mentally prepared. Our morning stakeout and follow had been enough for me. It didn't seem to affect Maisie, though. Her plate of beef lo mein was empty.

"Then let's go," Riya said. "I'll drive. My car is better for stakeouts."

Riya's car was the Batmobile. If anything, it stood out. It was a Chevy Camaro. It had just rolled off the transport truck when she got the keys to it. Red body. Black grill. Tinted windows. It was hot and made for Riya. Anywhere we took it, we always got looks. I didn't know if it was better than going in Maisie's lime-green Beetle. We'd driven there the last time in it, all neon green and shiny, and it had stood out like a sore thumb.

"Tell me about this date of yours," I said after we got in the car. She had started to tell us about him earlier at the restaurant. I sat up front, and Maisie sat in the back seat.

"I told you, it really wasn't a date," Riya said. "I was going to confront him."

"About what?" I said.

Maisie had a different question. "If you were going to confront him, why are you all dressed up?" she asked, her face between the two front seats. She knew what a confrontation with Riya meant.

"I'm trying to not jump to conclusions and to react calmly," Riya said, putting on her blinker and pulling the car out onto the road. "I wanted to be subtle. I was giving him the illusion that our date was something nice."

"He must not know you very well," Maisie said.

I looked at Maisie, acknowledging her statement. It was hard to imagine Riya being calm.

"Tell us what happened," I said again.

"Someone used my name to request drugs from the pharmacy cabinet," Riya said, looking straight ahead at the road. "I think it might have been him."

"What does that mean, used your name?" I said.

"Doctors request drugs—we don't have access to get them, the nurses do. So we tell them what we want prescribed. They get it. They administer it."

"And someone said you wanted drugs that you didn't request?" I asked.

"Yes."

"Pharmacy cabinet? Is that where they keep the drugs?" Maisie asked.

"That's what pharmacy means," Riya said. "And I can be in a lot of trouble if anything comes up missing. I wasn't even in the day the request was made."

"Why would they do that?" Maisie asked.

"How would I know?" Riya said. "I guess they wanted drugs and needed a reason to get them."

"And you think you know who did it?" I asked.

"Yes," she hissed. "He'd come down to the emergency department and 'visit' with me sometimes, so they were probably used to seeing him around."

"And you didn't tell him to give drugs to anyone?" Maisie asked.

"No. Of course not." She hit her hand on the steering wheel. "I don't know why he would have done that. It would jeopardize not only my job, but his, too."

"Was anything missing? Out of the cabinet?"

"I don't think so," Riya said. "At least they didn't tell me it was."

"You didn't requisition anything," Maisie said. "They shouldn't fault you. You're a good doctor."

"I don't know," Riya said. "They might. You can't just be a good doctor, you have to be a careful one, too, and me having my boyfriend hanging around is not good."

We pulled up in the parking lot of the nursing home and I gestured to Riya where to park. I wanted to position ourselves so we could see Glynis coming out, and see where in the parking lot she'd go to get into her car.

"What are you going to say to this guy when you see him?" I asked, picking up the conversation after we got settled, but keeping an eye on the door.

"I was just going to ask him if he used my name to get into the pharmacy cabinet."

"Just like that?" I asked. "Just ask him straight out. That's not subtle, you know."

"It is for Riya," Maisie said. "I commend her."

"Look," I said, spotting movement at the door. "That's Glynis. See her, Riya? That's who we're following."

"The one in that blue coat walking with that guy," Maisie added. "That's her."

"No. That's Noah," Riya said.

"Who?" Maisie and I said in unison.

"Is that why he stood me up? For her?" Riya was looking past me, out the window toward the nursing home entrance.

"What are you talking about?" I said, trying to see what was going on.

"Uh-oh," Maisie said. Evidently she knew. "Is that him? Your date?"

"Her date?" I turned around to follow what they were looking at. "Maisie!" I squawked. "Not the guy with Glynis Vale?"

That could only mean disaster for us. There was not going to be anything furtive about our being there if that guy was the one who stood Riya up.

"That's Noah Bean," Riya said. "The guy I told you stole my code."

"No," I said. "You said you weren't sure he stole it. Remember?" I was getting nervous.

Riya started taking off her earrings. I looked at her, then back at Maisie with sheer horror on my face. When I looked back at

Riya, she'd taken the rubber tie from her arm and pulled her hair through it into a ponytail.

"No, Riya!" I said, nearly pleading. I knew by her actions that Riya was upset enough to attack. "I thought you were going to try the calm approach."

"I'm calm," she said. "And I am going to calmly flip that no-good, two-timing . . ." She mumbled some other adjectives under her breath that I couldn't decipher. "Then I'm going to put my foot on his chest and find out what it is he thinks he's doing." She finished those last words strong.

"You don't know that he's doing anything," I said. "He just walked out of the building."

"With her," Riya said. "Look how they're smiling at each other."

"Look!" Maisie said. "They split up. She's going one way. He's going the other. I think they're getting into their own cars, Riya, and leaving."

"See," I said. "He's not going with her. Let's just follow Glynis. See what she's up to. She's going to that red Honda Civic. See it? I can see part of the license. GHS. Do you see that, Riya?"

But Riya wasn't paying any attention to me. Her focus was somewhere else.

"It's okay," Maisie said. "I've got apple juice in my bag."

"Just let him get into his car," I said. "And you calm down. You want some juice?"

"I need to talk to him," she said, lowering her voice.

"No, you don't," I said. "Not now. Not until you calm down. Plus, he's leaving and we're gonna miss Glynis."

"He better be glad he's leaving," Riya said.

"We're all glad he's leaving," I muttered.

"What?" she said, and turned to look at me, her eyes red, her nostrils flaring.

"Nothing," I said. Maisie pushed a bottle of apple juice between the seats. "Here." I cracked open the top and pushed the juice toward her. "Drink this and let's follow Glynis. Look." I pushed her head to the side. "She's leaving."

"Okay," Riya said. "Okay."

"Okay?" I said.

"Yes. I'm okay," she said. "I'm good. As long as he's gone and I don't have to see him."

"He's going," Maisie and I said at the same time.

"Don't worry, he's going," I said. "Everything is going to be okay."

But I feared for that man the next time she saw him. I knew Riya didn't know how to do calm.

# chapter THIRTY-FOUR

But Mr. Noah Bean didn't get in his car and drive away. Oh no. The fates weren't with us that night.

He walked over to it, sure enough, but then with a look as if he'd forgotten something, he turned around and headed back toward the door of the nursing home.

*Why would he do that?*

"There he goes again!" Riya said, her hand swooping down to grab the car handle. I had to grab the bottle of juice from her, otherwise it would have been all over the seat and floor of her pretty red car. "He just doesn't know what's good for him, does he?" She watched him through the windshield, the ends of her mouth curling under, her almond-shaped brown eyes getting narrower and narrower. I expected to see daggers shooting out at any minute.

"Riya," I said. "Calm down. This isn't how you are going to get information from him."

She turned and looked at me, and I could almost see the

smoke coming from her nose. "You should want me to get him. You can talk to him."

"About what?" I said. "I don't have anything to talk to him about."

"Maybe he stole succinylcholine out of the cabinet and gave it to Glynis," she said. "Didn't you say she was there the night of the murder?"

"Yeah . . ."

"Well, there was succinylcholine in that pharmacy cabinet that he forged a requisition for."

"There was?" I asked. But before I could get an answer from her, she had one foot out the door. She turned back and hissed, "I'll make sure you'll get the information you need."

"Oh no!" I tried to grab her arm, but she was out of the car and on the move in one fleeting moment. "I don't need any information," I tried to say, but it was too late.

I reached for my door handle, getting ready to chase her down and stop her, but noticed Maisie hadn't moved.

"What are you doing?" I looked back at her. "We have to go get Riya."

"I don't think we can," Maisie said matter-of-factly. She didn't move and no fear showed on her face. I couldn't understand that, since she knew as well as I did what Riya Amacarelli could do to a body.

"What do you mean, we can't?"

I saw a smile cross Maisie's face. "Look," she said. Her arm outstretched, she pointed through the windshield. "He thinks he can get away from her."

I followed her arm, and there was Riya chasing Noah through

the parking lot. He was running around cars, darting and dashing back and forth, ducking down between rows. Head in the air, arms and legs pumping, but no matter which way he went, Riya was right behind him.

No one could get away from Riya. Noah's sudden high-pitched, fright-laced squeal that came with a thud was evidence of that.

Riya had caught him. She did some karate/tae kwon do/judo foot sweep on him and he went down. He landed with his face in the concrete, and she was on top of him like she was at a rodeo event. He was squirming around yelping, but that wasn't going to help.

"We have to help him," I said, and bounded out the door. "C'mon!"

"Kindergarten all over again," Maisie said, shaking her head and following behind me.

"Riya, we don't want him maimed and tortured," I said, trying to get her off him after we got over to her.

She was sitting on top of him, her hand twisting his arm back, her legs splayed over him, her face filled with determination. She wasn't letting him go. "I thought you wanted to question him," she said.

"That was your idea," I screeched. "But even if I did, I don't want to do it through a séance. We need him alive to talk to him."

"He stood me up!" She took the side of her fist and came down on his back like she was hitting a tabletop. "He stole my pharmacy code!" She punctuated that the same way. "And he ki—"

"Whoa!" I said, and grabbed her arm. I had to stop her. It sounded like she was getting ready to say he killed someone. She was jumping to huge conclusions.

"Riya. Sweetie." I took to rubbing her arm. "Let him up."

"Hmpf."

"We can't talk to him like this." I turned my head to the side so that it was nearly at the same angle as his. He was breathing heavily and his eyes looked wild.

"Please?"

"OKAY, QUESTION HIM," Riya said.

We'd gotten Noah stuffed into the back seat of the car with Maisie. I was terrified that the police would come barreling up at any moment. I didn't doubt that Riya's whole assault thingy had been captured on security cameras.

"Question him? Me?" I said.

"Yes. About your mystery you're trying to solve."

"We came to question Glynis," I said.

"Well, Glynis is not here," Riya said. "So question him."

"He might not know anything about it," I said, my voice shaky. It couldn't be a good idea to get information from anyone when they're under duress.

"What do you know about the murder on Bell Street?" Riya said, turning to look at him between the two bucket seats. "Did you have something to do with that?"

She didn't know how to be calm or subtle.

"I'll ask him questions," I said. I glanced over at Maisie and pushed myself up to look over the seat. I really didn't know what to ask. But I knew I'd do better than Riya. "Do you know Glynis Vale?" I had to come up with something.

"Of course he does," Riya said. "He stood me up to go out with her."

"What is she talking about?" Noah said his first words.

"Why did you stand me up?" Riya asked. "To go out with that woman?"

Noah looked from me to Riya and back to me. "Help me," he mouthed.

"I thought you were going to let me ask the questions," I said to Riya.

"Go ahead." She gestured with her hand for me to continue. I opened my mouth to speak, but didn't get the chance to. "Why did you sign my name to get access to our pharmacy cabinet?" She jumped up in her seat to face him.

"Can she do this?" Noah looked at me.

"Riya," I said.

"I'm helping you," she said, turning to look at me as if she were possessed.

"No, you're not," I said.

"Okay, well I'm helping me," she said. "I could lose my job over this."

"I didn't *sign* it," he said.

"Yes, you did," she hissed. "Tell the truth."

"What do you mean?" I asked him. I noticed he had put emphasis on the word "sign."

"I just put her name on it," he said.

"Why?" Riya asked. She was on her knees peering over the top of the seat.

"I don't know," he said. "I just got it in my head that I could do it, and I couldn't lose the thought. It just stuck in my brain that I could, so"—he shrugged—"I did it."

"I've got something to stick in your brain," Riya said, and held up a fist.

His eyes got bigger.

"But she won't," I assured him.

"And how is that not forging my name?" Riya asked, her eyes nearly bulging out of their sockets.

"Because I didn't *sign* it," he said. "It wasn't your *signature.* Then it worked and I thought, I wonder what's in there."

"Narcotics, dummy," Riya said, and smacked him on top of his head. Her reflexes from all her years training in martial arts were too quick for me to try to stop her or for Noah to duck out of the way. "Duh."

"Did you take anything out of it?" I asked. I remembered that Riya had explained that succinylcholine wouldn't be in every area of the hospital, only places where surgery was going to be performed.

If he knew Glynis and he was inside of a pharmacy cabinet that belonged to the emergency department, then there was a good chance that he might have been the one to give it to her.

Maybe Riya tackling him was a good thing. Maybe we could find out if the drug used to kill Stephen Bayard was in that cabinet.

"How do you know Glynis?" I said, getting back to my original question. Riya started to ask one of her questions. "Uh-uh." I shook my head and put up a finger. "Don't say anything, Riya."

"Glynis works here," Noah answered my question, probably relieved I had stopped Riya from asking one of hers.

"We know she works here," Riya said, sliding back into her seat. "What? Are you dating her, too?"

Okay, maybe I wasn't any good at getting Riya not to talk.

"Dating her?" He scrunched up his nose. "I don't date people. I'm trying to work on my career."

"You don't date people?" Riya squealed. She popped up out of her seat and was trying to worm her way into the back. "What were you doing with me?"

"Oh my God! Maisie, can you help me?" She'd been sitting in the back listening the whole time, not contributing to the interrogation or helping me control Riya.

"Bad, Riya," I scolded, pulling on her legs. Noah had scooted back into a corner and was trying to defend himself from Riya's barrage of hand flapping. "B-A-D!"

"What is wrong with her?" Noah asked, his face red and puffy.

"She's working through some issues," Maisie said.

"You're telling me," Noah said.

"Why are you here?" I asked. I wedged myself between the two front bucket seats to keep Riya from going through them.

"I work here," he said.

"You work at the hospital," Riya interjected, talking around me. "At least you do until I tell the board you stole my code by looking over my shoulder."

"You can't prove that," he said, the only courage he'd shown throughout Riya's handling of him.

Riya tried nudging me aside, but she could only get me over enough to put her face between the seats. "Look," she said, gritting her teeth, "I can make you talk."

"Did you give drugs from that cabinet to Glynis?" I asked. I knew I needed to get my questions in because I didn't know how long I could keep Riya off him. Who knew if he'd still be able to speak when she finished with him?

"Drugs?" His eyes got big, and he let them float to each of our faces. "What are you trying to say?" I saw the blood drain out of his face. "I'm not saying anything else. Not until I talk to my lawyer."

"You don't have a lawyer," Riya said, rolling her eyes. She plopped back down in her seat. "And that wouldn't work with us anyway."

"That wouldn't work with *her*," Maisie said, and pointed a finger at the back of Riya's seat. "Win and I are good with you getting a lawyer."

# chapter THIRTY-FIVE

Maisie probably thought that the only way Noah could keep safe was if he got himself a lawyer. Or a police escort.

But after the Riya/Noah incident, I didn't think I'd be able to get any kind of information out of him. And if he told Glynis I was asking questions about her, she might panic and get rid of evidence, or even leave town.

If she even had anything to do with it.

Now I was at the shop. It was four thirty in the morning and I was supposed to be making ice cream. Instead, I sat at my makeshift desk staring at the monitor, elbows on desk, chin cradled in palm of hands, legs crossed, the one foot kicking out a measured beat.

I was trying to figure out what I could look up that would give me answers. But I was coming up with nothing even with all my snooping, googling and stalking, as Riya put it. I had yet to find out one single thing that could help. At least not enough to set Detective Beverly straight about my father as my initial plan had entailed.

I uncrossed my legs and let my arm fall onto the desk.

I began to think that at this point, I had probably lost the right to carry an amateur sleuthing ID card, if there was such a thing, and if I had ever deserved to have one in the first place.

I got up from the stool and blew out a breath. I was here to make ice cream and I figured I'd better get started.

Not bothering to turn off the computer, I went to the sink, washed my hands, then went over to the refrigerator. I grabbed a dozen eggs, heavy cream and milk. I placed them on the long aluminum prep table, then pulled down two bowls from the floating wooden shelf and plucked a whisk out of the drawer.

I cracked an egg, starting the crème anglaise for the base of my ice cream. But I realized I'd need to take on a more taxing task than separating eggs if I wanted to keep my mind from wandering back to the murder.

I thought about our suspects.

My conversation with Ari confirmed Maisie's and my suspicion of a motive. He didn't want to deal with Stephen Bayard anymore. Through blackmail or any other illegal enterprise. And with him not being at work, even if he really was sick, he had opportunity.

But using those same assumptions, so did my father. Daddy, I was sad to admit, had the motive, the opportunity and the means.

Making him still the best suspect out of the two.

I had nothing on Glynis other than the fact that she and her son were on the scene and she worked in a nursing home, and even though she knew Noah Bean, he didn't seem to be her connection to the drug. And I just didn't get how she could think it was okay to have her son lie and keep him from coming forward with what he knew. He had to know something. Have seen something. He was right there.

I hit the last egg on the side of the bowl.

*So were you, Win, and you didn't see anything . . .*

With Riya's info on where the drug could and couldn't be found, I'd probably have to cross Glynis Vale off my list.

I sprinkled sugar over the eggs, held the bowl in my arm and started to whisk.

*Unless Glynis had help,* I thought. Help from someone like Noah Bean. He seemed like a better accomplice for her than Danny, seeing as how he, with Riya's code, could potentially get his hands on the drug. But from what I knew, which, granted, wasn't much, Danny Clawson was the only one of the three who had a motive to kill him.

Well, in my mind at least. Who knows? Maybe Stephen Bayard was a good father to him. Maybe Danny just felt bad about what Stephen did to the other shop owners in the village, and that's why he helped them out. But he bore no ill will toward his stepfather.

And if the detective was right, and people were usually murdered by people they knew, then I was sure it could be just about anyone Stephen Bayard had ever run into. It seemed he was always doing wrong to people.

He'd wronged just about every shop owner in our little village.

This was all too complicated.

I put the bowl on the table and set the whisk down next to it. I picked up the eggshells and walked over to the trash can. Putting my foot on the lever to open the lid, I realized that I could see why the police would give up and just choose the person most likely to have done it. I was starting to understand what O had told me about how police detectives just leave it to the prosecutors and jurors to sort things out.

But with my father being a surgeon, if they just decided he

was the "most likely," there wouldn't be anything for them to sort out. He was the only one out of all the people I suspected that I was sure could have gotten ahold of that drug.

But, I thought as I absentmindedly poured the milk and cream into a saucepan and placed it over a low flame on the stove, Riya had said that a hospital or surgical facility wouldn't be the only place to get it. There was always the illegal route.

*What am I supposed to do with that information?*

I got a wooden spoon and stirred the mixture as it heated up.

*I should probably trust Riya. That's what I should do.*

When it came to the deadly drug succinylcholine, it seemed that Riya had the inside scoop.

And Stephen Bayard certainly indulged in the illegal . . .

I drew in a sharp breath.

Ari had said that Stephen had come to town because he wanted him to do a job. What if the job was stealing drugs? What if one of the drugs they stole was succinylcholine, which Ari then used to kill him? Then the murder weapon, as Detective Beverly referred to it, wouldn't have come from a place that did surgeries, like where my father worked.

Something like that, another way that someone could get access to succinylcholine, might help my father get off the hook. Give those pesky prosecutors and jurors some other circumstantial evidence.

I hurried over to my computer, sat down, but had to pop right back up. I'd forgotten to turn the eye off under my pot.

I turned off the burner, set the saucepan on another eye, then went back to the laptop. I plopped down on the stool and grabbed the mouse.

I decided to see if I couldn't find something about succinylcholine being part of a robbery. Or something. If it had, it would have made the news. It would surely be on the internet. And maybe, fingers and ice cream scoops crossed, the theft would have happened a few days ago and right here in Ohio.

Maybe even somewhere close to Chagrin Falls.

I clicked on the search box and typed in *Stolen succinylcholine.* I got a lot of articles about the drug, and the more I scrolled down the page, the more I lost hope.

Until I got to the last link on the page.

*Who's Responsible for the Nation's Biggest-Ever Drug Heist?*

My hand started shaking as I hovered over the link. Was this going to be it? What I needed to help me get my father off the hook?

*Couldn't be this easy,* I thought.

And it wasn't. The article was dated three years ago. I rested my elbow on the desk and used it to hold up my heavy head. This wasn't what I needed, but I read on.

The article said that a pharmaceutical warehouse in Columbus, Ohio, was robbed of over fifty million dollars' worth of drugs and that the theft was believed to have been orchestrated by someone working on the inside.

Someone named David Niven.

*David Niven.* Why did that name sound familiar?

I typed it in and found out he was the actor who had played the thief in the Pink Panther movie.

Wow. He named himself after the *thief.*

# chapter THIRTY-SIX

There was a *rap, rap, rap* on the side door and I had to stop reading to answer it. It was hard to tear myself from that article.

I glanced up at the clock. It was 6:37 a.m.

Who could that be?

"Hello," I said from the other side of the metal door. "Who is it?"

"Findlay Glass," a gruff voice answered back. "We have the plexiglass sheet for your wall."

"For my wall," I muttered, unlocking and pulling open the door. "Hi." I stepped back to let the two men in. "I thought that was coming on Monday."

"We're early," one of the guys said. "We can come back if you want."

"No. No," I said. "I don't want you to go. How did you know I'd even be here this early?"

"It's on our work order."

I was happy my plexiglass wall had arrived. I was tired of my line of sight ending with that particleboard. But they couldn't have picked a more inopportune time.

I glanced over at my laptop. That article was sitting on my monitor, ready to divulge information about Stephen Bayard and the drug that killed him.

Or so I hoped.

"Hold on," I said. "I have to put my food away and cover everything up."

I got the kitchen squared away and thought I'd get back to my reading. But I kept getting interrupted. First, they had questions—*What do you want us to do with the particleboard? Is it okay if we plug this up here?* And invoices for me to initial and sign—*here, and here, and here.*

Then my mother, who never comes in early, arrived. Early. I couldn't let her see me reading the article. And once the plexiglass—the beautiful, transparent, sparkling plexiglass—was installed, I had to get back to making ice cream.

I did learn, in bits and pieces, that the drugs stolen, from a place called LaGrosse Warehouse, were never recovered. That David Niven had worked at the warehouse only a few months, but the evidence pointed to him as the ringleader. It also said that Niven's wife was questioned and released. They were satisfied, it noted, that she had no connection to the robbery.

*Wow . . .*

"Win."

"PopPop," I said, fumbling to shut the laptop and turning to face him. "I didn't hear you come in."

"Busy looking up stuff, huh?" He pointed to my laptop.

"Nothing important."

"Well," he said, "it's a lot more civilized, and probably more efficient than chasing people down in parking lots."

"Huh?" I said.

"I know what you've been doing," he said.

"What have I been doing?" I asked. I looked at him out of the side of my eye.

"Conducting an investigation. Not a very good one, but one nevertheless."

"Oh my goodness, PopPop." I slapped a hand across my forehead. "How did you know?"

"I've been following you," he said. "I started out wanting to protect you from Stephen Bayard."

"Wait," I said. "Is that why you told me I didn't have to worry about him anymore?"

"I didn't know he was the one they found by the falls. I only knew he had approached you. I was going to stop him from doing that again."

"So all this time, you've been following me around?"

"Yeah," he said.

"Why didn't you stop after you found out he wasn't around anymore?"

"Because then my son was being accused of his murder, and you and Maisie—" His eyes flickered and he looked up to the ceiling. "God help that child, but you two seemed like you might be onto something."

"You mean that we were figuring out who it was that really did it?"

"No, you never seemed close to that," he said. "Especially after you took Riya along with you. I meant trying to look for the answer for yourselves."

"Yeah, that was bad with Riya," I said. "Why didn't you help stop her?"

"I started to," he said, "but I didn't want to blow my cover."

*His cover? Oh wow, I have another Maisie on my hands.*

"Then I saw that you and Maisie had gotten her calmed down. But I couldn't stop thinking how badly that could've gone wrong. Riya is a lethal weapon."

I chuckled. "I know. I really thought she wasn't so hot-tempered anymore."

"That's why I'm telling you now." He smiled at me. "Other than that one incident, you and Maisie were doing okay, I thought. Talking to people, going to Molta's, following Danny Clawson. Just seemed to me like all the right steps to take."

"I don't know if they were," I said. "We haven't solved it yet. Found out one thing of value yet."

"What were you looking at on there?" He pointed to my laptop.

I turned and looked at the computer, then back to PopPop. "I was trying to figure out where else someone might have gotten the drug that killed Stephen Bayard."

"What did you find?"

"I think I found that he was involved with a robbery. He may have stolen drugs from a pharmaceutical warehouse."

"The drug that killed him?"

"I don't know," I said. "It didn't say which drugs. But Riya told me that they could be at a warehouse."

"So she was some help, huh?" He grinned at me.

"The only thing I got from it," I said, "was that it happened in Ohio, and I believe Stephen Bayard was involved, under another name. Maybe even the ringleader. Maybe. And that he had a wife."

"That would mean the drug he stole was the one that killed him," PopPop said.

"Maybe he accidentally injected it himself," I said, doubt clouding my words even as I spoke them.

"Might be a possibility, but I'm sure they scoured those grounds around where he was found. Haven't heard any mention of evidence of him doing that being found."

PopPop chewed on his bottom lip, tilted his head and let his eyes drift upward. "Seems to me," he started, "you've missed the two most important people to talk to about all of this."

"Who?" I asked.

"Dan Clawson and Debbie Devereaux."

# chapter

# THIRTY-SEVEN

"PopPop," I said, awe, I knew, spreading across my face. "You've been thinking about this."

"Yeah, I have."

"You wanna help?"

"Why wouldn't I?" he said. "Graham is my son. I don't want anything to happen to him just like you don't. It would tear me up inside." He shook off the thought. "Especially if I could have done something that could've helped."

"So," I said, scooting up on my stool and licking my lips, happy to have my grandfather joining our little sleuthing group, "I had given some thought to Dan Clawson being involved and questioning him, but I thought he was too old to have done it. That's why I started following his son, Danny."

"Danny's too kindhearted to have done something like that. And I'm not suggesting you talk to Dan because he had a hand in it. But because he knew the guy. Better than anybody around here."

"He did?"

"Yeah, he did. Stephen Bayard used to hang over there with Dan all the time."

"I did think about talking to him for that," I said. "Not that I knew." I had figured my family was the way to get information on Stephen Bayard. "I did think that I needed to get to know Stephen Bayard better to help me figure out who killed him."

"Then you were thinking right. We should talk to Dan."

"Okay. And why should I talk to Ms. Devereaux?" I asked. "Do you think she might have done it? I had thought about that," I said, my voice low. I was talking fast. "But then Maisie and I thought that because of the way that drug acts when it's injected, it had to be a man who did it."

"That's some male superiority hogwash," he said. "You of all people should know about female determination."

I felt a blush coming on.

"Don't limit yourself when you're looking for a suspect," he said. "You might miss something."

*Geesh, he really is another Maisie. I wonder which shows he watches.*

"And that's the reason I said you should talk to Debbie," he was saying, "not because she could be a suspect, but because she doesn't miss anything."

"What do you two have your heads together about?" my mother said, interrupting us. She stood to the side of us, hands on her hips, her head cocked to the side.

I hadn't realized, but I had my face tilted up to PopPop's and his was bent forward toward mine. Both of us were leaning into the other, our conversation low, our bodies tense.

"Nothing," I said, and scooted back on the stool. I slumped my shoulders and let my feet slide off the bottom rail. "Just talking shop."

"Well, you must have been talking about how to burn it down and collect the insurance money without getting caught," she said. "Because that conversation was serious." She waggled a finger between us. "And I don't know how you could have even heard each other's words, you were speaking so low."

"We were trying to figure out a way to break the news to you, Ailbhe." PopPop walked over and placed a hand on my mother's shoulder before heading out to the front of the store. "We decided not to serve that strawberry nonsense you conjured up. Just doesn't fit the new sophisticated style we're going for."

My mother's mouth dropped open and she started hyperventilating. "The what?"

"He's kidding, Mom." I got up and put my arm around her shoulders. "Just joking. I've already ordered the strawberries."

My mother and I made ice cream while PopPop took care of the front. We had appeared in the local morning paper as catering the dessert for the President's Dinner and the sorority's ice cream social, and I think it brought people in. But in between customers, when my mother couldn't hear, we plotted and planned what we were going to do.

With all the business we were getting, we couldn't leave my mother to run the store by herself. I had my fingers crossed that Maisie would show up soon. I wanted to get back to looking into Bayard's murder. Especially with my PopPop.

But I could never let Maisie know that.

"Afternoon," Maisie said, bounding into our kitchen. "I just made it official."

"Made what official?" My mother looked up from changing the paddle on the mixer.

"I'm coming here to work."

"What?" I asked, raising an eyebrow.

"I quit Molta's"—she held her hand to the side of her mouth—"for reasons I can't announce publicly. Yet." She spread her arms out like an eagle. "And I'm working here. Although, I will still have to split my time between this and the community garden."

"Did anyone offer you a permanent job here, Maisie?" my mother asked. She didn't look up from what she was doing.

Maisie's smiled drooped. I went and stood next to her. "I did," I said, although I hadn't. "And I'm glad she's here. She's officially on the payroll as a *regular* employee."

"I'm happy she's here, too," my mother said. "I just wondered whether this was just another Maisie move. She changes jobs more often than OPEC changes the price of gas."

"She's stuck with the community garden," I said in her defense. I knew my mother wasn't being mean. She was just being a mother. Worrying about Maisie's welfare.

"That she has." My mother looked up. "So if we're paying you, you need to get busy. Don't just stand there."

"I need Win to go with me," PopPop came in the back and announced. I knew what he was up to, but it still surprised me.

My mother looked up.

"You okay, PopPop?" my mother asked. She laid down the orange half she'd been juicing and wiped her hands on her apron. "You need me to help you?"

"No. I just need to go over some . . ." He looked at me, rubbing his fingertips together.

"Things," I said. I knew if I told her the truth she'd tell my father, and that wouldn't be good.

"Okay, we've got this. Me and Maisie," she said. "But you know tomorrow I won't be in."

"I know," I said.

That was the day my father and his lawyer were going to speak with Detective Beverly at the police station. I wanted to go, but PopPop was going with them and there was no one else to run the store.

"Maisie and I will be fine."

"Okay," she said. "And I'm almost finished with this Orange Burst ice cream you wanted, then I'll go up front with Maisie."

"Where to first?" I asked PopPop as we stood by the door buttoning up our coats and putting on hats.

"Debbie Devereaux. We need to find out what she knows."

EXQUISITE DESIGNS BOUTIQUE was small, quaint, haute and stuffed to the brim with clothes, trinkets and scarfs—most of them shiny and sparkly.

We walked in, the small bell on the wood-and-glass door announcing our arrival.

"Okay," Ms. Devereaux called from the back. "I'll be right out."

She appeared out of the back and smiled when she saw us. She had on blue jeans and a winter-white-colored knitted top that had a three-tiered ruffle on each sleeve. She'd covered that with a brocaded black vest that opened at the front.

I started to tell her that she looked nice, but she always did.

"Well, hello," she said, walking up to the front. "What can I do for the two of you?"

"Hi, Debbie," my grandfather said. "You're looking good."

I smiled. Her usual appearance didn't stop him from complimenting her.

"Thank you, Aloysius," she said. "I feel good."

"Hi, Ms. Devereaux," I said.

I looked at PopPop, not sure how to start the conversation. I hadn't told him what she'd said to me the night she brought me the cup of tea. Saying "he got what he deserved." It had made her, in my mind, a possible suspect.

"Win's been looking into you-know-who's death after they thought Graham may have something to do with it."

"You come up with anything?" she asked me.

"Um. Not really?" I said it like it was a question.

"Walk with me," she said, her arm doing a gentle wave motion, her curling fingers gesturing her words.

I walked over to her, and when I got to her side, she nodded at my grandfather. "We'll be back, Aloysius. You watch my store."

"Alright," he said.

We walked to the back of the store, from where she'd just emerged. She went to a wall rack and pulled down her coat.

"Where are we going?" I asked.

"I have something I want to show you."

She slipped into the furry coat she'd worn the last two times I'd seen her. This time, though, she put on a cap that had "Diva" across the front in rhinestone cursive.

We went out her back door and across the alley to Bell Street and walked up it.

"You've been doing a little snooping around here, huh?"

"Yes," I chuckled. "For all the good it's done."

"Tell me what you found out so far," she said.

So as we walked, I did. I told her about Maisie and Ari and Lew and Mrs. Keller and Noah Bean. And she listened to everything, interjecting a question or two, but mostly signaling me to continue by saying, "Uh-huh." When I told her about Glynis and how she went into Dan Clawson's room, and how she came out the door from work with Noah, she told me she remembered Glynis from the falls that night.

"Did you see the killer?" I asked her. I knew she'd seen something that night.

"I saw Stephen Bayard."

"That night?"

"Yes."

"So you knew it was him at the bottom of the falls when you gave me the tea."

"I didn't *know*. But I had a feeling."

"And you told the police?"

"I did. I told them he had been lurking around out there. Loitering at the corner for ten or fifteen minutes. I knew exactly who he was and what he'd done to your family."

"You told the police what he'd done to us?"

"I did," she said. "Now, about what you say." She looped her arm in mine. "What is Glynis Vale's story?"

"I haven't the faintest idea what it is," I said. "Other than what I told you."

We turned down American Street.

"You probably should have a talk with her," she said. "Then you'd know."

"Know what?"

"What her story is. Whether she is the killer or if she saw the killer." She made a clicking sound with her tongue. "Or what that boy of hers has to do with anything."

I thought about Maisie's and my determination that the killer was a man, and then PopPop telling me not to rule anyone out.

"Maybe I will," I said.

Then I thought about her cryptic statement that night, too.

"What did *you* see that night?" I asked.

"Not that night," she said. "That morning."

"Morning?"

"Yes. I saw him with that puppy."

"You did?"

She stopped walking. "I did." Then she pointed. "Here," she said.

We were at her sister Dell's bed-and-breakfast.

"Is this what you wanted to show me?"

"Not the house," she said, and chuckled. "Something inside. My sister's not here right now." She reached in her pocket and brought out a ring of keys. "But I can get us in."

We walked up the steps to the front door. "Business is slow from October until the spring. So no one else is in the house either."

I looked around the porch while she unlocked the door. Then I walked into the foyer and took in the B and B. I'd never been inside before. The late-afternoon light streamed through the windows and I could see the place was sparsely furnished. A big overstuffed sofa and two chairs in a room off to the right. To the left, a huge dining room set made from light oak.

"Let's go upstairs," she said.

She was being so secretive. If I hadn't come to her with my

PopPop and she hadn't left him at her store, I might have thought she was taking me somewhere to do me in.

Maybe I just never noticed before and enigmatic was her usual persona.

She walked down the hall and found the skeleton key on her ring to the door we stood in front of.

"I think this is the right key," she said. The tumbler on the lock clicked and she pushed open the door and gestured me in.

"Why are we here?" I asked, looking at her.

"Stephen Bayard rented out this room."

"Oh," I said, and took in the room. "He did?"

"He did."

"And why are you telling me this?"

"Because I know you are looking for who killed him and I thought this might help."

"How do you know he stayed here?" I didn't know why I asked her that question. Debbie Devereaux, like my grandfather said, knew most things that went on in the village.

"My sister," she said, as if the answer was obvious.

"Do the police know he stayed here?"

"No," she said, and slowly moved her head from side to side. "Not yet. He registered as Peter Sellers. My sister didn't know at first who he was. But as soon as we discovered it, I told her she should ask him to leave. But he never came back."

I nodded. *That was probably because he died,* I thought.

"And I'll call the police after you've had a look around."

"Isn't that illegal?" I asked, walking around the room. "I mean, that's like evidence tampering or something."

"I think of it more as abandoned property. Anyone can go through that."

I didn't know how that made a difference, wasn't even sure what that meant. But I guess in her mind it made sense.

"How long did he stay?"

"Just one night." She gave me a head nod. "And it wasn't the night before he died either."

I had to think about that for a moment.

*Oh.* I glanced at her. That meant he had spent the night *somewhere else* the night before I saw him.

"And he left his things?" I didn't see anything much of any consequence—a shaving kit, a yellow notepad with nothing on it, a toothbrush and travel-sized toothpaste in the bathroom. Then I saw a dog collar and leash.

"That was his puppy he had with him?" I asked, picking up the collar with my gloved hands.

She shrugged.

"I did tell the police about him having one that day."

"Oh," I said, a look of realization lighting up my face. "That's why Detective Beverly asked me about the puppy."

She shrugged again.

"Why did he have this?" I asked more to myself than to her. I looked at the collar. It read "Blake." That must have been that little doggie's name. I flipped it over and saw a phone number.

"There's a number here," I said, and pointed to it.

"You want to call it?" she asked.

I blinked a few times. Call it? What would I say? And what if it were Stephen Bayard's number? It would ring at the police station, where his cell phone was. That wouldn't be good.

"I think I'll just take a picture of it," I said. I pulled out my cell phone and snapped a shot of each side. Why I thought I'd need it, I didn't know. But besides the email, I didn't have any physical evidence of anything. It was something to add to my investigation.

After that, we left. Ms. Devereaux locked the door behind us and we went back downstairs. We headed toward the front door, but as we neared it, she tapped her finger on a sign posted on the wall. It read: *No pets allowed.*

We walked in silence all the way back. I was lost in thought. I hoped Ms. Devereaux didn't think me rude.

When we got back to the store, it looked like PopPop was ringing up a sale. I couldn't tell, but there was a woman smiling at him, and he was handing her a bag over the counter.

I guessed he could take care of the store while Ms. Devereaux was gone.

"Thank you, Aloysius," Ms. Devereaux said.

"Happy to be at your service," he said, bowing slightly. That made her smile, then she winked at him.

"You ready to go?" he said, looking at me.

"Yes," I said. "I'm ready."

After we left, I asked him, "Did you know that she had that leash?"

"What leash?"

I thought I'd ask a different question. "Why did you have me talk to her? Did you know she knew about what was in the B and B?"

"Dell's B and B?"

"Yes," I said, getting exasperated. He seemed completely in

the dark about where I'd been and what I'd found out. "You didn't know what Ms. Devereaux was going to show me?"

"No," he said.

"Why did you take me there, then?"

"I told you. She always knows something. You should have started your questioning with her. You might have been a lot further along." He looped my arm through his, acting as if his comment wouldn't have any effect on me. "And before we proceed to our next interrogation," he said, "we have to stop and pick up Rivkah."

# chapter

# THIRTY-EIGHT

Who knew? My grandfather was a ladies' man. He had them smiling, winking and waiting for him to give them rides.

I wondered what my Grandma Kay would have to say about his behavior. I had no idea he was such a charmer.

"Maybe Dan wheeled himself out of that nursing home and got that awful man back for all the bad things he did to him," Rivkah said as she got into PopPop's car. We needed it to get out to the nursing home. Rivkah must have been coming along for the ride. According to my grandfather, she—as well as a myriad of other elderly people—enjoyed doing that.

I looked at PopPop and wondered how many people he had told about my "secret" investigation.

"I don't know if Mr. Clawson could have done that," I said to Rivkah as she settled in. "Isn't he pretty sick?"

"Where there is a will, there is a way," she said.

Same thing my grandfather had said.

But before I could get back to the Falls Park Senior Complex, Rivkah wanted to go to the grocery store. She'd brought out egg rolls from her restaurant for us. I declined her offer of one, upsetting her. My grandfather told her he'd eat both. That cheered her up. Somewhat.

I didn't know what she wanted to get from the store, but it was postponing my meeting with Mr. Clawson, and for some reason I was ready to get to it. Wouldn't that make Maisie proud? Me wanting to talk and not just watch. I had a feeling that the stop was so Rivkah could try to get some of whatever she bought at the store inside of me. Somehow.

"You two go in," PopPop said as he pulled into the parking lot of Season's, a kosher grocery chain. New to our parts, the store was one of the "revitalization" projects the city had taken on. Not that there was anything wrong with the village as it was. "You help her out, Win. I'll wait here."

"Do you have a list?" I said, still wondering why we'd stopped. If it truly was grocery shopping she needed to do, it seemed like she would have done it on the way back so nothing would spoil or melt. We stood by the carts.

"I only need a few things," she said, taking one of the shopping carts out from its bay.

"You want to tell me some of them, and I'll go and get them?"

"No. I know what I like. I'll get it." She looked at me and handed the cart over to me. "You take that one. Go find yourself some nice fruit. I'll buy it for you."

I didn't want any fruit, but I was sure she was telling me not to bother her while she did whatever it was she'd come to do.

I took the cart and she got herself another one and took off down one of the aisles. I stood there for a minute, not sure what to do. Then I decided to amble off toward the produce.

That's when I heard her.

That tobacco-stained voice coming around the corner of the aisle. I knew it was her even before I saw her face.

Glynis Vale.

"I'll get the bread," she called over her shoulder.

I didn't know who she was talking to. I wanted to go around the corner to see, but I didn't want to lose track of her.

She saw me, our eyes locked and it took her a moment to realize where she knew me from, but as soon as that realization hit, she turned around and went the other way. I followed behind her. I didn't know why. I didn't know what I wanted to do when I caught up with her. What I wanted to say.

Glynis looked back at me as she rounded the corner. Walking quickly, she ducked down an aisle. But I followed. When she got to the other end, she looked over her shoulder and turned right, and before I could get to the end of the aisle, I saw her pass back by going in the opposite direction.

I got to the end of the row and looked in the direction she'd first gone in. There was something that way she didn't want me to see. I looked the other way but couldn't see her.

"Win, what are you doing?" Rivkah came up behind me. "You have nothing in your basket. I saw you go down the other aisle. Now you're just standing here."

I didn't answer her. Instead, I turned my head, looking back and forth down the aisle trying to see if Glynis had come back that way.

"What is going on with you, Win?"

I looked at Rivkah, concern on her face, and I let the tight feeling I had inside of me go. I relaxed my face. "Oh, I don't know, Savta," I said. "I think I'm letting Maisie get into my head."

"What does Maisie have to do with grocery shopping?" she asked.

"It's nothing, Savta," I said. "I'm okay. Just being sil—"

*Bam!*

A cart ran into mine. I jumped back and put my arm in front of Rivkah to protect her. I looked to see what had happened and saw that it was Glynis. She was glaring at me. Her face looked as intense as my whole body had felt moments ago. Her eyebrows furrowed so deeply that they almost touched.

"Why are you following me?" she said, venom in that gravelly voice.

"I'm not following you," I said.

"Yes, you are!" she hissed. She moved her cart out of the way. She came and stood on the other side of mine. "You were at my job the other day. You beat up Noah. Why? What for? Are you crazy?" She pointed her finger at my face. "Now you're here!"

"You beat up someone?" Rivkah said.

"No," I said.

"Yes, you did!" Glynis said. "Right in the parking lot of my job!"

"Why would the woman lie?" Rivkah asked.

"Because she is a liar, Savta," I said. Glynis was making me angry now. I probably shouldn't have followed her in the store, but now she was attacking me. "And she is lying about this. It was Riya who beat that man up."

"Oh," Rivkah said, nodding. "That makes sense."

"I'm warning you," Glynis said, wagging her finger in my

face. "Don't cross me. And stay out of my way!" Spittle flew from her mouth with each word.

"I would be happy to leave you alone if you just told me why you lied that night."

"I don't have to tell you anything," she said.

"Your son may have seen a murderer. Don't you care about that?" I said.

"My son didn't see anything. And you need to not talk about him."

"How do you know he didn't see anything?" I asked. "Did you ask him?"

"I don't need to ask him," she said, talking over me. "I already know."

"What is it that you think you know?"

"Look," she said. "You need to learn to mind your own business."

"I am minding my own business," I said. I moved the cart out of the way and got up close and personal with her. Now my finger was in her face. "They are trying to blame my father for this. Put him in jail. This is about family for me. You understand about protecting *family*, don't you?"

Rivkah gently placed her hand on my arm. "Win," she said. "It's okay."

Then I felt those stupid tears welling up again. I was sure there was no crying in sleuthing.

"If this is about family," Glynis said, "then *you* should be the one who understands." Her voice had calmed down and it seemed her eyes showed me some empathy.

She moved back behind her cart, put her hands on the handles and pulled it out, readying to leave. "Jasper didn't see anything," she said, her voice lower, calmer. "He was running after his . . ." I saw her swallow hard before she spoke. "His mother." She lowered her head and swiped at the corner of her eye. "But then she disappeared, just like she always does. And that was all he saw that night. Her."

"I thought Jasper was your son," I said.

"He is. Now."

I didn't know for sure what she meant. But her face showed me her words were sincere.

"And now maybe everything will be okay," she said with a faraway look in her eyes. "I don't want to mess anything up for him ever again. I want him to be happy. That's all I care about."

She took off, and I wanted to go after her. I couldn't believe—didn't want to believe—that that boy hadn't seen anything, but Rivkah put her hand on my arm. "Let her be."

Rivkah didn't have much in her cart, but she was ready to go. We went through the checkout line and out the door. I spotted PopPop standing over by another car speaking to someone.

"C'mon, Savta," I said. "I'll put the groceries in the car."

I helped her in. The car was still running, so it was warm inside. I popped the trunk. PopPop waved, telling me he was coming, and I waved back, telling him I had it.

He had parked right next to a red Honda Civic. Just like the one that Glynis drove. I backpedaled to take a gander at the license plate. GHS. The first part of hers. The only part I knew. It was her car. I started putting the groceries in just as PopPop arrived.

"I got this," he said. "Get in the car."

Instead, I walked around to Glynis's car window, wanting to look in. I didn't know what I thought I might find. Jasper, maybe, sitting in a cold car. Would I question a little boy? One who, according to his caretaker, had had a hard life?

I didn't know, but that didn't stop me. I peeked inside and gasped.

"What are you doing, Win?" my grandfather said. "Come get in the car."

I looked over at him. He had his driver's-side door open, one foot in, waiting for me.

I looked back down in the window.

"What? Do you see something?" He started to take his foot back out of the car.

"I'm coming," I said. I hurried over to his car. I couldn't wait to tell him that I'd just seen Blake. That little Ori-Pei puppy that Stephen Bayard had the morning before he'd died was sitting in Glynis Vale's back seat.

THE FALLS PARK Senior Complex was half-new and half-old, just like everything else in the village.

They'd built the complex around the older building as the seniors became less capable but still wanted their independence, creating a little village of its own. As we walked the halls, I noted an antiseptic smell to the place, but it was clean and cheery, and the nursing home part didn't have a hospital feel.

We stopped at the desk this time and signed in. My grandfather seemed to know right where to go.

"You been here before to see Mr. Clawson?" I asked.

"A time or two," he said. "Came once with Danny."

Danny. He'd been my number-one suspect until PopPop shot that idea down. He'd said Danny Clawson wasn't that kind of man.

That had been how I thought I'd find out who killed Stephen Bayard. I'd look into what kind of person he was. So I couldn't argue that point with PopPop.

We walked down the hallways and I stayed closed to the walls. I didn't want Falls Park employees Glynis or Noah to see me, even though I'd just left Glynis at the grocery store. With a dog in her car. And not just any dog.

"This is his room." PopPop stopped in front of the same door I had hidden myself from just a few days before. "He didn't do it," he said.

"I know," I said.

"Well, when you question him, act like you know."

I wanted to remind him it had been Riya who didn't know how to interrogate people. But I just nodded my head and followed him as he pushed open the door.

"How you doing, Dan?"

"Aloysius," the man said. "Good to see you."

His hair was white. His body slumped. His crumpled clothes seemingly hastily put on. He sat with his wheelchair facing the window, but turned around on his own when we came in.

"Good to see you." PopPop put a hand on my shoulder. "You remember my granddaughter, Win."

"Course I do," he said. "She's all grown-up now."

"Hi, Mr. Clawson." He didn't look anything like I remembered, but I put on a smile and tried not to show how bad I felt that he was so sickly.

"We didn't come to stay," my grandfather said, not wasting any time. "You heard about Stephen Bayard?"

"Yeah, I did." He seemed to sit up a little straighter with his words. "Can't say I care much about that kind of stuff, or him, anymore."

"We need to find out about when you did care about that stuff," my grandfather said.

"What do you mean?" Mr. Clawson asked.

"Win's got some questions. They're trying to blame my boy for his murder."

"Graham?" Mr. Clawson said.

"Yep," my grandfather said.

Mr. Clawson frowned up. "He wouldn't do anything like that."

"Everyone knows that but that darn detective. He believes that Graham is his best suspect."

"How can I help?" Mr. Clawson asked. He grabbed the wheels on his chair and pushed them to face us better.

"Answer Win's questions," PopPop said. "She's been doing a little investigating of her own."

I went over and stood by a chair opposite him. "May I?" I said, pointing to the chair.

"Of course," he said. "Aloysius, you can sit there." He pointed to another chair in the corner.

"I'm fine," PopPop said.

"I hate to bring up bad memories," I said, sitting down. "But I heard that your wife left you for Stephen Bayard."

"Naw, that's not true," he said.

Leave it to my mother to get the information wrong.

"Diane left me, but not for him. He had a wife. The two of them were the perfect pair."

"How so?" I asked.

"She was just as much of a criminal as he turned out to be."

"Did you meet her?" I asked. I remembered reading in the article I'd found about the LaGrosse Warehouse heist that they had questioned David Niven's wife. I wondered if they were the same person.

"I met her a time or two. She'd show up at the shop. Go in the back room with him. Take care of their business."

"Back room?" I asked.

"That's why Diane left me," he said, hanging his head. "That back room."

"What'dya mean, Dan?" PopPop got in on my questioning.

Mr. Clawson let out a long sigh and shook his head. "Ain't nothing I'm proud of. But that guy was such a . . ." He seemed to search for the right word, then he chuckled. "Charmer," he said. "At least that's the word Diane used for him."

"Angel's smile. Devil's tail," I said, remembering my mother's words.

"That he was. So I let him put things in my back room. There was a wall back there that you couldn't tell didn't belong. That's where they'd store their loot."

"Who?" I asked.

"Whoever he was working with at the time."

"Did you know the things he put back there?" I asked.

"No," he said. "Didn't wanna know. To be honest, I don't know for sure what he did. I just know he'd come and go out of there every time he blew through town. I let him have full access to it. Couldn't let him keep coming through the shop, so I gave him a key to the side door."

"That's why your wife left." I had started feeling sorry for this guy. Stephen Bayard tore his family apart. My family banded together because of Bayard. His split apart.

"That's why she left. Took my boy with her. But at least he came back." I saw a smile come across his face. "After that, after she packed up saying she didn't want no association with a weak, spineless man, I told Stephen no more. I stood up to him. I told him I wasn't going along with whatever he was doing anymore. He said that wasn't going to make Diane take me back, but I told him I didn't care. It was over anyway. And I'd thought it worked. Didn't see him anymore. Then I closed up shop."

"Your store sat vacant for a while," PopPop said.

"Yeah," he said. "Couldn't decide what to do with it. Burn it down, or what. I didn't know, Stephen might have left something back there. Thought I might need to get rid of the evidence."

"You decided not to?"

"It's still standing, ain't it?"

"Yes, sir, it is," I said.

"That's when Isabella came to me."

"Mrs. Cro?" I said.

"Yep. Said she always wanted to own a flower shop." His eyes drifted off. "Diane loved flowers," he said, his voice cracking. "So I told her to take the building. Have lots of flowers. Pretty ones. Wash away all the bad things I let go on in there."

"It's a very nice flower shop," I said. "She always has the most beautiful flowers. And she's so happy to be there." Those words were because I wanted him to know he'd done a good thing.

"Good," he said. "I'm glad something good came out of it."

# chapter

# THIRTY-NINE

In twelve hours, I was supposed to serve dessert to one hundred benefactors attending the President's Dinner at Wycliffe University.

With five days' head start, I hadn't begun making any of it.

But it was all good.

We'd be fine. I had everything all figured out.

Twelve hours ago, Detective Liam Beverly had questioned my father about his involvement in the murder of Stephen Bayard.

After five days of investigation, I hadn't begun making headway on who the real murderer was.

That wasn't good.

I didn't know if my family would ever be fine again. I didn't have one single thing figured out.

The day before, I had been so busy I couldn't even think straight. I had colored sticky notes everywhere. I think Maisie pulled one off the back of my pants. Me and my crew—old and new—ran around getting everything together. We made sure the frozen cart was powered up and cold (all the while listening to Maisie wondering why I *just* didn't have a food truck, like I could take on another big project!), counting dessert plates I'd gotten from a party rental company and chopping up bushels of cherries, strawberries and nuts. I hadn't conducted one interrogation, as PopPop liked to call them, or collected one iota of evidence, as I liked to call pieces of paper and pictures of dog collars, and I had avoided my father, not wanting to hear what happened when he went to the station.

It was six o'clock in the morning and the three of us had already been at the shop for two hours.

Maisie, my mom and me.

My investigation had to be put to the back of the freezer. For now.

"Okay," Mom said. "I've got all the cakes ready. They're either in the oven, or ready to go in. Now what do you want me to do?"

And that was the way our day went. Hectic. Busy. Frenzied. Loud. But we got it done. We made fifty individual raspberry java ice cream cakes, and five each of the chocolate cherry and almond and the seven-layer strawberry tart ice cream cakes. Ten slices a cake. I figured we'd have enough to serve one hundred and fifty people. Surely, we wouldn't run out.

Felice slept the entire time and PopPop played backgammon.

When the store opened, PopPop went behind the counter for the first time to help Candy serve customers. Candy was my night help, but PopPop, who had insisted on volunteering, said he didn't want to work with Wilhelmina. I had to laugh. I was going to have to have a talk with that lady, I decided, flirting with my grandpop, making him nervous.

By three thirty, we were ready to roll out for the six o'clock dinner.

"You got everything?"

"I do," I said. "Except for the business cards I had Liken Printing do." I glanced out the front window. "They're coming UPS. I thought I might have them before we left. I wanted to pass them out."

"Don't worry about them," my mother said. "After they taste your desserts, people will be sure to find you."

"Fingers and ice cream scoops crossed," I said.

"Okay, then, I'm going home," my mother said. "You two are okay without me, right?"

"We don't really have to do anything," I said. "Clara's assistant, Sophie, called yesterday and said Ari's waitstaff would serve our dessert. We just have to plate it. Maisie and I can do that."

I had warned Maisie to be nice to Ari when she saw him, although I couldn't count on her listening to me. I knew, though, that she knew how important this was to me. Ever since word had gotten out about us catering the dessert at this event, the foot traffic in the store had picked up. And customers tasting our wares had come back with their friends and family in tow. And the weather hadn't mattered one little bit.

"You two aren't going looking like that, are you?" my mother said.

Maisie and I were covered from head to toe in chocolate and flour, and were sticky from sugar and eggs.

"Noo," I said warily. "But we hadn't planned on dressing up."

"You're not?"

"No," I said, sudden skepticism about that idea surfacing. "I just figured we'd get messy again. I got us some aprons with our logo on them and we're wearing matching white shirts and black pants."

"Oh," my mother said, nodding her head. "That'll be cute."

Glad that passed her approval, because it was too late to change.

Maisie and I dressed quickly upstairs in her grandmother's apartment and hustled out to the university's campus. Even though our food was the last to be served, I didn't want to do my setup while the guests ate their main course or while the speeches were going on.

We stopped at the front door of the University Center to unload and told the student who was working the desk who we were. He told us to go to the second floor. We packed the elevator and Maisie rode up with our stuff. I went back out and drove down into the underground garage to park. Nearly all of the parking spaces were reserved for the evening's guests, but there was also a spot reserved for me. I pulled in, hopped out of the car and, in my haste, made the mistake of trying to go up the stairwell from the garage and found after walking up that the door was locked. I peeked through the wire-threaded square window, but couldn't see anyone to get their attention. *Shoot!*

I went up one more floor and found that door was locked, too. I looked up and thought I didn't want to keep climbing just to find that I couldn't get in. I found, going back down, only the door on the first floor would let me back into the building. Once inside, I got in the elevator with a gaggle of apron-wearing Molta's waitstaff. They pushed four, I reached over to press two.

"Aren't you serving dessert?"

"Yep."

"The dinner's on four," he said.

"Oh. I thought . . ." I could have sworn the guy at the desk had told me two.

When I got to four, sure enough, it was where the dinner was taking place. Maisie wasn't anywhere to be found.

"What happened to you?" I asked when she finally arrived. I had run over to the elevator to help her.

"That dingbat told us two."

"That's what I thought," I said.

"Well how did you get here and why didn't you come looking for me?"

"Sorry!" I said. "And I was just about to come find you."

"Yeah, right."

We pushed and carried our stuff to a back corner and I explained I'd followed the waitstaff up.

"Ah," Maisie said, whispering and lifting a conspiratorial eyebrow. "The murderer is here."

I glanced at Ari and his crew. "Remember, be nice," I said as we started unpacking boxes and setting the dessert on the cold, frosty cart. "We're not investigating today."

"I know," she said. "I'll be nice. See . . ." She smiled and waved at Ari. Over the clanking of plates and silverware, he barked out orders, making sure everything was right.

He waved back.

"Yes," I said, smiling and nodding at him. "Be nice."

"Look," she said. "There's Althea." Maisie shook her head. "She doesn't look like she's working tonight." She was dressed all in white. Well, winter white, as my grandmother used to call it. Wool slacks, a beautifully crocheted sweater. Ankle boots with a silver buckle. “We should have warned her about him. She should be careful of that man.”

“No sleuthing,” I said. “That means no accusing either.” I glanced their way as I bent over to take another cake out of the box.

“I said okay,” she said.

“Hi, ladies.” It was Sophie, Clara Blackwell’s assistant. I did a quick check over our work to make sure everything was on schedule. Then gave the thermostat knob a little twist to set it lower.

“Hi,” we answered at the same time.

“Just wanted to check on you, make sure you didn’t need anything. I see you found somewhere to set up. I should have come earlier.”

“Yeah,” Maisie said, “because that boy downstairs at the desk said it was on two.”

She poked out her lips and tilted her head. “I’m sure that didn’t happen.”

“It did.”

“Why would he do that?” Sophie asked.

“I’d like to know.”

I gave Maisie a look that said, “Cool it.” This was the woman who gave scathing reviews. We did not need to be on her bad side.

“It’s all good,” I said in a singsongy voice. “We’re here and we’ll be all set up soon.”

She turned her attention back to me. “Good. I’ve got to run out on an errand for Ms. Blackwell.”

“That’s fine,” I said.

“Okay,” she said, and smiled. She looked around the dining room and back at the cart. “It looks delicious.” She pointed at the dessert cart. “I’m sure Clara will be pleased.”

"I hope so."

"Okay, so, if there's nothing else . . ." I shook my head. "Okay, I'm heading out." She pointed to a door with a red exit sign, the same doorway I'd tried to come through. "After I make a stop in the little girl's room."

"Those doors are locked," I said.

Sophie glanced at it. "Oh, did you try to come up from the parking garage?"

"Yep," I said. "I had to go all the way back down."

She chuckled. "Sorry about that. All the doors except for the garage and first floor levels are locked on the stairwell side. But for fire purposes, of course, you can get out that way from each floor."

"Oh," I said. "Good to know."

Sophie left and Maisie and I got back to work.

"You know, I hope they're not dating," Maisie said.

"Who?" I asked.

"Ari and Althea."

"I think they are," I said.

"Why would you think that?"

I sucked my tongue and stood up straight, resting my hands on my lower back. "I know we weren't mentioning anything about this, but . . ."

"But what?"

"She's his alibi for the night of the murder."

"What?" Maisie asked, her face contorted. "Althea?"

"She told me I shouldn't be judgmental about Ari, that he was a nice guy. And that she was with him the night of the murder."

"Why would she tell you that?"

I hunched my shoulders. "I don't know. Protecting her man, I guess."

"Ewww!" Maisie said, and feigned a shiver going down her spine. "When did she tell you that?"

"One day when I was taking out the trash, I was talking to Mrs. Cro and she walked up."

"Between the buildings?" Maisie asked.

"Yep," I said, then tapped her on the arm. "Hey! We're unpacking here." She had stopped to stare at Ari and Althea.

"Why would she come into the alley?" Maisie asked, turning back to help me. "That alley goes nowhere."

"She was looking for Mrs. Cro. I told you. She wanted to buy flowers. Probably for her man."

"There you go again, making me sick to my stomach," Maisie said. "She must be really desperate to date him."

"Ari is not a bad-looking guy, even if . . ."

"He's a murderer?"

"Maisie."

"I know. No murder talk today."

"We're going to put the dessert plates under here," I said. "Keep them chilled."

"Look at him looking at her like a little puppy," Maisie said. "Like he's just cute and adorable and not dangerous." Her mouth was turned up like she had a bad taste in it. "I think I should tell her."

"No, you shouldn't," I said. "Here, put these plates up."

"I might be saving her life," Maisie said.

"And Ari might kill you for doing it."

"I'm not afraid of him."

"You're not? Even though you think he killed someone?"

"I've got Riya on my team. That makes me practically invincible."

"Well Riya's not here." I tugged at her to get her back to the task at hand. "Oh. Did I tell you that I found the puppy?"

"What puppy?" she asked.

"The one Stephen Bayard had when I met him."

"How did you find it?"

"It was in Glynis Vale's car."

"No," she said, her eyes big—that got her attention diverted from Ari and Althea. "Get out of here."

"Yes," I said. "Now, how did that happen?"

"Glynis is the killer."

"Doesn't take much for you to jump ships."

"How did you see the dog?"

"She was at the grocery store. We'd stopped there so Savta could pick up a few things before we went to question Dan Clawson."

"Wait! What? I'm missing something here."

I grimaced.

I'd been busy that day and the day before and hadn't caught Maisie up on the time I'd spent sleuthing with my grandfather.

"If you promise to work while I talk, I'll tell you."

"I'm working," she said, and picked up a stack of the small plates. "Start talking."

I told her everything. I started with what I'd found out on the internet about the robbery, and ended with what Mr. Clawson said about his practically being a willing participant to Bayard's illicit activities while we were at the Falls Park Senior Complex.

"Oh my." She was standing there slack-jawed as I ended my telling of the events.

"I thought you were going to work while I talked."

"I'm too stunned to move." She leaned against the wall like she couldn't stand on her own. "Win, when were you going to tell me all of this?"

"Tomorrow," I said. "When we picked the investigation back up."

"Oh my goodness," she said, spreading her fingers. She shook her hands like she was trying to get something off them. "I have so many questions."

"Well, you can't ask them now."

"I am going to ask them now because if I don't I might burst," she said. "You may not answer them, but you can't ignore them."

"Argh." I looked at her. "Let's slice cake while we talk."

I knew there was no stopping her. I'd be serving cake with a hundred or so people in the room and she'd still be trying to ask me questions. I pulled out my ten-piece slicer and handed it to Maisie. "If you stop slicing, I stop talking."

"Deal," she said.

I rolled my eyes. I didn't know why I made that deal with her. She hadn't kept the one we'd made immediately before that one. "Okay, first question."

"What did Stephen Bayard keep in the back at Mr. Clawson's?" she asked.

I shrugged. "I don't know. I don't think Mr. Clawson knew."

"Was it what was stolen the day of the murder from Mrs. Cro?"

"Oh." I said the word in slow motion, and this time I was the one who stopped working. My mouth still in the shape of an "O,"

I was at a loss for words. I had forgotten there'd been a robbery that day at the Flower Pot.

"Maybe it was the succinylcholine and all the other drugs," Maisie said, her voice taking on a scary-story tone. "From the robbery. Maybe he went there to get it back."

I hadn't ever taken the time to put all the information I'd gathered together. Not that I would have thought the conversation with Mrs. Cro was part of our investigation. But it made sense that Stephen Bayard or someone who knew that he kept things in that safe broke in to get something left there. And it made sense, if Stephen Bayard was David Niven, the man who orchestrated the LaGrosse Warehouse robbery, that he might have stashed something from that heist there.

"He didn't get it and then inject himself with it," I said. "That's not your conclusion, is it?"

"No. No." She shook her head. "Someone else could have," Maisie said. "Someone who knew it was there—"

"And brought it along with a needle that night." I finished her thought.

"Ari said he worked on a job before with Stephen Bayard, didn't he?" Maisie said.

"I can't remember." I was too nervous and my brain synapses were slow firing. "But I do remember him saying he wasn't going to work on another one with him."

"So you know what that means."

"What?" But then I knew right away what she meant and filled in the blank. "Ari had been on the LaGrosse job," I said.

"Right," Maisie said.

"Stephen Bayard probably thought he could force him to do it. But Ari wasn't having it."

We both turned and looked at Ari. He had gone back to working and Althea was off to the side watching him.

"So, instead," I said, "Ari killed him."

"Finally!" she said, and palmed my forehead. "You get it. Ari is the killer."

"What about the dog?" I asked.

"What about the dog?" she asked.

"How did Glynis get the dog?"

We stared at each other. Trying to think.

"Maybe . . ." Maisie started, but said nothing else.

"Maybe," I said, "it was *her* dog in the first place. Maybe that was what the boy was chasing that night. The dog. He saw Stephen Bayard with the dog and he went to get it back."

Maisie's face frowned up. "Then the boy would have seen who killed Stephen Bayard, don't you think? And Detective Beverly wouldn't have asked you about the dog if he knew its rightful owner."

"It might be why Glynis Vale lied and had her adopted son lie in the first place," I said. "Or maybe the police didn't find out until after Ms. Devereaux let them into the B and B and they saw the dog collar with the phone number."

"And they called it," Maisie said in agreement.

"Right," I said.

"That couldn't be right," she said, her face now turning to one of disagreement.

"Why?" I thought we'd figured out another piece of the puzzle.

"Because you'd just left Ms. Devereaux when you went straight to the grocery store, right?"

"After we picked up your grandmother." I nodded my agreement.

"How would they have had the time to come over, secure the crime scene, bag the evidence and call Glynis Vale to let her know her missing dog had been with Stephen Bayard?"

"I don't know," I said, my words sounding a bit more fractious than I meant them to be.

"And where was the dog all this time?"

"I don't know. The dog pound, I'd guess."

"If he really took it there in the first place," she said. "You said when he left he went in the other direction."

"Still, the dog could have been there and no one knew who brought it in or who it belonged to. No collar, remember?" At the side of my neck, I tugged on an imaginary leash.

"It wasn't enough time." Maisie shook her head in opposition.

"You know," I said, "I don't know about your timeline, because I don't know about all that bagging evidence stuff, so I couldn't say how long it would take."

"But you have to admit that she had that dog pretty quickly after you left the bed-and-breakfast. I mean, Ms. Devereaux even went back to the store."

"So?"

"So she would have had to call the police and go back and let them in, right?"

"Yeah . . ." I looked at Maisie. "That is true. And that's not—"

"Enough time," Maisie finished my sentence.

"So what do you think?" I asked. "Glynis got the dog from him when she killed him?"

"Let's call."

"What?"

"The phone number that was on the collar. You took a picture of it. Let's call it."

"No." I shook my head vigorously.

"Why?"

I swallowed hard. "Okay," I said hesitantly. "But what if the police have that phone tapped?"

"Don't be ridiculous," Maisie said, and took my phone from me and put in my code. I could hear the camera on her phone going off. "Why would the police do that?"

"Because now they're thinking like we're thinking."

"Who? Detective Idiot?" Maisie asked.

"He's really not," I said. "I just agreed with you calling him that because he was being mean to my father." I swiped my hand across my forehead. I was standing next to a cart that was set at below freezing temperature and I was sweating.

"What's a phone call?" She held up my phone. "It's no big deal."

"Stop." I took my phone from her. "Let's think. There is another way to find out if he knew Glynis."

"How?"

"I don't know. Maybe he . . ."

"He what?"

"She! Maybe *she* was his wife." A light bulb went off in my head. "You know what?"

"What?" she said as if she was listening to a scary story.

"That dog's name was Blake."

She gave me a look as if to say, "So what?"

"Blake. Like *Blake* Edwards. The guy who wrote and directed the Pink Panther movies."

"Oh, wow." Maisie's eyes got big. "So that puts Glynis in on this whole Pink Panther charade thingy."

"Yep," I said, nodding. "*Mrs.* Nivens. From the newspaper. And according to O," I said, "we should be able to prove that with a quick check of marriage records." I shook my phone.

"Only if they got married in Ohio," she said.

"You should be able to look it up anywhere they got married," I said.

"Are we going to go through every state's records?" Maisie said. "That could take years."

"No, it wouldn't." I searched the web on how to get marriage records. "Okay, you go to the probate court records," I said, announcing my search result out loud.

"Oh my goodness," Maisie said. She starting pushing up and down on her toes, anticipation bouncing in her body, looking as if it were ricocheting around.

"Hold on," I said. "I just have to put the names in here. Wait. Okay. Last name. B-A-Y-A-R-D. Now the first name. S-T-E-P-H-E-N."

"Too late," she said.

"Too late for what?" I said, and pressed submit before I looked up at her.

"I called."

"You called?" I screeched. "How?"

"I took a picture of your picture," she said. "I got the number." She turned the phone so I could see. "Don't worry, I dialed *67.

Now shush, it's ringing." She looked at me. "You know Glynis's voice, right?"

"This is crazy, Maisie."

"Hey, somebody else's phone is ringing," Maisie said. I looked at her and she nodded over toward Ari's area, where his people were working. Walking right past them was O.

"This couldn't get worse," I said. "Hang up before O gets over here and finds out what we're doing."

"That's where the phone is ringing," Maisie said. "Right where he is."

Then someone picked up the phone.

"Hello?" I could hear the voice on the other end.

Maisie took my arm and started shaking it. "Oh my God! Oh my God!" she mouthed. "Look who picked up!"

"Hang up! Hang up!" I said in a strained whisper.

"Did you see that?" she said, pressing the end button.

"I saw that," I said, then glanced down at my phone. The marriage license record had come up. It showed that on August 1, in Cuyahoga County some twenty years ago, Stephen Bayard had married the same person who had just picked up Maisie's call.

Althea Quigley.

# chapter

# FORTY

My phone rang and Maisie and I almost jumped out of our skins.

"Oh my God!" I said, and put my hand over my heart. It was pounding under my apron.

"Who is it?" Maisie asked in a strained whisper, like the person on the other end could hear her asking.

"PopPop," I said, looking at the phone. "Geesh," I said with a nervous chuckle, "that scared the stew out of me." I tried to steady my hand as I pressed the button on my phone. "Hi, PopPop." Still a tremor in my voice.

"You okay?" he said.

Couldn't get anything past him.

"Yep." I swallowed down the jitters, then stole a glance at Althea. "Thought I had turned my ringer off. The phone scared me."

"I brought the business cards you ordered." Knowing I was fine, he moved to the matter at hand. "They came after you left."

"Oh. Okay," I said. "Thanks."

"Well, don't you want them?"

"Oh! Y-yes." I fumbled my words. "Of course I do, PopPop." I chuckled. "Sorry, just a little rattled."

"Okay, where are you?" he said. "I'll bring them to you."

"I'm at the University Center."

"I know that," he said. "What floor?"

"Oh, no, PopPop. I can run down and get them. No need of you trying to park and come up." I remembered how all the spaces were marked "Reserved."

"I'll wait for you." He didn't even say "Bye." Just hung up. It was what he always did.

"Being in the same room with a killer," Maisie said, "is quite unnerving."

"You're telling me," I said. "I have to go downstairs and get the business cards from PopPop."

"What are we going to do about—" She jerked her head a few times toward Althea.

"Good question," I said. "We should call Detective Beverly, but—"

"Would he believe us?" We said it at the same time.

"Hi." It was O. He'd made it over to us after stopping to talk to Ari. He just seemed to know everybody. "What'chu two up to?"

"Nothing," we said. We huddled together, our eyes trained across the room.

He swung around and looked that way. "It smells good over there."

I gave him a polite smile.

"I thought I'd check in on you guys." He nodded at the dessert cart. "Seems you've got everything under control."

"Uh-huh," Maisie said.

I smiled again.

"Okay," he said. "What's going on?"

"Why do you think something is going on?" I hit Maisie and pointed at the cart, telling her to do something. We could at least act as if we were working. "I was just on my way downstairs to get something from my grandfather." I untied my apron and pulled it over my head, my eyes still watching Ari's area.

O swung from the waist again and looked toward Ari and his waitstaff.

"Did Ari do something to you guys?" He squinted his eyes and tilted his head. "Did he say something off to you?"

"No," we said.

"Then what?" His face dropped the confused look. "Wait. Don't tell me you figured out who killed your Mr. Snowman? Is that why you're acting so nervous?"

"He's not my Mr. Snowman," I said.

"We did," Maisie said.

"And I'm not acting nervous." My head shot around to Maisie. We were talking at the same time, but I knew he'd heard what she said. "Maisie!" I said, and tugged on her arm.

"Well, we did."

"Tell me," he said. "Who did it? Ari?"

"No," I said. "We can't tell you."

"It was Althea," Maisie said at the same time.

"Shhh! Maisie!" I said, and glanced across the way. They seemed to be paying no attention to us, which was good since Maisie was trying to spill the beans.

"Have you called the police?" O asked.

"I don't know if your police friend would appreciate us snooping around or if he'd even believe me."

"You have to do something," O said.

"Agreed," I said, lowering my voice. "But in the middle of the dinner? And what if he won't listen to me? I will have embarrassed everyone here."

"You want me to call him?" O asked, not even knowing what we'd found out.

I glanced again at Althea, and thought about my father. Telling Detective Beverly would clear his name, which would make him happy. But my father wouldn't care that I had figured it out, he'd want me to be safe. The only way to do that, I knew, was to get Detective Beverly there.

"Okay," I said. "You can call him." I looked down at my phone. "First, though, I have to go and meet PopPop downstairs," I said. "Maisie, you fill O in on everything we found out." I turned to O. "Then I'm going to need you to get your friend Detective Beverly down here. I don't know how he'll take to me snooping and figuring out who the murderer is, if we really figured it out."

"We did," Maisie said.

"And can you tell him no sirens, please?" I said. "I don't want to disrupt the dinner."

"Why do you care about that?" Maisie said.

"Because it's my family's business at stake," I said. "And we could be wrong."

"We're not," Maisie said.

"And look at her," I said, talking about Althea, but then stopped Maisie from doing it. "Don't look now!"

"What?"

"She's all dressed up, chasing after Ari. She doesn't know we know anything," I said. "The detective won't have to chase her and it can all be handled quietly." My voice went down to a whisper. "Dinner won't be interrupted."

"Okay. Go," Maisie said, and gave me a push. "I'll tell O what we know." I could tell she couldn't wait to do that.

"Then I'll call Liam," O said.

"It's a plan," I said with a firm nod. "Okay, then. Be right back."

I WENT OUT the stairwell door. My mind focused on getting to PopPop and back up so that we could call the detective and let him know who the real killer was and save my father.

I didn't even hear her come through the door behind me.

"Don't think I don't know what you've been up to," she said, her voice ricocheting, echoing off through the tight space.

My foot, going for the next step, dangled in midair. My breath caught in the back of my throat. I turned and looked upward, right into Althea's eyes.

"Hi," I said, trying to mask my fear. "You mean the desserts?" No way she knew I'd figured out what she'd done. "Yep." I felt my throat tightening, my words barely able to eke out. "We did a lot of work."

"Don't play with me." Her lips barely moved when she spoke, her eyes cold and menacing.

That was when I saw the steak knife in her hand.

"Oh," I said with a fleeting breath. Tiny balls of pain formed inside my forehead, trying to push through. They were making me nauseous and weak. My legs trembling, I felt my knees buckling. I held on to the rail to keep steady.

"I—I have to . . . uhm . . . to meet my grandfather," I said, and pointed down the stairs. "He's waiting for me."

"Why? So you can tell him what I did?"

"No," I said, shaking my head. I eased down a step. "He has something for me." I swallowed. "I—I wouldn't . . . don't have anything to tell him about y-you." I pushed up against the wall, leaning on it for support, and took another step down.

"Now you want to act as if you don't know that I killed Stephen."

I gulped. "Y-you what?" I couldn't get the words out. I shook my head so hard I felt my brain hitting the sides of it. "Please! I . . . I . . ."

"Yes, be afraid," she said. She took another step down. Calm. Measured. She taunted me as she got closer. "You shouldn't have been snooping."

"I—I didn't . . . wasn't . . ." I sucked in as much air as I could so I could force my words out. "How could I"—I tried to speak above the pounding in my head—"think you did that when you were with Ari that night?"

"I know you know I wasn't his alibi." She looked off for a moment. Distracted. "But he needs me. He's in as deep as I am."

"He helped you k-kill . . . him?"

"No! I didn't need help to kill Stephen." Then she smiled.

*Oh my God, this lady is crazy!*

"But Ari was the reason Stephen was back in town. Stephen wanted him to help him with a job."

I already knew that, but how that figured Ari in on the murder, I didn't know. And I didn't care. I just wanted to get out. Get away from her. I used my hands to guide me as I slid down the wall, taking two more steps down. I needed to get to the first floor fast. It was the first door I could get to that was unlocked. I edged down one more step. Taking my eyes off her for only a second, I glanced down the stairwell. I still had three flights to go.

"Take another step," she warned, and jabbed the knife in the air at me, "and you'll be sorry."

I was already sorry.

Sorry I'd tried to figure this stupid thing out.

I felt my bottom lip starting to tremble. Tears were welling up in my eyes and my breath was only coming in short bursts.

She was going to kill me.

I glanced up over her head. Back up the steps. Where was Maisie? Hadn't she seen this woman come through the door behind me? Why hadn't she sent help?

"When did you figure it out?" she said, making me focus on her again. "When you saw me in the alley between you and the flower shop?"

"The flower shop?" Oh yeah, that was when she'd told me about the alibi. She must've known then what I was doing. What we were doing. *She* was the one who'd broken into the shop. To get the drugs. The drugs she used to kill Stephen Bayard.

"No," I said, a foam of saliva forming around the corners of my lips. I cleared my throat. "That's not when I knew."

She found that funny. I guess it was. I had just admitted that I did know. Surely, I wasn't helping my own cause.

"He wouldn't have had to die. All he had to do was let me in on the job. But no, he laughed at me," she said, her eyes seemingly reliving the conversation. "Said I had given him up after the LaGrosse job. Ratted on him."

"But you didn't," I said, trying to make nice with her, hoping she'd forget about killing me. I started clicking my nails.

She frowned. "Stop that!" Her words filled with spite, she pointed at my hand with the knife.

"Sorry," I said, and balled my hands into fists. Hoping to placate her, I kept talking. "I read in the newspaper that you said you didn't know anything about that robbery."

"I did say that, didn't I?" A creepy smile spread over her face. Then she took another step down. "And neither one of you would have had to die if you hadn't tried to make me look like a fool."

"I didn't," I said, tears running down my face. "I don't want to die." I went down another step, ending up on the landing between flights. "I wouldn't. I was just . . ." I swallowed again. "They thought my father . . ." I inched my way along the wall to the next set of stairs.

"Yes, you did." Her voice was so calm that it made me more afraid. "You tried to make me look foolish."

*How in the world did I do that?*

"I knew I didn't have to worry about that Maisie," she was saying. "She'd never figure out anything."

*She sure doesn't know Maisie.*

"But you!" she shouted.

My nail clicking went into overdrive.

And that's when she lunged. She vaulted over the railing, her knife slicing downward as she came. I shrieked and grabbed my arm. Bright red blood trickled down it.

But, even with her managing to cut me, Althea had lost her balance when she jumped over the banister.

It was time to run.

Before she could right herself, I scrambled down the stairs, holding on to my arm, tripping over the steps, stumbling over my own feet. "No!" I yelped. "Help! Somebody help me, please!"

I got to the second floor just when I heard her feet hit the stairs, but I knew that door wouldn't open. Rushing past it, I ran into the wall and pushed myself off to get momentum to get down the next flight.

I heard her hit the second landing and then I heard a *thud!* Then another and an *"Umpf."* Something metal skidded across the floor and hit the wall.

"Win!" I heard my name, but I didn't stop. I couldn't stop. I had to get out. "Win!"

I knew that voice.

"PopPop?" I sobbed. I stopped and leaned against the rail, squeezing my arm. I tried to calm down. *Is he really there?* "PopPop." My voice barely audible.

"It's me, Win." I saw someone leaning over the banister. "Look at me!"

"How?" I said. I'd started to hyperventilate. I looked up.

"I hit her with the door. The door smacked her, then she smacked the wall. She's out." He turned away for a moment, then his eyes met mine again. "I'll stay here." He held up the knife she had brandished. "Go get help."

I looked at the door below me. A big "1" painted in black.

My way out.

"But . . ." I looked back up the stairs. "How did you know where I was?" I asked.

"Some boy at the front desk told me the President's Dinner was on two, and then I heard you scream."

# Epilogue

I didn't need O to call that not-so-bumbling detective. The 911 dispatcher did it for me. He came so quickly to arrest Althea that she hadn't even regained consciousness. EMS bandaged my arm, and that student who'd sent PopPop to the wrong floor got a lifetime supply of ice cream, compliments of Crewse Creamery's founding father.

Luckily, the dinner wasn't disrupted. The rest of the night went off without a hitch. Ari kept on serving during the arrest like nothing had happened. If he was her boyfriend, he didn't seem the least bit concerned about her fate.

PopPop didn't leave my side the rest of the night, even after all my jitteriness wore off.

Our desserts were a hit. Of course. I passed out the business cards that PopPop had brought. They doubled as loyalty cards—another one of my fantastic marketing ideas—and I got so many promises that people would use them. Heck, it seemed like the entire campus was abuzz with praise for Crewse Creamery and my heroics, capturing a killer.

They didn't know Althea had captured me, and it was my grandfather who was the hero.

And more good came out of it. One guy, who saw our minivan with a plastic sign on the side, offered his business card in exchange for mine. His name, company name and contact info were on one side. "Flip it over," he said, nodding at the card. "I can get you a good deal."

*We Make Food Trucks* was embossed on the other side. "Nowadays you can't run a food business without it," he said.

*So says you and Maisie.*

I tucked his card safely away.

The night was a hit, and that translated, in my opinion, to sales.

*Cha-ching!*

In the days that followed, things didn't slow down.

Noah Bean working two jobs—at Lakeside Memorial Clinic and Falls Park—was due to him taking care of his sick mother. That was the reason he didn't date (but clearly he fooled around)—he didn't want to get distracted from her care. But thanks to his using Riya's number, he was fired from the clinic. Riya, feeling bad (yes, she does have a sweet side), made it her mission to make sure his mom got the medical care she needed. She started volunteering at Bobby's clinic so Noah's mom could be her patient.

Danny Clawson, good man that he was, got Mrs. Keller a puppy. The cutest little dachshund. She named him Max Two and quickly corrected me when I thought she meant she was naming him that *also.* Two, she said, was part of his name.

Maisie had to rethink her opinion about Ari. It seemed he may have done wrong in the past, but was now trying to turn his life around. Maisie said she'd consider reconsidering how she felt, but she wouldn't ever step foot in that restaurant again, let alone work there, and she was serious about signing on with us permanently. That was fine with me. With all the business we'd soon have, I was going to need another employee at Crewse Creamery anyway.

Jasper turned out to be Althea's son, and she was who he'd seen when he went running off that night Stephen Bayard died. She'd lost him in the dark and snowy night, which turned out to be a good thing for him since she was on her way to a rendezvous with murder. Glynis had been a friend of Althea's who had taken the boy in because she wasn't a very good role model. With guardianship papers filed when he was still an infant, she'd been the only mother he'd known. I had to admit, all Glynis had been trying to do was keep the boy safe, happy and mentally stable. That puppy, Blake, she'd thought would be good therapy and she'd welcomed it when Althea gave him to her.

Althea, aka Barbara Niven, was the wife interviewed by the detectives after the heist at the LaGrosse Warehouse. She'd been a good liar. The police officers had walked away from her none the wiser. And Stephen Bayard matched the profile of the David Niven the police in Franklin County had been looking for. How he'd gotten away without leaving any fingerprints was anyone's guess. Nevertheless, when he was arrested a year later and spent time in prison, no one knew he was the one they'd been looking for.

Just as Mr. Clawson had said, the pair had hidden their ill-gotten loot in the back of his store. And with it being vacant for so long, they just went in and out as they pleased, no one ever knowing they were in town, selling the drugs, as Maisie surmised, on the street and through the black market. They had free rein until an investigation into their drug vials being expired prompted them to lay low. Still, an expiration date hadn't stopped Althea from using the drugs to kill Stephen Bayard. And being expired, per my father and the Cuyahoga County coroner, didn't necessarily hinder a drug's efficacy.

Stephen Bayard had come back to town wanting Ari in on another job he was plotting to commit, but Ari refused to be a part of it. Althea, on the other hand, was raring to go. Only Stephen didn't want her help. Seemed like she hadn't been such a good wife during the eighteen months he'd been locked up—she'd gone through most of their stash without sending him a dime. But him excluding her just made her mad. Mad enough to kill. And, Detective Beverly told us one cold, snowy day when he came in for ice cream, for her, there was no coming back from that idea after Stephen Bayard took her puppy!

# Acknowledgments

Without God, my keeper and my friend, I wouldn't be where I am today. My mother, who keeps Him company, as do my sisters: I miss you much.

I want to thank my agent, Rachel Brooks, who found me, and I'm so happy she did. I also want to thank the whole BookEnds Literary Agency team. They rock!

And I couldn't ask for a better editor than Jessica Wade. She helped me through this whole process with encouragement and helpful emails and phone calls. I appreciate her so much. Thank you. To my publisher, Penguin Berkley, thank you, thank you. I am so happy to be a part of the family. And I just love having a penguin in my book.

I'd like to thank Dr. Alexia Gordon for her invaluable information on succinylcholine, how the emergency department is called the ED and not the ER by professionals, and how passing meds in the ED really works.

And I want to thank the wonderful cozy mystery authors who read my book and gave a blurb: Jenn McKinlay, V.M. Burns, Sofie Kelly, Bailey Cates and Juliet Blackwell.

As always, I want to thank my writing group, #amwriting, at South Euclid-Lyndhurst Public Library—Bernard, Rose, Molly, Melissa, Zach and Nicole—you guys are the best. And, of course, to Laurie Kincer and Kathryn Dionne, my friends and confidants through this writing journey—kisses, hugs and much love. And a special thank-you to Erin George. You set my feet on this path and I will always be grateful.

## *Crewse Creamery*

# ICE CREAM RECIPES

For these recipes, you don't need an ice cream machine. But if you do use one, be sure to follow the manufacturer's instructions. And if you don't have one, remember to use whipped cream to create a better texture. It'll take a little longer for your mixture to freeze properly, but it'll be fine. Just check on it every couple of hours and give it a good stir.

Here are a few other tips before you get started:

TIP #1: When it comes to the milk you add, embrace the fat content. Low-fat products don't freeze as well, don't taste as good and give the ice cream an icy texture. Always use heavy cream, whole milk or half-and-half.

TIP #2: If you use an ice cream maker, never pour your warm (or even room-temperature) base into your ice cream machine. A base that isn't chilled prior to going into your ice cream maker won't freeze. The colder, the better!

TIP #3: Don't overfill your ice cream machine. Remember, liquids expand as they freeze, and if your machine is filled to the top, it will end up spilling over the sides. Fill it no more than three-quarters of the way full.

TIP #4: Don't over-churn your ice cream. The ice cream will start to freeze as it churns in your machine, but it won't freeze to the right consistency. Churning too much will cause your ice cream to have an icy texture. Churn just enough until the mixture is thick, about the consistency of soft serve, before transferring it to the freezer.

# Grandma Kay's Snow Ice Cream

1 cup milk

⅓ cup granulated sugar

1 teaspoon vanilla extract (store-bought or homemade)

1 pinch salt

8 cups clean snow (during the summer or in warm climates, just use shaved ice)

Whisk milk, sugar, vanilla and salt together in a bowl until combined. Do not heat.

When it starts to snow, place a large bowl outside to catch falling snow, or scoop up fresh, clean snow from the ground.

Stir milk mixture into snow until the ice cream is fluffy.

Freeze or dive in!

# Riya's Upscale Cherry Amaretto Chocolate Chunk Ice Cream

1¼ cups milk

2 teaspoons pure vanilla extract

1 cup sugar

Pinch of salt

2 cups heavy whipping cream

3 cups fresh, ripe cherries, pitted and quartered

¼ cup amaretto liqueur

1 cup dark chocolate chunks

In a medium saucepan over medium heat, combine milk, vanilla and sugar. Stir occasionally until the sugar completely dissolves. Take off heat and add salt. Allow to steep and cool.

Whisk in the heavy whipping cream. Cover with plastic wrap and place in fridge about two hours, until completely chilled.

Using an ice cream maker, add the chilled ice cream base according to the manufacturer's instructions. Once the mixture has thickened, add the cherries and the amaretto. Continue churning until it is the consistency of soft serve, then mix in chocolate chunks and place in a freezer-proof container and freeze for at least two hours.

Enjoy!

# Chagrin Falls Pumpkin Spice Roll Ice Cream

⅔ cup pumpkin puree (not pumpkin pie filling)

1 teaspoon ground cinnamon

½ teaspoon ground ginger

⅛ teaspoon ground nutmeg

⅛ teaspoon ground cloves

1¾ cups milk

2 cups heavy cream

¾ cups sugar

1 teaspoon vanilla extract

In a large bowl, mix the pumpkin puree with the cinnamon, ginger, nutmeg and cloves.

Add the milk, heavy cream, sugar and vanilla to the bowl, and then beat using an electric mixer until the mixture becomes smooth (about two minutes).

Pour the mixture into an ice cream maker and churn until it reaches the consistency of soft-serve ice cream. Place in a covered freezer-safe container and freeze for at least two hours.

Enjoy!

# *Wilhelmina's Caramel Corn Ice Cream*

6 raw ears of corn

½ cup heavy cream

2 cups whole milk

1 teaspoon vanilla extract

¾ cup sugar

¼ teaspoon salt

8 large egg yolks

Salted caramel (see following recipe)

Cut kernels from the ears of corn, and chop the cobs. Combine cream and milk into a medium saucepan over medium-high heat. Add cobs and kernels to the cream mixture along with the vanilla extract. Let the corn steep. Heat the mixture until hot, but don't let it boil. Remove from heat and cool completely. Strain mixture into a bowl, discarding chunks.

Add sugar, salt and egg yolks, and whisk in a mixer on high for about three minutes. (Mixture should have tripled in size.)

Temper corn mixture into yolk mixture. Beat to combine. Pour mixture into a large saucepan; cook over medium heat until thick (do not boil). Stir constantly for about twenty minutes. Remove from heat. Place pan into a large ice-filled bowl for thirty minutes or until mixture comes to room temperature, stirring occasionally. Chill.

Churn the mixture according to your ice cream maker's instructions until mixed, then add the caramel. Transfer the ice cream to a freezer-safe container. Freeze for at least two hours.

## Salted Caramel

1 cup granulated sugar

6 tablespoons butter, cubed

½ cup heavy cream

1 teaspoon salt

Heat granulated sugar in a medium saucepan over medium heat. Stir constantly.

Once sugar is melted, add the butter. Caramel will bubble quickly.

Stir in the butter until completely melted. Slowly drizzle in the heavy cream while stirring. Allow mixture to boil for one minute.

Remove from heat and stir in salt. Allow it to cool before using.

Duke Morse Photography

*Wall Street Journal* bestselling author ABBY COLLETTE loves a good mystery. She was born and raised in Cleveland, and it's a mystery even to her why she hasn't yet moved to a warmer place. She is the author of the Logan Dickerson Mysteries, a southern cozy mystery series featuring a second-generation archaeologist and a nonagenarian who is always digging up trouble. She is also the author of the Romaine Wilder Mysteries, set in East Texas, which pairs a medical examiner and her feisty auntie who owns a funeral home and is always ready to solve a whodunit. Abby spends her time writing, facilitating writing workshops at local libraries and spending time with her grandchildren, each of whom is her favorite.

Abby is a member of Crime Writers of Color, and the Sisters in Crime national, regional and guppy chapters.

CONNECT ONLINE

AbbyCollette.com